More Than This

by Dominique Wolf

More Than This
Copyright 2021 Dominique Wolf
All rights reserved.

No part of this book may be reproduced or transmitted in any form or by any means, electronic or mechanical, including photocopying, recording or by any information storage and retrieval system, without permission in writing from the copyright owner.

ISBN: 979-8-462693-08-3

Published by Dominique Wolf
Formatting by Bob Houston eBook Formatting
Editing by TC Media
Cover design by Dominique Wolf (Picture supplied through Canva ProLicense - @muzzyco from Getty Images Pro)

CHAPTER 1:
Isabella

"I can't believe it's you," he said wide-eyed. "I had heard you were in Barcelona but that was months ago."

How the hell was Nate standing in front of me right now? I wiped away the tears that managed to escape and quickly took a moment to take him in. He had the same kind eyes he always had. He was sporting a light, well-groomed beard that he never had before. He always found it frustrating to maintain so he never allowed it to grow out. His light hair was pulled back into a bun. *He grew his hair out?* Since when? I was surprised by his appearance. He looked just like the man I used to know, but he also looked like a complete stranger.

Why was he here now? Why now when I was trying to wrap my head around what I just found out. I was still in shock.

"What are you doing here?" I managed to get out, reminding myself to keep my emotions in tact.

He pulled his bag over his shoulder nervously. "I'm working on a project here."

"Good for you," I mumbled.

It came out more hostile than I intended it to but how was I supposed to react to my ex-boyfriend, who dumped me only to get engaged to someone else, standing in front of me?

"I wanted to reach out to you," he said. "To see ho-".

"To see how I was doing?" I snapped. "Don't you think you're half a year too late to be asking me that?"

He averted his eyes. "I'm sorry about what happened and for leaving just like that."

I really didn't have the energy to deal with this right now. I wanted to get out of here. The air around me was becoming thin again and my breathing was starting to pick up. I was too focused on the fact that Casey was pregnant. What did that mean for Giovanni and I now? When last did he sleep with her? How far along was she? How could I trust him again? When did he find out? I had too many unanswered questions right now and the last thing I wanted to do was deal with Nate of all people.

"Don't you have a fiancé to get to?" I huffed, annoyed by his presence at that moment.

His eyes met mine. "You know?"

I scoffed. "Of course I know, Nate. You put your announcement on social media, did you think it would be a secret?"

"Isabella, I wanted to talk to yo-".

I lifted a finger to cut him off. "I don't care that you're engaged. I really hope you and Christina will be happy, but I'm sorry, I have to go right now."

I turned to leave, but he grabbed my arm. "Please wait."

"Wait for what?"

Before he could answer, my phone started ringing in my hand. I looked down to see Giovanni's name flashing on my screen. My heart contracted. I couldn't do this right now. I couldn't face him. How could I?

"Who's Giovanni?" Nate asked.

I jerked my hand out of Nate's grip. "That's really none of your business!"

And with that, I turned towards the exit, ignoring his calls for me to stop. I pushed through the crowds of people and finally made my way outside. Winter was quickly approaching and the icy wind was unforgiving today. I pulled my jacket closer to me, trying to figure out what my next move was. My phone started buzzing again. *Giovanni must already be here.* I didn't want to face him right now. I couldn't - not without completely breaking down. I was barely holding it together, but I knew I needed to until I got home. I didn't want to get into a car with him. I needed time to process this.

My phone buzzed for the third time.

I glanced down at the two missed call notifications and messages that popped up from Giovanni.

Izzy, where are you? I'm here.

And another one...

Baby, I've been trying to call you. Why aren't you answering? I'm in the parking lot just outside the exit.

I jerked my head up, looking towards the open parking lot filled with cars. Giovanni was somewhere out there. I pulled the hood of my jacket over my head and turned in the direction of the metro. My default setting to run away had kicked in and I just needed to get out of here as soon as possible. I walked down the stairs towards the underground and quickly purchased a ticket. My phone kept buzzing in my hand, but I couldn't bring myself to check it again. I knew it was him. I knew he was looking for me. I scanned myself in and made it to the platform. The train was going to be another five minutes and I was thankful that there were hardly any people around. I found a bench and took my place on it, dropping my head into my hands.

How could this happen? How could Casey be pregnant? The universe was playing a sick game and I hated it. I didn't want to believe it. I wanted to believe that there was no way the baby was his, but given their past physical relationship, I knew it would be naive to think otherwise. I felt sick to my stomach and the pain in my chest continued to escalate with each thought. It was aching for him.

A small part of me wanted to turn around and go find him. I wanted him to tell me this was just some sick rumour and that we were going to get through this.

But I couldn't do that.

He knew she was pregnant yesterday when he was with her and he didn't say a word to me. He lied about who he was with and to find out on the front page of a tabloid was an absolute slap in the face to me. My phone started to ring again and I knew I wasn't going to be able to dodge him forever. I stared blankly at his name on my screen, trying to figure out what I was going to say to him. I took a deep breath and answered.

"Isabella, thank God. I've been trying to reach you," he said frantically. "Where are you, baby? I'm here."

The tears started to pool in my eyes at the sound of his voice and a huge lump formed in my throat.

"Isabella? Can you hear me?"

"I can hear you." I managed to get the words out.

"Are you alright? Where are you?"

"When were you going to tell me, Giovanni?" I murmured.

I heard him take a deep breath in on the other end of the line before answering, "Isabella, where are y-".

I interrupted him, raising my voice. "When were you going to tell me that Casey is pregnant?

He was silent for a moment before he softly said, "How did you find out?"

I scoffed. "Is that really what you're concerned about right now? Maybe you should check the latest tabloids, Giovanni. Your picture with her at the hospital yesterday is spread across the front page. Isn't it ironic that I had to find out that way?"

I was overcome with my emotions and I couldn't control my tongue. He hated that his mother found out about his father's affair in the press and now here I was finding out about him and Casey in the exact same way.

"Baby, please you need to listen to m-," he started to say, but I cut him off again.

"When I asked you who you were with yesterday you said no one. You lied to me, Giovanni."

Tears fell from my eyes and I hung my head down, defeated by all of this. I couldn't hold it back any longer. I was struggling.

"I didn't know how to tell you, Isabella. I was just finding out for myself and I couldn't wrap my head around it. How could I have told you this over the phone? Casey pulls shit like this all the time for attention and I wa-".

"Oh, so she's not pregnant?"

"No, she says she is bu-".

The train pulled up to the stop and the few people around me started to get on. I stood up and grabbed my bag, pulling it closer to me.

"I can't do this Giovanni." I choked on the tears. "I've found my own way home."

And with that, I disconnected the call. I found myself a single seat in the back, away from the people that were on the train, and I buried my face in my hands.

Was this what true heartbreak felt like?

CHAPTER 2:
Isabella

I was a few blocks from my apartment when the rain started to come down. I quickened my pace and pushed myself through the building. The whole ride back I tried to wrap my head around everything, but I couldn't. It was too difficult for me to think about. The pain in my chest deepened with each thought and the tears were finding it difficult to stay put. I unlocked my front door to silence and shut it behind me. I couldn't make it one step further before the tears I was holding back consumed me. I leaned against the door and fell to the floor.

I cried.

I cried like I had never cried before. The pain consumed me - every thought of Giovanni made it worse. I love him. *Oh, how I loved him.* I always knew that the heartbreak I'd feel from Giovanni would be a pain I had never felt before and I was right. I never expected that this would be the way I would be welcomed back home. *What was I supposed to do?* How was I supposed to react in a situation like this?

I pulled my knees towards my chest, attempting to drown out the aching feeling. I didn't know how much time had passed before I finally managed to stop the tears from falling, a numb feeling settling over me instead. I leaned my head against the door, closing my eyes as I tried to find a moment of peace.

Suddenly, I heard the banging from outside my door and jerked my eyes open.

"Isabella, open the door," Giovanni shouted from outside.

I froze, unable to move. *What was he doing here?* I didn't want to see him. I couldn't see him. I wouldn't be able to keep it together.

"Izzy, baby, I know you're in there," his tone softened. "Please open up for me."

I unwrapped my arms from my legs and slowly brought myself up. I stared at the door handle. One swift movement and I would open the door to him. I would see him standing in front of me and I would be forced to have my heart broken all over again. I just couldn't bring myself to do it.

He knocked on the door. "Isabella, please."

I heard the desperation in his voice. I had never heard it before, but it was there along with an underlying subtle hint of sadness. It hurt me to hear him like that but I couldn't move. I couldn't open the door and allow him to come inside. I couldn't do that to myself. I needed time. I had to process all of this and figure out what the hell I was going to do. It was silent for a few minutes, but then I heard his voice through the door again.

"I know how this must look, but we need to talk about this," he begged. "I need to explain things. I need to figure this out but I need you, Isabella, please."

I shut my eyes in an attempt to stop the newly formed tears from falling, but I was unsuccessful. They started streaming down my face once more.

"I love you so much, Isabella," he murmured. "You don't realize how much I love you. Please open the door so we can talk. I can't lose you."

A part of me was screaming to let him in. One look at him and everything would be okay, she whispered in my mind.

But that wouldn't change the facts.

I covered my mouth with my hand in an attempt to control the muffled cries I couldn't contain. The tears kept flowing.

"Please don't run away from this. I know you must have a million questions, but I just need to see you, baby, please just open the door."

I did have a million questions and a million emotional reactions running through my head. I was the worst in situations like this. I couldn't help but run and cower away from it. It was my terrible attempt at dealing with pain and this was a different kind of heartbreak that I hadn't experienced before. I didn't move. He continued at my door but I couldn't bring myself to open it and face him.

Not now.

Instead, I reached up to the door and twisted the key, making sure it was locked. I was not going to let Giovanni in. My heart couldn't handle any more of this right now. I dragged myself to the couch and dropped down, burying my head against the pillow as I cried into it.

"I know you, Isabella, you run away when things get difficult, but I'm begging you not to do that now. Not before we've had a chance to speak. I need you, *mi hermosa,* please," he choked.

My heart contracted at the sound of his pain. Hearing his sadness only made me cry harder. I didn't know how long he continued at my door before he finally accepted defeat.

"I'll give you your space for now," he shouted. "But I won't stop, Isabella. We are going to figure this out together. I love you, please."

With each word from him, I cried harder into the pillow. The heartbreak consumes me more and more. I cried to the sounds of the footsteps of the man I love walking away.

CHAPTER 3:
Giovanni

D ragging myself away from her apartment killed me inside. I wanted to bang on that door until she got tired of me and was forced to answer. I needed to see her. This wasn't how it was supposed to happen.

The elevator to my apartment opened and I was welcomed by the deafening silence. I had nothing else to focus on but my own thoughts and it was driving me fucking insane. I opened up the cupboard door above my counter and reached for the bottle of whiskey. I didn't even bother getting a glass. I needed something to drown out the thoughts racing in my head.

I was angry.

I was angry at Casey for rocking up yesterday, unannounced and springing this on me. I was angry that the paparazzi caught us together and plastered the story on the front page. It made me sick to my stomach that Isabella was blindsided by this - that was the last thing I wanted. I wanted to be the one to tell her and for us to figure it out together. Not to have the opportunity to tell her ripped away from me and smeared across the tabloids. The parallels between this and the way my mother found out about my father were uncanny and it made me sick with guilt.

How the fuck did they even know she was pregnant?

How could she be pregnant? I couldn't wrap my head around that. Surely there was no way the baby was mine? The deep nagging in the pit of my stomach reminded me not to dismiss the possibility. I've always had a physical relationship with Casey and her words kept ringing in my ears over and over again.

"I haven't been with anyone else, it can only be yours. You're the father, Giovanni."

She said she was six weeks along now? Or was it seven? I couldn't even remember. Her words were a muffled blur of an echo in my mind after she told me the baby was mine. I told her there was no way. I repeated it over and over trying to convince myself it couldn't be true, but her continued repetition that the baby was mine made me feel sick to my stomach.

"You're lying," I said.

She shook her head. "No, I'm not, Giovanni. I would never lie about something like this."

"No, no, no!" I kept repeating. "This can't be happening."

"Do you think I wanted this to happen?" She spat, "Do you think a baby is what I need right now for my career? No, it isn't but we can't run away from this. I've had time to think about this and I'm keeping the baby, but I am not doing this alone."

The timelines were a fucking mess in my head, but the constant nagging feeling that she could be telling the truth was killing me. She sprung this on me right as Penelope was giving birth and I had to be there for Alvaro. I told her to leave and I hadn't heard from her since. I didn't want to believe Casey. How could she be carrying my baby?

"We slept together, Giovanni," she said. "That night after Mala Mía, we went back to your apartment an -"

I lifted my hand to cut her off. "Please stop!"

I didn't want to hear more. She was right and I was sick to my stomach with guilt. I remembered trying to get Isabella out of my head. From the first night I met her, she consumed my thoughts in a way nobody had ever done before and it fucking terrified me enough to turn to self-sabotage. As the weeks went on, I didn't want to give in to what was happening between her and me. I was adamant that I was never going to be with anyone. I couldn't. I couldn't trust anyone and I didn't want to. I tried to get her out of my head in any way I could and Casey was one of those ways. That was until that night at Paradiso when I saw her kiss Lorenzo and I realised I didn't want to see her with anyone else. I wanted her to be with me and I had to admit my feelings to myself.

I didn't want to accept that Casey was pregnant. The denial continued in my head - no matter how hard I tried to convince myself this wasn't true, all the evidence was pointing to the opposite.

And now Isabella knew.

Isabella knew and she found out in the worst way possible. I was overcome with guilt at the way this all played out. I never wanted to hurt her. I brought the bottle to my lips and tilted my head back, the alcohol burning down my throat. I didn't care about the burn - nothing could ever be worse than what I was feeling right now. I knew I shouldn't have lied to her yesterday, but how could I have told her what I knew over the phone? Without being able to hold her and remind her that no matter what, we would be okay. To remind her that this didn't change anything.

And yet, everything had already changed.

I was alone in my apartment with nothing but my drink for company. I took a sip again. And then again. And again. *How else was I supposed to drown all this out?* I couldn't face it. I couldn't accept it.

My phone buzzed in my pocket and I quickly pulled it out, hoping that I would see her name on the screen. I glanced down and a rush of disappointment came over me. Sergio's name flashed on the screen and I placed my phone on the counter. I didn't want to talk to anyone right now. I only wanted her. I hung my head in my hands as my phone continued to buzz. This time Alvaro's name popped up.

They must have seen the news.

There was no way they couldn't have seen it. Casey's public persona in the country made her a hot topic for the news outlets and unfortunately, this new story of hers involved me in the worst way. I let the calls go to voicemail. They were going to drill me about the story and I wasn't ready for that yet. I had enough guilt already without needing to be reminded of it. My phone buzzed once more and a message popped up on screen from Alvaro.

Gio, please give me a call. Is it true? Is Casey really pregnant?

I reached for the bottle again. I needed proof that she was pregnant - the scan, a positive test or whatever the fuck she had. I needed that clarification, but I couldn't think of anything right now except Isabella.

I needed Isabella. I needed her and I needed her now.

I placed the bottle down and reached for my phone, my movements slower than I expected. A sudden dizziness started to set in but I ignored it. I dialed her number and was immediately greeted by her voicemail.

"Isabella," I slurred. "Isabella, please talk to me. I need you to talk to me. We need to talk."

I couldn't string together a coherent sentence and it was frustrating me. I stood up and ran my fingers through my hair.

"Baby, I love you and I need you to know that. Please, we have to figure this out together. I'm sorry."

I repeated my apology until the line disconnected. The burning anger inside of me reached the surface and I couldn't hold it back anymore. I reached for the bottle on the table and threw it against the wall, shattering the glass everywhere. I didn't care. All I cared about was Isabella and she wasn't here right now.

I hung my head in defeat.

CHAPTER 4:
Isabella

I was so happy. Hand in hand with Giovanni, we walked through the city, taking in the sights. I laughed at a bad joke he made and he smirked, showing me that deep dimple of his that I loved so much. He caressed my hand with his thumb and brought my hand to his lips, leaving a sweet kiss on it. My heart swelled with happiness. He pulled me into his arms and I was content. There was nothing else that I needed but to be here with him.

He pulled away to face me. "I love you, Casey."

Casey?

My eyes flung open and I was greeted by darkness. My heart ached at that cruel dream. My cheeks were stained with tears again. I cried for hours before sleep finally found me and then I was greeted with that? I reached for my phone to check the time and found the battery had died. I dragged myself off the couch and went over to my bag, digging through it until I found my charger. I plugged it in by the counter and left it to charge. I had no idea what time it was or how long I had been asleep. The hovering sadness I was feeling settled in again and the dull ache in my chest wasn't going to be leaving me anytime soon. I dragged myself to the shower and turned it on. My appearance in the mirror caught my eye and I was saddened by it.

I looked defeated.

Dark bags under my eyes and bloodshot stained eyes from all the tears I couldn't hold back. I stared back at my reflection and I wanted to apologize to the sad girl in front of me for getting her into this mess in the first place. I wanted to apologize to her for allowing her to fall for Giovanni. I wanted to apologize for the pain she was feeling right now. I turned away from my reflection and removed my clothes, stepping into the shower. The hot water hit my skin as I took a deep breath in. I closed my eyes and stepped forward, tilting my head back against the water. For a brief moment, I felt calm and collected as I focused on the hot water. I thought of nothing more for those few seconds, but it was short-lived before memories of Giovanni and I flooded my mind. The memories of that night in Valencia under the hot water. A night filled with passion and love - at the time we hadn't said that to each other, but we were already in that place. The warm tears stained my cheeks again.

"Come on, Isabella," I reprimanded myself. "Stop crying."

I quickly finished up in the shower and turned the water off. I started to feel more collected as I stepped outside, wrapping my body with the towel. I thought back to earlier when Giovanni was banging at my door. I should have opened the door. I knew it was the right thing to do, but I couldn't bring myself to face him.

You can't run away from this.

That phrase echoed in my mind. I needed to rip the band-aid off and speak to him. I needed to find out everything I could about Casey's pregnancy and what that meant for us. The thought of Giovanni with Casey in any way were thoughts I hated to entertain so the idea of the two of them starting a family together was killing me inside.

I made my way to my room and quickly changed into something more comfortable and much warmer. Within days winter had started to make itself comfortable in the city. As I pulled a hoodie over my head, I heard my name from the kitchen.

"Isabella?" Reyna shouted. "Izzy, where are you?"

"I'm here," I replied as I strolled down the hall and came into view.

"Oh, thank goodness!" She threw her arms around me. "I've been trying to call you, but you weren't picking up."

"Sorry about that, my phone died."

She pulled away to meet my gaze. "I saw the story about Casey."

I remained silent. I didn't know what to say. My boyfriend got another woman pregnant and it was out there for everyone to see. It made me feel sick to my stomach.

"Is it true?"

I nodded.

"I'm going to kill him," Reyna announced.

"Rey, please."

"I'm serious, Izzy," she reiterated. "What happened? How far along is she?"

"I don't know."

"How long has he known?"

"I don't know that either. I think since yesterday, but I could be wrong," I mumbled.

She pulled me to the couch to sit down next to her, never letting go of my hand.

"Have you seen him?" she asked softly.

"He arrived to fetch me at the airport but I couldn't face him when I found out so I took the metro home. He followed me here and spent a while outside banging for me to open the door but I just couldn't. I don't know why, Rey, but I just couldn't bring myself to open the door."

A stray tear escaped my eye and I quickly wiped it away. I didn't want to continue to cry. I was already tired of it and my eyes were burning from having to constantly wipe my tears away.

"I understand you need time to process this," she started.

"Thank y-".

She quickly interrupted me to continue her thought. "But, Izzy, you have to go and speak to him. You run away when things get difficult and I don't want to be the friend that lets you do that this time. Especially not with something like this."

I hung my head. "I know. I just don't know what to do. I'm so angry at him and the blurred lines of our timeline together. I love him so much, but could I really stand by and watch while he and Casey raise a child together?"

That thought alone brought on another wave of nausea.

"How could I put myself through that?" I continued. "I hated to see him with anyone else and now they're bringing a baby into this world. Shouldn't they at least try to be a family for the sake of the baby? I don't even know what I'm supposed to do in this situation."

This time the tears streamed down my face again and I couldn't hold them back. Reyna pulled me closer to her, allowing my head to bury itself in her shoulder. I held onto her and allowed my emotions to overcome me. I had to go and speak to Giovanni, but I couldn't afford to break down in front of him. He'd want to comfort me and how would I be able to leave his arms?

"Listen to me, Izzy," she said as she ran her fingers through my hair. "I am going to be here for you okay? Whatever you decide to do, you need to go and see him. You are going to drive yourself crazy with all these unanswered questions."

She was right. I wasn't going to be able to figure anything out if I didn't get the answers that I deserved. I pulled away from her and took a deep breath in. I wiped my tears and tried to prepare myself for the conversation I was going to have to have.

"I'll call him now," I said and went to my phone on the counter.

I turned it on and all my notifications started to come through. Missed calls from Reyna, messages from Katrina and Sergio and there was a recent voicemail from Giovanni. I took in another deep breath and brought the phone to my ear.

"*Isabella,*" he slurred. "*Isabella, please talk to me. I need you to talk to me. We need to talk.*"

He sounded as if he had been drinking as he continued. "*Baby, I love you and I need you to know that. Please, we have to figure this out together. I'm sorry.*"

My heart ached for him. I hated hearing him like that. We needed to talk about this and I wasn't going to be able to wait until tomorrow to do so. I felt bad that I hadn't opened up earlier, but I didn't know what the right way would be to handle this situation. I scrolled to his name and stared at it on my screen for a few seconds. Giovanni Velázquez, the man who changed it all for me, and now I had this terrible feeling inside that I was going to have to let him go.

How could I do that?

I pushed that thought out of my mind and dialled his number.

After the second ring, he answered, "Isabella?"

"Hi, Giovanni."

"You called me. Fuck, thank you for calling me back. I tried to call - I've been trying to call you, I wa-" he rambled on, slurring his words.

He was definitely drunk. I leaned against the counter trying to put together what I wanted to say. Just hearing his voice was already painful enough, but I was adamant to keep it together, even if it was just for this phone call.

"I needed some time to wrap my head around what's going on," I explained. "And I have some questions."

"I'd be surprised if you didn't," he joked in an attempt to lighten the mood. "Can I see you? I need to see you."

"Yes, I'd like to meet up and talk." I kept my tone as clipped as possible.

"Can I?" he asked as he mumbled again. "Can I come to you again?"

Through his constant slurring and mumbling, he was in no condition to get behind the wheel right now. As much as I wanted him to come to me so I could be in the safety of my own place, I didn't want him going out and endangering himself or others.

"No, I'll come to you," I said. "I'm going to leave now."

"Okay, thank you so much, baby," he murmured.

"See you soon."

"I love you, Isabella."

I shut my eyes in an attempt to stop the new tears that had formed. "I'll see you, Giovanni."

I ended the call. I couldn't say it back to him, no matter how much I wanted to. It pained me to hear him say it. The three words I had waited so long to hear him say. The three words I had been longing to hear and now they brought on a wave of pain I didn't think I would have to experience. I wanted to tell him I love him and that we would make it through this. I wanted to tell him that no matter what happened, we would have each other, but I couldn't. I didn't know if I could keep my word and I refused to lie to him.

My phone hadn't charged much, but I disconnected it and reached for my keys.

"Do you want me to come with you?" Reyna offered.

"That's okay, Rey, this is something I have to do myself."

She pulled me in for a hug again. "I love you, Izzy, and you'll be okay."

"I love you, too. I'll see you in a bit."

I grabbed my big jacket on the way out and closed the door behind me. I hailed a taxi as I reached downstairs and gave the driver Giovanni's address. I leaned my head against the window as I stared up at the dark sky.

A storm was brewing.

CHAPTER 5:
Isabella

I tried to talk myself out of going upstairs as soon as I arrived at his apartment. I was suddenly too scared to have to face him and deal with this. I knew that once I did, there was no going back and the fact that I could leave there today without having him in my life was a thought that I didn't want to entertain. I couldn't accept that and yet, I knew it was a strong possibility. I took in one last deep breath before calling on the elevator. The doors opened and I stepped inside. The air around me started to become thin again and I had to focus on my breathing to keep myself from having a complete breakdown.

In and out.

I repeated that over and over until the doors opened to his apartment and there was nowhere else left to go. His apartment always had a particular smell that I couldn't quite identify, but I had started to associate it with home. He felt like home to me and I had always felt so comfortable here. Walking in now, I felt like a stranger. I stepped inside and slowly walked towards the kitchen. My breath caught in my throat at the sight of broken glass all over the floor. I turned towards the counter and there he sat with his head in his hands. There were a few bottles on the counter. Some empty and some still had alcohol in them.

"Giovanni?"

He jerked his head up in surprise and his sad eyes met mine. I had never seen him like this before and it broke my heart. A part of me wanted to throw my arms around him, but I remained where I was.

He ran his hands through his hair nervously. "Isabella, sorry I didn't even hear you arrive."

He slid off the chair and used the counter to keep his balance. *How was I going to have a conversation with him if he was this intoxicated?* I walked over to his fridge and grabbed a cold bottle of water. He was leaning against the counter so I stepped closer to him and handed him the bottle.

"I think you could use this," I murmured.

He took the bottle from me and opened the lid. He leaned back and finished it in one go. I looked around his apartment and it was unusual for me to see how messy it was. He always had everything so neatly kept. There was liquid on the floor dripping off the wall and some amongst the broken glass. I figured that the bottle must have been thrown against the wall.

"Why didn't you open for me earlier?" he asked.

"I needed time, Giovanni. I wasn't going to call you today until Reyna convinced me that we needed to talk."

"She probably hates me now."

"She doesn't hate you," I reassured him.

"Do you?" He looked up to meet my eyes.

"Do I what?"

"Do you hate me?"

Instinctively, I reached out and cupped his face with my hand before I realised what I was doing. My hand dropped and I turned away from him.

"Of course, I don't hate you, Giovanni." I sighed. "It's because I love you so much that this is difficult for me."

It was true. I was so in love with Giovanni that the thought of him having a baby with another woman was enough to shatter my heart into a million little pieces.

"I'm sorry about the way you found out, Isabella," he started. "You know I would never want to hurt you like that. I didn't know that was going to happen."

I ignored what he said and focused on why I was there. "So, you were with Casey yesterday?"

"Casey rocked up at the hospital uninvited," he clarified. "Penelope had just gone in and I went to fetch my jacket from the car. On my way back she stopped me on the steps by the entrance. That was the picture you saw. I didn't know the paparazzi was there, but it wouldn't surprise me if she had them there on purpose."

"On purpose? What do you mean?"

"She's done this before. In order to stay relevant, she sends tips to them herself to make sure they are there to take pictures of her. Usually, it's for events and shit like that, but I wouldn't put it past her to do something like this."

I wasn't entirely surprised by the possibility. Just from that small interaction I had with her that night at *Mala Mía,* I got a sense of a spiteful nature to her. But to set Giovanni up like that? Surely not. I pushed that out of my mind and focused on finding out more.

"So, she stops you on the steps and then what?"

"She told me she needed to speak to me about something important. I brushed it off and told her to leave. I knew you wouldn't be happy with her being there, but she ended up blurting out that she's pregnant and the baby is mine."

It didn't get any easier hearing that over and over again. I wish I could dismiss this entire thing as nothing but a lie, yet I couldn't. Giovanni had a history of a physical relationship with Casey. One she had no problem reminding me of.

"And then you called me," he continued. "I was caught off-guard by what she had just said. I couldn't wrap my head around it."

"That was when you lied and said you were with no one," I reminded him, even though that was not the biggest problem we were dealing with right now.

He averted his eyes. "I know that I shouldn't have lied to you, Isabella, but Casey had just told me she was pregnant. I was in shock."

I walked over to his couch and sat down. I needed to moment after the constant nausea rushing over me. He remained standing against the counter.

"How could I have told you over the phone?" he continued. "I couldn't bring myself to do that."

I remained silent for a moment. I understood his reasoning behind it, but I would have much rather heard it from him than the way I did find out. It was humiliating.

"And then what happened?" I managed to get out.

"I didn't believe her. I told her to leave, but she said I was the father and that we had to talk about what we were going to do."

"You slept with her while we were together."

"No, don't say it like that, Isabella," he objected. "You and I weren't together at the time. I would never have betrayed you like that. When I realised I was falling for you, I stopped seeing anyone else. It was only you."

My face remained unchanged as I tried to process what he was telling me. I was so angry. I was angry at the blurred lines of our relationship. I couldn't believe this was happening. I didn't want to accept it. I wish I could believe that this was all a lie, but I couldn't. Giovanni slept with Casey - those were the facts.

"How far along is she?"

"I don't remember what she said. I think either six or seven weeks along."

I tried to rack my brain with the timeline of our relationship and the overlapping of theirs. How long have Giovanni and I been seeing each other? Surely it was a few months now? The more I thought about it, the more I realised how little time had actually passed. Our relationship took an unusual trajectory and the intensity of it made me feel like we had been together for years. I struggled to put the pieces together and it was frustrating me. I was angry at the inconsistencies in the timeline. I was angry at the consequences of such casual relationships and that I was caught in the middle of this.

"Isabella," Giovanni murmured softly. "Please say something."

I kept my gaze on my hands in my lap. "What do you want me to say, Giovanni?"

"Anything. I need to know what you're thinking."

"You want to know what I'm thinking? Where do I even begin?" I laughed. "I'm thinking that this whole situation is fucked up. I'm thinking that Casey was right that night at *Mala Mía* when she said you guys always find your way back to each other."

"We don-," he started, but I interrupted him.

"I'm thinking that you're a liar because suddenly the timelines of your relationships don't make sense. You said it had been a while since you had slept with her, but clearly it wasn't as long as you thought cause now there's a fucking baby on the way."

"Isabella, I didn't-".

"Oh, would you stop?" I snapped. "I feel like such an idiot now. You were the only one I was ever thinking about and that wasn't the same for you. You were sleeping around and I was nothing more than a stop to you."

"That's not fair, Isabella," he objected. "I didn't know I was going to fall in love with you. When I told you how I was feeling, you were the only one I had been with."

I remained silent.

"I know I have fucked up, okay? I fought my feelings for you for so long because that's what I always did. I ran away from any commitment and I fucked things up. I shouldn't have slept with Casey, but how was I supposed to know what was going to happen between us? I fucked up. I am telling you that I know I fucked up and-".

"I told you I never wanted to be a casualty of your fuck up!" I snapped. "If I had known that this was going to happen, I would have stopped seeing you a long time ago."

His face fell. "You don't mean that."

I was saying things I didn't mean, but I couldn't stop myself. I couldn't hold back anymore. Everything I was feeling consumed me and I gave into my emotions.

I felt bad for what I had said so I softened my tone. "Bottom line is that you're having a baby with another woman, Giovanni, what does that mean for us?"

He walked over to the couch and sat down next to me, careful to keep some distance between us.

"I don't know what it means, Isabella, there is still so much that I don't understand right now," he said, exasperated. "But we can work through this. We can figure it out together."

This time he reached for my hand and I couldn't stop the tears that escaped my eyes. I couldn't see light at the end of this tunnel. What did he expect from me? Was I supposed to be a step-mother? Was I supposed to watch him have this constant connection to Casey for the rest of my life?

"I know that you probably don't believe me now, but I promise that when I realised what I was feeling for you, I couldn't even look at another woman. You were the only one for me and I would never have intentionally done anything to hurt you."

I hung my head in my hands. I believed him. I never believed Giovanni would be the kind of man to betray me. He wouldn't - he wouldn't make the same mistakes his father made, but the inconsistencies and blurred lines of his hook-ups now had consequences. One that I never thought I'd be caught in the middle of.

"Baby, please don't cry," he murmured and reached for my cheek, wiping away my tears.

His touch burned against my skin. It seemed like forever since I had felt his touch and I never imagined that the next time I felt it, it would be like this.

"Do you see the mess we're in now because of your hook-ups?" I choked. "You slept with Casey and look what happened."

He averted his eyes. "Isabel-".

I stopped him. "I don't think I can do this, Giovanni."

His breath caught in his throat for a second. "We can figure this out."

"I can't watch you raise a kid with Casey," I said as the tears streamed down my cheeks. "I can't do that to myself."

"Isabella, I know what you're going to say," he choked. "Please, don't."

Hearing the clear emotion in his voice was breaking my heart even more. I finally looked up to meet his gaze and they were brimming with sadness and fear. I didn't want to say it. I never thought I would have to say it to him, but how could I not? How could I stay with him now when everything has changed? I was so angry with him. I was angry that we were in this situation. My heart has completely shattered now.

"Giovanni, I'm sorry," I whimpered.

He tightened his grip on my hand. "Please don't leave me."

My heart ached and the pressure in my chest worsened. I didn't want to leave him. I wanted to spend the rest of my life with him. I had thought for so long that Giovanni was it for me. He was all I needed and there would never be anyone else. I wanted a life together. I wanted that with him.

But not like this.

I couldn't put myself through that and I knew there was nothing else that he could say to change my mind.

"I'm sorry, but there is no way I could stand by and watch you start a family with Casey. Just the thought of it makes me sick to my stomach and I could never watch you raise a child with her. I'm sorry but I ju-".

"Isabella, please just take time to think this through. You don't have to make any decisions right now. There is still so much to figure out."

"Nothing is going to change." I let go of his hand and stood up, pacing past him. "You can't change what's happened."

"I'm sorry, Isabella," he murmured. "I never wanted this to happen."

Neither did I. Never in a million years did I think I would be in this situation. No matter how much I loved Giovanni, everything was different now and there was no going back. I could have never prepared for something like this.

"I'm sorry, Giovanni, but I can't be with you anymore."

I didn't think it was possible for my heart to break even more, but the pieces that were left of it shattered once again. It was killing me inside to have to do this, but I had to walk away from the situation. I couldn't be involved, not like this.

"Isabella," his voice cracked and he stopped for a moment. "Please don't do this."

I couldn't bring myself to look at him. The emotion in his voice was already sending me off the edge and I just wanted to take it all back. I wanted to go back to a time when we were happy. When we were in each other's arms and we didn't have to deal with any of this.

But that would never happen again.

"I can't, I'm sorry," I said and turned toward the elevator.

He ran after me and reached for my hand, stopping me in my tracks.

Desperation filled his eyes. "Please don't leave like this."

"There is nothing else to say," I objected.

"Except that, I love you, Isabella!" he shouted.

"That's not enough, Giovanni!" I shouted back. "It's not enough that you love me. Look at the situation we're in. You're about to become a father and for the sake of that innocent baby, you need to figure out how to be a family, in whatever way works, but I can't be a part of that."

I pulled my hand out of his grip and he didn't reach for me again. He was defeated. I stepped into the elevator and faced him one last time. Never again would I be welcomed into this apartment. Never again would I be able to throw my arms around his neck and be close to him. Never again would I be able to breathe in that cologne of his that I loved so much. Would this be the last time I saw those deep brown eyes I loved or that dimple that made an appearance any time he smiled? My heart was broken at the reality of the situation and I wondered if I would ever find happiness again.

The elevator doors closed me off from the man I love for the last time.

CHAPTER 6:
Giovanni

*T**hat's not enough, Giovanni. It's not enough that you love me.*

Her words replayed in my head over and over again. Isabella made her mind up and I watched her walk out of my life. I couldn't think of what to say to make her stay. I told her I loved her and that wasn't enough.

I couldn't handle it.

A rush of emotions overcame me and I lost it. I walked over to the counter and grabbed anything in sight. The empty bottle in my hand met the wall in a fit of rage. And then the next one. And then one more. I tossed them all at the wall in an attempt to release the pain I was feeling inside but nothing worked. There was nothing I could do but face it head-on and it consumed me in a way I had never been consumed before.

I love her.

Fuck, I love her in a way I never thought possible. Just thinking about the fact that I would never be able to call her mine was destroying me inside. I just wanted her to be happy. I just wanted to hear that laugh of hers - it was contagious. It was the kind of laugh that brightened up your day. Her happiness was all I cared about. I just wanted to be the one to make her happy and now I never could be. I finally found someone I wanted more with and now I had lost her. I ran my fingers through my hair and a huge lump formed in my throat.

"Joder," I muttered.

I would not give in to the emotions pushing through - I couldn't. I had never been good at that. I needed to drown it out. I reached for the bottle on the counter that I hadn't tossed against the wall and I was thankful for the alcohol still inside of it. I took a sip of it as I fell onto the couch. I couldn't accept that Casey was pregnant with my baby. I was so angry at myself for being so stupid. If I had just allowed myself to feel what I was truly feeling at the time, I never would have hooked up with Casey again but in true Giovanni fashion, I had to go and fuck it up. I was so afraid to face my feelings that I sabotaged things whenever I got too close to anyone.

I didn't want to be that way - I fucking hate that I was like that which was why I had been working so hard to not fuck things up with Isabella. I realised I had fallen in love with her and I did my best to show her that she was the only one for me. There was no one else, but I couldn't change what I had already done. I couldn't change the very clear mistakes I had already made. It pained me that Isabella even thought for a second that I would have betrayed her while we were together. I could never have done that. I would never have done that. I wasn't my father.

I never should have slept with Casey that night. I was running away from my true feelings and even when I was with her, it felt wrong to me. That was the first time I had ever felt like I was betraying someone even though we had no obligation to each other back then. That was how I knew I was already in too deep and I would do anything right now to take back what I had done.

Isabella was right, this was all my fault. I had always fucked around and I never stopped once to think about the consequences of what I was doing. I had accepted a long time ago that a relationship would never be for me so when she waltzed into my life, I did all I could to push her out of my mind. I learned quickly that she was not going anywhere.

Our relationship had escalated quicker than I realised. It was intense and all-consuming that it blurred the timelines. It felt as if we had been together for years, but the reality of how little time had passed was actually insane. I couldn't believe how hard I had fallen for her in such a short space of time and it was driving me crazy to know that I had now lost her. I knew in my heart that she was the one for me.

I continued drinking.

The alcohol burned through me, but I couldn't stop. I wouldn't stop until it burnt away the pressure I was feeling in my chest in the absence of her.

There was no way this was it for us. It couldn't be. We had come so far for it to end like this. *No fucking way.* She would come around and we would figure it out. We had to - this was not the end for us.

The more the alcohol made its way through me, the more the voices started to become nothing more than a faint echo. I thought about nothing else but Isabella.

I was going to win her back. I had to.

CHAPTER 7:
Isabella

It had been days since I left Giovanni and yet, the pain was like a fresh wound. I wallowed in my own self-pity. I was the one who broke up with him. I didn't want to - how could I have possibly wanted to leave the man I loved more than anything in this world? But I needed to. I didn't have it in me to watch him have a baby with Casey.

For days I followed the same routine of crying, barely eating, and finding what little sleep I could manage. I didn't leave my bed if I could avoid it. I didn't want to face the world. I didn't even bother checking my phone. I didn't even know where it was. If I unlocked it, I would be greeted by a happier time between Giovanni and me. That time by the fountains where we took our first picture together - that memory was now a snapshot in time that I had made my wallpaper. I would never be able to get over him. I tried so hard to push him out of my mind, but it was proving to be impossible. He invaded my thoughts and my dreams.

For the first time in my life, I felt truly broken.

That evening after breaking up with Giovanni, I couldn't stop crying. I was at war with myself - a part of me regretted walking away from him, but the other part of me was absolutely terrified of him having a baby with Casey. I wasn't strong enough to put myself in that situation. How could I have ever prepared for something like that?

As the days went by, the heartbreak didn't weaken. It intensified with each passing moment without him. I was empty inside. Nothing but a hollow void was left where my heart used to be. Was he thinking about me? Has he gone to see Casey yet? What did they talk about?

By the fifth day after our breakup, I was starting to drive myself crazy thinking about the two of them together and the inevitable joy that came along with having a baby. I constantly felt sick to my stomach. Reyna had tried, unsuccessfully, to distract me, but by the time the end of the week rolled around, she was finally successful in actually getting me to leave my bed. I didn't want to but I had to start doing something more than wallow in my own heartbreak. She was headed to finish off the last few walls at the coffee shop so after a little pep talk between me and me, I dragged myself out of bed and attempted to have a normal day.

"Don't forget to dress warm," Reyna shouted from the kitchen.

I walked over to my dressing table and pulled out another jersey to pull over the one I already had. I had underestimated how unforgiving Barcelona's winter could be.

Just like Giovanni said it would be.

No. Don't think of him. I pushed that thought away and reached for my hairbrush, focused on getting this hair under control. I pulled it into a high ponytail and stepped in front of the mirror.

A stranger with empty eyes stared back at me.

With dark bags under my eyes and my skin clinging to my cheekbones, this was the first time I had noticed my sudden weight loss. *When was the last time I had a decent meal?* I couldn't even remember. It surprised me to see myself like that. Not a flicker of life inside of me.

"Izzy, you ready?" Reyna shouted.

I turned away from the hollow girl in front of me.

"Yeah, let's go."

***

The last couple of roads from the metro, we were forced to huddle together under the one umbrella we brought with us. Thankfully, we pushed ourselves through the door before the storm opened up to the world completely. Reyna dropped the umbrella at the door and I shrugged my jacket off. I looked around and everything was just as it was the last time I was here.

With Giovanni.

I remembered the happiness I felt that day. His contagious energy and the way we moved together so comfortably. The way he danced with me that day just like we had at *Mala Mía* the first time we met. The way his strong arms lifted me onto the counter and his lips...

Isabella, stop!

I couldn't allow myself to think any further. The tears had already started to form in my eyes and I quickly wiped them away before Reyna could see. I didn't want to cry anymore. I was so tired of crying.

"Okay, so we've got the last few walls to do and then the fun begins," Reyna announced and escaped to the back.

I pulled the plastic onto the floor and reached for the tray that Reyna came back with. I placed it on the ground as she reached for the rollers and handed me one.

"Thank you," I murmured and dipped it in paint.

"We should probably start thinking of a name," Reyna said. "Do you have any suggestions?"

My mind wandered back to Giovanni...

> *"Have you guys decided on a name yet?" he asked.*
>
> *"Haven't decided yet. I'm really leaning towards calling it Aroma."*
>
> *"Aroma," he repeated. "That's a great name."*
>
> *He took another spoonful of ice cream and passed the tub over to me. I took it from him and continued eating.*
>
> *"You're the first person I've shared that name with."*
>
> *"Well, I'm honored to be part of your inner circle," he quipped.*
>
> *I smiled and as I brought another spoonful of ice cream to my mouth, it dripped off onto my chest.*

I couldn't allow the thoughts of that memory to go any further so instead, I shook my head and replied, "Haven't given it much thought."

Every memory with him hurt to think of. It hurt to think of the man I no longer had.

"Well, I'm sure we'll come up with something," Reyna continued and I knew she was trying to keep the conversation as light as possible.

I hadn't spoken much since I got back that night. Reyna knew we broke up, but I couldn't bring myself to share anything more. I just wanted to disappear. I was so distracted by everything that happened with Giovanni that I completely forgot about Nate being in Barcelona.

"I forgot to tell you that I bumped into Nate," I said casually.

Reyna stopped and turned to me. "I'm sorry, did you say Nate?"

I nodded.

"Nate Cameron?" she repeated. "When? Where?"

"At the airport actually. He's in Barcelona for a project."

"*Joder*, what are the chances?" She couldn't hide her surprise.

"Right?" I agreed.

"What did you guys talk about?"

"Honestly, it wasn't a very long conversation, it was right after I saw the..." I stopped for a moment and took in a deep breath. "The news of Casey's announcement so I wasn't really focused on him being there."

"That's understandable," she comforted me. "But I'm still surprised. Nate ending up in Barcelona was something I never expected."

"Me neither." I shrugged.

"It couldn't have been easy seeing him though." She eyed me. "He dumped you and then got engaged to someone else."

I should be angry about that, but it all seemed so insignificant compared to everything else that had happened.

"I didn't really care. I didn't feel anything when I saw him," I admitted.

I was so wrapped up in what I had found out that there wasn't space for me to feel anything for anyone else. The last thing I cared about was Nate being in Barcelona. He wasn't in my life anymore. We continued painting in silence for a while before Reyna brought her roller back down and turned to me.

"Izzy, I need to know that you're okay. You broke up with Giovanni, but you haven't said anything about it since then and you're worrying me."

She had given me these few days to wallow in the sadness, but I knew I wasn't going to be able to escape her questions forever.

"I don't know what you want me to say," I admitted.

That was the truth. *What was I supposed to say?* The situation was a fucked up one that I was forced to live with.

"What happened that night when you went to him?" she asked softly.

"We broke up." I sighed and placed my roller on the floor."I wish I had more to tell you, but I don't. Bottom line is I can't watch him have a baby with Casey. I'm just not strong enough for that. I just love him - loved him -".

I had to start talking about us like we were in the past because that's the only place our relationship lived now.

"I loved him too much to put myself through that."

"Did he cheat on you?" she asked. "Cause I'll burn that apartment of his down right now."

"You don't need to do that." I managed a smile. "We weren't together at the time. That's what makes me so angry about this whole situation... I, technically, can't even be angry because we had no obligation to each other at the time."

Every time I thought about that, it made me feel like even more of an idiot. I couldn't help the connection I had to him from the first moment I saw him, but it wasn't the same for him. I wanted to be angry at him for the situation - hell, I was angry at him, but how could I be? Neither of us thought our relationship was going to become what it was.

"And you never wanted to try?"

I was surprised by her question. "Try what Reyna? A relationship with him? How could I?"

"I'm not trying to fight with you, Izzy." She reached for my hand. "I've just never seen you the way you were with him."

I turned and walked towards the counter, pulling myself up onto it.

"I've never felt that way for anyone," I murmured.

The love I felt for Giovanni was one I never thought I would experience. The all-consuming love that often took my breath away. He was the only man to ever capture my body, heart and soul and now I was left with broken pieces of them.

Reyna came to join me. "And I've never seen Giovanni like that with anyone. You changed him."

I shut my eyes to keep the tears from falling. I didn't want to be reminded of that. Giovanni was the man everyone warned me to stay away from and yet, we fell in love with each other. He loved me and I had waited so long to hear those words from him. It pained me to know I would never hear that again.

"Could you have done it?" I asked her.

"Done what?"

"Watched Diego raise a child with someone else?"

She remained silent.

"You know Casey told me once that she and Giovanni always found their way back to each other and that I was just wasting my time."

"You don't believe that," Reyna retorted.

"I didn't at the time, but I do now," I admitted.

"Do you know how far along she is?"

"Giovanni said six or seven weeks. He couldn't remember exactly."

I noticed her deep in thought.

"What are you thinking?"

She snapped out of it and turned to me. "Nothing. It doesn't matter. All I care about now is being there for you and making sure you get through this."

I reached for her hand and squeezed it. "Thanks, Rey, I could really use you right now."

"Well, I am here." She smiled. "But right now, we need to finish these walls cause we have been putting them off for weeks."

For the first time in days I smiled and for that brief moment, it didn't hurt so bad.

CHAPTER 8:

Giovanni

I woke up with my face against the cold floor. I tried to open my eyes, but the blinding light from the sun shining through forced me to shut them closed again.

Where the fuck was I?

I slowly rolled over, the throbbing headache reminding me that this was alcohol-induced and completely self-inflicted. I finally managed to get my eyes open and I stared at the ceiling of my bathroom.

Well, at least I was home this time.

Not like the last few days where I had ended up passing out on whatever bar counter I could find. Okay, it wasn't always on bar counters - some were other people's couches and sometimes even floors. I couldn't remember one person I had seen this week - everything was a blur since she walked out of my life.

I didn't want to think of her. That was the whole point.

I dragged myself off my bathroom floor and slowly moved through my room. I stopped in my tracks as I noticed two females in my bed.

Fuck Giovanni, what have you done?

I walked downstairs to find sleeping bodies scattered across my apartment. I was the only one awake and I didn't recognise a single person, but judging by the copious amounts of empty bottles, the party had moved to my apartment last night.

I opened my cabinet doors in search of another drink, but was out of luck.

"*Mierda*," I mumbled.

This agitated me more than I realised and I suddenly needed everyone out of my apartment.

"Hey, get up," I said as I started tapping the sleeping bodies. "You need to get out of here."

I was greeted by a chorus of groans, but I didn't give a fuck. They needed to leave.

"Party's over," I announced. "Get out!"

Slowly they started dragging themselves out of my apartment. I turned to go back upstairs to the two females occupied in my bed. I was thankful that they were both at least clothed.

Did I sleep with them?

I couldn't have, and yet, the holes in my memory were making it impossible to confirm that.

I strolled over to my bed. "Hey, you guys need to leave."

The blonde one rolled over and reached for my hand. "Come back to bed."

Fuck. *Was I even in bed last night?*

"No, you guys need to get out. Now!"

The brunette one sat up and gave me a dirty look. "You're a dick!"

"So I'm told." I shrugged. "You know where the exit is."

They both mumbled insults as they made their way out of my room. I followed behind them to make sure everyone else had left. After they stepped into the elevator, I was left with nothing but the thoughts in my head to keep me company. I strolled into my kitchen for one more inspection of the bottles scattered across the counter. I managed to find one with some alcohol left inside and I lifted it to my lips as my phone rang from the other end of the counter.

Days ago, I would have thought it was Isabella calling to tell me she made a mistake, but I stopped wishing for that when I realised that was never going to happen.

She wasn't coming back.

The ringing stopped for a moment, but started up again. The piercing tone was driving my headache fucking crazy.

"*Joder,*" I muttered and grabbed my phone to answer. "*¿Qué tú quieres?*"

"There you are," Casey's nasal tone greeted me. "I've been trying to get a hold of you."

I rolled my eyes. Casey was the last person I wanted to speak to right now.

"What do you want?" I snapped.

"Giovanni, I've given you some time to come to terms with the news," she said calmly. "But we need to talk now. You can't avoid me forever."

"Unfortunately not," I muttered.

She ignored my comment. "We need to talk about this and how we're going to move forward as a family."

I scoffed. "Casey, we are not a family."

"Well, not yet, but once the ba-".

I interrupted her. "Stop. I don't want to hear anymore talk of family. I agree that we should probably speak about what we're going to do about this situation."

"I can come to you," she suggested. "How about tonight?"

"Fine. Meet at my place."

I didn't bother to wait to see what else she had to say as I ended the call. Casey was fun for a hook-up back then but there was nothing more to her. I had never been into her in the way that she was into me. I always made my intentions clear, but that never stopped her from trying.

I never wanted more with her - I never wanted more with anyone until Isabella. I took another swig from the bottle when I heard my elevator open. I wasn't expecting company so who the fuck was here?

"Giovanni!" Sergio's voice boomed through my apartment.

I turned to face him as he walked around the corner, coming into view.

He stopped and looked around my apartment. "*¿Qué carajo?*"

I shrugged and turned back to my bottle. I didn't feel like the company right now.

"What the fuck happened here?" he asked, walking around to the other side of the counter so he was directly in front of me.

"I had a party." I shrugged.

"This place looks like a shithole."

"No one asked you to be here, Sergio," I snapped. "Why are you here?"

"I've been trying to call you for days. Did you not get any of my messages?"

I shook my head. That was a lie, but he didn't need to know that. I got his messages, but I chose to ignore them. I chose to ignore everyone.

"What the fuck happened?" he asked. "You got Casey pregnant?"

My blood boiled every time I heard that. It reminded me of the fuck up that was my life right now.

"Casey *says* she's having my baby," I clarified.

"Did you seriously cheat on Isabella? I thought you l-".

"I never cheated on her," I said through my teeth. "I would never fucking do that. This shit with Casey happened before I realised how I was feeling for Isabella."

I would never have betrayed her like that. I could never. I could never have made the same mistakes my father made and it angered me that the pattern looked to be exactly the same. I was so angry at myself for the situation we were in. I knew I was starting to fall for Isabella a long time ago, but I ignored it. I didn't want to feel anything for anyone so it was easier for me to push her away, but I couldn't deny it for much longer. When I accepted I was falling in love, there was no one else and there never would be.

"And what's going to happen with the two of you now?"

"Oh, you didn't hear?" I took another sip. "Isabella dumped me."

The pressure in my chest resurfaced, reminding me of its on-going presence when it wasn't hidden behind copious amounts of alcohol. Sergio was quiet for a moment. I avoided eye contact with him and kept my eyes on the bottle in my hand. I was ashamed of what I had done and how I had destroyed my relationship.

"That explains a lot," he muttered.

I ignored his comment. "Why are you here, Sergio?"

"I know you, Giovanni, and when shit like this happens, you self-destruct and I'm not going to let that happen again."

"Just go," I mumbled.

I didn't need his help. I didn't need anyone's help. I was perfectly capable of dealing with the happenings in my life in any way I saw fit. I didn't need a fucking babysitter.

"Come down to the gym with me," Sergio suggested. "We can go a few rounds in the ring."

I was ready to shut down any suggestion Sergio made in an attempt to get him to leave me alone, but boxing actually sounded like a great idea. My pounding headache was begging me not to go, but I was itching to get rid of all this pent-up tension. At least whatever pain I felt in the ring would outweigh what I was really feeling, even if just for a little.

"Fine," I mumbled. "Let me get my gloves."

***

One black eye and a busted lip later, I dropped onto my couch in exhaustion. Sergio didn't go easy on me in the ring today and I matched his energy. I finally had an outlet for my emotions that didn't involve drinking myself to sleep. I managed to knock Sergio a few times too. We always pushed each other in the ring. We had been doing it for a few years now. We were used to throwing a few punches around and the small injuries that came with it. Sergio and I met in my final year of business school. He was a late transfer and we hit it off right off the bat. He was always the one who had been there for me when I needed him. When the shit went down with my parents, he let me stay by him until I figured out what my next step was. He was well-aware of my self-destructive tendencies and had always tried to show me there was another way. I often ignored his attempt at help, but today I was thankful for it.

Sergio tried to ask questions in the ring, but my constant physical interruptions showed him I wasn't in a talking mood. I didn't want to talk about anything. I wanted to get rid of the unnecessary amount of emotions that had built up over the past few days. My breathing was still heavier than usual since we finished up. I didn't realize how unfit I had become. I was just thankful that my mind has reached a moment of ease for the first time in days. I clung to that brief calmness for as long as I could.

I checked the clock on my wall and I had a bit of time before Casey was going to be here. I was dreading it, but I had to face her. No matter what was going on, there was a baby involved now and I couldn't escape that responsibility. I had to figure out what the fuck I was going about this entire situation.

I dragged myself off the couch and upstairs to my bathroom. I turned the water on and pulled my shirt over my head, tossing it into the basket. The steam started to surround me as I stepped out of my sweats and into the shower. The hot water hit my skin, burning as it ran over me. I turned it down a bit and leaned my head back, allowing the water to flow through my hair. I closed my eyes and thought about that night in Valencia. Her hands on my body allowed me to focus on nothing else, but her. I didn't want to think of anything that night - I couldn't. Her simple touch set my arousal on course and I was consumed by my desire for her.

"*Joder,*" I muttered.

I shouldn't think of her in that way anymore, but I miss her body. The feeling of being buried deep inside of her was addictive. Our emotional attachment intensified our physical relationship in a way I had never experienced until her. I had never loved anyone like I loved her.

The pressure in my chest returned and the calmness I was feeling slipped out of reach. I took a deep breath in and attempted to put her out of my mind. I focused on the hot water as I brought the soap over my body. I quickly washed it down and turned the water off. I reached for the towel and wrapped it around my waist as I stepped out of the shower. I needed to gather my thoughts and how I was going to approach Casey's arrival. I couldn't help the unexpected guilt that washed over me at the mere thought of her being here.

Isabella would hate it.

I wanted Isabella to be here. I wanted her to be here with me, holding my hand and assuring me that no matter what happened, we would figure it out together. I looked up at the reflection staring back at me. I was alone now and it would always be that way.

I had no one else but myself to blame for that.

CHAPTER 9:
Isabella

"Should we go and get something to eat?" Reyna suggested.

I locked up the door of the coffee shop and placed the keys in my handbag. Night had fallen upon us and we had successfully managed to finish the last of the walls in the shop. I was impressed with our progress and I felt a flicker of excitement at the prospects of where we could go with our little place now that things were starting to come together.

"Yes please, I'm starved." My stomach growled in agreement. "But can we take it home? I could really do with a shower."

"There's a great pizza place up the road," she suggested.

"Lead the way."

I breathed in the cold nighttime air and an unexpected wave of calmness made its way over me. I had focused on nothing else today but getting those walls painted and I was surprised that I hadn't thought of him.

Until now.

I was completely distracted today and it worked. For a while, there was no pain. There was no sadness and no tears. The hollow feeling in my chest remained, but I knew that wasn't going anywhere. It was a reminder of the part of me that I no longer had. What was he doing right now? Was he thinking of me?

You left him, Isabella.

The voice echoed that in my head and a rush of guilt presented itself. I hurt him that night and I would never be able to get his sad eyes out of my mind. The last thing I would have ever wanted to do was hurt him and now I would never be able to forget the way he looked as I walked out of his life.

"I'm so glad we finally got those walls done," Reyna said, bringing me out of my thoughts.

"Me too. Now we can at least start with the next phase."

"There's a lot to discuss. We have to pick a name, find suppliers, make sure the equipment is right, bring it ba-".

"Please, don't say it all at once," I chuckled. "It's overwhelming."

"Sorry." she smiled sheepishly. "We'll make a list."

"Sounds good to me."

We entered *La Pizza Pazza* and my stomach reacted to the smell of tomato and basil in the air. I hadn't eaten properly in days and I was finally starting to feel my appetite slowly return. There were a few tables in the restaurant filled with people, but we joined the take-away line. Reyna stepped up and we were next to be served.

"I'll wait for you by the entrance," I said.

She nodded and turned to the older man behind the counter to place our order. I strolled to the entrance and leaned against the wall, a sudden wave of exhaustion washing over me. I had struggled to get a decent night's sleep these past few days and now it was catching up with me. Every time I closed my eyes, Giovanni was all I saw.

A moment later I heard my name and turned to see a familiar friendly face.

"Lorenzo?"

"*Hola, Isabella.*" His eyes lit up and pulled me in for a quick kiss on each cheek. "I didn't expect to see you here."

He placed his hands in his pockets casually. I was taken back by his appearance. It had been weeks since I had seen him and yet, he seemed much older. He allowed his dark beard to grow out more and his dark hair was hidden beneath a black beanie. He had on that strong cologne he had the first time I met him and I couldn't help but breathe him in, remembering how much I was intoxicated by it. I suddenly became self-conscious about my own appearance. I wasn't wearing any makeup and the old clothes I painted with weren't exactly the most attractive look. He, on the other hand, looked surprisingly good.

"Are you here alone?" I asked.

He shook his head and pointed to the table he came from. "Just here with a couple friends."

He turned back to me and reached out for my arm causing an unexpected amount of electricity to flicker inside of me.

"I wanted to call you," he said softly. "I saw the story about Giovanni and Casey."

There it was again. That burning pain inside my chest at the reminder of the two of them. Would I ever get used to hearing about them?

"How are you handling it?" he asked.

"I don't think I am handling it," I admitted.

"Well, I'm sure you and Giovanni will figure it out," he said politely.

A lump started to form in my throat as I could feel the tears starting to build. I used every ounce of self-control I had to push them away. I didn't want to cry right now, especially not in front of Lorenzo.

"Giovanni and I aren't together anymore."

He jerked his head back in surprise. "Oh, *lo siento*. I didn't know."

"That's okay." I brushed it off.

He reached for my hand and squeezed it. "I can't imagine any of this could be easy."

I was surprised by his touch and the unexpected reaction I had to it. I clearly had some attraction to him, how could I not? My gaze met his and I was warmed by the sincerity in his light-brown eyes.

"It's not, but I don't think there is a blueprint for how I'm supposed to deal with it," I attempted to joke.

He smiled. "No, there isn't."

Reyna strolled in and stopped next to me. He dropped his hand from mine as Reyna extended hers to Lorenzo.

"I don't think we've officially met."

"Lorenzo," he said and pulled her in for the typical Spanish greeting.

"Nice to meet you, Lorenzo. I'm Reyna." She turned to me. "They said about 10 minutes so I'm going to run to the ladies room quickly."

I nodded and she turned to make her way through the restaurant. I stood awkwardly as Lorenzo stepped closer to lean against the wall next to me.

"Well, if you ever want to get away from all this shit, please give me a call."

A small smile played on my lips. "You mean it?"

"Oh yeah, I have plenty we could do to distract you," he said proudly. "Or even if you just need a friend to talk to."

"Why would you do that?" I asked softly.

It's not that I didn't appreciate his friendly suggestions, they were just unexpected. We had only seen each other a couple of times, and yet, he was offering himself to me like an old friend.

"Why wouldn't I?" he creased his brow. "I care about you."

"You don't even know me."

"But I want to."

He didn't bother hiding his interest. It was as clear as day burning in his eyes just like it was the first night I met him. I was in no place to reciprocate his interest, but I did appreciate his kind nature. It was refreshing.

"And I'm not coming here with any romantic intentions," he clarified. "That's not what you need right now."

Thank goodness. The last thing on my mind would be anything romantic with anyone. I didn't think I'd be able to recover any time soon from my current heartbreak.

I reached for his hand and squeezed. "Thank you. I appreciate that."

Reyna strolled over to us and I dropped my hand.

"Let me not keep you any longer," Lorenzo said. "Hope to see you soon, Isabella."

"Bye, Lorenzo."

He said his goodbyes to Reyna and returned to his table in the corner of the restaurant.

Reyna turned to face me with her eyebrows raised.

"What?" I asked.

"Isn't that the guy you made out with at *Paradiso*?"

The heat slowly started to spread across my cheeks. "Yes."

Reyna chuckled. "Well damn, I forgot how cute he is."

I flicked my eyes over to Lorenzo again. "Yeah, I guess he kinda is."

I was thankful for the older gentlemen calling our number to stop the conversation from going any further. Reyna strolled over and fetched the box for us. I was starting to feel a pang of guilt inside at the interaction with Lorenzo.

Giovanni would hate it.

I pushed both Giovanni and Lorenzo out of my mind. I didn't want to think of either of them. All I cared about right now was that delicious smelling pizza in Reyna's hand.

We pushed through the exit and turned to make our way home.

CHAPTER 10:
Giovanni

The last thing I wanted to do right now was have to deal with Casey, but I had avoided her for long enough. At the end of the day, I had to figure out what the hell I was going to do about this. There was a baby on the way now and I couldn't escape that responsibility. I strolled downstairs into my kitchen and started clearing up the empty bottles. Sergio was right - this place did look like a shithole. As I put the last of the bottles in the trash, I heard the elevator doors open. I took a deep breath in and gathered all the energy I had to focus on this one conversation. I was going to need all the help I could get.

"Giovanni!" Casey shouted, turning around the corner coming into view.

A year ago I would have been happy with the beautiful blonde walking into my apartment, but now the sight of her brought on a wave of guilt I couldn't control. Her bitchy nature and constant need for drama washed away any previous attraction I had towards her.

Now she reminded me of everything I had lost.

"Well, hello handsome." She smiled and sauntered over to the kitchen counter.

"*Hola,* Casey," I said bleakly.

She placed her bag on the counter and walked over to me. "What? No kiss?"

I rolled my eyes. "Please, don't start."

She flicked her hair over her shoulder and walked over to an empty barstool. "Now Giovanni, there's no need to be like that."

Not even two minutes into the conversation and I already wanted her to leave. *How the fuck was I supposed to raise a child with her?* The thought made me sick. There's just no way I was going to be a father. I tried to push that thought out of my mind. Instead, I walked over and opened up the cupboard door, reaching for the new bottle of whiskey I bought.

"You can't ignore me in person," she muttered. "Are you not going to say anything?"

I placed the glass on the counter and poured some whiskey into it. I looked up at her as I brought it up to my lips, taking a small sip.

"What do you want me to say, Casey?" I asked.

She crossed her arms. "Well, we have a lot to figure out now that we're starting a family together."

I tilted my head to the side in an attempt to control the anger that one statement brought over me. *Was she fucking delusional?*

"Let's get one thing clear here, you and I will never be a family. A baby doesn't change that."

She widened her eyes. "A baby changes everything."

Okay, she was right, but it didn't change things in the way she was clearly hoping for. This entire situation fucked up everything in my life and now I was stuck trying to pick up the pieces.

"How did the paparazzi get a picture of us at the hospital?" I asked. "Did you set that up?"

She peered at me. "Do you honestly believe I would have wanted people to find out like that?"

"Yes, I think that's exactly what you would have wanted."

She ignored my comment. "Well, I'm just glad I don't have to hide now."

I was convinced that Casey set that up. She only cared about remaining relevant. There was nothing beneath her outside beauty. She was a selfish, fame-hungry model that was adamant to stay in the limelight.

"I have a doctor's appointment coming up," she continued. "You're welcome to tag along."

"How many weeks are you Casey?"

"About seven weeks now I think."

"And you're sure that you're pregnant?"

She rolled her eyes. "Of course I am, Giovanni. You think I would lie about something like that?"

"And you're sure it's mine?"

"Don't insult me, Giovanni," she scowled. "You know how I've felt about you. It was always more than just a hook-up to me."

I ignored her comment and brought the drink to my lips again. The reality of the situation was starting to set in and I hated every moment of it. Casey had always wanted more from our arrangement, but I had never seen her that way.

"Look, Giovanni, I know we've had some hiccups along the way, but we can have a good relationship. I know we can make this work for the sake of the baby."

I laughed. I couldn't stop myself. She was fucking insane. What did she think was going to happen here?

"Casey, I need you to listen to me clearly now because you don't seem to understand." I leaned against the counter in front of her. "Just because there is a baby involved now doesn't mean that you and I are suddenly going to be a couple. You and I will never be together. I am in love with Isabella and that's not going to change."

"That girl from *Mala Mía*?" she scoffed. "Oh, please."

I met her piercing gaze and her spiteful nature shone through. She was crossing a line that I would rather she stayed far away from. I focused on staying calm. I couldn't afford to lose my cool now.

"Casey, don't," I warned.

"No, please, Giovanni. I'd love to understand what you think is going to happen here. Do you really think Isabella is going to be a stepmother?" She laughed.

I remained silent.

"Where is she? Shouldn't she be here then?" she probed.

"Because of your little setup, I wasn't able to tell her myself about your situation," I muttered. "She found out along with the rest of the country."

"I told you yesterday, Giovanni. I didn't know you weren't going to tell her right away." She crossed her arms. "But she knows now and she isn't here with you so I'd say it's not going very well for you two."

I was livid. Casey knew exactly how to get under my skin and I was starting to lose it.

"My relationship with Isabella is none of your business."

"Your relationship?" she repeated. "Giovanni, please, you have never been able to maintain a relationship in your life. That little fling with her certainly wasn't it."

"That was the most real thing I had ever known. You don't know a thing about how I feel about her," I spat.

"Her absence and your deflection of why she's not here speaks wonders."

The anger spread across my body and I clenched my fists in an attempt to control it. I wouldn't consider myself an angry person, but I had also never been pushed to this point before and I wasn't sure how to handle it. I was consumed by emotions and I hated it. I couldn't get it under control.

I downed the rest of my drink. "This is not going to work. You will not speak to me about my relationships. We will deal with this situation day by day. You can send me the details for the doctor's appointment. I don't want to know anything else. You and I will never be together in the way you're hoping for, so you better start accepting that."

She narrowed her eyes at me and her nostrils flared. She had a resting bitch face that had settled back in place and I knew I had struck a nerve.

She reached for her bag. "Clearly this was a waste of time. You need more time to process, but remember this, Giovanni, I'm going to be in your life forever now. You better get over whatever it is you're going through because we have a baby on the way and I already told you that I am not doing this alone."

She slid off the barstool and walked over to me, standing in close proximity. "You may not believe it now, but we are going to be a family, Giovanni, whether you like it or not."

Her words echoed in my head as she turned and left my apartment. This was not the way I imagined starting a family. I didn't want it this way and I especially didn't want Casey to be the mother of my child.

Did I even want children?

I had never thought of it up until now. Up until a few months ago I was convinced I was going to be a terminal bachelor and I had accepted that.

Then I met her.

Isabella came along with her beautiful smile and witty tongue and changed everything for me. She was who I wanted a future with. For the first time ever, I wanted it all. I wanted to come home to her every day and start a life together. The reality that I could never have that was suffocating me again and I didn't know how I was going to make the pain stop.

CHAPTER 11:
Giovanni

I was drenched in sweat. Sergio was adamant to keep up our training so after going a whole hour with him in the ring, I was exhausted and ready for a shower. I pulled my gloves off and took a seat on the bench trying to catch my breath.

"You did not go easy on me today," Sergio muttered as he lightly touched his busted lip.

I shrugged. "Only fair since you gave me a black eye the other day."

Sergio chuckled and took a seat on the bench across from me. He reached for a water bottle and took a sip, looking deep in thought for a moment. I had known Sergio for years so I always knew when he had something to share.

"I know you have something to say."

He ran his fingers through his hair nervously. "Yeah, I actually wanted to talk to you about something important."

I leaned against the wall and waited for him to continue.

"I wanted to tell you the other day, but then you told me about you and Izzy and I wanted to be there for you."

My face remained unchanged. Every mention of her name reminded me of that burning in my chest at her absence in my life. I didn't know how long had passed without her, but it didn't matter, the wound was just as fresh.

"I'm going to ask Katrina to marry me," he said nervously.

"Oh fuck," I gasped.

"Not exactly the response I was hoping for."

I leaned forward. "Shit man, I didn't mean it like that. I just didn't expect it - you've only been going out for a few months now."

He shrugged. "We've been together for almost a year, Giovanni."

Has it seriously been that long? Fuck, I should really start paying attention.

"You could at least say congratulations."

I stood up and reached for him. "I'm sorry. Congratulations! Seriously, I am happy for you guys."

He returned my hug before quickly pulling away. "Thank you."

"I'm serious, Sergio, I'm really happy for you guys," I repeated. "And hey, once she says yes, please feel free to use *Mala Mía* for the engagement party. I'll cover it all."

Sergio was one of my oldest friends and as much as we pushed each other around, figuratively and literally, I would always be there for him. He had changed since being with Kaulua - in a good way. She brought out the best in him and I had always thought they were good together. No matter the mess in my own life, I had to be happy for my friend.

"I appreciate that," he said.

"Do you have a ring yet?"

He nodded. "I've had it for a few months now."

"A few months?" I couldn't hide my surprise. "So you've been planning this for a while then?"

He shrugged. "When you know, you know, Giovanni."

He was right.

CHAPTER 12:
Isabella

Halfway through my latest binge-watch on Saturday night, Reyna's excited shrieks echoed through the apartment. I jumped out of bed and quickly ran to the lounge where she was on a video chat.

"Reyna, what's going on?"

She shrieked again and turned the phone to face me, Katrina's beaming face greeted me.

"I'm engaged!" Katrina cried out.

My jaw dropped. "Oh my god, Katrina, congratulations!"

A chorus of excitement surrounded us as Reyna and I huddled closer to both face Katrina on the screen. She had tears of happiness streaming down her face as she covered her mouth in shock, her huge engagement ring now on display.

"Kat, that ring is stunning!" I exclaimed.

She placed her hand closer to the camera so we could get a better look. Sergio had done well with the size of that diamond. A single band surrounded the oval-shaped diamond and fit perfectly on her skinny finger.

"I am so happy for you, *hermana!*" Reyna shrieked.

Another wave of tears rushed over Katrina. I mirrored her happiness and excitement, but a large part of me was infested with jealousy at their happiness. I would give up anything to feel the happiness they were feeling right now. Don't get me wrong, I was so happy for them. Sergio and Katrina were perfect for each other, but their engagement just reminded me of how far I was from that again. I had nothing.

"Where's Sergio?" Reyna asked. "Let us congratulate him."

Sergio popped onto the screen.

"Congratulations!" Reyna and I said together.

"Wishing you two all the best," I said.

"Thank you guys so much." Sergio was beaming. "We're going to have a proper celebration so I hope you guys are ready."

Reyna continued the conversation with Sergio as I strolled over to the kitchen in search of a bottle of water. My mouth was dry and I was using all the self-control I had to control the tears that were starting to form. Thoughts of Giovanni entered my mind and I couldn't stop them. I thought of a happier time with him - there were so many moments. I had spent so much time in absolute bliss with him that the reminder I was completely alone now was starting to tear me apart inside again.

I found a cold bottle of water in the fridge and took a sip. The cold liquid forcing me to focus on just that for now.

Reyna walked over to me. "Say goodbye to the happy couple."

I said my last goodbyes to Sergio and Katrina before the call disconnected. Reyna placed her phone on the counter and pulled herself onto a stool.

"Did you know Sergio was going to propose?" I asked.

She nodded. "When he flew out to Madrid it was because he wanted to chat to my parents and get their blessing."

"And you didn't tell me?" I lifted an eyebrow at her.

She averted her eyes. "With everything going on with you and Giovanni, I didn't know if I should."

I felt guilty. I didn't realise that my own sadness had kept me from being involved in the happiness of others.

I reached out for her hand and squeezed it. "No matter what's going on in my life, you know that I'm happy for Katrina."

She smiled at me.

"Your little sister is getting married before you," I teased.

She rolled her eyes. "I always knew it would be like that."

"I'm really happy for them."

A small lump started to form in my throat so I took another sip of water. I didn't want to get emotional right now. It wasn't about me. I already felt bad about how I had allowed my own sadness to get in the way.

"Who would have thought? A whole engagement from a one-night stand." She chuckled at the thought. "If you know, you know."

She was right.

CHAPTER 13:
Isabella

How could I go to Mala Mía?

I would have to see him and that thought alone brought on a wave of unexpected nausea. Sergio and Katrina were having their engagement party tonight and I was stuck in my bedroom trying to talk myself into going. Sergio explained that Giovanni offered the club to them for the evening. They were having a private party tonight in the VIP section with all their friends and then a lunch with both their families in the next week or so when Katrina and Reyna's parents arrived.

Both Katrina and Sergio told me that they would understand if I chose not to join, but how could I do that to them? How could I not go and celebrate with them? They were two of the closest people in my life and I needed to suck it up and be there for them. I was dreading having to leave the apartment tonight, but I kept reminding myself that it wasn't about me. This was their night. The thought of seeing Giovanni again riddled me with nerves though. How would I react? Would I have to say hi? Of course, I'd have to say hi, I couldn't be rude. Or was I supposed to avoid him? Would he avoid me?

These thoughts continued in my head and I needed to take a seat on my bed to stop the dizziness that occurred. I lay back against my bed and closed my eyes.

In and out.

I focused on my breathing in an attempt to get it under control. I was not going to be able to get out of going tonight and for the sake of my friends, I had to push everything aside and remember that.

This was about Sergio and Katrina.

After a couple of reprimands from the voice inside my head, I finally managed to get a handle on my breathing.

You will be fine, Isabella.

I hadn't quite figured out exactly what I was feeling towards Giovanni. Obviously, my heart was broken, that much was clear but there was a hint of anger too. I was angry that we were in this situation. I was angry that Casey was pregnant. I was overwhelmed with emotions - anger, sadness, hurt, but overall there was still love. That hadn't changed. How could it have? A few weeks ago I was the happiest I had ever been and completely in love with him. Now, I didn't have him in my life anymore, but my heart still belonged to him. I will be civil tonight. I was going there for them and I would be polite if I had to, but overall I planned to avoid him. I had to. I couldn't be around him without the constant reminder of what we used to have.

"Izzy?" Reyna shouted from outside my door.

"You can come in, Rey." I sat up as she strolled into my room with a towel wrapped around her and a bottle of tequila in her hand.

"What the hell is that for?" I asked, my face inadvertently pulling to form a look of disgust at the thought of the taste.

"This is for you and me," she announced. "I know you're worried about seeing Giovanni tonight and quite frankly, you could use something to take the edge off and me being the great friend that I am, I can't let you drink alone."

I chuckled. "Oh sure, that's the only reason."

"Okay fine, you caught me. You know how much I enjoy tequila."

She placed the shot glasses on top of my draws and opened the bottle as she filled the glasses to the top.

She handed one over to me. "You'll be fine tonight."

I smiled and took the shot from her. "Thanks, Rey, I appreciate you."

We both brought the glasses to our lips, tilting our heads back allowing the burning liquid to travel down our throats. I couldn't help the face that I pulled. The taste was awful, but I knew it would help. It was an unhealthy escape, but it was an escape nonetheless.

"Come, let's find you something to wear," Reyna said, turning to my cupboard.

***

Three shots later, we pulled up to the entrance of *Mala Mía*. Reyna had me wearing her tight long sleeve black dress that clung to my curves in ways I never would have wanted, but the alcohol in my system was giving me this newfound confidence. I stepped outside the taxi and I could feel I was already tipsy. The alcohol had made its way through me and my movements were more delayed than I expected. I was surprised at how low my tolerance was but it probably had something to do with the lack of food in my system.

Pull yourself together, Isabella.

I pulled my coat closer to me and took a deep breath in. *I can do this.* Tonight was about celebrating Sergio and Katrina and I was focused on doing just that. Reyna linked her arm with mine and led me into *Mala Mía*, reminding me of the first time she brought me here. I was consumed by it that night - loving every moment of the on-going drinks and handing ourselves over to the music. I will never forget that night.

The first time I met Giovanni.

Instinctively, I scanned the area for him and was disappointed to find he wasn't anywhere in sight. The music was blaring through the club as we pushed through the crowds to get to the VIP section that was booked out just for us.

"You're here!" Katrina shrieked and threw her arms around Reyna and me. "I'm so happy to see you guys."

"Let's see the ring." Reyna reached for her hand, displaying the huge diamond that now had a permanent residence on her left ring finger.

"It's so beautiful, Kat." I squeezed her arm before pulling her in for another hug. "I'm really happy for you guys."

"Thank you, Izzy."

Sergio stumbled into the conversation, wrapping his arms around his fiancé's waist. Katrina was glowing with a new refound happiness. The two of them were completely smitten with each other and it reminded me that I needed a drink. Now.

"Congratulations, Sergio." I pulled him in for a quick hug. "I wish you guys nothing but the best."

"Thank you. That means a lot." He smiled. "And hey, listen I'm sorry about Giovanni and everything that's going on."

"You don't need to apologize."

"I know bu-".

I politely cut him off. "Seriously, it's fine. I think we should all get a drink though."

I needed a subject change. I didn't want to be that sad friend that everyone pitied. I wanted to forget all about that and focus on celebrating them. We strolled over to the bar and Sergio ordered us a round of drinks. I tapped my nails on the bar nervously. A part of me was dying to see Giovanni, just to get a glimpse of him again. That was all I wanted. Just one last look and then I could move on.

As if it was that easy.

I knew it wouldn't be, but I could at least try. Diego arrived just as we took our shots and I was suddenly very aware of the fact that I was a fifth-wheel tonight. I hated it. I grabbed my drink off the bar and downed a bit of it. I didn't want to think right now - I wanted to forget it all. I took one more sip before placing it back on the bar and pushing my way through the crowd. I wanted to dance. I stopped and signalled Reyna to let her know I was headed to the dance floor. She nodded and turned back to say something to Diego before following behind me. I turned down the stairs and made my way to the middle of the dance floor that was already packed with people. I was under the big chandelier and I threw my hands in the air, allowing the music to overcome me. I moved my body from side to side and focused on nothing, but the beat surrounding us.

I didn't know how long I had been on the dance floor for before Reyna escaped back upstairs to grab our drinks. I managed to push everything out of my mind and there was nothing else but the music consuming me. Until I closed my eyes and all I saw was him. Fragmented thoughts of his hands on my body entered my mind and the way he would pull me closer to him, moving side to side. I ran my fingers through my hair and down my neck, tracing the places he used to leave kisses against. I was being suffocated by the memories of him. I never realised how much I needed his touch before now. The only man to light my body and soul on fire. I slowly opened my eyes and there he was.

Giovanni...

He stood at the top of the stairs overlooking the dance floor. His gaze met mine and my breath caught in my throat. *Fuck, he looked so good.* Even from this distance, I could see he was wearing that leather jacket that he wore the first night I met him. He knew how much I loved that jacket on him. I couldn't think of anything else, but that first night with him. My body awoke at just the mere sight of him. I couldn't control my thoughts anymore - not in this inebriated state. Every inch of me ached for him. It had been so long since I had my body set alight and that was all I wanted right now. I wanted his hands on my body, his lips against mine.

I missed him.

I missed him so much it hurt. I couldn't look at him any longer. I turned away from him but the aching in my chest reappeared and I needed to make it go away. I didn't want to feel like this anymore. The heat from all the dancing spread across my body and I suddenly needed some air. I pulled my coat off me and turned towards the exit. I was so aware of his presence. I couldn't go back to our section now. *What would I even say to him?*

The world was spinning as I stumbled up the stairs, finally pushing through to get outside. I leaned against the wall to help get my balance again. Heels and drinking were a terrible combination. I closed my eyes and leaned my head against the wall, trying to regain my composure. I focused on the cold wind that hit my arms. It was refreshing. For a moment I focused on nothing but my breathing. My heart was beating erratically in my chest. *In and out.* I knew I had to go back inside and I was going to have to face him. I had to make sure I could keep it together. There was no way I wanted to lose control around him. Not again.

After a few minutes, I was feeling better. I finally started to get my breathing under control and the cold air helped get rid of the unnecessary amount of heat I was feeling. I was going to be fine. I would go back upstairs and focus on celebrating with Katrina and Sergio. If I bumped into Giovanni then I would politely greet him otherwise I would avoid him as best as possible. It seemed like a solid plan and I was adamant to follow it.

I turned to make my way back inside as Reyna stepped outside, drinks in hand. "Are you alright?"

I nodded. "Sorry, I just needed some air."

She handed me my drink as we turned and made our way back inside.

CHAPTER 14:
Giovanni

Where did she go?

I leaned over the railing trying to find her in the crowd again. I was thankful for the many drinks I had upstairs before finally convincing myself to come down. I was dying to see her again and when my eyes met hers on the dance floor, I couldn't look away.

Until she took off towards the exit.

I know she saw me. There was no way she didn't. Her gaze met mine and in that moment, there was no one else around. It was just her and I and I wanted nothing more than to go up to her and pull her into my arms.

But I couldn't.

I turned to the entrance and she caught my eye as she slipped back inside, hand in hand with Reyna. *Should I go to her? Am I allowed to do that?* Fuck, I didn't know how I was supposed to act around her. I watched her make her way back to the dance-floor as Reyna slipped past her. I couldn't take my eyes off her and right now, I needed all the help I could get to try and rid myself of the constant pressure in my chest. The alcohol was the perfect illusionist and it helped to not think of the pain. It wasn't a healthy outlet, but it was the only one I had right now. I couldn't pull my gaze from her and I was reminded of how much I wanted her. She threw her hands in the air and moved her body to the music. I was intoxicated by the sight of her. It had been so long since I had felt her body and watching her throw her head back the way she was, reignited the desire I had worked so hard to push away. I wanted to push through the crowd, grab her hand and lead her back to my place so I could have my way with her.

But that would never happen again.

I felt a hand on my shoulder and turned to meet Reyna's judgemental gaze.

"*Hola, Reyna,*" I said politely.

"Don't *Hola Reyna* me." She leaned against the railing and faced me. "Giovanni, what happened?"

For fuck sakes. I was so tired of that question. I hated that what went down with Isabella was public knowledge. I was reminded of my fuck up at every turn and it was making it harder to escape.

"I don't want to do this right now, Reyna. I'm only here for Sergio."

I didn't want to come tonight. I had to talk myself into it because I knew I would have to see her and that it would leave me feeling exactly how I was feeling right now.

"I wouldn't be doing my duty as best friend if I didn't tell you what I thought." She crossed her arms. "You fucked up."

"I hadn't noticed." The sarcasm dripped off my tongue.

"But I'm still rooting for you two."

I turned back to her, surprised by her statement. "What?"

Before Reyna could answer, Sergio and Katrina joined us holding shot glasses in their hands.

"Come on guys! It's a celebration!" Katrina exclaimed and handed me a shot.

I wanted to know what more Reyna had to say. I never thought I would say that because her opinions were often unwelcome ones, but it surprised me that she was rooting for us. If anything, I would have expected her to give me an earful about how I hurt her best friend. Sergio handed a shot to Reyna and turned back to me, handing one over as his gaze reached past me.

"Perfect timing!" Sergio shouted. "Isabella, come have a shot with us."

I turned around and there she was coming up the stairs. *Fuck, she looked so good.* I had never seen that dress before, but it clung to the curves of her body, sending my imagination into a frenzy. She had pulled her hair into a low bun with curly strands of hair falling forward. Her gaze met mine briefly and there was something missing in her deep hazel eyes. She was the Isabella that I knew and loved and yet, she was like a stranger to me now. She walked past me and stood on the other side of Sergio, taking the shot from him. She avoided my gaze.

"Thank you guys for being here," Sergio shouted and lifted his shot glass up.

There was a chorus of congratulations that went around as I brought the glass to my lips. It burned going down, but I was thankful for something to help take the edge off. I could feel I needed something stronger because it was taking every ounce of self-control I had not to look over at her again. Just knowing she was so close, but I couldn't do anything about that was driving me fucking crazy. Instead, I turned around to face the dance floor full of people again. I was happy this place was still able to fill up, no matter the cold weather outside.

I tapped my foot anxiously, trying to focus on anything but the thoughts of her. I didn't want to think of her and that dress. I wanted nothing more than to rip it off her right now. I swallowed and clenched my fists in an attempt to hold back my arousal. I headed for the bar to order a drink.

"Whiskey, neat," I asked the bartender.

I leaned against the bar and scanned my surroundings for her again. I couldn't help it. I hated that I wasn't able to go up to her. I thought I would feel better about being able to see her again, but this was fucking torture. She stood in the crowd with Reyna and Diego. I watched her as she engaged in conversation with them, throwing her head back in laughter. From here, she looked perfectly fine to me, laughing as if nothing had changed. To an outsider, she just looked like a beautiful woman enjoying the company of those around her.

How was she so okay?

Here I was falling apart inside and she didn't even seem phased by it. The pressure in my chest returned along with a flicker of anger and I had to turn away from her.

Why did I do that to myself?

The bartender placed my drink in front of me. I reached for it and brought it to my lips. This was going to be a long night.

CHAPTER 15:
Isabella

I noticed him out of the corner of my eye. He stood by the bar with a drink in his hand. Probably a whiskey, neat. That was always his drink of choice. I tried to forget about the fact that he was here, but I couldn't. He was in such close proximity and yet, it was like we were complete strangers. I hated it. I allowed my gaze to flick over to him again. I was drawn to him just like I was the first night I met him. His oozing sex-appeal didn't disappear and knowing that I couldn't have him only made me want him more. I watched as he tilted his head back with the glass against his lips. His strong arms flexed as he brought it up and back down again. I was gawking at him now. Why couldn't I look away? I needed to look away but it was too late. He turned to meet my gaze.

Fuck, I missed him.

We were so far from each other, but I felt him calling out for me. The tension surrounded me, making it difficult for me to breathe. I couldn't believe how the instant desire had overcome me from something as simple as eye contact. I wanted nothing more than to walk over to where he stood and throw myself at him.

But I couldn't.

Nothing had changed. I was the one who walked away from him. I pulled my gaze away from his. I couldn't look at him anymore. I walked over to an open seat in the corner booth and slid onto it. This was torture. I hung my head in my hands, the sudden dizziness washing over me. A few minutes later I heard his voice close to me.

"Isabella?"

I looked up and met those deep brown eyes I loved so much. I was surprised by his choice to come up to me. I could never have done that.

"Giovanni."

He stood awkwardly in front of me, one hand in his pocket and the other holding his drink.

"Do you mind if I sit?" he asked politely.

Please, don't. It was already torture having him this close to me. I thought the alcohol would have helped me tonight, but all it did was intensify everything I was already feeling and I immediately regretted my decision.

"Go ahead," I said.

What was he doing? I didn't want him this close. It was already painful just to have him in the same room and now he was only inches from me. He slid onto the couch across from me and leaned against it, bringing his drink to his lips. His beard was thicker now and his strands of hair fell forward like it always did. He turned his head to the side to face the crowd and I noticed the new ink he was sporting behind his neck.

"You got a new tattoo?" I shouted over the music.

He ran his hand over the open wing on the side of his neck and down the back. "Yeah, got it last week."

I nodded, not sure what I was supposed to say next. I tapped my nails anxiously against the couch. I had no idea how to act around him and it was unnerving.

"You look like you're doing well," he remarked.

If only he knew.

"Yes, I'm fine," I lied.

He scoffed. "Must be nice."

I was thrown off by the hostility behind that statement. He had no idea what I had been going through these last few weeks, but I wasn't about to give him the satisfaction of knowing he had broken me to the point of no return. I didn't know how I was ever going to get over him. The thoughts were spinning in my mind and a rush of dizziness overcame me again. Alcohol and emotion were a terrible combination, but it was already too late for me. A spinning wheel of emotions spun around in my head and landed on anger.

"And you? I'm sure the elusive Giovanni Velázquez has found many ways to entertain himself."

I was being petty now, but my inebriated state was in charge and I wasn't able to control what I was saying. My filter had slipped away about three shots ago.

He raised an eyebrow. "What the hell does that mean?"

I shrugged. "I highly doubt you've been without company."

He stopped with his glass halfway to meet his lips. "My company is hardly any of your business anymore."

Ouch!

My heart contracted, but my face remained unchanged. I was caught off guard by his bitterness towards me. I had never seen him like this and it was making it harder for me not to burst into tears. I tried to convince myself that he wasn't being intentionally cruel to me, he just wanted a reaction.

"Thanks for the reminder," I scolded sarcastically and reached for my coat.

"Where are you going?" he asked.

A pretty young red-head stopped by our booth, flashing a quick smile to me before turning to face Giovanni.

Before I could answer, she interrupted, "I haven't seen you here in a while."

She was an unfamiliar face to me, but then again, I didn't know everyone who interacted with Giovanni. He dismissed my presence and turned to reply to her. I was shocked and disgusted by his behaviour. *Has he not hurt me enough?* I felt a lump start to form in my throat.

"Well, that's my cue," I muttered and stood up without a last glance towards him.

Reyna and Katrina were laughing by the bar so I walked over to join them. The entire interaction with Giovanni was unnecessary and made me feel so much worse. I had started to get used to the pain I was feeling over the last couple of weeks, but that interaction brought on a fresh wave of sadness. I was reminded of how much love I still had for him. That didn't matter anymore though because he had clearly forgotten about me.

Reyna reached for me. "Please, can you tell my sister that a winter wedding would be a terrible idea?"

Katrina chuckled. "I'm just playing around with ideas, nothing has be-".

The rest of the conversation became white noise as I couldn't help but watch Giovanni and the red-head stand up and leave the area together. Jealousy reared its ugly head. *Are you fucking kidding me?* Was this not the reason we were in this situation in the first place? I couldn't believe the audacity. I cried over him every day and here he was leaving with someone as if our relationship meant nothing to him.

I turned to the bartender. "Can I please get a shot of tequila?"

"I'll have one too!" Reyna shouted. "Katrina?"

"*Joder,* no, please. I'm pretty sure I'm already drunk."

"Well, drunk sex is great so I'm sure you and Sergio are going to have a gret time tonight." Reyna winked, laughing.

Katrina's jaw dropped. "Reyna!"

I couldn't help but laugh at her reaction. Katrina was so polite and more reserved than Reyna was.

"Please don't act like you just hold hands." Reyna rolled her eyes. "Your relationship literally started with a one-night stand."

Katrina blushed and couldn't help but giggle. "I know, but you don't have to be so loud about it."

The bartender handed us the shots and we took them straight away. Sergio walked over and pulled Katrina in for a kiss. I averted my eyes. I didn't want to see other people's romances right now. It was making me feel sick and I was struggling to hold back my jealousy without my sober filter.

I turned to Reyna. "Where's Diego?"

"He's here somewhere." Reyna chuckled, but then turned to me. "But how are you handling tonight? It must have been hard seeing Giovanni earlier."

I was thankful for the copious amount of alcohol working its way through my body right now. It helped take away the initial sting I would usually get from those kinds of questions. I wish everyone would stop bringing him up to me.

"I don't care about Giovanni anymore," I slurred.

That was a lie, but I was so angry at him. He went out of his way to come and sit with me and for what? To make snide comments and flirt with some random person? I glanced around the area, but I couldn't find him or that red-head anywhere. My blood was starting to boil over with jealousy.

"You don't mean that," Reyna said softly.

I turned back to her. "Yes, I do. He was bad news from the beginning. I should never have gotten involved with him."

Reyna reached for me. "Izzy, I think you've had too much to drink. Can I get you some water?"

I pulled away from her. "No thanks. I'll be right back."

I didn't wait for her response before turning and heading for the stairs. I was drowning in jealousy and incredibly angry that Giovanni had the audacity to put me in this situation. *Who the fuck did he think he was?* He came into my life and bulldozed all over my heart. I searched the dance floor for him and he finally caught my eye at the bar with the same woman.

"Fucking asshole," I mumbled.

I was way past the point of rational thinking and right now I couldn't do anything except react to my emotions. I was sick to my stomach with jealousy, but I refused to give him that power. We were in this mess because of him and this was how he chose to act? Before I knew it I was pushing my way to the dance floor again. There were plenty of attractive men here and I needed one of them to make me forget all about Giovanni. He wasn't the only man in the world.

These drunk ramblings continued in my mind as I threw my head back, trying my hardest to focus on the sexy beat blaring through the speakers. The crowd had gotten bigger and I was brushing up against the people around me. I made eye contact with an attractive man across from me and I didn't look away. I welcomed his inquisitive gaze as he moved himself over to me. I didn't care about who he was at all. I just wanted to feel something other than what I was feeling. I slowly moved myself to meet him. I turned with my back to him as his arms found my waist, pulling me against his body. I closed my eyes and leaned my head against his chest. Our bodies moved as one and my mind wandered back to the first time I danced with Giovanni right on this dance floor. His hands on my body set me alight in a way I had never felt before and I was consumed by desire. I would give anything to feel that again. I opened my eyes and met Giovanni's piercing gaze from across the dance floor. Even from here, I could see he was seething. *Good to know I could still get a reaction out of him.* He turned away from me and back to the woman he was still with. I watched as he led her to the back.

He's probably taking her home.

I shut my eyes to keep the tears from forming. *What the fuck was I doing?* I didn't want to be here anymore and I wished I had never come in the first place. Seeing Giovanni like this was too painful and I was going to have to work to start getting over him all over again. Not that I had much luck up till now, but this just made everything worse. I didn't have the strength inside of me to move on, but I knew there was no other option. Not being with him was destroying me from the inside out.

I didn't know how much time had passed before I broke away from my mystery dance partner and started pushing my way to the back of the club. The idea of him with someone else brought on a wave of anger and there was no way I could stop myself now. I was too intoxicated for that. He didn't have the right to take someone home. Especially right in front of me?

Who the fuck did he think he was?

He couldn't break my heart by getting Casey pregnant and then still have the audacity to do what he was doing. I pushed the button on the elevator and tapped my nails against the wall, the nerves washing over me. The elevator opened and I stepped inside.

What are you doing, Isabella?

A faint echo of my sober self tried to get me to turn around, but it was too late. I had no right to be doing what I was doing, but I couldn't help the increasing amount of jealousy working its way through me. It was taking everything I had not to burst into tears. The elevator doors opened to the familiar smell of his apartment, suddenly bringing on a rush of unwanted memories.

"Giovanni!" I shouted. "Where are you?"

I stumbled through his living room. The curtains were open and the only company I had was the bright moon shining down on me. I looked around and everything was in its place again, unlike the last time I was here.

"Giovanni!" I shouted again, but was greeted by silence.

I stormed up the stairs and pushed open the door to his bedroom. The bathroom door was drawn closed and I could hear the shower on as the steam seeped out from under the door.

Please let him be alone.

I wouldn't be able to handle it if I opened this door and he was with someone else. I didn't need those visuals in my mind. I stood outside the door, contemplating what to do next. What was I going to do? What was the point of me coming up here? I was not supposed to be here and yet, I couldn't pull myself away.

I banged on the door. "Giovanni, I know you're in there."

The water turned off suddenly and I heard bustling from behind the door. I knocked on the door again and he opened it, his wet body greeting me.

"Isabella, what the hell are you doing here?"

He tightened the towel around his waist and I couldn't help but tug at my lip at the sight of him. I couldn't take my eyes off his body. I was surrounded by the suffocating tension that suddenly filled the room. It made my mouth dry and I couldn't gather the words I needed right now.

"I wa..."

I couldn't finish my sentence, not with a sexy wet Giovanni standing in front of me. I flicked my eyes to meet his.

"You what, Isabella?" he murmured.

I wanted to throw myself at him. I wanted him to take me in his arms, lay me on his bed and have his way with me. I was dying to feel his body against mine. I missed him. I missed what it felt like to have him inside of me.

But I couldn't and I suddenly realised what a mistake I had made coming here.

"I'm sorry." I turned to leave, but he reached for my arm.

"There's obviously a reason you came here." He pulled me closer to him, not letting go of my arm.

His touch burned against my skin and a ripple of desire made its way through me, increasing the pressure between my legs.

"You left with someone else," I whispered.

He jerked his head back, confused. "What are you talking about?"

I pulled my arm away from him. "That red-headed woman. I saw you guys leave together."

"I didn't leave with her, Isabella. I had to show her my office because she's the new manager."

New manager?

Relief washed over me with those words. The idea of him with someone else drove me crazy enough to come up to his apartment and I suddenly felt incredibly stupid for giving into my jealousy. I was acting like a deranged idiot right now and it was embarrassing.

"Oh well, that's gr-".

He cut me off. "Did you really think I would leave with someone else?"

I averted my eyes.

"And what do you care, anyway? You were perfectly happy grinding up on that guy on the dance floor."

"I was not grinding," I objected.

He scoffed and rolled his eyes. I suddenly felt so guilty over what I had done. I knew I wanted a reaction out of him, but it was so petty and out of character for me. I hated that I was acting this way.

"I don't know what you're doing here, Isabella," Giovanni muttered and walked past me towards his cupboard. "Even if I had brought someone else home, that really has nothing to do with you since you were the one who broke up with me."

My stomach dropped. "Please don't act like I had no reason to break up with you, Giovanni."

He ignored me and reached for a pair of shorts from his cupboard and tossed them on the bed.

"Are you trying to hurt me?" I murmured softly, trying hard not to allow the tears that were building to spill over.

He stopped for a moment before turning to face me, a defeated look on his face. "Of course not. I've never wanted to hurt you."

Tears filled my eyes again and I took a deep breath in trying to keep them at bay. I couldn't break down - not here.

"The fact you believe I would have brought someone home with me proves that you really don't understand how I feel about you at all."

My heart swelled at his words. A flicker of happiness appeared before quickly being replaced by the reality of our situation. Nothing has changed and now I feel worse than before.

I turned to leave. "I'm sorry, I shouldn't have come."

"Don't do that." He stepped in front of me. "You're running away again."

Yes I was.

"I shouldn't have come," I repeated.

He grabbed my wrist, his touch burning against my skin as he pulled me closer to him. He was so close now that I could smell the fresh body wash on him mixed with his intoxicating natural scent. My pulse was racing at the close proximity we were in and I couldn't move. I didn't want to.

He slowly cupped my face with his hand. "Fine, you can leave then."

Was he serious?

How could I possibly pull myself away from him now? He slowly ran his thumb against my cheek and along my jaw, each touch causing my heart to beat erratically.

"Giovanni," I breathed.

"I'll let you leave if that's what you want, Isabella, but I don't think you want to."

He was right. Leaving was the last thing I wanted to do.

His eyes traveled down to my mouth. "But you have to tell me what you want."

My eyes met his and his desire mirrored my own. Whatever sane thoughts I was supposed to be having slipped away and were replaced with my deepest desires. I couldn't think of anything else but his body and how I needed to feel it against me. I tried to fight it, but there was no stopping me now.

"You." I threw myself at him, my lips crashing against his.

I was scared he was going to push me away but instead, his arms encircled my body and he pulled me closer to him. My tongue flicked over his as I was overcome with the sudden urge to have all of him. *God, I missed him.* My hands found their way to his hair and I tugged at it. His strong arms came around me and lifted me up, my legs wrapping around his waist as he pinned me up against the nearest wall. His hungry kiss sent a rush of heat through me and I exploded with desire. The towel he had wrapped around his waist fell away, revealing what he was truly feeling. I felt him hard against me as he leaned closer, my legs wrapping tighter around his waist. His lips left mine and made their way to my neck.

"Giovanni," His name rolled off my tongue as I leaned my head back, the familiarity of the situation overcoming me.

He didn't slow down. He worked his way over me with an insatiable appetite, both of us giving in to our animalistic desires. My hands tangled in his hair again and I pulled it, hard. I needed him to know that I needed him and I had to have him. There was no going back now. His lips sucked at my neck before moving across my collar bone as he carried me towards the bed. He tossed me against it and didn't slow down as his hands made their way over my body. As I reached out for him, he quickly grabbed my arms and pinned them down over my head.

"Stay," he commanded.

The heat tore through me and my body handed itself over to him. I was consumed by him and there was nothing I could think about except his lips against mine. He ran his hand down the side of my body where my zip was. In one swift motion, he pulled it down and allowed me to move my hands in order to push my way out of my dress. I peeled it off my arms and he grabbed the rest of it, pulling it down my body before tossing it onto the floor. He brought himself over me and pinned my arms above my head again. His kiss was rough and greedy as he explored my lips. His tongue flicked over mine and I arched my hips against him, needing to feel more of him. I needed to feel what I had done to him. I needed to feel his desire for me.

I needed him inside me.

"Giovanni, please," I moaned.

His hand slipped behind my back and I arched it, allowing him enough space to unclasp my bra and pull it off me. It didn't take him long before he reached my underwear, sliding it down my legs. He ran his hands up my legs, reaching my knees and slowly spreading them. I was so ready for him. Just the sight of him hovering between my legs made my heart skip a beat. He was overcome with a hunger I had never seen before and I didn't know what he had planned. He moved closer to me, so close now that I could feel his breath against my skin. He flicked his eyes up to me and they were burning with desire.

Without breaking eye contact, he leaned forward between my legs and I knew what was coming next. I tried to squeeze my legs together, trying to get a handle on the overwhelming electricity coursing through my veins, but he wouldn't let me.

"You just can't stay still can you?" he murmured seductively.

I bit down on my lip, keeping myself from reacting.

"Don't keep quiet, Isabella, you know I love hearing you."

He brought himself closer and I felt his tongue flick over me. My eyes rolled back and I gripped against the bed as he continued his hungry rhythm against me. Licking and sucking me before bringing his fingers into the mix. I tightened around him as the tension between my legs rapidly increased with each flick of his tongue. My hands found their way into his hair again and I pulled, not being able to control my reaction. He explored me greedily and without barriers. He pushed me further and further and I was fast approaching my climax.

"Don't stop, Giovanni."

And he didn't. He pushed me closer and closer until I couldn't hold it back any longer. I came undone and moaned his name into the night. My body was reeling from the pleasure that overcame me, but he didn't stop. He reached for a condom, tore it open, and rolled it over himself. He spread my legs and positioned himself between them. My breathing was ragged and my pulse was racing. The sight of him above me sent my desire reeling. I never thought I would be able to feel him again.

He leaned closer to my ear. "You're mine."

He claimed me as his again by burying himself deep inside of me. I threw my head back in ecstasy - this was what I had been craving. I craved him inside of me. I wrapped my arms around his neck and pulled him closer to me as we moved. There was nothing delicate about the rhythm we had chosen. We didn't care about that. I wanted to rip into him. My nails dug into his arms as he pushed deeper inside of me, reaching the spot every time. I increased the pace of my movements, needing more of him. His hand ran from my hair, across my cheek and gently wrapped at the base of my throat.

Small breaths escaped him and I felt the pleasure building deep within the pit of my stomach again. I wrapped my legs around his waist, forcing him deeper. I didn't want this to end. I wanted to stay wrapped up in this euphoria for as long as possible. He pushed deep inside me and I cried out in pleasure as my body came undone again. I couldn't hold it back any longer. He didn't stop, he continued to move faster and faster. My legs shook as the pleasure tore through my body, down to my very core.

I moaned his name as the pleasure continued to spread. I moaned for him - the man I would always love. The man who introduced me to the kind of overwhelming passion and pleasure I had never experienced before. The man who had my heart and always would.

His hand was buried in my hair, pulling at it as he reached his own climax. He dropped down, his body hot against me. His chest rising and falling with mine. At that moment, I thought of nothing but how much I love him. I slowly ran my fingers through his hair the way I always used to, not wanting this moment to end.

    I didn't know how long we stayed like that before he finally removed himself from me and lay against his bed, staring up at the ceiling. I turned to lie on my side, facing him. I slowly ran my finger across his chest, over every marking as I moved along his arm. Without a word, he reached out and pulled me closer to him, my head resting against his chest and my leg draping across his. He tightened his arms around me and we said nothing. We didn't need to say anything. We just needed each other right now. I listened to the sound of his heartbeat as I drifted off into darkness.

CHAPTER 16:

Giovanni

I woke to the soft sounds of her breathing. She was no longer on my chest, but she had moved her head onto my pillow, sharing it with me. I turned to face her. She lay on her stomach facing me. She was in a deep sleep and I soaked in the moment. I couldn't believe she was in my bed again. That was the last thing I thought would happen tonight. Stray strands of hair fell forward and I slowly moved them behind her ear. I caressed her cheeks softly, careful not to wake her. I turned to face the ceiling trying to wrap my head around what happened. She sought me out after she thought I had taken Ali home. It bothered me that she thought so little of me. I thought I had made it clear that I was in love with her, and yet, she still believed I would do something like that. The thought of me with someone else was enough to get her to storm through my place though. She was also the one who kissed me first.

What did that mean? Did that change anything?

I wasn't sure, but all I knew was that I had missed her. I didn't want her to leave. I wanted her to stay in this bed with me forever.

A light buzzing from across the room caught my attention. Isabella didn't move - she was too deep in sleep to notice. I slowly moved off the bed and walked over to where her bag was. I opened it and it was her phone that was buzzing. I turned it over and Reyna's name flashed across the screen. I noticed it was well past midnight and figured Reyna was probably worried about where she was. The call ended, making that the fourth missed call.

I dialled Reyna's number as I slipped outside the room. After the second ring, I was greeted by Reyna's voice.

"Isabella! *Joder*, I've been worried sick ab-".

I interrupted her. "It's Giovanni."

She was silent on the other end and I didn't blame her.

"Reyna? Are you there?" I asked.

"I'm here. I'm just confused right now. Why do you have Isabella's phone?"

"Uh, she's here with me," I mumbled awkwardly.

"What are you doing, Giovanni?"

I could just picture her rolling her eyes.

"What do you mean?" I asked. "She was the one who came to me."

She let out an exasperated sigh. "Of course, she came to you. She's still in love with you."

Hearing that brought on a quick rush of happiness, reminding me of the first time I heard Isabella say that.

"But this is a terrible idea. This isn't helping either of you at all. You need to let her move on."

"I don't want her to move on, Reyna," I retorted.

"I know that," she muttered. "Can I ask you something?"

"Go ahead."

"I didn't want to say anything about this to Isabella in case it comes back with the results she doesn't want and I've gone and gotten her hopes up for nothing but why haven't you asked Casey for a paternity test?"

A paternity test?

I was surprised by her question, but I was more surprised that I hadn't thought of doing that in the first place.

"A paternity test?" I repeated.

"Yes, Giovanni, a paternity test. How do you know the baby is yours?"

"She said I was the father."

She scoffed.

"I slept with her, Reyna," I said sheepishly.

"Yeah and you were a fucking idiot for doing that," she muttered.

"I kno-".

"But surely there could be a chance that she's lying."

As Reyna said it, I started to feel dumb for never having questioned Casey before. I was so wrapped up in my own guilt over this that I didn't even think of her as being someone that would lie about something like this. Surely she wouldn't? It never crossed my mind but for the first time in days I felt a flicker of hope.

"And what if she's not lying and I've gone and gotten my hopes up for nothing?"

"You'll never know for sure unless you find out."

"Can that be done while she's pregnant or do I have to wait till after the baby is born?" I asked. I was clueless about shit like this. I had never been in this situation before.

"I don't know," she continued. "But listen to me carefully, you do not breathe a word of this to Isabella. There is still a strong possibility that the baby is yours and I would hate it if she got her hopes up for nothing. It would crush her."

She was right. The last thing I would want to do is give false hope only to have everything ripped away from us again. I didn't even want to think too much about the possibility that this nightmare could be over. I had slept with Casey so it wasn't impossible to think the baby could still be mine.

"Giovanni?" Reyna brought me out of my own thoughts. "Promise me you'll keep this from her?"

"Yes, Reyna, of course."

"Good. Now I'm assuming the reason you answered was that she must be asleep. I just wanted to make sure she was okay."

"I'll take care of her, Reyna."

"I know you will," she said. "And hey, for what it's worth, I really hope it works out for you two."

"Thank you. Bye, Reyna."

I disconnected the call and leaned against the wall, reeling from that conversation. *Why the fuck didn't I think to ask for a paternity test?* My initial reaction was to believe that Casey wouldn't lie about something like this and all the evidence pointed to it being true.

Careful Giovanni.

The voice in the back of my head warned me that this could still be a possibility and I had to treat it that way. I didn't want to think of that right now. I wanted to revel in the fact that the woman I love was in my bed again. I slipped back into the room and laid back against my pillow. Her eyes fluttered open briefly as she pulled herself onto my chest again. My arms wrapped around her and I hoped this moment would never end.

CHAPTER 17:

Isabella

My head was killing me.

I slowly opened my eyes as I was greeted by the day. The sun was peeping through the curtains and the memories of last night came flooding back.

Oh fuck.

I sat right up, looking around Giovanni's room. The abrupt movement really wasn't helping the pounding from behind my eyes. I pulled the blanket over my naked body. I ran my fingers through my hair, trying to get a handle on my thoughts. I remembered brief fragments of storming through his place trying to find him. I remembered his hot, wet body as he stepped out of the bathroom. I remembered him pinning me against the wall.

My cheeks flushed at the memories of what came next.

"Isabella," I groaned to myself and hung my head in my hands.

What were you thinking?

How could I have allowed myself to end up in Giovanni's bed again? This was such a bad idea and I needed to get out of here. I slowly moved off his bed and scanned the room for my clothes. I quickly found my underwear and bra and slipped back into them. I was searching for my dress again and this was reminiscent of the first night I slept with him. *What was I going to say to him?* This should never have happened, and yet, the reminder of his presence between my legs was making it difficult for me to want to leave at all. I found my dress and pulled it over me, zipping it in place. My bag and shoes were waiting in the corner and I quickly reached for them. I slipped out of his room and slowly made my way downstairs. I had to keep my movements slower than usual - the raging headache and lingering dizziness were begging me to. As I turned around the corner towards the kitchen, there he stood behind the counter.

"Morning," he said with a smile on his face.

He had nothing on but a pair of grey sweatpants, hanging perfectly at his waist. He has got to be doing this on purpose. He knew how much I loved the sight of his body and I couldn't keep my eyes off him.

"Uh hi," I mumbled awkwardly.

"You're not trying to run away again are you?" he joked. "'Cause this feels very familiar."

I couldn't help but smile at his reference to the morning after we first slept together. This was reminiscent of that day. I was so adamant to keep to Reyna's rules that I really thought I could run away without him seeing. That was definitely not what happened next, but I couldn't allow myself to think of that.

He placed a glass of water and two tablets on the counter. "I was going to bring this to you."

I walked towards the counter. "Thank you."

I picked the tablets up and brought the water to my lips, washing them down my throat. I was really hoping they would start kicking in soon because my head was pounding.

He leaned against the counter and flicked his eyes to meet mine. My breath caught in my throat, I was sick to my stomach with nerves. I had no idea how I was supposed to get out of this.

"Breakfast?" he asked. "I can order us something or we can go out and ge-".

"Giovanni," I interrupted him."I'm sorry, but I think I should leave."

"Why?" His eyes were saddened.

I averted my eyes. Coming here last night was so selfish of me and now I was overcome with guilt. No matter how much I was dying to be in his arms again, all I've done now was put us both through a continued and inevitable heartbreak. It wasn't fair on him either. I was the one who walked out on him.

"Last night shouldn't have happened," I said softly.

"That's not true," he objected.

"I'm serious, Giovanni." I looked up to meet his eyes. "That was a mistake."

He ran his hands through his hair. "You're lying to yourself, Isabella. You know that wasn't a mistake. We are meant to be together."

He walked around the counter to where I stood. I turned with my back against it as he stepped closer to me. My heart ached for him. Last night wasn't supposed to happen. It was a poor lapse of judgment and all I've done is broken my own heart over again knowing that we were still in this fucked up situation.

"This doesn't change anything," I murmured and slipped past him.

I needed to get out of here. The continued tension was suffocating me and I didn't know how to handle it.

"How many times are you going to break my heart, Isabella?"

His voice was riddled with pain and it made the tears fill my eyes. I turned to face him.

"I never wanted to break your heart, Giovanni," I choked. "But what am I-".

Before I could finish my sentence, the sound of the elevator opening made both of us turn towards the exit.

"Giovanni? Are you ready to go?" Casey shouted.

She sauntered around the corner and a rush of nausea washed over me.

"Oh, you're here," she muttered, stopping in her tracks.

I turned back to Giovanni and his eyes were screaming an apology from across the room. This was exactly the kind of situation I wanted to avoid and yet, here I was.

"I was just leaving," I mumbled and turned towards the exit.

"Isabella, wait," Giovanni shouted and rushed over to me. "Casey, please can you just give us a moment?"

Casey scoffed and strolled into the living room. Her blonde hair falling effortlessly over her shoulder. She was wearing a large coat that hid her stomach and I wondered if she was starting to show.

Giovanni reached for my arm, stopping me from getting into the elevator. "Isabella, please don't leave like this. She's only here because we have a doctor's appointment."

I didn't want to hear that. I didn't want to hear anything about them and their baby. I hated it.

"I should never have come here last night," I repeated.

"Please don't say that," he murmured. "You know that last night wasn't a mistake. You and I being together is not a mistake, Isabella."

"Nothing has changed, Giovanni," I repeated. "I want no part of this."

I pulled my arm out of his hold and stepped into the elevator.

"Isabella, please," he pleaded.

"I'm sorry."

"If you walk away now then that's it." He took a deep breath in. "You either want to be with me or you don't, but I can't keep watching you leave."

My eyes met his and I could see I had hurt him again. Worse than I did before. All I wanted to do was get out of the elevator and wrap my arms around him. I wanted to comfort him and tell him how much I love him.

But I didn't.

Instead, I stayed silent and the elevator doors closed, shutting me off from him again. As soon as he was out of sight, I felt my heart break all over again. The tears spilled over and I couldn't hold them back any longer. I was so angry at myself for allowing this to happen. I was angry that this was our reality. I was so happy being in his arms last night. It felt like that was exactly where I belonged but that was short-lived. This morning reminded me exactly of why I needed to stay away from him. Casey walking in so casually made me feel sick. Every time I saw her, it reminded me of what she said at *Mala Mía*.

We always find our way back to each other.

By the time I stepped out of the elevator, the sadness had slipped away and I was now overcome with a wave of all-consuming anger. I was angry that we were in this situation in the first place. I wiped away my tears. What good would crying do? Nothing was going to change and I had to accept that Casey had won. I turned to hail a taxi as my phone buzzed in my bag. I gave the driver my address and glanced down at my screen, surprised to find a text from Lorenzo.

Hey Isabella, how about coffee?

Any other day I would have probably politely rejected his offer, but after seeing Casey at Giovanni's apartment, I was reminded that I needed to start forgetting about Giovanni. He and I would never be end game and I was torturing myself here. I needed a distraction and Lorenzo would be perfect for that. I took a deep breath in and texted him back.

Where should I meet you?

CHAPTER 18:

Giovanni

How many times was I going to have to watch her walk away from me?

I stood frozen, staring at the closed elevator doors. I gave her one last chance to make the right decision for us and she chose to walk away again. It killed me more than it did the first time because I stupidly allowed myself to have a flicker of hope last night. I was so angry. I was angry that I ever allowed myself to think things would be different. I half-expected her to fight for us but that was a foolish thing to think. She clearly had her mind made up.

"She didn't have to leave like that," Casey shouted from the lounge, bringing me out of my own thoughts.

I completely forgot about the doctor's appointment with Casey today. The last thing I wanted to do was have Casey rock up here while I was with Isabella. I took a deep breath in as the anger rolled through me. I turned and walked back to the kitchen. Casey had made herself comfortable on the couch and leaned her arms over the top, facing me.

"Why did she run off in a hurry?"

"Casey, don't." I reached for the headache tablets from the counter and popped two onto my hands.

She stood up and walked over to the counter. "Well, I think it's a good thing she left. I don't know how comfortable I would be with her tagging along to *our* appointments."

I reached for the glass of water and downed my tablets. Each word coming out of Casey's mouth was piercing me and I was struggling to keep myself from snapping. I didn't want to fucking deal with her. I wanted to fix things with Isabella. That was all I wanted to do and the fact that she was the major obstacle in my way was driving me crazy.

"Isabella won't be coming around anymore," I muttered.

There was no point in hiding that from her. Isabella had her mind made up and last night didn't change anything for her.

Casey's eyes lit up. "Did you guys break-up?"

I averted my eyes and said nothing.

I noticed her smiling from the corner of my eye. She could be a real bitch sometimes. I kept hoping she would keep her mouth shut now. I didn't want to hear one more word from her about Isabella and me. I placed my empty glass back on the counter and turned to make my way upstairs.

"We need to leave in five minutes," she changed the subject. "I don't want to be late."

I didn't even make it past the first step before I stopped in my tracks, remembering what Reyna mentioned last night. How did I know I was the father? What proof did she have of that?

I turned back to Casey and walked over to where she was standing.

"What?" she asked.

"What's your doctor's name?"

"Dr. Gonzalez."

"Do you think Dr. Gonzalez could do a paternity test for me?"

Casey jerked her head and her eyes brimmed with anger as she processed what I had just asked her.

"You want a paternity test?"

I nodded.

"Are you fucking kidding me?" Her eyes narrowed, fuming with anger.

"No I'm not, Casey." I tried to keep my voice as calm as possible. "I think it's fair for me to ask that of you. How do I know this baby is even mine?"

"Of course it's yours!" she objected.

"We don't know that for sure."

Her jaw dropped and her hand suddenly came up, connecting with the side of my face. I froze as the stinging continued to spread across my cheek. The anger tore through my veins and it took all the self-control I had left to remain expressionless.

"How dare you say that to me, Giovanni?"

I turned to face her and noticed the underlying hurt now taking up residence in her eyes. I didn't even feel bad. Any attraction or feelings I had towards Casey had disappeared a long time ago.

Truth was, I didn't really care for her at all.

"I think it's fair of me to ask that, Casey," I repeated calmly. "I'm going to get changed and then we can go to the appointment."

Without another word, I turned and made my way upstairs.

CHAPTER 19:
Isabella

I pushed through the door to the sound of Reyna's laughter. I closed the door behind me and slipped off my coat as I walked into the kitchen. Diego was seated across the counter and Reyna was handing him a plate full of food.

"Good morning," Diego said politely.

"Hey guys," I mumbled.

Reyna raised an eyebrow at me. She probably had so many questions, but instead of delving straight into that, she pointed to the kettle.

"Want some coffee?"

I nodded and strolled over to take a seat next to Diego. I might as well get the third-degree over with now so I can push last night out of my mind for good. I was thankful for the numb feeling that settled over me on the drive home. There was no pain and no anger. There was nothing.

"Where did you disappear to last night?" Diego eyed me out of the corner of his eye.

I flicked my eyes over to Reyna who was now glaring at Diego. They had obviously discussed this, but I had expected the questions to come from her. I had come to enjoy Diego's company since hanging out with him at *Vai Moana*. Their relationship had just escalated since then which meant wherever Reyna was, nine times out of ten, Diego was close by.

I hung my head in shame. "I made a big mistake last night."

Reyna handed me my coffee and leaned against the counter. "Giovanni?"

I nodded.

"We already knew that," she shrugged.

"How did you know that?"

"Well, you ran out last night and for hours I didn't know where you were," she explained, a hint of annoyance in her voice. "I had called you a number of times, but you didn't answer until I got a call from your number and it was Giovanni on the other end."

I wrapped my hands around my mug, clinging to the heat that was coming from it.

"I made a mistake," I repeated. "I should never have ended up at his place."

"What were you doing there?" Diego asked politely.

"I don't want to talk about it."

My mind wandered back to last night. His hungry kisses still lingered against my lips and my body still burned for him. There was an animalistic desire that consumed us last night that we had never experienced previously. I couldn't get enough of him and now I was stuck with such recent memories of him. I hated it.

"Izzy, please don't give me that," Reyna snapped. "What are you doing? You broke up with him."

"I know that!" I retorted. "Trust me, I don't need that reminder okay? I fucked up. I should never have slept with him last night."

"You didn't," she groaned, leaning her head against her hand.

Her reaction wasn't helping the copious amount of guilt that was working its way through me. I knew I fucked up bad by going there and saying it out loud was only making it more of a reality.

"Look, I don't need you guys to make me feel worse," I snapped. "I'm well aware that I shouldn't have done that. I was drunk and high on emotion. I couldn't help it."

I took a sip of my coffee. Last night was a moment of weakness that I should have never allowed. And then to have to see Casey this morning just poured salt in the wound. It reminded me of what a fuck up this all was in the first place.

"We're not trying to make you feel worse," Reyna said softly. "But what are you going to do now?"

"Nothing. Nothing has changed. That much was clear by Casey arriving this morning for their doctor's appointment."

The nausea returned. It was a knee-jerk reaction every time her name came up. I didn't want to think of them going to the doctor together. I didn't want to think of them seeing the scan of their baby. I didn't want to think of any of that.

"That couldn't have been easy," Diego said.

"Obviously not," I mumbled sarcastically.

Reyna nudged Diego and shook her head. He was quite obtuse when it came to stating the obvious in situations. The previous anger I was feeling started to work its way back as it tangled itself in the overall guilt and sadness that was already hanging over me. I didn't want to have to deal with Giovanni and Casey again.

"Well, I'm not going to sit here and reminisce on the adventures of Isabella," The sarcasm continued. "I have plans."

"Plans?" Reyna looked confused. "What plans?"

"Lorenzo and I are going for coffee."

Diego looked confused and glanced over to Reyna for answers. Reyna tried to keep her face unchanged but that was never something she was very good at.

"Coffee with Lorenzo?" she repeated.

I nodded.

"Do you think that's a good idea?"

I rolled my eyes. "Well, it can't be worse than the other decisions I've been making."

I grabbed my mug off the counter so I could take it back to my room with me. My raging hangover and emotional overdrive were making me very tired of this conversation.

"Just think about what you're doing, Izzy," Reyna said softly.

I nodded and made my way to my room, leaving their concerned gazes behind me. I didn't need my actions to be questioned. I was well-aware of the mistakes I had been making but going for coffee with Lorenzo wasn't going to be one of them. He was being polite and friendly, what was the problem with that? I didn't want anything romantic. I just wanted a distraction from the pain.

Was that too much to ask for?

CHAPTER 20:

Isabella

I pulled my coat closer to me as I turned down the street towards the address of the coffee shop I was meeting Lorenzo at. The sun was shining down and although that didn't take away the chill in the air, it definitely assisted with giving what little warmth it could manage. I was thankful that the headache tablets had started to work themselves through my system. My raging hangover wasn't something I intended to have for the day, but that was self-inflicted.

As I turned around the corner, the *La Sagrada Familia* came into full view. It was breathtaking - apart from the cranes from the on-going construction. I was always mesmerised by it. How could you not be? It was one of the most impressive architectural structures ever. I strolled down the street past the various tourist shops that popped up around a sight like this. In Summer, the area was flooded with people trying to get in, but today there were only a handful of tourists flocking around it.

I continued towards my destination and stopped at the red door that came into view. *Cafe Belmont* was a quaint little café across the road from the *La Sagrada Familia*. I peeped inside and noticed how small it was. I didn't mind that - the less people, the better. I scanned the area trying to see if I could notice Lorenzo but instead I was surprised by the increasing amount of Christmas decorations that lined the streets.

Wait, what was the date?

I had been so wrapped up in the last few drama-filled weeks that I didn't even realise the festive season was upon us. How did I not notice any of this sooner? I continued to look around trying to really pay attention to anything else I could have missed.

"Why do you look so confused?" Lorenzo popped up from behind me.

I turned to see his friendly smile.

"Would you believe me that I only noticed the Christmas decorations now?"

He chuckled. "That's surprising since they started putting these things up well into November already."

"That's even worse," I admitted, laughing along with him.

He was casually sporting a grey hoodie that was hidden beneath a denim jacket he had pulled on over it. There was no beanie this time round as he had his dark hair perfectly styled in place. His beard had grown longer since I last saw him - it was as dark as his hair and really complimented his complexion. I was surprised by his appearance. When I had first met him, there was nothing dark and alluring about him, but I was clearly mistaken. I could admit that there was something about him.

"Have you been waiting long?" he asked. "Sorry, I couldn't find parking so had to park a few streets up."

"No, I just got here." I smiled. "Shall we?"

"Yes, please." He stepped back and allowed me to enter first.

I strolled inside and was welcomed by the aroma of freshly made coffee in the air. There was only one other couple inside and a staircase in the far corner.

I turned back to Lorenzo. "Where do you want to sit?"

"Oh no, we're not sitting down here," he explained. "The best part of this place is upstairs."

He gestured to the staircase. "Follow me."

He led the way as we climbed the stairs. It didn't take long to reach the top and the area was scattered with chairs and tables, but that wasn't what caught my eye. The large windows were opened wide displaying the most perfect view of the cathedral. It took my breath away. The four gothic designed spires were in the distance and from where we sat, you didn't notice the ongoing construction. It allowed for the archaic view that the architecture wanted. From the outside of the coffee shop, you wouldn't expect much from it, but they had one of the best views I had seen.

"What do you think?" Lorenzo asked, bringing me out of my gawking state.

"It's breathtaking," I gasped.

"Right?" He agreed and led me past the tables to the closest one to the window. "I love coming here for this very reason."

"I didn't even know this place existed."

"I'm here all the time," he explained. "Nothing beats sitting here with a good book."

"You're a reader?" I asked, surprised.

"Oh yeah, big time."

That was good to know. Giovanni wasn't much of a reader.

Why are you thinking about him?

The voice echoed through my mind and she was right. I needed to stop that. I was still feeling the emotional after-effects from this morning, but I was working really hard to try and push that out of my mind. I was wrapped up in the guilt and the sickening feeling of Casey arriving for their doctor's appointment. Of course, he was going to accompany her - it's his baby too, but the thought of them together would never be a welcomed one. She got under my skin and filled me with a jealousy-fueled rage. Giovanni and Casey had to plan for their baby's arrival now and I had to work on moving on from him, if that was even possible.

I pushed him out of my mind as I took a seat across from Lorenzo.

"How do you take your coffee?" he asked.

"No sugar. Just milk please."

He turned to the younger male waiter that had followed us upstairs from the entrance. *"Un café sin azúcar y un espresso por favor."*

With a friendly smile, the waiter turned to place our order. My gaze wandered outside again and I was calmed by the sun peeping out from behind the spires.

"I hope you like the place," he said sheepishly. "It was the only one I could think of that would be nice to meet at."

I turned back to him. "Lorenzo, it's perfect."

"I'm so glad." He smiled, his eyes brimming with sincerity. "I thought you could use a change of scenery with everything going on."

"These last few weeks have been quite the rollercoaster," I admitted.

"You're welcome to talk about those things if that's what you want." He alluded to the Giovanni and Casey situation. "You know I'm here for you."

I sighed. "I don't think there is much else for me to say. Giovanni and I are not together anymore so I shouldn't be bothered by what happens in his life."

My sadness had turned to anger recently. The constant reminder of the two of them was starting to piss me off more than anything else. I tried to distance the pieces of my heart from it. It was easier to be angry at him than to admit that he hurt me. That was too closely connected to the amount of love I had for him and I couldn't think of that anymore. That was irrelevant now.

"But it's okay to have been hurt by what happened."

I averted my eyes. "Yeah, but it doesn't change anything."

Lorenzo reached for my hand across the table and squeezed it gently. There it was again - that unexpected electricity at this touch. What was that? Was it an attraction? Obviously I found Lorenzo attractive, but was I *really* attracted to him? I flicked my eyes to meet his gaze. I probably could be if I allowed myself but I didn't want that.

"How about we don't talk about them?" he suggested, bringing me out of my thoughts. "I'm happy to be here for you to vent to but I think you could do with a distraction."

I nodded. "Yes, please. Last time you promised me that you could distract me and I've been so intrigued since then."

He smirked and ran his fingers through his hair. "I promised you distractions, I just never promised you that my company would be any good."

"Of course it is." I smiled at him. "But if I'm being honest here, Lorenzo, I don't really know anything about you."

"Now, that's not true," he objected playfully. "You know I enjoy tequila."

When I first met him at *Paradiso*, he ordered us a shot of tequila as well as a drink that was laced with it. He drank that with no problem, unlike me who couldn't control my facial expressions.

"That's true," I laughed. "And you know that I don't particularly enjoy the taste of tequila."

"Oh, that much was clear since you failed to take a shot without making a face last time."

"I tried really hard!" I objected and he threw his head back in laughter.

"I also know that you have some killer dance moves," he teased. "I have those moves to thank because without them I wouldn't have even met you."

The heat started to spread across my cheeks. "You say killer dance moves, everyone else says terrible dance moves."

He scoffed. "Oh please, I know you can dance."

He flicked his eyes to meet mine and I knew he was referring to when we danced together that night. He pulled me close to his body and knew exactly what he was doing with it. He moved with the music and it was hypnotising. I took a deep breath in, trying to keep my mind from going to what it was like to dance with Giovanni. Those memories were pushing through and I didn't want to allow them in. I couldn't - I couldn't think of his body against mine when not even 24 hours ago, I had exactly that.

"Those were alcohol-induced moves."

I was thankful for the waiter arriving with our drinks to stop that conversation from going any further. Lorenzo had a friendly energy to him, but he couldn't hide his very clear interest in me. I knew he didn't expect me to reciprocate it, but I also didn't want to give him the wrong idea.

"So, do you live in the area?" I asked casually, trying to change the subject.

"Yeah, I'm not too far from here. It's not too far from where I work either."

"What is it that you do? Last time I saw you, you were in a fancy suit."

He chuckled. "Yeah, that was rare. My boss likes us to dress up like that when we have an important meeting. I'm actually the head of marketing at a company called Augmented Media. I mainly work in the digital marketing space."

"That's pretty cool. How long have you worked there?"

"Been there for a couple years now. It's not bad. We work with some pretty cool clients."

He continued to explain more about the business and name-dropped a few of the bigger brands that I was quite familiar with. He spoke with such ease and confidence. There was never an element of arrogance to him, only sincerity and I was enjoying his company. I didn't know much about him which opened up the opportunity to keep the conversation going for as long as possible. I needed all the distractions I could get at this point.

"And you? Where do you work?"

I sipped on my coffee. "Well, I have a casual job as a waitress at this place close to where I stay. I worked at a publishing house back in London but I'm still trying to find my feet here now."

The conversation around my lack of career always caused a small stir of anxiety inside. The constant lingering fear that I didn't quite know where my life was going often made me feel uneasy.

"And Reyna and I actually own a little coffee shop together."

His eyes lit up. "Really? Why didn't we go there instead?"

"Oh, it's not ready yet," I answered quickly. "There is still a lot to be done before it will be ready for the public."

"That's amazing though. I'd love to come by and see it."

"I don't think it'll have a view as nice as this but of course, you should definitely check it out."

He smiled at me and leaned back in his chair. "That would be great."

The conversation between us flowed so easily. Never stopping to reveal any awkward silences or scraping to find a new topic. It was refreshing to find someone so easy to talk to. We zipped through a number of topics - covering the basics of our favourite types of things. Colors, food, weather, movies. We covered it all and I was starting to get a better understanding of him. We had so many similarities - more than I thought I would have with him.

He signaled the waiter for another drink before turning back to me. "You mentioned that you used to work in London, how long were you there for?"

"I'm actually originally from London. I moved here earlier this year," I replied.

"I remember you mentioning something about your ex when we first met."

I ran my mouth a bit too much when Lorenzo and I first met it seems.

"Yeah, my boyfriend of six years left me because he didn't want to get married."

"Why do I feel like there is more to that story?"

"Oh, there's so much more to that story," I groaned. "None of the details I feel like boring you with."

"Learning more about you is not boring." He flicked his eyes to meet mine.

I couldn't control the unexpected heat that spread across my cheeks again. Every now and then he made these comments that had an underlying hint of flirtation to them. As much as I wanted to continue the conversation with him, I didn't feel like explaining my family drama. It was draining.

I sighed. "I promise I owe you the full story, but it's just too recent for me to want to talk about now."

This conversation was reminiscent of when I first explained my family dynamic to Giovanni. He learned all there was about me and had a first-hand account of what my family was really like. His patience at the hospital with my mother was commendable. She held nothing back when it came to sharing what she thought and he handled it in the best way. Not once did he ever disrespect her, even when he had every right to. There was always a dull ache in my chest whenever I thought of him. He was my comfort during those days with my father. He was the only one that could have gotten me through that. I longed to go back to what we were.

"That's perfectly fine." He reached across the table and grabbed my hand. "I'd never want to push you to talk about anything you weren't comfortable with sharing."

"I appreciate that."

My hand slipped out of his as I leaned back against my chair. I brought my coffee to my lips, trying my hardest to focus on Lorenzo and his attempts to distract me from what constantly hovered in my mind.

Forget about Giovanni.

The voice in my head continued to whisper that, but my heart knew it was easier said than done.

CHAPTER 21:
Giovanni

We drove in silence. Casey didn't utter a word to me since I asked her for a paternity test. I didn't even feel bad about it. If she had nothing to hide, then what would be the problem in getting confirmation? Every part of me was hoping that this was all a big misunderstanding and that I wasn't the father. That would mean that Isabella and I could be together again.

She keeps walking away from you.

That phrase echoed in my mind over and over again. Every time she walked away from me, she broke me a little more. Having the hope that I would be able to call her mine again being ripped away from me over and over again was torture.

If you walk away now then that's it, Isabella.

I was angry at her. I was angry that she walked away from me again. Did our relationship mean that little to her? She had no problem leaving and I couldn't accept that. We were supposed to be together. My hands tightened around the steering wheel and I took a deep breath in trying to get a handle on my emotions. The last person I wanted to show emotion in front of was Casey.

"You take the next left," she muttered, bringing me out of my thoughts.

She turned away from me and crossed her arms. She was hurt - that much was clear but I didn't care for her feelings the way she hoped I would. Our relationship had always been purely physical - since the first day I met her. She was attractive and interested and I didn't need anything complicated. I should feel bad that she went on to develop feelings for me but I didn't. I had made it clear from the beginning what this was going to be. Her feelings were not my responsibility.

I turned around the corner and she pointed to the building up ahead.

"You can just park on the street," she said.

I maneuvered into an open parking spot along the street and turned the engine off. A rush of nerves settled over me at the thought of going inside. I had no idea what to expect and that wasn't something I welcomed. I needed to be in control of a situation and everything about this out of control situation was driving me insane. Casey grabbed her handbag and stepped outside the car. I reached for my wallet and followed her lead. I pulled my coat closer to me as we walked through the front doors. It was a small clinic. There were a handful of empty chairs scattered along the walls of reception. I followed Casey to the counter where a petite receptionist sat behind. She glanced up at us, peeping from behind her large round glasses.

"*Hola, Casey Fonseca - tengo una cita con el Dr. González,*" Casey said.

The receptionist nodded and politely pointed to the waiting room. "*Ella estará contigo ahora.*"

We took a seat and I couldn't help but tap my foot nervously against the floor. There were pictures of babies hanging on the walls. Tons of babies. There were sleeping babies, smiling babies, crying babies - they were everywhere. Pressure spread across my chest at the sight of them. I was pretty sure I didn't even want children. Or maybe I did but it was never something I had thought about. I certainly never expected to be stuck having a baby with someone I didn't love. No matter the decisions I had made in the past, if I was ever going to bring a child into this world, I would have imagined it going differently.

I took a deep breath in and ran my fingers through my hair.

"Can you stop?" Casey muttered. "You're making me nervous."

"Good. I don't want to be the only one nervous."

She said nothing more and we sat in silence until a dark-haired doctor stepped through the door. She was a much older woman but I was thankful for her welcoming smile as she looked over at us.

"*Buenos días,* come on in." She stepped back and gestured towards her room.

Casey stood up and greeted Dr. Gonzalez as I followed closely behind them.

"Dr. Gonzalez, this is Giovanni." Casey pointed to me. "The baby daddy."

I extended my hand. "That is still to be confirmed."

Casey turned to gape at me but Dr. Gonzalez just smiled and shook my hand, her face remained unchanged at my comment. I was pretty sure she had seen some complicated situations in line of work.

"Casey, you can lie down on the bed like you did the last time you were here," she instructed. "How are you feeling? Has the morning sickness stopped?"

Casey removed her coat and pulled herself onto the bed, leaning against it. "It's not as bad as it was, but I still get it every now and then."

Dr. Gonzalez nodded and slipped on a pair of gloves. I sat on the only other chair in the room and observed them. Casey lifted her top to reveal the small bump that started to form by her stomach. I hadn't noticed it before and the sight of it made me feel sick.

"Okay, we're just going to check on the little one," Dr. Gonzalez said as she started spreading gel on Casey's stomach.

I couldn't watch. I wasn't feeling queasy at what they were doing, I was just unsettled by the situation. I wasn't ready to be a father, that much was clear to me now. I didn't want to accept it. If I accepted that then that would mean that I would have really lost Isabella forever and I wasn't ready for that.

"And there it is," Dr. Gonzalez announced.

A small heartbeat started to come through the machine and I turned to face the screen. The black and white lines across the screen were making it difficult for me to focus on what they were looking at.

"Lo siento, I don't know what I'm looking at," I said sheepishly.

Casey chuckled and waited for Dr. Gonzalez to explain.

She smiled at me before turning to the screen, pointing. "Do you see this little thing over here? It's like a small little kidney bean?"

That I could see, now that she was pointing at it. I nodded as she continued.

"That's it," she announced. "That's your baby."

I looked back at the screen and focused on the kidney bean. It was so tiny and I couldn't understand how that small little thing developed into a baby. I felt a rush of unexpected emotion come over me at the sight of it. It wasn't the bean's fault. It was an innocent bystander in this situation.

"You're just over nine weeks now," Dr. Gonzalez explained to Casey. "Your baby is about the size of a kidney bean which is around one point five to two centimeters."

"That's so tiny!" Casey gasped.

Dr. Gonzalez chuckled. "Yes, it's small for now, but it's going to grow significantly over the next few months."

I pulled my eyes away from the screen and turned to Dr. Gonzalez. "And what about a paternity test? Can that be done while she is still pregnant?"

Casey glared at me. "Giovanni, please."

"I have every right to ask this, Casey," I snapped and turned back to Dr. Gonzalez.

Her face remained unchanged again and I was impressed with how she managed to keep it together, but she had clearly been doing this for years.

"There are a couple of options that can be done while the mother is pregnant. I would recommend doing a NIPP - a non-invasive prenatal paternity test," she explained. "We would need a blood sample from each of you and we can compare that to the fetal cells present in the mother's bloodstream."

"And how accurate is it?" I asked.

"It's the most accurate test we can do. The result is more than ninety-nine percent accurate."

"And how early can we get that done?"

"After the eighth week of pregnancy. So you're already at the point where the test can be conducted, if you wish."

Casey crossed her arms. "Come on, Giovanni, this is hardly necessary."

"I have the right to know," I retorted. "If it's mine like you say it is, then you have nothing to worry about."

Even from here, I could see her nostrils flaring in anger. I wasn't here to care for Casey's feelings. I was here for answers.

I turned back to Dr. Gonzalez. "Well, let's do this then."

***

After we each gave the blood samples needed for the test, we were on our way back from the clinic. It was going to take a few weeks to get the test back so all I could do now was be patient. Casey was seething as she sat next to me. Her arms were crossed and she refused to look in my direction.

"I don't understand why you're so angry, Casey," I muttered. "You know I have every right to get this done."

"The fact that you think I would lie about something like this is upsetting to me, Giovanni!" she shouted.

"There's no need to raise your voice," I snapped. "If you're not lying then you have nothing to worry about."

She huffed and crossed her arms again. "Please just drop me at my place."

We drove the rest of the way in silence. She wasn't too far from the clinic so I only had to endure this energy for a little while longer. I didn't feel bad that she was angry at me. Why would I? I needed answers and I was going to get them. I tried not to focus too much on the test. I didn't want to put my hopes into something that had a chance of coming back with the results I didn't want.

I stopped outside her apartment building. "Here we go."

Casey didn't move. She kept her arms crossed as she turned to face me. "That little kidney bean is ours, Giovanni."

"Cas-". I started to say, but she cut me off.

"You've always known how I've felt about you. Those were more than just casual hook-ups for me."

I could see the flash of emotion in her deep brown eyes. I had always known that it meant more to her, but I didn't care. At the time, she was a convenient means to an end. I could see how badly she wanted this to be true and that's what concerned me. She only had eyes for me, even when I didn't want that. I could have said anything - anything that would probably be hurtful to her and popped that bubble she was living in, but I decided against it. I didn't have to be a dick.

"Enjoy the rest of your day, Casey."

Without so much of a goodbye, she reached for her handbag and stepped outside my car, slamming my door as she turned on her heels.

I rolled my eyes at her unnecessary reaction and turned my car back on. My phone started to ring and Alvaro's name was flashing on the screen of my handsfree kit. I turned down the road and answered the call.

"*Hola, hermano,*" I greeted.

"*Hola,* Giovanni," Alvaro greeted. "Where are you?"

"I just dropped Casey off. We had a doctor's appointment."

"And how did it go?"

"Well, I asked for a paternity test so you can imagine how that went down," I muttered.

"A paternity test?" he asked, surprised. "I'm sure she didn't like that."

"Nope," I changed the subject. "But what's up?"

"Listen, *Mama* went back home earlier today, but I'm not sure how she's going to handle being alone. She's been up and down these last few days and I don't think she's figured out exactly what she is going to do," Alvaro explained. "I know *Papa* is meant to come back tomorrow so I wanted to ask if you could go by their place and just check on her before he gets home."

With everything that has happened over the last couple of weeks, I had completely forgotten about the mess that was my parent's relationship. My father had been out of town for business for a while now which gave my mother time to try and figure out her next step. I still carried all the anger towards my father over what he had done and I hadn't seen him since. I had chosen to avoid him because I didn't know how I would react if I had to see him again. I was still so angry.

"Yeah, of course," I replied. "I'm on the road now so I'll head over there and check on her."

"Thank you," Alvaro said. "She knows about the whole Casey and Isabella situation by the way so be prepared for some questions."

I rolled my eyes. "Wonderful."

I had been dodging my mother's texts about it up till now, but that certainly wasn't going to be easy in person. I turned in the direction of my parent's house as Alvaro remained silent for a moment.

"How's Mateo and Penelope?" I asked.

"Both are doing great now. You should come by soon and see him."

"I will."

"And you?" Alvaro asked. "Have you seen Isabella?"

The ache in my chest returned at the mention of her name again. I wondered if I would be able to hear it without the pain that accompanied it. I could tell Alvaro what happened last night but, truthfully, I didn't have the energy for it.

"Briefly," I murmured. "Listen, Alvaro, can I call you later?"

"Sure."

We said our goodbyes and I disconnected the call. So much had happened in the last twenty-four hours and I finally had a moment to myself to wrap my head around it. Turns out, I didn't want to though - I didn't want to think of any of it so instead, I turned up the volume and focused on the music blaring through my speakers.

CHAPTER 22:
Isabella

"How far are we from your shop?" Lorenzo asked.

We were walking side by side along the promenade as I led him in the direction of the coffee shop. He parked underground and the parking was a couple of blocks away from where we were headed. We continued our casual conversation. The sun was still shining down on us and the reflection against the sea in the distance brought on a wave of calmness that I needed.

"It's at the end of the road on the corner." I pointed in the direction. "You could have parked closer."

"I don't mind the walk."

We sat at the cafe for a while before our stomachs started needing something more than caffeine. We ordered a couple of pastries for the table as we continued our getting to know each other. He circled back to wanting to see the coffee shop so I suggested we headed over there. Neither of us had anywhere else to be and since I didn't feel like being alone, I was happy to continue to enjoy company.

"Now, I have to prepare you because the place is a mess," I explained. "We only just finished up with the painting of the walls so there's stuff scattered everywhere."

He chuckled. "That's really fine, Isabella."

I pulled the keys out of my bag as we reached the door. I quickly unlocked it and we were welcomed by the smell of fresh paint. There were plastic covers across the floor and counters.

"Welcome to-". I stopped to think for a moment. "Uh, we actually don't have a name yet."

Lorenzo smiled and stepped inside, taking in the surroundings.

"It's quite a big space," he commented.

I closed the door behind us and placed my bag on the counter. "It is. It was falling apart when we first got it, but it's getting there."

He casually placed his hands in his pockets as he strolled across the room.

"I'm actually thinking of putting a couple of bookshelves along that wall over there." I pointed to where he was. "We can sell some classics and maybe a few new ones."

"That's a great idea. You can actually line them up across this whole area." He pointed to the vacant area. "If you have them spread out, there will be enough space."

It wasn't a bad suggestion. Reyna and I had plenty to discuss when it came to the direction of this place so I made a mental note to include that.

"That's a good idea. We are going to have a couple chairs and tables here." I gestured to the area in front of the counter. "And probably a couple outside for when the weather is good."

He nodded and strolled over to me. "I think it's going to be great."

"Thank you. I'm hoping that we can get this going soon enough. I'd be happy to work here full-time."

"Well, you can count on my support." He pulled himself up onto the counter.

I leaned forward against it, facing him. "The view here isn't as magical as where we just were."

He looked over at me. "I beg to differ."

My gaze met his and the heat began to spread across my cheeks again. He wasn't afraid to continue his flirting, but I wasn't sure how to react to it. I was careful to never give him the wrong idea and focused on just enjoying his company. He was easy to be around and this day was turning out better than I thought it would be. It was probably selfish to want to be around him knowing his clear interest, but he was the perfect distraction.

Before I could answer, his phone started to ring and I was thankful for that.

"Sorry, it's my sister. Can you give me one sec?" he asked.

"Of course."

He jumped off the counter and brought his phone to his ear. *"Hola, Milana. ¿Qué pasa?"*

I pulled myself onto the counter thinking back to the last time I was on here. That day with Giovanni was one that I would never forget. His spontaneous energy and care-free nature was something I couldn't help but fall for. He made me laugh. He was sexy in so many ways but he had me hooked with his humor. Between his witty charm and dirty jokes, I fell for him. Hard.

I sighed and allowed the sadness to seep in for a moment. It was the only way to remind myself that what we had was actually real.

"Sorry about that," Lorenzo said, quickly bringing me out of my thoughts before I sunk too deep into them.

"Don't apologize. Is everything okay?"

He nodded. "I just have to go and fetch her though. She has a flat tire and my dad is out of town so I'm the next emergency contact on her list."

I chuckled. "Big brother problems."

"You'd be surprised how often things like this happened." He smirked. "I'm sorry to have to cut this short."

"That's okay," I said, but a part of me was disappointed at just the thought of being alone with my thoughts. There had to be something I could do to continue the distraction I needed.

"Can I drop you at your place on my way out?" he offered.

I nodded. "That would be great, thank you."

CHAPTER 23:

Giovanni

A familiar reggaeton beat came on next and my mind wandered back to the time with Isabella in her coffee shop. That would always be one of my favourite memories with her. I was trying to show her how much she already meant to me and after finally getting Reyna to tell me where she was, I couldn't help but seek her out. The surprised look on her face as she peeped around the corner. Her contagious laugh and bright smile. She was so care-free and relaxed that day. I remembered the way we danced and what it felt like to have her body close to mine.

I just wanted to feel her close to me again.

A part of me was screaming to pick up the damn phone and tell her about the paternity test. Tell her that there's a chance this nightmare would be over, but I couldn't do that. It would be selfish of me to put her through that knowing that the outcome could be an unfavourable one. She had decided to keep herself out of this situation and I couldn't blame her. If the roles were reversed, could I have watched her have someone else's baby?

No fucking way.

Just the thought of her with someone else made me feel like I had been kicked in the stomach. I never wanted to think of her with anyone but me and it was tearing me apart inside that she wasn't mine anymore. I waited so long to find her and now I have lost her. I didn't think I would ever be able to get over that. I never even believed in love before I met her. She showed me what it was like to give yourself over to someone entirely and how terrifyingly exciting that could be.

Now all I was left with was the heartbreak of having fucked that all up.

My hands tightened around the wheel as I pulled into the driveway of my parent's house. I followed the path to the back parking where I always parked my car. When Alvaro and I moved out of the house, they decided to find a smaller property outside of the city. I hadn't spent much time here since my relationship with my father started to go downhill. I chose to avoid him after what happened the first time. I was still angry at the fact that he never took responsibility for the pain he caused my mother and our family. I always seemed to be the one who was ready to protect her.

As I pulled closer to the top, two figures caught my eye at the top of the back stairs. My father was only expected back tomorrow but if he was here already, I needed to avoid him. I didn't have the energy to deal with him right now. I had managed to avoid him since that night in Valencia. Whenever he tried to call, I ignored it and I had no intention of speaking to him again.

What was I supposed to say?

I stopped my car just out of view but where I could still get a good look. I squinted, trying to make out who it was. I wanted to go closer but a strange, unwelcomed voice urged me not to. I leaned forward over the steering wheel as my mother turned to the figure in front of her with a smile on her face. I couldn't make out exactly who it was but I could see that it was a male figure that was unfamiliar to me. He stood in close proximity to her and he reached out and caressed her cheek. The figure turned and revealed his side-profile. Even from here, I could tell that it was definitely not my father.

What the fuck was going on?

My mother looked up at him and before I knew it, they were locked in a passionate embrace that I should never have witnessed. My mother stood at the top of her stairs making out with someone who was not my father.

"Are you fucking kidding me?" I muttered in shock.

First, I caught my father and now here I am catching my mother being unfaithful. My family was slipping further and further away from what I once knew it to be. A wave of overwhelming anger consumed me at the sight of her and there was no way I could face her now. My mother has always been the voice of reason in my life. She has always been the voice that guided me in the right direction and to make better decisions. I had always believed her to be an angel to me and now she revealed herself to be someone I didn't know at all.

Was this a fucking joke?

Instead of parking and getting out of the car, I put my car in reverse and pulled out of the driveway before anyone noticed.

I couldn't think straight. I was trying to put the pieces of my parent's relationship together. My father was unfaithful to my mother and now it turns out that she had been doing the same? How long had this been going on for? Was it before my father or after? Did that make a difference?

"Joder!" I banged my hand against the steering wheel.

I didn't know how I was supposed to react, but I was angry. I was angry at both of my parents. Why couldn't they be like normal couples and get a fucking divorce if they were so unhappy together?

But to continue to be unfaithful to each other? What a fucking joke. I didn't know anything about my parents and their relationship. The family that I had grown up with was nothing more than a distant memory. I never remembered my parents being unhappy with each other when I was younger. But now? Now I had caught both my parents betraying each other. It didn't have to be this way and why did I have to be the one to find this out? I could have happily remained ignorant. My parents were no longer just my parents - now I was viewing them in a different light and I wasn't sure how I felt about that.

I was spiraling in my own thoughts and all I could focus on was how much I needed Isabella right now. She was my only comfort and the only one to keep me from slipping into my self-destructive ways.

Without a second thought, I turned in the opposite direction toward her apartment.

***

I arrived at her apartment building and parked in front of it. I hadn't quite figured out what I was going to do but I couldn't be alone right now. I didn't know how to begin to work through everything I now knew. When I caught my father in Valencia, I was in a fit of rage. I was angry because of what he was putting my mother through again. I had expected this from him but not from her. She was better than this. She was better than him.

I slammed my door, locking my car behind me as I pushed through the door to her building. I called on the elevator and ran my fingers through my hair, trying to get a handle on my emotions. The doors opened and I stepped inside, pressing the button for the fourth floor.

"Come on." I tapped my foot nervously.

I didn't focus on the fact that we were broken up. She was the only one that would understand what I was going through right now and I needed that. I needed someone who could be there for me and keep me from turning to my darkest thoughts. The thoughts that dismissed all relationships and the good in them. The thoughts that I could never deal with because of my constant inability to face my emotions. She helped me that night in Valencia. She kept me from doing something I would have later regretted. Punching my father once was not my intention - I was ready to beat the fucking shit out of him. She was there for me whether I was venting or staying silent. She held my hand through it all and I never knew I needed that kind of comfort until her.

I stepped out of the elevator as it opened onto her floor. I walked up to her door and knocked on it lightly at first.

No answer.

"Isabella?" I shouted, knocking a bit harder. "Isabella, please open up."

Still no answer.

I continued at her door for a little while longer before I had to accept that there was no one home. I tried the door handle but it was locked.

"Fuck," I muttered.

Where the hell was she?

I leaned against the door and took a deep breath in. I could easily call her, but what are the chances that she would even pick up? She had made it pretty clear earlier that she was done with us but I needed her right now. No matter how selfish that was, I was already at her door and there was no turning back.

I made my way back downstairs. I needed to wait for her to come home. I just needed to talk to her. She would know what to say. She always knew the right thing to say. I pushed through the door onto the street, welcomed by the cold breeze picking up its pace. I looked around trying to figure out my next move. A bar down the road caught my eye and it was calling for me.

If she wasn't going to be there for me right now, I knew what would be.

CHAPTER 24:

Isabella

"I'm not going to lie, that wasn't the best song choice," I admitted sheepishly.

"Seriously?" Lorenzo laughed and looked over at me. "So, you don't listen to this kind of music?"

"Hip hop isn't really my genre. I'm more into the reggaeton stuff."

He indicated and turned down my street. "I'll have to tailor a playlist just for you then."

I smiled and placed his phone back down. I was zipping through his playlist all the way from when we left and if there was one thing I had learned about Lorenzo, he had a very interesting taste in music. I was surprised by how different our tastes were. We had plenty of similarities between the two of us but music was not one of them.

"We'll have to do some kind of music exchange," I suggested. "I'll introduce you to some of my favourite artists and you can do the same."

"That sounds like a plan," Lorenzo agreed. "How about ne-".

Lorenzo continued talking, but the black Audi R8 parked outside my apartment caught my attention, forcing my focus away from him.

Giovanni was here.

My breath caught in my throat and the nerves started to zip through my veins. What in the world was he doing here? Did he come to see me? Surely not. But who else would he be here for? He wouldn't casually be in the are-

"Isabella?" Lorenzo snapped me out of my thoughts. "What do you say?"

He pulled into an empty parking spot a couple cars down from where Giovanni's car was parked.

"About what?" I turned to him.

"Our music date?" he repeated sheepishly. "I don't mean date *date*, just like we can get together and exchange music."

"Oh yes!" I exclaimed. "We can do that."

I was trying my hardest not to focus on the very obvious fact that Giovanni was in the area.

Maybe it wasn't even his car?

I was pretty sure other people in the world had that car and here I was just assuming it was his. Lorenzo stepped outside the car and I followed his lead. I came around to his side as he leaned against the car.

"That was fun," he announced.

I pulled my coat closer to me. "Yeah, it was. You were a very enjoyable distraction."

"Well, I'm glad to hear that." He reached for my hand and squeezed it.

Before I could reply, I heard his voice boom from behind me. "Are you fucking kidding me?"

I turned to meet Giovanni's dark seething eyes. He stumbled towards us and I quickly pulled my hand away from Lorenzo's, suddenly overcome with an unexpected wave of guilt.

"Giovanni, what are you doing here?" I gaped.

He pointed his finger at Lorenzo. "What the hell is *he* doing here?"

Giovanni stumbled closer to me and he reeked of alcohol. He had clearly been day-drinking.

I stepped in front of him, and lifted my hand up, stopping him from taking another step towards Lorenzo."Giovanni, stop."

He stopped against my hand and looked down at me, his deep brown eyes swimming with emotion. There was a hollowness to them that I hadn't noticed before.

"Isabella, do you want me to stay?" Lorenzo asked politely.

I turned back to him. "No, it's okay. I'll deal with this."

"You shouldn't even be here in the first place," Giovanni spat.

"I'm here for Isabella," Lorenzo retorted, trying to remain as polite as possible but I could tell he was starting to get annoyed. "You're the one who shouldn't be here."

Giovanni stepped closer to him, trapping me between the two of them."What did you say?"

"Giovanni, stop!" I shouted and pushed myself closer to him, trying to get him to focus on me and not Lorenzo.

There was a couple staring at us from across the road and who could blame them with the volume at which Giovanni was speaking. He didn't keep his eyes off Lorenzo. His jaw clenched and if it wasn't for me standing between the two of them, who knows what he would have done. I had seen Giovanni angry before - the night when he caught his father in Valencia and he was borderline that kind of anger again. I didn't understand it. It was completely unwarranted.

I turned around to face Lorenzo, completely embarrassed that he was caught in the middle of this. "I am so sorry about this."

"If you need me to stay, Izzy, just say the word," He looked down at me, his eyes full of concern.

Giovanni scoffed from behind me, but I ignored him. I was so humiliated by his behaviour. He had no right to rock up here and start acting like this. I really didn't want to drag Lorenzo into my problems. I would deal with Giovanni.

"I promise I'll be okay." I reached out and squeezed Lorenzo's arm. "Thank you for today."

He smiled at me. "I'll call you later."

"Just get out of here, Lorenzo," Giovanni shouted. "She doesn't wa-".

"Giovanni, for fuck sakes!" I snapped.

Lorenzo pulled off down the road and I was thankful he didn't have to witness what was going to happen next. I was disgusted by Giovanni's behaviour.

I turned to face him. "You had no right to say that to Lorenzo."

"Don't give me that shit, Isabella," Giovanni snapped. "Not even twenty four hours ago you were in my bed and now you're out with him?"

Now I was seething.

The anger rolled through me at his tactless comment. He had no fucking right to come here unannounced and start making baseless accusations. He ran his fingers through his hair and pushed past me towards his car.

"Where do you think you're going?" I shouted.

"Home!"

"Are you kidding me? You're in no condition to drive right now!" I shouted back.

He leaned against his car, fumbling for his keys in his coat pocket. He was infuriating. I took a deep breath in and tried to regain my composure. There was no way he was getting behind the wheel right now. That would be completely reckless.

I walked over to him. "Giovanni?"

He ignored me and unlocked his car, reaching for his door handle. I leaned against his door, stopping him from opening it.

He jerked his head up. "What the fuck are you doing?"

"First of all, you do not speak to me like that," I warned.

His face fell and he mumbled an apology.

I ignored him and continued, "And second of all, you're not getting behind that wheel."

"Oh yes I am," he retorted.

I rolled my eyes and reached for his keys, but he pulled his hand away.

"How much have you had to drink?"

"Why do you care?" he muttered.

I sighed. "Please don't argue with me right now, Giovanni. Give me your car keys so I can take you home."

"You're gonna take me home?" His eyes now brimming with sadness and surprise.

My heart ached for the beautiful sad man in front of me. I couldn't help the constant affection I still felt towards him pushing through. He needed to get home but I certainly couldn't allow him to endanger his own life and the lives of others on the road.

"Well, I'm definitely not going to let you get behind the wheel so hand it over." I opened my hand and waited for him to give me the keys.

He was apprehensive. "Are you going to be able to handle this car?"

I rolled my eyes and grabbed the keys from him. "It's just a car."

I stepped towards the door to grab it open but he stepped in front of me, closing the proximity between us. He smelled of alcohol and his faint cologne. My breath caught in my throat, the familiarity of the situation overcoming me. Whenever he was around, I was consumed by him. No matter how hard I tried not to be, it was just what happened.

"No one else has ever driven my car," he slurred. "So be careful."

"I'll be fine."

My eyes flicked up to meet his. I allowed myself a moment to soak him in. I only noticed now that his dark beard was thicker than usual and he had a new rugged look to him. His hair was out of place and the bags under his eyes displayed his very obvious lack of sleep. It saddened me to see him like this. The man I love so much now overcome with all this sadness. I wish things could have been different. I only wanted him to be happy. I wanted him to be mine, but I couldn't put myself through the complications of his life now and the sooner I accepted we were over, the sooner I could attempt to move on with my life.

If that was even possible.

His eyes wandered down to my lips, causing the tension deep inside of me to reignite. It was a knee-jerk reaction around him. He caused the air around me to become thin as the desire suffocated us.

Isabella, get your shit together.

I snapped out of the trance I was in and focused on getting him home.

"Get in," I ordered.

"Fine," he mumbled and stumbled over to the passenger side.

CHAPTER 25:

Giovanni

She followed closely behind me as I stumbled into my apartment. The world was spinning as the nausea worked its way through me. I had managed to down a significant amount of alcohol before I saw Isabella arrive back at her apartment. Seeing her get out of Lorenzo's car caused jealousy to rear its ugly head. I fucking hated seeing it. What was she doing with him anyway?

I made it to my couch and fell against it. I closed my eyes trying to get the world to stop moving. My thoughts were a fucking mess right now. Between what happened with my mother and now the realisation that Isabella had spent the day with Lorenzo, I was fucking done with everything.

"Where are my car keys?" I shouted.

"On your counter," she replied, her voice getting closer to me. "Here, sit up."

I peeped an eye open as she stood over me, a glass of water in her hand. I closed my eyes again. I couldn't even think of moving right now.

"Giovanni, you need to drink this," she ordered.

I tried to sit up, but my body wasn't having it. It was heavy and with the world spinning, I didn't know how I was going to manage that without throwing up. I lifted my arms up, trying to get her to assist me.

"I can't sit, I need to si-," I slurred, not being able to manage a coherent sentence.

She sighed and I heard the glass against the table as she placed it down. With my eyes still closed, I felt her hands in mine and she gently pulled me up. I leaned against the backrest and slowly opened my eyes. She sat next to me on the couch, her hazel eyes full of concern. Her hair was straightened and hung over her shoulders effortlessly. She had on a full face of makeup and I noticed for the first time how dressed up she was in her tight leather pants and cream-colored coat. She looked so good and it killed me that the effort was for Lorenzo.

She handed me the water and I took it from her, slowly bringing it up to my lips to take a sip. "You and Lorenz-".

"No, Giovanni," she stopped me. "We are not talking about me and Lorenzo."

Her dismissal of their very obvious relationship was angering me. How could she have moved on already? And with Lorenzo of all people? We fucking slept together last night and today she was out galavanting on a date with someone else. What the fuck?

"Oh yes, we are," I snapped. "You were out with him today. Are you really dating already?"

She sighed and ran her hands through her hair. "No, I'm not dating. We just went out for coffee. We're just friends."

I scoffed.

"We are friends, Giovanni," she repeated. "And that actually has nothing to do with you anymore. Wasn't that the same thing you said to me last night?"

I swallowed and kept my eyes firmly on my hands. She was using my own tactics against me and it hurt me to hear. The constant reminder that what happened in her life was none of my business fucking drove me crazy. I didn't want it to be that way.

I took another sip before placing the glass back on the table. "You don't get to fuck me and then go on a date with another guy."

She lifted an eyebrow at me and I could tell I had struck a nerve. "Giovanni, you need to st-".

"No seriously, Isabella, you're fucking with my mind here."

"I'm fucking with your mind?" she snapped and stood up, pacing across the room. "No one told you to rock up at my apartment."

I remained silent.

"What the hell were you even doing there anyway?" she shouted. "You think you can just come and go as you please? You have no right to do that anymore."

"I needed to see you!"

She opened her mouth to say something, but quickly closed it. Her eyes softened as she took a deep breath in. She was way better than I was at containing her emotions. I was spiraling right now and it frustrated me. I was usually the one who was good at keeping those intact, but not when it came to her. She made me vulnerable.

"Giovanni, you can't just do that," she said softly. "I'm sorry about last night. I know that I shouldn't have come here and that it was a mistake."

"Stop saying it was a mistake!" I snapped.

"It was!" She groaned. "We can't keep doing this to each other."

She was sticking to the fact that us being together was a mistake and I didn't believe her.

How could we be a mistake?

Our relationship was the most real thing I had ever known. I had never loved anyone the way I love her. She told me she loved me, but she also walked away from us like it was nothing. The pressure in my chest started to build again and I was itching for another drink. It was my unhealthy coping mechanism. I needed something to take the edge off. I needed something to stop the pain. My mind was racing and when I thought of her with Lorenzo again, the pain quickly turned to anger.

"You're lying to yourself if you think that you and I are not meant to be together," I muttered."You can run around with Lorenzo as much as you want, but you will never have with him what you and I have."

She jerked her head back in surprise. "I'm not *with* Lorenzo. We are just friends!"

I rolled my eyes and pushed myself off the couch, ignoring the dizziness.

"Where do you think you're going?" she shouted.

I ignored her and strolled over to the kitchen counter. Everything was as it was this morning before she left. Our empty glasses still scattered on the table and the box of headache tablets next to it. Thank goodness. I reached over and grabbed the box, fumbling to get tablets out to stop the pounding in my head.

"Giovanni, let me help you." She walked over from the couch and tried to reach for the box, but I pulled away.

"I don't need your help," I slurred.

"Fine then!" she snapped. "I don't even know why I'm here!"

She turned and grabbed her bag off of the counter. I didn't want her to leave. That was the last thing I wanted, but I couldn't control my mouth right now. I had so much anger inside of me towards my parents' fucked up relationship, the fact Isabella and I weren't together, and my constant ability to fuck up any situation with her.

"Isabella, wait!" I shouted.

She turned to face me, crossing her arms. She was angry at me and I hated to see it. I didn't want to anger or upset her. I just wanted to tell her what happened. I couldn't help that she was the only comfort I needed right now.

My heart belonged to her.

CHAPTER 26:
Isabella

"What, Giovanni?" I snapped.

I crossed my arms across my chest, waiting for his response. He tells me he doesn't need my help and yet, that was exactly what he needed. Not even a few minutes ago I was helping him sit up because he couldn't do it himself. I hated to see him self-destruct like this. That was the last thing I ever wanted for him and I felt so guilty about it.

He leaned against the counter and hung his head in defeat. "I needed to see you, Isabella."

My heart warmed at his words. A few weeks ago I would have reveled in those words, but now it was torture. My heart was calling out for him, but my head was warning me against giving into my emotions again. Every time I did that, I made it more difficult to pull myself away from him.

"And I'm sorry I rocked up at your place unannounced, but I didn't know what else to do."

He looked up and his sad eyes met mine. "Alvaro asked me to go check on our mother earlier today. She went back home after staying with him and I needed to make sure she was okay with being alone."

I had completely forgotten about everything that happened with his parents. So much had happened over the last few weeks that it never occurred to me that this was still a situation in his life to be dealt with. I relaxed my arms and walked over to the counter, placing my bag back down.

"Turns out my mother is also having an affair." He looked away.

No. Way.

"As I arrived, I saw her at the top of the stairs kissing someone who was not my father."

I couldn't contain the shock that spread across my face. My hand covered my mouth as I tried to process what he just told me. He caught his father and now his mother being unfaithful and suddenly his behaviour made sense to me. He had never been one to have a healthy outlet for his emotions. He was impulsive and self-destructive. He was in a fit rage when he caught his father. He had so much that he hadn't dealt with and catching his father again when he did just made it all worse. I couldn't imagine what it must have been like to catch his mother. The person who was closest to him and the very person he worked so hard to protect.

"Giovanni, I'm sorry," I murmured.

"And I know that we're broken up," His voice was laced with sadness. "But you were there for me in Valencia and I just didn't know who else to turn to."

That was the last straw for me. I couldn't hold back my emotions any longer and I walked over to him, positioning myself in between his legs as I wrapped my arms around his neck. He buried his head in my shoulder and wrapped his arms around my waist. Nothing felt more right than being able to hold him again. He held onto me tighter and I allowed myself to be consumed by my feelings for him again. I had worked so hard to push it away but it was proving to be a very trying task.

"Does your mother know you were there?" I asked softly.

"No," he murmured into my shoulder. "I left before anyone realized I was there."

He pulled away to face me, but still kept his arms around me. "I don't know how I'm supposed to feel about this."

"There are no instructions on how you're supposed to feel." I brought my hand up to cup his cheek. "You just feel what you feel."

His eyes were brimming with sadness and I wanted to take it all away. I hated the hollowness in those deep brown eyes of his. There was no life in them and it killed me that I had contributed to that. I watched how it broke him when I broke up with him. It was the worst thing I had ever done but what was I supposed to do? I couldn't be a stepmother. I couldn't be a part of him and Casey bringing a baby into the world. I knew myself and I knew that would be something I wouldn't be able to handle. My heart was broken too and I had yet to figure out what I was going to do to pick up the pieces.

"My family is a fuck up," he muttered.

I pulled myself away from him and reached for an empty glass. I placed it on the counter and took the cold water out of his fridge again. I filled it up and handed it to him. He took it and quickly downed the water.

I leaned against the counter across from him. "No family is perfect."

"No, they aren't and that's the problem."

"Have you told Alvaro?" I asked.

He shook his head. "I came to find you as soon as it happened."

A small part of me was happy that I was his comfort. Things went wrong and I was the first person he turned to. I always wanted it to be that way.

You broke up with him, Isabella.

The rational voice in my head continued to whisper that over and over again to remind me of the reality of the situation. It was easy to forget what was going on when it was just him and I. Outside of this apartment, there were so many reasons to keep us apart, but when it was just the two of us, it was easy to forget them all.

"I think you should tell him," I suggested."You shouldn't have to deal with this by yourself."

"I'll leave him a message and ask him to come by tomorrow."

He reached for the cupboard door above the counter and pulled out a bottle of whiskey.

"Don't you think you've had enough to drink?" I asked softly.

He placed the bottle on the counter and turned to face me. "Nothing else helps."

"You're not going to find the answers at the bottom of the bottle, Giovanni."

"You'd be surprised what you can find." He pulled two glasses from the cupboard. "You want one?"

Any other day I would have rejected his offer, but I couldn't disagree that it certainly took the edge off. I extended my hand and he handed me a glass. I wasn't big on whiskey, but I could do with anything that would make me forget our new reality. I brought it to my lips and the bitterness spread across my tongue.

"How can you drink this?" I muttered, pulling a face at the strong taste.

He shrugged and brought his glass to his lips, taking a small sip.

"You know this doesn't help right?" I repeated, knowing I was trying to convince myself of this, too.

"I don't need something that helps right now. I just want to forget everything." he sighed. "Don't you wish you could just forget?"

I brought my glass to my lips again. "Of course I do."

He flicked his eyes to meet mine and I had never longed for anything more. I wanted to forget everything that had happened between us. I wanted to go back to the day he told me he loved me. Hearing those three words made me happier than I ever realized I could be. I would give anything to go back to that.

He placed his glass on the counter and walked over to me. "I'm sorry for how I spoke to you earlier. I shouldn't have acted like that. You don't deserve that."

I lifted my eyes to meet his. "It's okay."

He stepped closer to me. "I hated seeing you with Lorenzo."

"We're just friends," I murmured.

He lifted his hand and ran his thumb across my cheek as his hand cupped my face. "I don't want to see you with anyone else, Isabella."

My breath caught in my throat. He was standing so close to me that I could smell that cologne of his. I couldn't help but breathe him in. He leaned closer, allowing stray strands of his hair to fall forward. He was inches from me now and my body was burning to have him closer. My eyes met his and I could see his desire mirrored my own but instead of making another move, he dropped his hand.

"I'm sorry," he murmured.

I shook my head. "It's okay."

"It's so difficult to have you so close to me and know that I can't rip your clothes off right now."

The desire deep within the pit of my stomach was screaming at me to hand myself over to him. Hearing those words roll off his tongue caused an aching pressure between my legs and I didn't know how I was going to pull myself away from him.

"And I know I shouldn't do this but fuck it." He reached out and cupped my face again, bringing his lips to meet mine.

I should have pushed him away. We were broken up and we couldn't keep doing this to each other, but I was in no position for any rational thinking right now. My body was calling out for him so I kissed him back. His hands found my hair as I flicked my tongue over his. It was exhilarating to be able to do this again. I knew it was wrong - fucking wrong to be exact, but I couldn't help it. I couldn't help that my body and heart called out for him. No matter how much I convinced myself I could be without him, I was afraid that would never be true. His hand left my hair and traveled down to my coat, pushing it back as I allowed it to slip off me onto the floor. My hands found his hair as his lips moved down to my neck. I threw my head back and basked in the way he was making my body feel. My arousal shot through my veins melting away any thoughts warning me that this was a bad idea. I couldn't concentrate on anything else, but the feeling of his lips against my skin. I pushed him against the counter as I brought my lips back to his with a new sense of urgency. I leaned against him and felt him come alive. My hands ran down his body and pushed under his shirt. I wanted more of him. I needed more of him.

Before I could take this any further, my phone started to ring, breaking me out of the bubble of desire I had found myself in. I pulled away from him, both of us breathing heavily.

"You want to get that?" he asked.

I leaned over the counter to my bag and pulled my phone out, Reyna's name flashing across my screen. I stared at it, contemplating whether I should answer or not. In that moment, my voice of reason managed to push its way to the front, screaming at me to stop whatever it was I was going to do with Giovanni. I couldn't answer Reyna right now without having to explain myself to her again so I placed my phone back down and allowed the call to go to voicemail.

"I'm sorry," Giovanni said softly.

I turned to face him. "We can't keep doing this to each other, Giovanni."

"I know."

The right thing to do would have been to walk away. I should leave and go back home because I knew that what we were doing was only making things worse on each other. I was allowing myself to continue to give in to the overwhelming love I had for him. Even now, it consumed me to the point where I felt I couldn't breathe. Seeing how overcome with sadness he was,

was killing me inside. I couldn't just turn away from him. My heart wouldn't allow it.

"But I don't want to leave right now," I admitted.

His eyes lit up. "You don't have to."

"But you can't kiss me again," I warned. "I want to be here for you but not like that. We're not together anymore."

"Fine."

"I'm serious."

I didn't want to say it. I didn't want him to stop kissing me. It was taking all the self-control I had left to not throw myself at him, but I had to stand my ground. We were broken up and we had to start acting that way. Nothing was going to change.

"Fine, I won't kiss you again. Not until you tell me that's what you want."

My stomach flipped with butterflies. Of course, I wanted him to kiss me - all day, every day, but I couldn't give into that.

"I won't."

I was trying to convince myself that I could stick to that. I was adamant.

CHAPTER 27:
Giovanni

Hours later I woke to the sound of the credits rolling from the movie we had just fallen asleep to. We spent the rest of the day keeping things fairly mundane. We kept the conversation light except for when we delved into the situation with my parents. I didn't know how to process the information, but apart of me knew that I had to accept the fact that the family I once knew was now a fuck up. My parents couldn't continue running around, betraying each other like this. A part of me was saddened by their relationship. It didn't have to be that way. Their relationship brought up the underlying fear and insecurity I always had when it came to relationships at all. My failure to want to commit to anyone still lingered when I was reminded of theirs, but then I'd look at Isabella and remember all the reasons why it would work. She and I were meant to be together. I couldn't shake that feeling. I believed that with every fiber of my being.

Eventually, we ordered some takeout and put on a bad movie. For the first time in weeks, things actually felt normal. We moved together like we always had and just having her here was what I needed. I immediately felt more at ease. I was better with her around.

She was asleep on the couch next to me and I soaked in her presence. I thought back to the kiss earlier. I knew I shouldn't have done it, but I couldn't help myself. Her words were telling me that she didn't want me but her eyes were saying something different. I knew her and I knew when she wanted me, but it wasn't up to me now. Even after everything, she still chose to stay here with me so I would respect her choice to not want to do anything more.

The choice would always be up to her.

No matter how badly I wanted her, I would do anything just to have her in the same room with me, if that was all that was given to me. The alcohol had finally made its way out of my system and all that was left was the pounding headache I had become accustomed to. I slowly pushed myself off the couch and strolled over to the counter. I reached for some pain medicine and popped a couple pills into my hand. I walked over to the fridge and pulled it open, grabbing a bottle of water before closing it behind me. I leaned against the counter and downed the pills. I took another sip as I heard murmurs from where Isabella lay.

"Giovanni?" She murmured into the night.

"I'm here." I walked over to the couch and leaned against it, looking down as she turned to face me.

She opened her eyes slightly and reached her hand out to me. "I miss you."

"I'm right here, baby."

I shouldn't have called her baby. I had no right to do that but it was just so natural to me. That's what she was to me.

She opened her eyes completely and I noticed the tears that stained her, now, red cheeks. "Not like that. I miss what we once were."

My heart contracted at her words and the pain in my chest from the reminder of what we no longer had continued to ache. Her voice was laced with sadness and it tore me apart. I hated that I had caused her this pain. We were in this mess because I slept with Casey and I wanted nothing more than to go back in time and change what happened. If I had accepted early enough that what I was feeling for Isabella was real, I wouldn't have fallen back into my old ways. I was angry at myself for fucking up the only good thing in my life.

Without letting go of her hand, I lifted my leg and climbed over the couch. I pulled her closer to me, her arms instinctively dropping across my torso and her head finding my chest.

"I miss you too, *mi hermosa*," I murmured, bringing my lips against her hair.

A lump started to form in my throat and for the first time in a while, I felt the tears start to build up. I had really fucked up with her and yet, she was still here. She was still giving me the time of day and allowed me to have her in my arms. She didn't push me away. Instead, she held on tighter and I never wanted to let her go.

"You have to know that I never wanted this to happen," I whispered.

"I know."

"You are all I ever wanted."

She sniffed and I felt her chest rise and fall as she cried into my chest. I pulled away enough to face her as she tilted her head back, her sad eyes meeting mine.

"Baby, no." I brought my hand up to her face and wiped away her tears. "I don't want you to cry."

She took a deep breath in and tightened her arms around me. It was well past midnight and the TV reached the timer I had on and automatically turned off. The only light was the moonlight peeping through the open curtains. What was I doing to myself? Having her here in my arms was all I ever wanted, but at what cost? Tomorrow morning she was going to leave and I was going to have to watch her walk away from me again. How many times was I going to put myself through that?

"I don't want you to cry because of me," I murmured.

"It's not because of you, Gio. It's everything. I hate that we're in this situation."

I leaned my head back. "Trust me, I hate it, too."

We said nothing further. Instead, we lay in each other's arms and soaked in the last moments we could get with each other. I love her so much. I love that even though we weren't together, she spent the night with me because she knew I needed her. It was selfish of me to have asked her to do this, but she did, no questions asked. She let me rant about what I needed to get off my chest and she allowed me to be silent when I wished not to continue speaking about it. I had never met anyone like her. The most beautiful woman inside and out. She was compassionate and kind. She was everything I could have ever wanted in someone.

I pulled her closer to me and kissed her forehead. "You don't have to say it back, but you need to know that I love you, Isabella, and I always will."

I didn't expect her to say anything in return. I had accepted that I would never hear those words from her mouth again.

She surprised me by whispering into the night, "I'll always love you too, Giovanni."

CHAPTER 28:
Isabella

"I know I shouldn't have spent the night, but he needed me, Rey." I leaned my head against my hand. "I couldn't help it."

"I understand, Izzy," she murmured on the other line. "But you know you're only hurting yourself."

I sat in the bathroom leaning against the counter. I had gotten out of the shower and was changing back into my pants and a random shirt that Giovanni gave me to wear when Reyna called me. I left her a message last night letting her know that I wasn't going to be home and I would explain tomorrow. She didn't wait long this morning before calling me to find out what was going on.

I took a deep breath in trying to keep the tears that were forming from falling. "I don't know what to do."

"You're the only one who can figure that out. I know you love Giovanni, but I also know how much it broke you to find out about Casey's pregnancy. You said you couldn't watch him raise a baby with her."

I couldn't. Every time I thought of them together, it sent me into an emotional frenzy that I couldn't control. I couldn't hold back the deep pain it brought me and the constant rolling anger. How was I ever going to get over that? I loved Giovanni more than I had ever loved anyone, but nothing had changed and I was angry that I kept allowing myself to be pulled back into this.

The tears escaped my eyes and rolled down my cheek. "I can't put myself through that."

"Then you know you have to walk away and for real this time," she advised. "The two of you are only making this harder on yourselves."

She was right. I knew she was right but I hated to hear it. I didn't think it was possible for my heart to break anymore, but it did. Every time I was reminded of the reality of our situation, the pieces cracked even further and there was nothing I could do to stop it. I had to make a decision and stick to it. I couldn't keep doing this to myself. I couldn't keep doing this to him.

"I love him so much," I cried.

"I know you do, Izzy." Her voice was laced with sadness.

There was nothing that could be said to make this better. It didn't help that I loved him and he loved me back. The fact was I couldn't stand by him while he had a baby with another woman and that was the truth. That was never going to get easy to hear and it certainly wasn't going to be easy when the baby finally arrived. I had to accept that Giovanni and I were done for good.

Maybe we just weren't meant to be.

Reyna and I said our goodbyes and I wiped away the rest of my tears. I stood up and reached for the shirt Giovanni left for me. I held it to my chest and breathed in the smell of him that lingered. It smelled like home to me and the tears formed again. I was breaking inside and I just wanted to make the pain stop. I pulled the shirt over my body and reached for the towel to wipe away the last of my tears. I had to contain myself before I left the bathroom.

After finally pulling myself together, I slipped out the door and went over to the bed to pull my boots back on. I slowly ran my fingers over his bed. The memories of him and I together flooded back. The way he held me in his arms as I fit perfectly across his body. My head on his chest as it rose softly when he was in a deep sleep. I tried to stop my mind from wandering further but I couldn't hold it back. I thought back to the way he lay me down and took control of my body. His lips across my skin, his hands in my hair pulling it back as he entered me.

"Isabella?" Giovanni's voice broke me out of my walk down memory lane.

I jumped at the sound of his voice and turned to face him as he stood against the door frame of his room.

"Sorry, I didn't mean to scare you," he said sheepishly. "Alvaro and Penelope are here."

"I'll be down in a sec."

He nodded and left the room. I took a deep breath in, preparing myself for what was coming next. I could be here for Giovanni a little longer, but I needed to remove myself from the situation. There was only so much pain I could put myself through and I had reached the quota. My heart would never be what it once was.

I grabbed my coat off the bed and hung it across my arm as I turned to make my way downstairs. The chorus of voices from the bottom got louder as I reached the bottom of the staircase.

"Isabella!" Penelope shrieked and walked over to me, pulling me in for a hug. "It's so lovely to see you again."

"You too, Penelope." I pulled away and was surprised by how great she was already looking. "You wouldn't say you just had a baby, you look amazing."

"First time wearing makeup in a couple weeks and it helps to have these bad boys sucking everything in." She laughed and lifted her shirt to show her high-waisted tights.

Alvaro stepped out from behind her and leaned forward to greet me. "Didn't expect to see you here, but I'm really happy you are."

"Thanks, Alvaro."

"How's your dad doing?" he asked.

"Oh, much better. He's been home recovering for a while now, so thankfully everything is back to normal."

"I'm so happy to hear that." Penelope reached for my hand and squeezed it.

Giovanni was bent down by the couch before turning around revealing his nephew in his arms. He was wrapped in a blanket and had the smallest beanie over his little head. He held onto the baby with such care and his dark eyes lit up at the sight of him.

"Isabella, meet Mateo," Giovanni murmured and slowly walked over to me.

My eyes swelled at the sight of him. He was the most precious little thing I had ever seen. His tiny hands peeked outside of the blanket and his eyes fluttered open.

"Oh my God, he is beautiful." I slowly reached for his little hand and rubbed my thumb over his soft skin. "Congratulations you guys."

Penelope smiled. "Thank you. You should have seen how tiny he was when he was born. You wouldn't say given how huge I was."

"He just seemed big because of how small you are Penelope," Giovanni teased.

Penelope laughed and Alvaro strolled into the kitchen."Coffee anyone?"

I politely declined the offer, but both Giovanni and Penelope asked for a cup. Penelope went to assist Alvaro.

I couldn't take my eyes off Giovanni with Mateo. He was a natural as he held onto his nephew. My heart warmed at the sight of him and I longed to have the same. Seeing Giovanni with Mateo reminded me that at the back of my mind, I always wanted this and I wanted it with him.

But I couldn't have it.

He was going to have this, but it wasn't going to be with me. The sadness consumed me and I suddenly felt the air around me become thin again.

"Please excuse me for a moment."

I turned towards the door that led out onto the balcony from his living room. I pushed it open and was welcomed by the cold air brushing up against me. I took a deep breath in, filling my lungs with the air it needed. I leaned against the railing and tried to contain my emotions. I didn't expect to see Giovanni with Mateo. I didn't expect to react like this, but I couldn't help it. It was the final straw for me.

"Isabella, are you alright?" Giovanni asked from behind me.

I kept my eyes firmly on the building in front of me. I couldn't look at him right now. Not when I was on the verge of breaking down.

"I'm fine," I lied.

He stepped forward and stood next to me. "No, you're not."

The tears that had formed in my eyes escaped and I was consumed by my emotions. My heart was breaking and there was nothing I could do to stop it.

"I think I need to leave," I murmured.

"Leave?" he repeated. "Why would you want to leave?"

"Seeing you with Mateo just reminded me of what you and I will never have." I turned my head to meet his gaze. "I can't keep putting myself through this."

I expected him to ask me to stay. I expected him to try and fight for us again, but instead his eyes swelled with sadness and he whispered.

"I know."

He had accepted the reality of our situation just as I had to. There was nothing more for us to say or do. We were in this mess and it was time to start moving on, without each other.

"And I meant what I said last night. I will always love you, Giovanni, but I'm sorry, I just can't watch you raise a child with someone else. No matter how much I love you, I can't put myself through that and we need to stop what we're doing because this isn't helping either of us."

He reached out and pulled me into his arms. I buried my head in his chest and I allowed myself to cry.

"I understand, Isabella," he murmured into my hair. "I just wish things could have been different."

"Me too."

CHAPTER 29:
Giovanni

Isabella said her goodbyes to Alvaro and Penelope and she left my apartment. I had lost count of how many times I had watched her walk away from me, but I knew that this time was different. As much as I loved having her here last night and being able to hold her in my arms, it wasn't right. It wasn't right for me to keep putting her through this. I could have stopped her from leaving. I could have told her that I asked Casey for a paternity test and that there's a chance that this could all be over. But just knowing there's a chance this baby was mine was enough for me to keep that to myself. I watched her cry. I watched how broken she was over this. I had broken the heart of the woman I love and I could never live with myself if I did that again. It was selfish of me. It was selfish of me to involve her in my own drama again. All I wanted was for her to be happy and she had made the decision to leave. I loved her with every part of who I was and it was because I loved her so much that I had to let her go and move on with her life.

No matter how much it killed me to watch her leave, it was the right thing to do for her.

"I didn't expect to see Isabella here," Penelope commented and placed a cup of coffee in front of me as I pulled myself onto one of the barstools by the counter.

I reached for it and wrapped my hands around it, soaking in the heat. "Yeah, it's a bit complicated."

Alvaro had Mateo in his arms as he took a seat on the barstool across from me. He was already a natural with the baby. I remembered how stressed he had been the day Penelope went into labour. I couldn't get that look out of my head but it made me happy to see how relaxed he was now. In the end, everything worked out the way it was supposed to.

"Are you guys back together?" Alvaro asked.

I shook my head. "No, and I'm pretty sure that's the last time I'll be seeing her."

"I thought you asked Casey for a paternity test?"

"I did, but I couldn't tell Isabella that." I brought the cup up to my lips and took a small sip, the hot liquid burning my tongue. "How do we know the baby isn't mine? And if I tell her about the test and it comes back saying I'm the father then I've gone and dragged her through this all over again. She's made it clear that she doesn't want to be involved."

The deep sadness around my heart had returned again. There was a hollowness that now lingered in my chest and I knew it was going to be a permanent resident.

Penelope reached out and squeezed my hand. "I'm sorry. I know how much you love her."

I said nothing and brought the coffee to my lips again. They both got the message that I didn't want to keep talking about Isabella and me. There was nothing more to say anyway.

"Did you go and see *Mama* yesterday?" Alvaro asked.

I placed my cup back on the counter and leaned my chin against my hand, looking over at him. "I did and I saw her. I also saw her making out with someone that wasn't our father."

Penelope's jaw dropped. "No!"

Alvaro's expression remained unchanged except for the swimming confusion in his eyes.

"What do you mean?" Penelope couldn't hide her shock. "Marcina would never do that."

"Clearly she would," I muttered.

I had become numb to the mess that was my parent's relationship. I went through all the emotions last night with Isabella - denial, anger, sadness, shock and now, I felt nothing towards it. I had always wanted to protect my mother from the pain that my father caused. I watched how it broke her the first time and my instinct was to do what I could to defend her. It never occurred to me that she would do the same to him.

Alvaro finally spoke. "What did you say to her?"

"She didn't see me. I saw her at the top of the back stairs. I didn't recognise the man she was with, but when I saw them, I left."

He remained silent as he tried to process this. The fact that I had to break it to my brother again that another one of our parents was unfaithful to the other was a fucking joke.

"I don't know why I always have to be the one to catch them," I attempted to joke. "But seriously, our parents need to get a fucking divorce."

"What are they doing to each other?" Alvaro asked, the anger making its way into his voice.

Penelope walked over to him and placed her hand on his shoulder as he continued.

"It was bad enough when we found out about dad the first time and then again a few weeks ago, but for *Mama* to do the same? She's so much better than this."

"Can you blame her though?" Penelope chimed in. "Your father was the one who did it first."

"Two wrongs don't make a right Penelope," I snapped.

"She should have left him after the first time," Alvaro interjected. "Why did she stay with him if this was what was going to happen?"

"We don't know how long this has been going on for," I added.

Alvaro stood up and passed Mateo to Penelope who took him in her arms. He paced up and down the kitchen. My brother was usually very good at containing his emotions so it surprised me that he was more affected by this than I expected. I couldn't blame him though - it was a fuck up.

"They need to get divorced," Alvaro repeated my suggestion. "They clearly aren't happy together, and to continue to betray each other like this isn't going to work."

He stopped and leaned against the counter. "I don't remember their relationship ever being this bad."

"It wasn't. Or maybe it was and we just never realised."

"The *Velázquez Constructa* Christmas party is coming up now. You know we're going to be expected to attend right?" Alvaro reminded me.

Every year my father's business hosts a lavish Christmas party with all of its employees, the top people in society and any press that was itching for a story. The point of the party is to raise funds for various different charities that my father was involved in. The man may have some questionable tactics when it came to his family but I couldn't deny that he did what he could to give back to those less fortunate. This party has been happening for years now and was always a compulsory family affair.

"I forgot all about that," I admitted.

"Well, we're going to need to bite our tongues until after that party. There's always press there and quite frankly, I'd like to keep them out of our family's business this time around," Alvaro continued. "We need to make it through this last public appearance as a family and then they need to get a divorce because what they're doing isn't right."

I was about to object to his idea to hold off on saying anything but instead, I agreed. The press had no problem ripping into my family the last time a scandal like this rolled around and even though it was a fucked up situation, I would still protect my family and we had the right to go through this privately.

"Fine, but as soon as that party is over, we're going to have a family meeting and sort this shit out."

CHAPTER 30:
Isabella

The tears wouldn't stop.

It felt like I had lost Giovanni all over again and my heart was completely shattered. I tried to think of what kind of future we could have together and I couldn't. I tried to grip onto some kind of scenario where this could work for us, but there was nothing. Knowing that Casey was going to be a part of his life and they were going to share something as precious as a baby together was too much for my fragile heart to handle. It was just a constant reminder that no matter what, he would never truly be mine. It was selfish of me, but I wanted to be the only one to have it all with him. I wanted a family one day and I wanted it to be with him.

But not like this.

This was something I just couldn't bring myself to be a part of and it destroyed me inside. It reminded me of his relationship with Casey and the blurred timelines of his relationship with both of us. I knew we weren't officially together at the time, but just the idea of him with someone else, while I was completely taken with him, made me feel like a complete idiot. I didn't want anyone else to have him.

I finally managed to drag myself upstairs to my apartment. I unlocked the door, pushing it open as I stepped inside. I closed the door behind me and my phone started to ring. I pulled it out of my pocket and my father's name flashed across the screen. My heart contracted at the sight of it as the memories of him in the hospital came flooding back.

"Hi Dad," I answered, wiping my tears away.

"Bella, how are you?" His warm voice made me smile. "We haven't spoken in a while so I wanted to check in."

"I'm sorry I haven't called," I said, the guilt washing over me. "Things have been crazy this side."

I didn't want to explain it to him. I couldn't bring myself to do it. The last thing I wanted was for my mother to find out about Giovanni and me. Who knows what she would have to say then?

"But how are you doing?" I quickly changed the subject.

"I'm getting there, Izzy. Day by day. Yesterday I struggled a bit, but I'm going to see my doctor at the end of the week for a check-up."

"That's good. You need to take care of yourself, Daddy."

"I am. It's nice to have this time off to relax." I could hear him smile through the phone and it made me smile.

"I'm sure. You and Mom work way too hard."

"She told me about your new boyfriend," he said casually.

A lump formed in my throat and it took all my self-control to keep my tears at bay. *How could I tell him what happened with Giovanni?* He never even met him and I was not about to tell him that he's having a baby with someone else. I just couldn't bring myself to do that right now.

"I'm surprised she mentioned him. How is she doing though? And how's Camila?" I deflected.

"Everyone is good. I wish you were coming home for Christmas."

I leaned against the counter and took a deep breath in. "I know, Dad and I'm sorry I'm not going to be there. There's just a lot of friction with Mom right now and I need some time."

"I understand." I heard the sadness in his voice. "You know I just want you to be happy, Izzy."

"Thank you. Please just know that I love you very much and we'll see each other soon okay?"

"I love you, too."

We said our goodbyes and I disconnected the call. I placed my phone on the counter and leaned my head into my hands, allowing the tears to consume me. I was putting myself through a vicious cycle here. I thought I was making progress starting to get over Giovanni, but that was a lie. I was nowhere close to getting over him and spending last night in his arms was the worst thing I could have done. It just reminded me of what it was like to be his.

The front door opened and I jerked my head up toward it as Reyna slipped inside. She turned and made eye contact with me.

"Oh, Izzy." She walked over to me and wrapped her arms around me.

I was so tired of crying, but the tears wouldn't stop falling. I held onto her and cried into her shoulder.

She ran her fingers through my hair. "What happened?"

"Nothing new, but you were right. I should never have gone there."

"That's not something I wanted to be right about," she murmured and pulled away, taking a seat next to me.

"I don't know why I keep doing this to myself," I muttered.

"You love him."

A new rush of tears overcame me upon hearing that. "I do."

She reached out and held my hand in hers, squeezing gently. "I've asked you this already, but I'm going to ask you again because I can see how unhappy you are without him. Do you not want to try at all?"

I looked up and met her gaze. "I thought about it a lot since I left his apartment. I really tried to imagine myself with him now that he was having a baby with Casey and I just couldn't get past that. I know there are plenty of women out there who could probably be okay with being a step-mom, but I'm not that person. And it's not because of the stepmom part of it, it's because I can't put myself through watching him and Casey share something as special as a baby. That's next level connection stuff and I already hated the idea of him with someone else. I just can't do that to myself."

"I understand, Izzy." She comforted me. "I can't even imagine what that must be like. I'm so sorry. I just want you to be happy again. That's all I want."

She pulled me in for another hug. The pain consumed me and I wondered if I was ever going to be able to make it stop.

CHAPTER 31:

Giovanni

Countless days had passed since I last saw her. I was starting to become used to the numb feeling that now lived inside of me. The constant hollowness reminds me of her absence. Every day I fought the urge to pick up the phone and call her. I fought the urge to rock up at her apartment and bang on her door until she opened up for me. I fought the urge to tell her that this could all be over.

But I couldn't bring myself to put her through that again.

I watched how it broke her over and over again to be reminded that Casey and I were having a baby. I was the continued reason for her pain and it killed me. All I ever wanted was to make her happy and I knew I could. I knew she and I had something special, but one wrong move and I had lost it all. For days, I allowed myself to wallow in the sadness, but I had to start pulling myself out of it. I had people relying on me and even though I didn't want to face the world without her, I had to.

I casually strolled into the office building of *Velázquez Constructa*. We had closed the deal for the building in Valencia for the expansion of *Mala Mía* and I needed to pick up the blueprints for the original one from my father's office. I hadn't seen him since that night in Valencia and I wasn't sure what to expect from him. If I knew him well enough, it would be a brief and curt conversation. He would hand them over to me and I would be on my way. Weeks ago I would have wanted to have a full-on conversation about what happened, but I just didn't have it in me. I didn't have it in me to deal with my parent's broken relationship right now.

I stepped into the elevator full of people and pressed the button for the top floor. After stopping for everyone else, I was the last one to get out as the doors opened up. I stepped out and strolled over to reception. I didn't recognise the petite blonde that sat behind the desk, her big blue eyes peering up at me.

"*Buenos Dias,*" she greeted politely. "How can I help you?"

"I'm looking for my father, Cecilio Velázquez. Is he in yet?"

"I didn't know he had a son." She batted her eyelashes, not even bothering to hide her very obvious interest. "He's in the conference room for a meeting but he should be done soon."

"*Gracias.*"

I turned down the corridor that led to the conference room. The entire floor space was scattered with offices that were separated by glass walls. My father had plenty of people working under him, but very few had a permanent residency in this office space. The door to the conference room was still closed, but I could see him inside seated with a couple of other people I had never met before. I walked to his office in the corner and pushed through the door. I had been here many a time and everything was just as I remembered. A large oak desk sat by the far wall with a leather chair on the opposite side of it. A large painting of the *La Sagrada Familia* hung on the wall behind it and file cabinets were scattered along the left wall. There was a large window that looked out onto the city on the right side. In the distance, you could see the four spires of the cathedral. His office had the best view.

I turned to the murmur of voices getting louder behind me as my father walked towards his office.

"Giovanni, I didn't know you were going to be here." He was surprised, but he kept his tone clipped and formal as always.

"I just came to get the blueprints for *Mala Mía*. I need them for the team in Valencia."

He nodded and strolled past me to his desk. Out of the corner of my eye, I noticed a formally dressed man down the hall in conversation with another employee. He looked so familiar to me and yet, I couldn't quite place him. He started to approach the office and I got a better look at him. His light hair was pulled into a neat bun and despite his full-beard, I could tell that he was definitely younger than I was.

Why was he so familiar to me?

It was starting to annoy me that I couldn't place him. I was usually very good at remembering faces and where I had met people but he was lost on me. He walked with purpose and control as he stopped at the door frame, noticing me for the first time.

"Apologies sir, I didn't realize you were meeting a client," he said politely, a hint of an English accent coming through.

"Nonsense," my father dismissed. "This is my son. We'll be done soon so you can wait outside."

He nodded and waited outside the door. He didn't make any movements to suggest he was going to introduce himself to me so I shrugged and turned back to my father as he handed me a blue folder.

I took it from him. *"Gracias."*

"You know the office Christmas party is coming up this weekend, Giovanni. We haven't received your RSVP." My father took a seat behind his desk.

I rolled my eyes. "Don't worry. I'll be there."

"Are you bringing a plus one?" he asked, leaning back against his chair. "I've seen the news so, I'm not sure it's going to be the same one I met last time."

I could have reached across the table and punched him in the fucking face again. The anger rolled through me and I had to use all my self-control to stay calm, especially with unwanted company around.

"Yeah, and I'm sure it will be interesting to see who you bring as your plus one or is it a family occasion for this event?"

My father's seething eyes met mine. "Watch yourself, Giovanni."

I dismissed his warning as nothing more than an empty threat. The fact he could act so arrogant when he knew what he had done was beyond me. He was a proud man so if there was one thing I had learned about him, it was that he would never own up to his mistakes.

He dismissed my presence and called for the waiting man outside his office. "Nate, you can come in now. We're done here."

Nate?

I turned to face him as he entered, this time extending his hand out to me.

"Nate Cameron," he said politely.

Why did that name sound so familiar?

Wait a minute...

I suddenly remembered where I had seen him before. On the engagement announcement that Isabella showed me when she revealed her ex was now engaged. And now he is here in Barcelona working for my father.

What are the fucking chances?

"Giovanni Velázquez," I replied and shook his hand.

"Nice to meet you, Giovanni."

"And you." I played along. "Welcome to Barcelona."

He looked confused by my welcoming, but he smiled politely and turned to my father. I didn't even bother saying goodbye. Instead, I slipped out of his office and made my way to the exit. *What the fuck was Nate doing here?* Did Isabella know he was here? Surely this was grounds to reach out to her?

By the time I reached my car, I had already convinced myself it was okay to call her. I pulled my phone out and dialed her number. It didn't even ring and instead went straight to voicemail. I tried her again, but I was out of luck. I tapped my fingers nervously on the steering wheel and dialed the next best thing.

"Giovanni?" Reyna's voice came through the other end after the second ring. "What can I do for you today?"

"Before you say no, I need to know where Isabella is."

"Why would you even ask me that?" she huffed. "You know you're supposed to be leaving her alone."

"I know that, but I can't since her ex-boyfriend now works with my father," I blurted out.

"No fucking way!"

"Yes, exactly," I muttered. "I tried to call her to let her know, but it went straight to voicemail."

Reyna was silent for a moment.

"Reyna?" I asked.

"I'm here," she replied. "And Isabella knows Nate is in Barcelona."

This was news to me.

"She does?"

"Yes. She bumped into him at the airport." A voice in the background called Reyna's name. "Listen, I have to go. Isabella is at the coffee shop today, but don't tell her I told you."

"Thank you, Reyna."

We said our goodbyes and I turned my car on, heading in the direction of her coffee-shop.

CHAPTER 32:
Isabella

I swept the last of the dust into a pile in the corner. I had finally managed to clean this place up and was disgusted by the amount of dust that had accumulated. I placed the broom against the wall and bent down to reach for the dustpan just as the bell by the door jingled to let me know that someone had just stepped inside.

I turned around and to my surprise, Giovanni stood there casually.

"Hi," he said awkwardly.

What in the world was he doing here?

And why did my heart flutter at the mere sight of him? He stood by the door with his hands in the pockets of his jeans. He had a dark green hoodie under his black leather jacket and his dark hair was hidden underneath a dark beanie. He didn't even try and yet, he still managed to take my breath away.

"Uh hi." I wasn't sure how I was supposed to respond to him. "What are you doing here?"

It had been a while since I had last seen him. I had been working so hard to focus on everything but him. I picked up extra shifts at the restaurant again and ended up coming here every time I had a spare moment. I didn't want to have time to think of him and the emptiness I felt in my life.

"Did you know Nate was in Barcelona?"

Nate?

Out of all the reasons for him to be here today, I definitely didn't think it would be to ask about Nate. How the hell did he even know Nate was here?

I stood up and dusted my hands off. "Yes, I did."

"When did you find out?"

More Than This

"The day I got back from London."

He jerked his head back. "And you didn't tell me?"

"I kind of had a lot on my mind that day, Giovanni." I sighed.

I alluded to our situation. Why would I care about Nate being here if I had bigger issues to deal with? I walked over to the sink behind the counter and washed the dirt off my hands. Giovanni walked over and leaned his hands against the counter. I didn't want to look at him. I'd have to be reminded of how fucking great he looked in his leather jacket and grown out beard. I didn't want to meet his deep brown eyes and be reminded of the love we once shared. I didn't want to be reminded of anything.

"Wait, how do you know Nate is here?" I asked, confused.

"Oh, well I just met him," he said casually. "He works for my dad."

I stopped what I was doing and turned to him. "No way."

"That seems to be the general response to that information," he mumbled sarcastically.

"He said he was working on a new project here," I explained. "I just never thought it would be with your dad of all people."

"Well, apparently the universe has nothing better to do but throw plot-twists our way."

I smiled at his attempt to lighten the mood. I was surprised by this though. Out of all the places Nate could end up, why did it have to be at my ex-boyfriend's father's company? My heart contracted as I referred to Giovanni as my ex. I hated it.

"Well, it doesn't really matter that he's here. It's not like he and I are on speaking terms or anything. He has his own life now."

"I just never expected to bump into your ex."

I reached for the nearest cloth and wiped my hands. "I don't think you guys are going to see each other much. You don't work with your dad."

"I'll probably see him at the Christmas party," he quipped.

"Christmas party?"

Before he could answer, my phone started to ring. It was on the counter in front of us and Giovanni's eyes wandered over.

"Lorenzo's calling," he muttered, the sadness in his eyes returning. "I should probably let you get back to that."

"We're just friends, Giovanni," I murmured.

I didn't know why I said it. I didn't owe him an explanation but I couldn't stop the guilt that washed over me.

"That's none of my business anymore, Isabella."

My name rolled off his tongue and my mind was transported back to the first time I heard him say it. It was intoxicating and I just wanted to hear him say my name over and over again. My name would never sound so sweet coming from anyone else.

"I'll be on my way." He turned towards the door.

"I mean it, Giovanni. There is nothing going on between Lorenzo and me."

I didn't want him to think there was. Even though we weren't together, I didn't want him to think I would just move on with someone else so quickly. I could never.

He turned to meet my gaze across the room."I just want you to be happy, *mi hermosa.*"

My eyes welled with tears at his endearing name for me. With one last longing look between us, he turned and left.

I was left with nothing but my sadness for company.

***

"Lorenzo, I heard you helped Izzy with the equipment today," Reyna said.

"Yeah, we managed to bring most of it in, but it's definitely gonna need to be cleaned and tested."

He leaned against the table and shifted closer to me, his arm brushing up against mine. We were all huddled around a high-table at *Paradiso*. Lorenzo arrived shortly after Giovanni left. He was helping me out with the coffee-shop today while Reyna was stuck at work. After that awkward encounter with Giovanni outside my apartment, I expected Lorenzo to have a lot of questions but when we met up again, he didn't breathe a word of it. We had spent the last few days together doing anything we could to keep my mind off Giovanni and I was starting to enjoy his presence in my life. He was always willing to help and tried his best to keep a smile on my face. The rest of the day was spent cleaning out the rest of the shop. We made really good progress together and we were able to start moving some of the equipment back in.

"But the place is really coming together." I joined the conversation.

"I'm so excited!" Reyna exclaimed. "Diego and I are going to spend some time there this weekend so if you guys want to join. We can make a day of it."

"That would be great." Lorenzo turned and smiled at me.

I didn't expect it but I had recently grown very fond of Lorenzo. I enjoyed his company. It was unproblematic. There was no drama when it came to him and I liked that. He had an on-going positive aura to him and it was contagious. The sadness I felt from seeing Giovanni lingered for the rest of the day but Lorenzo was a nice distraction from it. He was happy to spend his day with me doing unpleasant jobs like cleaning up and never once complained.

"Can we get a round of shots please?" Diego stopped the waitress as she walked past our table. "Anyone want another drink?"

I shook my head and lifted my glass. "I'm still good, thanks."

Reyna and Lorenzo both ordered another drink. We had been here for a while but I was still on my first drink. I sipped on it as I allowed myself to enjoy the beat blaring through the speakers. I was determined to have a good time tonight. Reyna invited us to meet her and Diego and said that Katrina and Sergio would be joining a bit later. It was strange at first to have Lorenzo tag along. It made me feel an unnecessary amount of guilt but we were all friends here so what was the problem with me inviting another friend of mine to join? I pushed all unnecessary thoughts to the back of my mind and focused on my drink and the company.

"Are we getting fucked up tonight?" Diego asked, excitedly.

I couldn't help but laugh at his excitement. "I really don't feel like having a hangover tomorrow."

"As my sister always says, we'll just be stealing happiness from tomorrow," Lorenzo chimed in.

Diego rolled his eyes. "Don't be so boring guys."

Lorenzo chuckled. "I never said I had a problem with that."

"See, that's better!" Diego lifted his hand for a high five, and I chuckled at their little moment.

"We had such a great time the last time we were here!" Reyna exclaimed and turned to Lorenzo and me. "Isn't that the night you two met?"

A small blush spread across my cheeks as I thought back to that night.

Too much alcohol and too much confidence was the real highlight of the night.

Lorenzo nodded. "Yeah, it was. Your friend over here was taking people out with her dance moves."

I rolled my eyes and laughed. "That's a little dramatic."

"There was more strength than you realised behind that little." He stopped and mimicked how I flung my arms in the air that night.

We all burst out laughing at his terrible demonstration and how he was forced to stop when the waitress stopped behind him with the shots on a tray. He just missed knocking her and that made me laugh even more.

"You're the one who needs to tame your moves," I warned playfully.

He moved back against the table sheepishly as she placed our shots in front of each of us. We reached for them and lifted them together before taking them. The alcohol burned going down my throat, sending chills up and down my body.

"You have got to work on that poker face of yours." Lorenzo nudged me playfully.

"It seems to be getting worse," I joked.

We placed our empty glasses back on the table as Katrina and Sergio pushed through the crowd to join our table.

"You guys took shots without us?" Sergio pretended to be hurt. "Now, we have to order another round."

I groaned and Lorenzo burst into laughter at my reaction. I introduced Lorenzo to Katrina and Sergio. I could see Katrina eyeing me as if she was waiting for more information.

I leaned closer to her. "We're just friends."

"Well, he's pretty cute." She nudged.

I rolled my eyes, a small smile on my lips. Yes, Lorenzo had many attractive qualities to him and the outside packaging was pretty good to look at too but I wasn't in that place. Or at least I had convinced myself that I couldn't be. Not when the emptiness in my heart remained as a constant reminder of what I once had.

Sergio ordered us another round of shots and the waitress brought them around a lot quicker than before. I hardly even had time for the last shot to kick in. I brought the shot to my lips and repeated the motion. It didn't get better. It still burned just as much going down but I started to feel the warm feeling washing over me. The alcohol blanket that made you forget about everything you didn't want to remember. Before I knew it, Reyna was ordering another round.

Oh, this was going to be a long night.

CHAPTER 33:

Giovanni

I finished up with the last of the meetings I had for the day about the expansion of *Mala Mía* in Valencia. Our investors were happy and now that the building was available, we had the green light to make it happen. For a brief moment today, I was happy.

I was happy that things were starting to make progress on the business side again. It gave me a healthy distraction from everything else I didn't want to focus on but now sitting in my car alone, trying to figure out what to do next just reminded me of the emptiness. I had no plans and I didn't know what to do. I was fine when I was around people but when I was alone, I was forced to focus on reality. Seeing her didn't help either but I had to tell her about Nate. I didn't know that she was well-aware of him being here and I would have rather wanted to know about his presence in Barcelona from her than from bumping into him. The last place I thought that would happen would be my father's office, but clearly, the universe was enjoying the games it was playing.

I tapped my fingers against my steering wheel, agitated that I had nothing to do. I was itching for another drink. I had managed to keep myself away from the alcohol for a few days but I was slipping further and further from my self-control. I had ordered quite a few drinks throughout the one lunch meeting and I could feel the alcohol in my system still lingering in the back. I was happy to have something to take the edge off but it made the thoughts of her more obtrusive in my mind. Jealousy reared its ugly head today when I saw Lorenzo's name light up her screen. I fucking hated it, but I had to keep it together in front of her. I didn't want to make another scene like I did last time. I was attempting to do better for her sake.

"Fuck it," I mumbled and pulled my phone out of my pocket to dial Sergio's number.

I needed some kind of distraction that didn't involve drinking alone. I was well aware of how unhealthy my coping mechanism was, but I couldn't stop. The phone rang for a couple minutes before Sergio finally picked up.

"Giovanni?" he shouted over the blaring music on his side of the line.

"Sergio, where are you?" I asked. "Can you hear me?"

"Sorry man, it's really loud here," he shouted.

"Where are you?"

"Paradiso bu-". The rest of his sentence got lost in the loud music and voices on his end.

"Sergio?" I repeated his name a couple times and got fragments of his voice coming through before I eventually gave up and ended the call.

The place sounded packed. There were just voices, laughter, and loud music on the other end so there was no way I was going to be able to have a conversation with him. I tapped my fingers again trying to decide my next move.

I could go and meet him.

Sergio was my friend and I knew he wouldn't mind if I met up with him. The tricky part was figuring out if Katrina was there and if so, was Isabella there? A small voice in my head was urging me not to go. It would be a bad idea if she was there, but the louder voice was pushing me towards it.

You have every right to meet up with your friends.

I had a feeling I was probably making the wrong decision, but I didn't care. The lingering alcohol already in my system was pushing me towards going. I turned my car on and pulled out of the parking lot, heading in the direction of *Paradiso*.

CHAPTER 34:
Isabella

"You're getting better at this!" Lorenzo exclaimed as I placed my shot glass on the table after successfully managing to not pull a face after taking it.

I was intoxicated now. The alcohol had made its way through me and I was definitely on a level. We had made it through a number of shots and after a while, I was starting to enjoy them.

"I don't know if it's starting to taste better or if I am just getting more drunk."

Lorenzo laughed. "I think it's definitely the drunk thing."

"And you?" I poked his arm. "Are you even feeling the alcohol?"

He leaned against the table, facing me. "Yes, but I have a higher tolerance for it than you do."

"You don't know that," I objected.

"Do you feel like dancing?" he asked, suddenly changing the subject.

"Yes!" I exclaimed.

He burst out laughing. "See, that's how I know you're already quite drunk. Sober you hates dancing, but drunk you, well, drunk you has some moves."

I could feel the heat spread across my cheeks. "So, you don't want to dance then?"

"Oh, of course I do."

He held out his hand and I slipped mine in his. The warmth of his hand against mine was a feeling I welcomed. He was right, sober me would never want to be on the dance floor but I was way past the point of making good decisions. He pulled me onto the dance floor and stepped closer to me, his one hand resting in mine and the other rested against my lower back. I was surprised by the tingling sensation that made its way through me as he pulled me closer. It felt good to be held again. I flicked my eyes up to Lorenzo, but his eyes were focused in the distance as we moved together to the music. There was no denying his attractiveness and a part of me was attracted to him. Since the first time I met him, I was definitely taken by him but nothing compared to the way Giovanni made me feel. I felt guilty for thinking about him while in the arms of another man but I couldn't help it. The alcohol washed away any barriers I had up to keep the thoughts of him out.

Isabella, enough now.

The voice in my head continuously reprimanded me and she was right. I was fighting a losing battle here and it was time to move on. I closed my eyes and pushed the thoughts of him to the deepest part of my mind. I focused on the music surrounding us. I focused on the way Lorenzo pulled me closer to him as we moved together. I breathed in the smell of his cologne as I opened my eyes to meet his. There was an intensity in his eyes that wasn't there before and I could feel the tension starting to creep in around us.

"What are you thinking, Lorenzo?" I asked.

A smile tugged at his lips before he answered. "You don't want to know what I'm really thinking, Isabella."

I lifted an eyebrow, intrigued. "Now you have to tell me."

"I'm thinking back to the first time we danced like this." He leaned closer to my ear. "Do you remember?"

I nodded.

"I couldn't keep my eyes off you that night," he shared. "You looked so beautiful just like you look right now."

My breath caught in my throat and he pulled back to meet my gaze. We were close now, inches away from each other and the tension surrounded me. I knew the alcohol was contributing to this situation and I wasn't sure how to react. I was terrified of the possibility that there may be a flicker of interest from my side. Or was I just enjoying the feeling of being in someone's arms again?

"And I know I shouldn't be saying this," he continued. "But you deserve to be told how beautiful you are."

"Lorenzo," I opened my mouth to continue, but he stopped me.

"You don't have to say anything, Isabella. I just wanted you to know."

I smiled and the heat continued to spread across my cheeks. I couldn't help it. He was always upfront about his very clear interest and it was up to me not to lead him on if I wasn't in that place. A part of me wanted to forget about everything and just pull into him again. I wanted to get caught up in the tension, but thankfully the rational voice in my head was still around to stop me. Instead, I leaned my head against his chest and enjoyed the moment with him. I was doing just that until I heard him say.

"What is he doing here?"

I lifted my head and turned to follow his gaze to meet Giovanni's across the room. Instinctively, I jerked away from Lorenzo and immediately felt guilty about doing that. I turned back to Lorenzo who couldn't hide his disappointment from my reaction.

"I have no idea why he's here," I said quickly. "He's not supposed to be."

"He just can't leave you alone can he?" he mumbled.

I avoided looking back at Giovanni. I didn't want to focus on him. I didn't even want him to be here. Not when I was intoxicated enough to give in to my true feelings. The familiarity of the situation brought on a wave of unwanted nausea. The last time I was here was when Giovanni brought Casey. I wanted to be done with him that night. I should have been done with him. It would have saved me all this heartache if I had pulled myself away from him for good. The world was spinning and I had to use all the energy I had to focus on Lorenzo and nothing else.

"Just forget about him." I reached out and placed my hand on his arm. "Let's get a drink and I'm sure he'll leave soon."

Please, let him leave.

Just knowing he was in the same room as I was enough to make the air around me thin and my heart beat at an incessant pace.

"Okay." Lorenzo grabbed my hand and led me to the bar.

CHAPTER 35:

Giovanni

Lorenzo was here with her. The rage rolled through me at the sight of her in his arms on the dance floor. They quickly broke away and I watched as they made their way towards the other side of the bar. She told me over and over again that they were just friends, but how could I believe her? Why was she here with him? I clenched my fists in an attempt to contain the wave of emotions rushing over me. I couldn't make a scene. I didn't want to be that person.

I pushed myself through the crowd, but stopped as someone tapped my shoulder. I turned around and met Reyna's piercing gaze.

"What are you doing here?" she shouted over the music.

"I'm looking for Sergio."

"Did he invite you?"

Technically, no but she didn't need to know that. Who was she to dictate where I could and couldn't go?

I ignored her question. "I didn't come here to start trouble, Reyna."

"No, but you probably will." She rolled her eyes. "You can't keep showing up like this. You need to let Isabella move on with her life."

"I don't want her to move on," I snapped. "You were the one who told me to ask Casey for a paternity test and I did."

She jerked her head back in surprise. "I didn't know you did that."

"Of course, I did and all I want to do is tell Isabella about it."

Her eyes softened. "You can't tell her, Giovanni. I've watched her get her heart broken over and over again and you will not put her through that again. You need to let her move on."

I scoffed. "With Lorenzo?"

"They're just friends," she objected.

"I've heard that before."

I didn't wait to hear what else she had to say. I was so sick of everyone saying they were just friends when clearly there was something more going on here. I was itching for a drink and I pushed my way through the crowd towards the bar.. I noticed Sergio leaning against it as he spoke to Katrina. I reached out and tapped Sergio on the shoulder.

"Giovanni!" He turned, surprised at my unexpected arrival. "What are you doing here?"

"I've come to get a drink with you guys." I leaned forward and greeted Katrina. *"Hola, Katrina."*

"Hi, Giovanni," she said politely. "Does Isabella know you're here?"

I shrugged my shoulders. "I'm not here for her."

Sergio called on the bartender. "Another round of shots for the three of us, please."

I could do with a shot. Actually, I could do with multiple ones. I could do with anything that would make me forget that across this bar stood Isabella and Lorenzo together. I fought all my urges to look over at them. I didn't want to see them in close proximity to one another. I hated that he was with her.

Fuck, it was torture.

Sergio handed me a shot and the three of us lifted them before I brought mine to my lips, tilting my head back and allowing the alcohol to burn through me. The warmth washed over me and I leaned my head from side to side, shaking off the tension. I had every right to be out here with my friends. She didn't get to decide what I was allowed to do. If she was going to move on then so was I.

I signaled for another round to the bartender and he was off.

"So, how's the wedding planning going?" I asked Katrina, trying to politely have a casual conversation.

"We haven't even started that yet. That is next year's focus."

I placed my hand on Sergio's shoulder. "Well, you've got a good one here, Kat."

She smiled and looked over at Sergio, her eyes shining with love and affection for him. I was never one who cared about that kind of stuff, but now the jealousy washed over me. I never wanted that until I met Isabella and I hated that all I was left with was the memory of what we once had.

We could have been great together.

I pushed that out of my mind as I downed my next shot. I wanted to burn away the pain I was feeling inside. I had done well to push her out of my thoughts over the last few days, but it was too late now. I was consumed by her and I couldn't think of anything else to help take it away.

As the night went on, I continued chatting to Sergio and Katrina, but I was always constantly aware of Isabella's movements across the bar. I watched out of the corner of my eye as Lorenzo leaned closer to her, whispering something in her ear. My anger reignited and my knee-jerk reaction was to order more shots. Or to storm across the room and punch him in the fucking face but I didn't want to be that guy. Instead, I stuck to the shots even though I was well-aware that it was a terrible way of dealing with this. The conversation continued to flow and the bartender kept delivering until I could feel my movements had become jagged and delayed.

I stumbled reaching for my next shot and had to lean on Sergio for support.

"Whoa, Giovanni," he said. "I think you've had enough."

"Nope." I reached for the shot and downed it.

Katrina placed her hand on my arm. "Giovanni, you can't drink away your problems."

I rolled my eyes. "You don't know anything about my problems."

"I know that you're clearly not handling this break-up very well."

"You don't know anything, Katrina," I snapped.

"Hey, don't talk to her like that," Sergio interjected. "We're not your enemies, Gio."

They were starting to piss me off. I didn't need to keep hearing how badly I was handling this break-up. I was well aware of it. I was the one going through it, not them, so who were they to tell me what I should and shouldn't do to get through this?

"There you guys are!" Reyna was hand-in-hand with Diego as they pushed themselves to join our group.

Reyna turned and looked at me. "You don't look good, Giovanni. Can I get you a bottle of water?"

My mouth was dry and I could feel the alcohol weighing me down. Every movement was slower than usual and trying to put together a sentence was proving to be a difficult task. They were all looking at me with concern and it was fucking pissing me off. I didn't come here to be babied. I came here to distract myself from my problems.

Even though my problem was sitting right across the room.

Lorenzo and Isabella had moved to a high-table on the other side of the bar and I couldn't keep my eyes off her. She leaned close to him and I watched as she threw her head back in laughter. I was at a crossroads here. I loved seeing her laugh. I just wanted her to be happy, but I wanted to be the one to do it. I didn't want fucking Lorenzo of all people to be the one making her laugh. The jealousy was eating at me.

"Hello? Earth to Giovanni?" Reyna snapped me out of my thoughts and forced me to look back at her. "Stop staring at her like that."

"Why is she with him?" I slurred.

"Don't do that to yourself." Sergio placed his hand on my shoulder.

I shrugged out of his grip. "No, seriously. She can't be with Lorenzo already. We haven't been broken up that long."

"Giovanni, what happens in Isabella's life is none of your business right now," Katrina said as politely as she could manage. "You're only torturing yourself by -".

"You told me to get a paternity test." I turned to Reyna. "And now you're telling me to leave her alone?"

"Giovanni, keep your voice down," Reyna warned. "You don't know those results yet do you?"

I remained silent.

"That's what I thought. You can't say anything to her until you know, Gio. You can't get her hopes up like that. It's not fair."

I ignored her and turned back to Isabella at the precise moment that Lorenzo leaned into her.

No fucking way was I going to let that happen.

Before I knew it, I was headed towards them. The voices around me told me to stop, Sergio even tried to grab my arm but I was already making my way across the room. My anger and jealousy were raging and without my sober barriers, I was being led by my emotions straight to their table.

No one kisses my girl.

I watched as Isabella pulled away from him with a look of surprise on her face. Lorenzo lifted his head and noticed me as I approached them.

CHAPTER 36:

Isabella

"What the hell are you doing here?" Lorenzo scowled.

I jerked my head up to meet the angry eyes of Giovanni as he approached our table. I didn't expect Lorenzo to kiss me, but for a second I allowed his lips against mine. I tried to allow the attraction I had for him to come forward but instead, nothing but guilt washed over me. I realized my mistake by allowing him to kiss me and I pulled away. Before I could say anything, Giovanni was standing at our table and I knew he just witnessed what happened

"What the fuck do you think you're doing?" he shouted and reached for Lorenzo, grabbing him by his shirt. "You shouldn't be with her."

"Giovanni, please don't do this again," I begged and tried to step in between the two of them.

I couldn't have a repeat of what happened the last time the two of them saw each other. I didn't plan on kissing Lorenzo and I definitely wouldn't have wanted Giovanni to see, but he did and he was seething.. My head was spinning and I was far too intoxicated to have to deal with this right now. Lorenzo pushed Giovanni back, forcing him to let go of his shirt.

Giovanni turned to me. "You told me you were just friends. You're not *just* friends, Isabella."

"We are!" I argued, knowing that the evidence was against me right now.

"Look at the two of you! " he shouted. "Fucking making out as if I'm not even here."

Making out? That was a little dramatic.

Lorenzo stepped towards Giovanni this time, closing the proximity between the two of them.

"She can do whatever she wants," Lorenzo said, speaking for me as if I wasn't standing right here, "I think you should leave now before you embarrass yourself further."

I didn't want to be in the middle of this. The animosity between the two of them surrounded us and it started to suffocate me. Lorenzo had no intention of backing down and I knew Giovanni well enough to know that there was no way he was going to allow Lorenzo to get the better of him.

The anger raged in his eyes. "You should learn to mind your own fucking business."

"Isabella's business is my business."

I watched Giovanni snap as he pushed Lorenzo back. Lorenzo bumped against the table and our drinks spilled over.

"Hey!" I shouted.

They both ignored me as Lorenzo shoved him back. The crowds around us dispersed as the two of them were now face to face. We were drawing attention to ourselves and I was pretty sure we were about to get kicked out.

"You will never have what Isabella and I have!" Giovanni shouted. "Don't fucking fool yourself here."

Lorenzo shoved Giovanni again. Were they seriously going to fight right now? What the fuck was wrong with the two of them?

"Stop!" I shouted and pushed myself between the two of them. I couldn't believe they were putting me in the middle of this right now. Alcohol-fuelled rage burned between the two of them.

I turned to Lorenzo and grabbed his hand, forcing him to look down at me. "Lorenzo, please."

"He needs to accept that you guys are over," he spat. "He's the one who fucked up."

"What did you say?" Giovanni snarled from behind me. "I broke your nose once, Lorenzo, do you want me to do it again?"

I remembered when I first learned of their history. Giovanni shared it with me the night he came banging at my door at two in the morning. I already knew how they both felt about each other and I should have known better than to have the two of them in the same room.

I turned to Giovanni and placed my hand against his chest. "Giovanni."

One of them needed to put an end to this embarrassment. Giovanni dragged his eyes away from Lorenzo and met mine. His deep brown eyes were blazing with anger and I needed to get him to calm down. He was seeing red right now and I didn't want this to go any further. Neither of them had the right to act like this.

"Please stop," I murmured.

"Isabella, you need to move out the way," he hissed.

Lorenzo reached for my hand and I turned back to him.

"Izzy, let's get out of here," Lorenzo suggested.

"You're not taking her anywhere," Giovanni spat and reached for me.

Were we in fucking middle school here? God - why would they put me in the middle of this stupid tug-of-war.

"And who are you to stop me?" Lorenzo retorted.

"STOP!" I shouted and pulled my arms away from their grip. "Both of you need to stop. Neither of you gets to dictate what I will do. It's my fucking choice and right now I don't want to be around either of you."

I was sick of both of them and their back and forth. They were going at each other as if I was not here and it was riddled with anger. I turned and made my way towards the exit. I was using everything I could to focus on not falling over as I stumbled outside. I pushed through the door and was welcomed by the cold air surrounding me. I took a deep breath in and took off down the street, needing to put some distance between me and the pissing contest that was going on inside.

"Isabella, wait!" Lorenzo shouted from behind me.

I turned and he jogged to catch up to me.

"I'm sorry, I didn't mean to behave like that." He reached for my hand. "He just gets under my sk-".

I pulled my hand away from his and stopped his apology. "I think we've all had too much to drink."

"I'm sorry."

I turned to him. "Why did you kiss me, Lorenzo?"

There was a part of me that was always curious about kissing him again. A very small part that was interested in the possibility of what could be, but as soon as his lips touched mine, I knew how wrong that was. I wasn't interested in him in that way and he didn't light my body up like Giovanni did. He didn't light my heart up like Giovanni did and I shouldn't have allowed that to happen.

He looked confused by my question. "You know why I kissed you, Isabella. You can't act like there isn't anything between us."

"We're friends, Lorenzo."

"Friends," he repeated and shook his head.

I didn't know what to say. Kissing him was a mistake. I tried so hard not to give him the wrong impression, but that clearly didn't work. I expected him to say something more about that but instead, he changed the subject.

"Can I take you home?" he offered.

I shook my head. "No, thank you, but I think I should go."

He couldn't hide the hurt on his face. I didn't mean to hurt him but I was angry at him and the way he acted with Giovanni. I didn't expect this from him. He always had a calming nature to him and to see him trying to get under Giovanni's skin was something I didn't like. Giovanni was not innocent in all of this, but he was no longer my problem to deal with.

"Izzy, please," Lorenzo murmured. "I'm sorry about what just happened."

"I know you are and it's fine, Lorenzo, I just think this night is over now."

He looked defeated.

"Look, Isabella, I care about you okay? I just don't want you to get sucked in with him again. I know he has a hold on you and I don't want him to keep hurting you."

I sighed. I felt so guilty for dragging him into my mess. I felt guilty for giving him the wrong impression about the two of us. I knew he wanted more and I just couldn't reciprocate his feelings. I didn't know if I would ever be able to. He was right about one thing - Giovanni definitely had a hold on me and I didn't know how to begin to shake him. It wasn't as if I broke up with Giovanni because I stopped loving him. That hadn't changed.

"I'm sorry you got dragged into this," I murmured.

"You don't need to apologize." He squeezed my hand. "I'm going to go now but please promise me you won't let him get to you again. You're better than him."

A part of me appreciated how he cared for me but the other part of me that was on team Giovanni was annoyed at the cheap shots he kept taking. I didn't have the energy to further the conversation with him so I let it slide.

"Thank you, Lorenzo."

He pulled me in for one last hug before crossing the street and hailing a cab. I was actually thankful for the moment to myself. It allowed me to attempt to compartmentalize my thoughts. I was angry. I was angry at Lorenzo, but I was also angry at Giovanni for causing a scene yet again. He was so confusing. This morning when I saw him he said he just wanted me to be happy and now he was here causing scenes in public.

What the fuck?

His back and forth was driving me crazy. I leaned against the wall in an attempt to stop the world from spinning. I closed my eyes and breathed the fresh air into my lungs. *In and out.* I focused on my breathing and slowly started to get a handle on the dizziness. I opened my eyes and watched as Giovanni pushed himself through the crowds of people along the street.

Where was he going?

He didn't get to bulldoze all over my evening and then just fuck off. Not on my watch. Before I realised what I was doing, I took off in his direction. I quickened my pace and pushed myself through the crowds.

"Giovanni!" I shouted.

He turned the corner and I took off in a light jog, turning the corner to an empty ally.

"Giovanni, stop!" I shouted again, this time catching his attention.

He stopped and turned to face me. "Isabella."

I stormed up to him. He made me so angry. I was angry with him and with his random outbursts of jealousy. I was angry that he stood here in front of me looking hot as hell. I was angry that the smell of his cologne was intoxicating and the way my name rolled off his tongue. My eyes flicked up to reach his and they were full of emotion, mirroring my own. I was way past the point of rational thinking and I had handed myself over to my true thoughts and desires. There he was again, completely consuming me.

"What were you thinking?" I asked. "Why did you come here tonight?"

"I came to meet Sergio."

I rolled my eyes. "Did you know I would be here?"

"As a matter of fact, I had no idea you would be here. I certainly didn't know you were going to be here with Lorenzo."

"Don't bring Lorenzo into this."

"Why?" He snapped. "He seems to constantly be making an appearance in your life. You had no problem kissing him."

"He kissed me!" I clarified. "There is nothing going on between him and I."

He stepped closer to me, closing in on the distance between us. "You keep saying that but I don't believe you."

I flicked my eyes to meet his. "You can't keep doing this, Giovanni. You can't keep appearing while I'm trying to move on."

He scoffed. "You think you can move on just like that?"

"Well, I'm trying!" I objected. "But how am I supposed to do that when you keep pulling shit like this?"

He took a step closer to me. "Then why are you standing here with me right now?"

My breath caught in my throat.

"Why didn't you leave with Lorenzo?" he said in a low voice. "You didn't have to come after me, but you did."

I took a deep breath in. Everything he was saying was right. I didn't want to move on from him. That was the last thing I wanted, but what else was I supposed to do? He and I would never be able to be together, not now that everything has changed, but I just can't keep dragging myself away from him. I didn't want to anymore.

He took another step closer to me. "You'll never have what we had with anyone else and you know it."

The air around me became thin as the tension surrounded us. He reached out and caressed my cheek with his thumb. His touch was soft, but it still burned against me.

"He can't make you feel like this," he murmured. "You can deny it, but I know you want me."

My lips parted and a small gasp escaped. I swallowed trying to form the words needed to tell him that wasn't true, but I couldn't. He knew.

"Your eyebrow has lifted the way it always does when you hear something you like. Your cheeks are flushed and I can hear your breathing has picked up."

He leaned closer to me, our faces now inches from each other and I held my breath in anticipation.

"I told you I wouldn't kiss you again, not until you wanted me to."

Instead of leaning into me like I thought he would, he pulled away and turned down the alley again.

Are you fucking kidding me?

I was so ready for him. My body was calling for him and there was no way I could stop the desire rolling through me.

"Where do you think you're going?" I shouted.

"I'm going to find my car."

I followed behind him into a dark parking lot. "You can't possibly drive right now."

"Watch me," his voice echoed.

He pulled his car keys out from his pocket and approached his car. There were a couple other cars parked in the lot, but his car was alone in the corner, away from any others. There was a dim light keeping the area illuminated, but we were the only two people here.

"Don't be an idiot, Giovanni." I picked up my pace and reached his car as he unlocked it.

He ignored me and pulled the door open, getting into the driver's seat. I let out an exasperated sigh and walked over to the passenger side, pulling the door open and slipping inside. My head was screaming at me to turn around, but my heart was in charge now and I was following it. I shut the door behind me and breathed in the familiar smell of leather mixed with his cologne.

"What the hell do you think you're doing?" he asked, a flicker of annoyance in his voice.

"You're not going to drive this car," I repeated. "Not with me in the passenger seat."

He tugged at his lip and let out a frustrated sigh. "Why did you follow me?"

"I didn't follow you," I objected. "You're the one who arrived tonight uninvited."

"I meant why did you follow me to my car?" he clarified. "And how do you know I wasn't invited? Sergio is my friend."

"And Katrina is mine."

"You and your endless supply of friends," he mumbled sarcastically.

I knew he was taking a dig at my friendship with Lorenzo again. He was infuriating. Here we sat next to each other in his car and despite all the anger inside of me, all I could think about was how close he was to me. His hand rested on his knee and he had his head tilted towards me. I was dying to reach out and touch him. I didn't care that we were broken up. I didn't care that he had just made a scene. I didn't care about anything right now except him. The anger I had towards him right now was only fuelling my desire in a way I had never experienced before. He definitely picked up on the tension that seeped its way into the car.

"What's on your mind, Isabella?" he asked in a low voice.

I tugged at my bottom lip and tried to get my breathing under control. The desire rolled through me and the pressure between my legs increased at an intensity that was new to me. I couldn't stop it and I didn't want to. I just wanted him. God, I wanted him so much it hurt.

I leaned closer to him. "You said you're not going to kiss me again."

"Nope, not until you tell me that's what you want."

He leaned closer to me. We were inches away again and his eyes wandered down to my lips. All the previous anger in his eyes had disintegrated and was replaced with a desire that mirrored my own. I reached out and ran my fingers across his rough beard and into his hair. Just being able to touch him again was beguiling. The rational voice in my mind telling me to stop slipped away into nothing more than a faint murmur. I didn't care about anything, but him right now. This was toxic, but I couldn't stop. My desire was fuelled by my love for him and I couldn't hold it back. I shouldn't have said what I said next, but we were past the point of no return.

"I want you to kiss me."

And so he did. He didn't wait one more second before he leaned into me. The moment his lips met mine, I was overcome with a deep euphoric feeling. This was what I wanted. I melted at his touch as his hands found my hair, tugging at it as he matched my intensity. Fuck, I had been craving him and I needed him. *Now.* He pushed his chair back as I leaned closer to him. He pulled me onto his lap, my legs straddling on either side. My hands found their way into his hair and I couldn't help but pull at it. I didn't want gentle right now. I wanted him and I wanted it rough. It had been far too long since I felt him. It was as if I had been drowning and now I was gasping for air that only he could provide. His lips left mine and made their way to my neck as his hand rubbed over my breast, squeezing it.

"Giovanni," I breathed.

Every sense of mine was heightened by my intoxication. Every kiss was elevated and brought on new waves of arousal. I rocked my hips and I felt him hard against me.

I couldn't help but moan at knowing what I had done. I loved feeling him alive beneath me. To know that I still had the effect on him gave me a sense of control I didn't think I had. I flicked my hips up against him and brought my lips back to meet his. I didn't care that we were in a car in a public place. I didn't care that we were broken up and that this was wrong. I didn't care about anything but him. I needed to have him now. I ran my hands down his body and pushed his jacket back. He leaned forward, never breaking the kiss as he pulled his jacket off him and tossed it to the side. My hands slipped under his shirt and I felt his hot skin against mine.

He pulled away to meet my eyes. "What do you want, Isabella?"

I rocked against him again, feeling how ready he was for me. "I want you right here, right now."

He tugged at his lip before a naughty smirk settled against his lips. "You sure?"

I nodded and he brought his lips back to mine. His hands ran along my stockings that I had on underneath my dress. I was so thankful I was wearing a dress because I needed to have him and this was going to make it so much easier. I hadn't felt him in so long and my body was calling out for him. The throbbing between my legs continued as I rubbed against him, trying to find some sort of relief. He pushed my coat back and pulled it off my arms, throwing it to the side. He lifted my dress up and reached for the opening of my stockings. I lifted my hips and allowed him to push it down, my underwear along with it, slipping them off one of my legs. I was elevated higher than him, my head against the roof of his car. I expected him to release himself to me already but instead, I felt him brush a finger over me. I gasped at his touch as he slipped a finger inside of me. He pushed deep inside, hitting right where I needed him to. I moved with his rhythm, throwing my head back, basking in the pleasure he was building up inside of me.

"I've missed you," I gasped.

"I've missed you, baby."

He removed his fingers and reached for the button of his pants, pushing them down to his knees. His underwear followed after that and there he was, ready for me. I was consumed by my desire as I positioned myself above him. He had his hands on either side of my hips and brought me slowly down on him, stretching me as he filled me up.

My eyes rolled back as I pushed him deeper inside of me.

Fuck, I had missed him.

My hand cupped the back of his neck as I started to bring myself up and down on him. I was in charge here and I knew the intensity I needed it at. I picked up my pace as I heard small breaths escaping his lips. I threw my head back as I continued to move, he matched my rhythm and continued to push deeper and deeper. I tightened around him as the pleasure started to build already. My hand leaned against the fogged window, leaving a handprint against it.

"Isabella," My name rolled off his tongue and I was just about ready to explode at just that sound.

I met his eyes and we both clung to this moment. I soaked him in. Every crease around his eye and the dark facial hair across his cheeks. Those deep brown eyes hidden beneath the long eyelashes. The dimple in his left cheek that made an appearance every time he smiled.

I love him so much.

I flicked my hips, pushing him deeper inside of me. I used this opportunity to ride him as we both fought for a release. His hand made its way to my hair again and he pulled it back, forcing my head to fall backward as his lips reached my neck again. I was consumed by the overwhelming pleasure rolling through me. We continued and the pressure between my legs built with each movement. I was reaching my climax and I didn't want it to end. I wanted to stay like this forever.

"Yes, Giovanni," I moaned.

I didn't care if anyone heard me. I didn't care about anything in that moment except him and what it felt like to have him inside me again. I picked up my pace and it wasn't long before I reached my climax, burying my face in his shoulder as my body was overcome with pleasure. He took control of the movements and pushed deeper inside of me. He couldn't control the small moans escaping his lips as he reached his own climax. He wrapped his arms around me and pulled me against him, both of us soaking in the euphoria of being in each other's arms again. My heart swelled with love and I was overcome with emotion. This wasn't a mistake. Him and I being together could never be one.

I didn't want this moment to end.

CHAPTER 37:

Giovanni

I kept my arms wrapped around her. I wanted to hold onto this for as long as I possibly could. The feeling of being inside of her again after all this time was unlike anything I had experienced before. I could have stayed like that forever. I wanted nothing more than to get lost in her and never find my way back.

She slowly pulled away to face me, running her hands through her hair as she moved it out of her face. "I don't want this to end."

I flicked my eyes to meet hers and they were filled with a longing that we were both feeling. She slowly moved off of me but still kept her legs straddled over mine. I was already ready to bury myself inside of her again.

I slowly cupped her face as she leaned into my touch. "It doesn't have to. Come home with me."

She thought for a moment and I could see her trying to decide if that was a good idea or not. I knew it was a terrible suggestion but I didn't want her to leave. I wanted to take her home with me and spend the rest of the night having my way with her. I wanted to cherish her body and make her scream my name.

I wanted her again. I wanted her forever.

"Don't think about it too much, Isabella," I said. "You followed me tonight because you still want me."

"Of course I still want you," she breathed.

"Then who cares about everything else?"

"We're only torturing each other."

Then clearly I was a sucker for punishment.

She was right though. It was torture having her walk in and out of my life over and over again. It wasn't healthy but I didn't care about that. How could I when I had her in my arms again? She was everything I needed and more.

"If you want to go home, I'll respect that," I murmured.

She shook her head and wrapped her hand gently around the back of my neck. "I don't want that. I want you."

A dormant happiness flickered inside of me at her words. She still loved me. Here she was in a parking lot with me instead of having left with Lorenzo. I was still angry about the kiss but I couldn't care too much about that right now. I was still what she wanted and I couldn't help but feel exhilarated. There was hope for us. As foolish as that may seem, I still believed that.

I leaned forward and started kissing her neck again, my desire reigniting. "Then let's get out of here. I can think of plenty more things for us to do with a little more space than this car."

She giggled. "Yeah, it's a bit small for things like this."

"To be fair, I never had car sex in mind when I bought it but maybe I should reconsider some things."

She smiled before bringing her lips down to reach mine again. The alcohol still lingered inside of me so every kiss burned on my lips, causing a rush of heat to my groin. My lips left hers and continued along her cheekbone as she leaned her head back, not being able to hold back the small gasps escaping her lips. I was so ready to have her again.

"Take me to your place, Giovanni."

I happily obliged.

CHAPTER 38:
Isabella

The rational voice in my head was screaming for me to turn around. It begged me to back out and leave right now.
What are you doing, Isabella?
Hand in hand with Giovanni, we walked into his apartment and I was welcomed by his home again. We were both far too intoxicated to get behind the wheel so Giovanni called a cab to bring us here. We said nothing further on the way here but the tension was suffocating. He held my hand the entire time and I was happy to feel his touch again. Even something as small as the way in which he caressed my hand with his thumb was enough for me. I didn't want to think of all the reasons for us not to do this. Tonight, my heart had won the battle. I just wanted to be with him again.

He let go of my hand and strolled over to the curtains in his lounge, pulling them closed as he shut us off from the outside world.

"Can I get you a drink?" he asked, dropping his jacket onto his couch as he walked back into the kitchen.

I walked over to the counter and placed my coat on it.. "What do you have?"

"I'm not going to offer you whiskey again cause I know you didn't enjoy that." He opened up the fridge. "I have white wine though if you'd like."

With the alcohol still pulsing through my body, I shook my head. "I'm actually fine for now."

He walked over to where I stood and leaned his hands on either side of me as my back was against the counter. He smelled of faint alcohol mixed with his cologne. It was still so strong and I loved it. Just breathing him in intoxicated my senses. He wore a black shirt that fit perfectly around his arms, showing every curve of his muscles. I allowed my eyes to wander over the dark markings against his skin before I flicked my eyes up to meet his. He was already looking down at me and my breath caught in my throat at the intensity in his eyes. He wanted me.

I reached out and ran my hands up his shirt and over his chest. "I like your shirt."

He smirked. "Really? It's not that great."

"Oh, I'm sorry, I should have been more specific," I murmured seductively, a new refound confidence washing over me. "I meant I'd like your shirt if it was on the floor."

"Well, that can easily be arranged." He reached over his head and pulled his shirt off, dropping it to the floor.

My breath caught in my throat at the sight of his naked body. *Fuck, I loved his tattoos.* They captivated my attention. I ran my fingers along his chest and down his arms, making my way over each of them. He stepped closer to me, closing in the proximity between us.

"Your turn," he murmured.

"I can't just pull mine over my head like you did." I turned around so my back was facing him and slowly moved my hair to the front. "You'll have to help me with the zip."

"I can do that for you." He reached for my zip and slowly pulled it down, his fingertips brushing over my skin.

I peeled the dress off my arms and allowed it to fall to the floor. He pulled me closer to him and we were skin to skin now. I could feel the heat radiating off his body. He leaned into my ear and nipped at the top of it causing me to gasp, arousal rolling through me. He moved his lips down my neck and I reached my arm behind me, finding his hair. I leaned my head back and soaked in what he was doing to me. Every kiss sets my body alight. Pulling me closer to him, I could feel him hard against me.

The rational voice in my head slipped into nothing more than a distant echo as my hunger for him pushed its way to the front. Every red flag that reminded me of what a bad idea this was had disintegrated. I just didn't care anymore. I only cared about him.

I turned to meet his eyes that were now filled with nothing but salacious desire. He ran his hands down my body and reached my stockings. He slowly pulled them down my legs as I kicked my boots off. He brought himself up again after removing them, leaving me in nothing but my underwear. His strong arms came around me as he lifted me onto the counter, my legs instinctively wrapping around him as he pulled into me. My body was cold against the granite counter but the heat between us was enough to make me forget all about that.

My tongue flicked over his as I felt his hands run up my body to cup my breast in his hand, rubbing and pinching at an intensity that excited me.

He pulled away. "Lean your hands against the counter."

I followed his instruction as he unhooked my legs from his waist. He reached for my underwear and started pulling it down. I arched my body to give him enough space and it fell to the floor. My heart was beating incessantly at the anticipation of what was coming next. He was in control and I was more than happy to hand my body over to him.

"What do you want, Isabella?" he murmured seductively.

"I just want you, Giovanni."

"Only me?"

"Always."

He smirked and brought my right leg up onto the counter, keeping it bent as he leaned closer to me. I pulled at my lip as the throbbing between my legs intensified. He leaned closer to me and I already knew what was coming. I felt the hunger for him down to my core and my body was screaming for a release. He positioned himself between my legs and brought his tongue over me causing me to lean my head back as the heat tore through me. He brought my other leg onto the counter and pulled me closer to him, his hungry tongue exploring me. I arched my hips towards him and I would have given anything to be able to see this from an outsider's perspective. I was spread across the kitchen counter as his head buried itself between my legs - an image that was sending my body into a frenzy along with what he was doing to me. He knew exactly what to do - each flick over me was a calculated rhythm that set my body on fire. He increased the intensity and my hand found its way into his hair, tugging at it as I tried to contain the pleasure building inside of me.

"Don't hold back, Isabella, I want to hear you."

I groaned at his encouragement and flicked my hips against him, matching his rhythm. My knees felt weak and I was unable to control the growing sensation between my legs.

"Yes, Giovanni," I moaned. "Don't stop."

And he didn't.

He picked up the pace and moved with my rhythm as I approached my climax. His beard was rough against me as he flicked over me one last time before I came undone. I threw my head back and allowed myself to be consumed by the delirious pleasure that shot through every inch of my body. He removed himself from between my legs and pulled me closer to him, his lips crashing against mine. He had no intention of stopping and I was dying to feel him inside of me again.

He explored my lips with a rough and greedy energy to it. I loved it. The ripple of electricity pulsing through my veins pushed my desire for him further and further. I gripped at his arms, digging my nails into them. My legs wrapped around his body and he lifted me, moving us to the couch. He lay me down and removed his pants and underwear, finally sharing himself with me again. I bit my lip at the sight of how ready he was for me. He didn't even bother with a condom and frankly, I didn't care. There was nothing like being able to feel him skin to skin inside of me. Nothing could compare.

I lay against the couch and opened my legs for him, inviting him where he needed to be. He brought his body over mine and positioned himself between my legs. I held my breath as I anticipated the feeling coming next. He wrapped his hand around the back of my neck and pushed himself deep inside of me. My eyes closed as I tightened around him, my body already sensitive to the enthralling pleasure on its way again. He leaned his arm against the back of the couch above my head and moved his body with mine.

"Lift your hips for me, baby," he murmured.

I happily obliged. I wrapped my legs and arched my hips up, following his movements. My body was already weak, but that didn't stop the constant desire pushing its way through me. It rolled over every inch of my body the deeper he went, knowing exactly where he was meant to be. With each thrust, we became one and my heart attached itself to him. This was so much more than just a physical connection. It always has been. No matter how much I tried to pretend it wasn't true, my heart would always belong to him.

I dug my nails into his arms, trying to contain the pressure building between my legs again.

His name rolled off my tongue the way it always did. I didn't hold back - I never had. He needed to know how he was making me feel. Strands of hair fell forward and I watched as he tilted his head back, soaking in the pleasure. It was captivating to watch him as he approached his climax. The greedy hunger pushed its way through both of us as we increased our intensity.

"Yes, yes, yes," I repeated over and over as he worked his way inside me.

His lips crashed against mine as I found my climax again, the pleasure rolling through me. I gasped against his lips as he joined me and fell against my body, both of us trying to catch our breath. I ran my fingers through his hair as he lay against my chest. I stared at the ceiling above me trying to get a handle on my breathing. The feeling that washed over me was incomparable. Nothing could take away the memory of what it felt like to have him again . He lifted his head and I brought mine forward to meet his gaze.

"You're the only one for me, Isabella," he whispered.

I was so overwhelmed with emotion that I had to shut my eyes to stop the tears that were starting to form. Giovanni was everything to me and there was no escaping the way I loved him. My heart had shattered into a million pieces and yet, when I was with him, I forgot all about that. I forgot all about all the reasons for us not to be together. It was just him and me and I didn't want to lose that. I felt whole again.

"And I know you love me, Isabella." He sat up and leaned against the couch. "We keep finding our way back to each other because you know we're meant to be together."

"I've tried to forget you, Giovanni. I've tried my hardest to move on but I always seem to find my way back to you."

"You say that as if it's a bad thing."

Given the fact that we were broken up, it was a bad thing. It was bad that we constantly found ourselves in this situation but I couldn't fight my feelings for him. The more time I spent apart from him, the more I realised just how much I needed him in my life.

I shifted closer to him. "I just want to be here with you right now. I don't want to think of tomorrow or what we're going to do. I just want this."

He pulled me into his arms and I rested my head against his chest, listening to the sound of his heart beating. It was easy to forget what we had to deal with when it was just the two of us. When there was no reminder of Casey and the baby, I was happy with him but I couldn't fool myself into thinking our problems were just going to disappear. I was putting my heart through hell here but I didn't care anymore. I wanted to hold onto him for as long as I could. The voice in my head reminded me that I couldn't continue this back and forth with him for much longer. I had promised myself we were done the last time I walked out of here but it was proving to be difficult to drag myself away from Giovanni. I love him. More than I had ever loved anyone before. That hadn't changed and it was never going to.

As much as I wanted to remain in blissful ignorance, we both knew this couldn't go on like this. I had some decisions to make now. For real this time.

CHAPTER 39:
Giovanni

"Can I make you some coffee?" I peeped my head into the bathroom as Isabella was showering.

"Yes please, I'm almost done," She shouted over the running water.

"You'll find me downstairs."

I closed the door behind me and couldn't help but smile. She was here again and as selfish as that was, it made me happy. This was what I had always wanted. We still had so much to figure out but something about last night felt different. She didn't leave with Lorenzo when it came down to it. She chose me and I knew she would continue to choose me. All the outside elements aside, we were meant to be together and I wasn't going to let her go without a fight. I tried to let her move on with her life. I tried to stay away but I couldn't. I couldn't live with the hollowness that was inside of me in the absence of her in my life.

I reached for a hoodie from my closet and pulled it over my head as I strolled downstairs. The sound of the elevator opening caught my attention and I stopped in my tracks trying to think of who it could be. *I seriously needed a front door.* I didn't want another unwelcome guest while I was with Isabella so relief quickly washed over me as my mother turned around the corner.

"*Mama*, what are you doing here?"

I was surprised by her arrival. I didn't know she was going to stop by today. I hadn't seen her since the last time I was at the house and I learned about her affair. I hadn't confronted her about it either. Alvaro and I agreed to deal with this after the Christmas party so I had to keep my mouth shut.

"*Hola, cariño.*" She walked over to me and kissed both my cheeks. "*¿Cómo estás?*"

"I'm good. I was just about to make some coffee, can I make you a cup?"

She followed me into the kitchen and stood by the counter, placing her bag down. "*Sí, por favor.*"

I brought the kettle to a boil and grabbed three cups from the cupboard, placing them on the counter in front of her.

"I haven't seen you in a while," she said with a flicker of sadness in her voice. "Not since what happened with your father."

I kept my face as neutral as I could manage as I reached for the tin of coffee and a teaspoon.

"Yeah, Alvaro said you went to stay with him for a couple of days."

She nodded. "It was nice to have some time to think."

I was dying to ask her what she was doing. Was she planning on leaving my father? When did her affair start? Why didn't she leave him earlier? So many questions were running through my mind but I couldn't breathe a word of it to her. She pulled herself onto the barstool and I noticed she wasn't the same today. She was usually so full of energy and a positive light in my life but that had started to dim since I told her what happened. It saddened me to see her like this. She deserved to be happy, too.

"But what about you?" she asked. "Don't think I haven't seen the news, Giovanni. Are you really having a baby?"

I sighed. This wasn't the first time she asked me about this. I had plenty of messages from her that I didn't know how to reply to. I had avoided her questions long enough. I didn't want to disappoint her but I couldn't get out of this one. Not with her sitting right in front of me. She peered at me from behind her glasses and I half expected there to be judgment in her dark brown eyes but instead, there was only concern.

"It's complicated, *Mama.*"

"What about you and Isabella? She seemed so lovely."

I reached for the kettle and brought the hot water to the cups. "I really want to explain everything to you but I don't think now is the be-".

Before I could finish my sentence, Isabella strolled into view. "I hung the to-".

The rest of her sentence disappeared as she noticed my mother sitting at the counter.

"Isabella!" My mother exclaimed.

"Hola, Mrs. Velázquez." She pulled her in for a hug.

"Mrs Veláquez," she scoffed, "Please call me Marcina."

Isabella looked over at me and smiled before she followed my mother back towards the kitchen counter.

"I didn't expect to see you here." My mother's eyes lit up at her presence. "It's so lovely to see you again."

My mother knew what Isabella meant to me. I had told her all about her and it was the first time I had ever introduced anyone to her. There was no one else that measured up to what Isabella meant in my life. I couldn't explain everything to my mother right now, especially not with Isabella here. I didn't want to bring Casey up in front of her. I was terrified to bring up anything that might cause her to leave again and I was hanging onto every moment with her for as long as possible.

I noticed she had helped herself to one of my jerseys. It sat oversized on her body and I loved to see her in my clothes. I was so taken with her. She didn't even have to try and she was breathtaking to me. She didn't have any makeup on and her wet hair had started to curl. Having her here just felt right.

I placed a cup of coffee in front of her.

"It's lovely to see you too. I'm sorry to interrupt, Giovanni didn't tell me you were coming by." Isabella said.

"I didn't know," I interjected.

She wrapped her hands around her cup and leaned casually against the counter.

"I was in the area and I had to drop off the keys for this weekend." My mother fished out a set of keys from her bag. "*Papa* rented out a couple of the cottages on the property for us to stay after the party."

The *Velázquez Constructa* Christmas party was this weekend and there was no getting out of it. It was tradition and the one event of the year that we were expected to all attend - as a family.

"Party?" Isabella looked over at me, a confused look on her face.

My mother jumped in before I could answer. "The *Velázquez Constructa*

Christmas party. We do it every year and this year's theme is *'casino'*."

She placed the keys on the counter and reached for her cup, bringing it up to her lips. "Oh please tell me you're coming, Isabella? It would be so wonderful to have you join us this year. Giovanni has always been the only one without a date over the years."

"*Mama*, I haven't even told her about it."

I tried to get my mother's attention with my eyes. I didn't want to put Isabella in an awkward position, but my mother had no boundaries.

"Well, what more is there to tell?" she asked. "It's just outside the city. The party is on Saturday, but people usually make a weekend out of it, hence the keys here. Your father has booked it out for you guys from today till Monday."

Isabella didn't say a word and instead just smiled politely as she sipped on her coffee. I wouldn't have even thought of asking her to join me. Of course, I wanted her to but we were broken up and I didn't have that kind of privilege with her anymore.

"And you can order a dress from the family designer, I'm sure she can ge-".

"*Mama,* please," I stopped her as politely as I could. "I'll chat to Isabella about it but I'm sure she has plans already."

Isabella's eyes met mine and I couldn't figure out what she was thinking. Her face remained unchanged, but I noticed a flicker of disappointment in her eyes before she looked back down at her coffee.

My mother reached out and squeezed Isabella's hand. "You're still here with him after all this, there must be a reason."

God, she was relentless. I ran my fingers through my hair and let out an exasperated sigh.

"*Mama,* I love you, but Isabella and I have a lot to talk about."

She realised she had started to cross a line and she covered her mouth in surprise. "*Lo siento,* I didn't mean to-".

Isabella reached out to her. "You don't need to apologize for anything. Thank you for the invite."

I was thankful that my mother's phone started to ring, giving us a break from her running commentary. I didn't want to get into anything with Isabella this morning. I was just planning on having a casual breakfast with her, but now there was awkward tension surrounding us that we weren't going to be able to ignore.

"That was the new driver, Edmundo, he's downstairs with the car so I have to get going," my mother announced and reached for her bag, slipping it onto her shoulder. "I just needed to give you the keys. Your father and I are headed out to *Vic* later this afternoon."

The question of where their relationship stood was partly answered in the fact that she was traveling with him tomorrow. Her eyes met mine and I could tell she was begging me not to ask any questions. My whole family was living a lie right now and we just needed to get past this weekend before we would all be forced to deal with the reality of it. I walked around the counter and pulled her in for a hug. No matter what, she was still my mother and I loved her. All I wanted was for her to find her happiness again.

"Travel safely, I'll let you know when I leave." I pulled her in for a hug.

She cupped my face with her hand and smiled before turning to Isabella, pulling her in for a hug.

"It was so nice to see you with Giovanni again," she murmured.

"Take care, Marcina," Isabella replied politely.

We said our last goodbyes to my mother as she stepped into the elevator and the doors closed her off from us. There was definitely a palpable awkwardness in the air and as much as I wanted to avoid it, we couldn't.

"I'm sorry about my mother," I said.

"You don't need to apologize."

We strolled back into the kitchen and she brought herself onto the barstool in front of the counter. I leaned against it on the opposite side of her and reached for my cup.

"So, you're going out of town this weekend?" she asked.

"I'm supposed to. The Christmas party is on Saturday and it's a family affair," I scoffed at that thought. "My family is a fuck-up right now, but we have to show face on Saturday and pretend that all is well in the Velázquez household."

"And you're going to have to see your father then."

"I saw him yesterday when I met Nate."

"And? What was it like?"

I shrugged. "Like nothing had changed. My family has a very good way of brushing things under the carpet, but that's not going to continue much longer. Alvaro and I agreed to get through this weekend, but then we would call a family meeting because I'm sick of pretending that everything is fine when it's not."

"Are Alvaro and Penelope going to be there?"

I nodded and took a sip. "They've hired a nanny who is going to come with them to take care of Mateo during the party."

She didn't say anything further. Instead, she sipped on her coffee and I watched her intently, trying to figure out where she was at. I couldn't get a good read on her today and it was making me nervous. I didn't know what to say. I didn't want to say the wrong thing and have her leave. Was I supposed to invite her to come with me? Was she mad I didn't mention it in the first place?

"How far away is the place you're going to?"

"*Vic* is about an hour out of the city."

She kept fishing around for information and was tapping her nails against the counter the way she always did when she was nervous. Good to know I wasn't the only one feeling it.

She brought her mug to her lips and peered at me from behind it. "Do you need me to come with you?"

I was surprised by her offer but I tried to keep my face expressionless. I didn't want to seem too eager and have her go back on her offer. Even though we broke our own rules last night by not staying away from each other, I didn't expect that she would want to extend our reunion.

"Do you want to come with me?"

She shrugged her shoulders. "I know how you feel about your parents right now and you could probably use a…" she paused for a moment before saying. "Friend."

Friend?

I hated her use of that word. Isabella and I could never be just friends. She made that perfectly clear in the past and now with all that had happened between us, it was even more true. But if she was offering herself to me for the weekend, the last thing I was going to do was reject her offer. I'd take anything I could get.

"Are you sure you want to come with?" I asked softly.

I needed to make sure this was what she wanted. I would never want to put her in a situation where she was uncomfortable or where she was somewhere she didn't want to be. That's the last thing I would want.

"Do you want me to come with you?"

I laughed. This back and forth could continue forever. I placed my cup back on the counter and walked over to her. "Of course I do, but I don't want you to feel obliged to have to come with me because of my mother, I'd really understand if you do-".

"I want to come."

A flicker of happiness came to life inside of me and I tried to hold back my smile. I didn't want to seem too eager but this was giving me hope that we still had a chance here.

"But I do have a problem," she said.

"What's the problem?"

"I have nothing to wear."

I chuckled and pulled her into my arms. "I'm sure we can sort something out."

CHAPTER 40:
Isabella

I didn't know why I suggested tagging along with Giovanni to his family's event, but it just felt like the right thing to do. When I woke up in his arms, I was reminded that I was meant to be there. It just felt right to me. I know I was the one who walked out on him and that I still had to deal with the whole Casey situation, but it didn't have to be today. It didn't even have to be this weekend. I had convinced myself that I could have this time with him and then I'd figure out what to do next. Right now, I just wanted to be with the man I love.

A voice in the back of my head reprimanded me for even suggesting this. My heart knew I wouldn't be able to handle it when reality came knocking, but I didn't have it in me to walk away from him again. I never wanted to walk away at all. All I wanted to focus on was a weekend with him out of the city. Away from everyone we knew and away from our problems.

You're only putting off the inevitable.

The voice in my head was right, but I drowned her out. I pushed through the doors of my apartment building with a bag packed for the weekend. I left Reyna a message telling her I was going out of town and that I'd answer all her questions when I got back. I didn't want to have to explain myself to anyone. I just wanted to follow my heart and it kept leading me back to him. He was casually leaning against his car, but walked towards me as I came into view.

He reached for my bag. "Is this everything?"

"I think so. I wasn't even sure what to pack. Are you sure I'll be able to get something to wear there?"

My phone buzzed in my back pocket. I pulled it out and Lorenzo's name flashed across the screen. I had been avoiding his calls this morning, but I just didn't know what I was going to say to him. I wanted to avoid everyone this weekend.

Giovanni shut the boot and walked over to the driver's seat, pulling his door open as we both slipped inside.

"My mother has already organised everything for you. We have a family friend who is a designer so they're going to send some options up for you."

I pulled my seatbelt across my chest and clipped it in. "That seems a bit excessive."

He shrugged. "My family is excessive. Trust me, you'll have everything you need."

He secured his seatbelt and leaned his arm across, resting his hand on the back of my headrest as he turned to reverse out of the parking. He leaned closer to me and I took a moment to soak him in. I'd never get enough of looking at him. He tugged at his bottom lip for a brief moment while he concentrated and the car moved back. He brought his hand to the steering wheel again and turned onto the road, joining the rest of the cars.

He handed me his phone. "You're in charge of the music."

I took his phone and unlocked it, surprised to see a picture of me staring up at me. It was a freeze-frame moment of me laughing and I was surprised at how happy I was here. I was also surprised I was even his wallpaper.

"When did you take this?" I asked.

"That day at the fountain," he replied sheepishly. "Sorry, I probably should have removed that."

I didn't even know he had me as his wallpaper, but the fact he did made my heart burst with happiness. I didn't want him to remove it. I didn't remove mine either - I couldn't bring myself to do it. It reminded me of a happier time and I never wanted to forget that.

"I loved that day," I murmured.

He glanced over at me and reached for my hand, bringing it up to his lips. "Me too."

I couldn't hold back my smile as he let go of my hand. Every little moment with him made my heart swell and I was consumed by my feelings for him. It was suffocating at times. I scrolled through his music and landed on a reggaeton playlist that I knew we would both enjoy. I kept his phone in the compartment in between us and fished mine out as it started to buzz again.

Lorenzo was calling.

"Do you want to get that?" Giovanni asked.

I placed my phone on silent and locked it. I needed time to figure out what I was going to do next and I didn't want to have to answer to anyone right now. I had decided I was going to spend the weekend with Giovanni and that was as far as I had gotten when it came to making decisions. I had no idea what I was hoping to achieve from this weekend, but I was happy to live in blissful ignorance for the next couple of days.

"Nope."

"Was it Lorenzo calling?"

I nodded and kept my eyes straight ahead. I felt guilty for what happened with Lorenzo last night. I should never have let him kiss me. It wasn't what I really wanted, but my feelings were a mess and I wasn't thinking straight.

"Do you have feelings for him?"

I was surprised by his question and how calmly he asked me. I turned to him, as he moved between looking at me and keeping his eyes on the road.

Did I have feelings for Lorenzo?

I enjoyed his company and was happy when he was around, but it didn't feel romantic to me. I could definitely acknowledge how attractive he was and there were moments when I thought there could be something more. Soft touches and longing looks - there was something there, but the kiss last night just confirmed that it was nothing more than friendship on my side.

"You're the only one I have feelings for."

"Even after everything?" he asked softly, the vulnerability shining in his eyes.

"My feelings for you haven't changed, Giovanni." I reached for his hand and squeezed it. "I just don't know what the future holds for us."

He was silent, but he never let go of my hand. Neither of us had that answer right now.

"But, I don't want to think about that." I tried to lighten the mood a bit. "We agreed that I'd come with you as a friend so I think we should try our best to keep it that way."

He lifted an eyebrow. "You told me once that you and I could never be friends."

He was right. Even in that moment, I was holding his hand as if it was the most normal thing but it wasn't. Not for two people who were broken up. I could never be just friends with him. How could I be when I was still completely in love with him?

"I don't want to be just friends with you, Isabella," he murmured. "But I'll respect your boundaries because I'm just happy to have you in this car with me."

I smiled, but pulled my hand slowly away from his. I couldn't think of being just friends with him when I could feel the heat between us already. I needed to keep my desire locked away for now. I couldn't keep handing myself over to him.

"You mentioned that Nate works for your Dad," I changed the subject. "Does that mean he is going to be at this Christmas party?"

"It's a possibility. I'm not happy about your ex being here," he admitted.

"It's not like you have to worry about him. Our relationship ended long ago and he's engaged," I reminded him. "And I don't really care about Nate that way anymore. I'll admit it was weird to see him again but there were no longing feelings or anything like that. I was over Nate way before we broke up."

That was the sad truth. I had definitely loved Nate in the beginning, but it didn't last. I wasn't in love with him and our relationship was more of one of convenience. I was actually happy that he found someone else. He deserved to be happy, too.

"So, we might have your ex to deal with and I have to watch my parents pretend they aren't fucking each other around." Giovanni took a deep breath in. "It's going to be quite an interesting party to attend."

He was right.

Who knew what this weekend was going to bring?

CHAPTER 41:

Isabella

Giovanni wasn't kidding when he said his family was excessive.

By the time Saturday rolled around, his mother had sent stylists with plenty of dresses for me to choose from. She also made sure to send someone over to do my hair and makeup. I was overwhelmed by the entire process, but as I got ready for the party, I started to feel a flicker of excitement inside. I was enjoying these last couple of days with Giovanni. We were away from anyone that could remind us of the ongoing drama in our lives and I loved it. We were staying in a quaint cottage on the property. It was a massive property and the main party hall was central to all the other cottages and rooms scattered across the land. Ours was the furthest away and I was enjoying soaking in the countryside. There was not even a flicker of city life insight and I felt a welcoming sense of calmness rest over me. We had managed to keep things as platonic as possible over the last couple of days except for the fact that there was only one bed that we had to share. I was proud of myself for not giving in to my temptation, but that part of me was starting to lose her mind. Every time I was close to Giovanni, he reignited my desire for him. Every sense was alive in anticipation of what was coming next.

But nothing did.

He stayed true to his word and respected my boundaries. If I wanted something, I was going to have to be the one to initiate it.

"Your hair is all done, miss," the young hairstylist with a thick Spanish accent announced as she stepped back from me, examining her work.

She brought my hair forward to fall against my chest and ran her fingers through the curls. *"Tan hermosa!"*

"*Gracias,*" I replied and turned to face the mirror.

I was surprised by my appearance. The team that was sent clearly had superpowers I was unaware of because I couldn't recognize the woman staring back at me. They had given me a confidence I didn't think I would ever be able to have.

"You guys are amazing," I gushed as the other stylist walked back into the room, dress in hand.

They both smiled at me.

"Time for the dress," she announced.

I stood up and removed my gown. In the back of my mind, I was clearly hoping for something more to happen between Giovanni and me, given the sexy black matching underwear I had decided on. I knew I shouldn't think that way but I couldn't deny that I wanted him again. Especially after sleeping next to him for two nights and not having done a single thing. The voice in my head was screaming to give into him, but I stood my ground.

The two of them helped me into my dress and it fit the curves of my body perfectly. I turned to the mirror again and a confident young woman stared back at me. I had decided on a long red dress with a plunging neckline and thin straps. The tightness of the dress held my breasts perfectly in place and I was happy with how it looked. I would never have had the confidence to wear something like this a year ago, but I wasn't the same woman I used to be.

A light tap at the door came from behind me and I heard Giovanni's voice on the other side. "Isabella? Are you almost ready?"

"Almost," I shouted back.

Giovanni had been banned from the room for the afternoon as the ladies worked their magic. I was sick with nerves wondering what he was going to think about how I looked. He still made me so nervous. I leaned down and slipped on my gold strappy heels and slid on the gold bracelet they had laid out for me.

"You look beautiful, miss," the hairstylist said with a kind smile.

"Thank you so much." I smiled. "And thank you guys for all your hard work. I appreciate it."

With one last smile and a friendly nod from each of them, they slipped outside the room and left me alone with my reflection.

"Isabella," Giovanni said from outside but slowly started pushing the door open. "Are you re-".

He stopped his sentence as his eyes landed on me. I noticed him in the mirror and my breath caught in my throat. He was wearing a slim-fitting black suit. He wasn't wearing a tie and instead had one button undone. He styled his hair and I noticed he cut the length of his beard a little. The facial hair was still spread across his cheekbones, but he had neatened it.

God, he looked so good.

"You look gorgeous," he gaped.

He was gawking at me now as he strolled over to me. I turned to face him. I couldn't explain how he was making me feel at that moment. His eyes were swimming with desire and I knew it mirrored my own. The tension between us was practically suffocating us now.

"You clean up pretty nicely too," I teased.

"No seriously, Isabella." He couldn't take his eyes off me. "How the fuck are you so beautiful?"

The heat spread across my cheeks and my heart skipped a beat. The tension deep inside my stomach was slowly creeping its way over my body.

"It's taking all the self-control I have right now not to kiss you," he murmured.

My eyes flicked up to meet his. I was dying to kiss him. We were inches away and all I had to do was lean into him, but I couldn't. I was adamant to stick to my rules.

"Permission to hold your hand?" Giovanni held his hand out to me.

I giggled. "Permission granted."

I slipped my hand in his and allowed him to lead the way.

CHAPTER 42:

Giovanni

She looked so fucking good.
It was taking every inch of self-control I had not to pull into her. I was dying too. Being so close to her and not being able to worship her body the way she deserved was torture for me. And now here she was looking sexy as hell. She deserved to have the floor she walked on worshipped. I would happily bow down to her if that was what she wanted.

I went around the other side of the car and opened her door for her. I held out my hand and she slid her hand into it and smiled. There was happiness in her hazel eyes and I watched as she was slowly returning to the Isabella I once knew. The woman she was before I broke her heart. I wanted the light back inside of her. I just wanted to make her happy again.

There were tons of people in line to enter the villa where the Christmas party was taking place. My parents were always excessive when it came to this party. It was the one time of the year for them to make a big statement in society and hide it behind a good cause.

We stood on a red carpet that was rolled out. A big feature was created with balloons and other creative pieces put together in a half-moon shaped entrance that resembled various elements in a casino - cards, chips, roulette tables. Everything added to the theme perfectly. I nodded to the security at the front that were standing with clipboards in their hands. My father had been working with the same security company for years now. He used it for the business and every event we had so they knew who I was.

"Don't they need our names?" Isabella asked.

"They work for my dad so they know who I am."

"Okay arrogant one," she teased and playfully nudged my arm.

I chuckled and led her into the large hall. They really kicked it up a notch this year. They had managed to create a mini-casino inside the hall. You couldn't help but glance up at the large chandelier that hung in the middle of the room. It was extravagant and a real centerpiece for the room. There were tables of blackjack and roulette scattered throughout. Crowds had already started to form around them as well as the dinner tables laid out. The dance floor was packed with people throwing their hands in the air enjoying the music the DJ was blaring through the speakers. Each year these parties got bigger and bigger. A sign wishing everyone a Merry Christmas was standing on the left side of the stage and next to it was the long table with the silent auction.

"You should check out the silent auction," I pointed to the corner where the table was set up. "We do it every year and there are some pretty cool items."

"Pretty cool expensive items I'm sure," she replied. "My bank account can hardly compete with the people in the upper-class society that are attending tonight."

I laughed. "Then maybe you should try a couple of these games? How about blackjack?"

"And lose all my money?" She lifted an eyebrow playfully. "A strong no from me."

"I'll have to make some bets for us," I teased.

I glanced over the seating arrangement as we continued through the hall. We were at table one with the rest of my family. I looked around but couldn't see any of them. My mother and father were definitely around here somewhere. They'd never be late to their own party.

A young waiter carrying a tray of champagne stopped in front of us and offered us each a glass. I reached for two and turned to Isabella, handing her one.

"To our first Christmas party together." I leaned my glass to hers and she returned the gesture before bringing it up to her lips.

I didn't want to think about the possibility that this could be our first and last. I had a strange sense of hope that had settled over me. The last couple of days with her have been just what I wanted. I wanted things to feel like they had before and it did. It felt right with her next to me.

Isabella was the one for me and I wanted her to be mine again.

CHAPTER 43:
Isabella

I watched as he brought the glass of champagne to his lips and leaned his head slightly back, allowing the alcohol to move down his throat. I watched as he swallowed, his Adam's apple moving with the motion and ran his tongue over his lips in a quick movement. He flicked his eyes to mine and there was something different to them now. They had been swimming with sadness and anger recently but not tonight. Tonight there was a flicker in them and I couldn't quite place what it was. There was a constant interest in his eyes whenever he looked at me and I knew he was working hard to hide the desire that was pushing its way through. I knew because I was feeling the same. Seeing him so well-groomed and in this well-fitted suit was sending my mind into a frenzy. The pressure between my legs deepened with each longing look.

I needed him.

I took a deep breath in and brought the champagne to my lips. I focused on that instead of Giovanni. I wouldn't be able to control myself much longer if I allowed my mind to continuously wander back to where it wanted to be.

"As a friend, I'd like to tell you how beautiful you look tonight," Giovanni said, leaning closer to me so I could hear him over the blaring music.

His voice brushed against my skin, sending an electrifying arousal up and down my veins. Before I could thank him, he opened his mouth to continue.

"But as someone that's in love with you, I have to tell you that it's taking every inch of self-control I have not to take you back to our room and have my way with you."

My breath caught in my throat and I couldn't help but tug at my bottom lip to contain the growing sensation inside of me.

I flicked my eyes to meet his. "You can't say things like that."

He leaned closer to my ear. "I can't help it. Not with that dress on."

The blush spread across my cheeks and I couldn't focus on anything but his breath against my skin. I thought about what it felt like to have his lips against me, exploring every inch of my body that was possible. The way he ran his hands over me, knowing exactly what he was doing. The way he felt insi-

"Isabella!" Marcina exclaimed, stopping my thoughts in their tracks. "You're here!"

"Hi, Marcina." I leaned forward and kissed both her cheeks as we greeted each other.

She turned to greet Giovanni. "I'm so happy that you two are here."

She was smiling and this time, her smile met her eyes. When we saw her the other day, there was something missing. She didn't have the same contagious energy that she had when we first met. I couldn't blame her, not with everything going on.

Cecilio Velázquez walked with an air of arrogance to him as he approached us. I watched as Giovanni tensed up - it was a slight change that no one but me would have been able to notice. His jaw clenched and displayed his cheekbones hidden underneath his facial hair and his breathing was more controlled. I could see he was trying to control himself. I shifted closer to him and slid my hand into his, interlocking our fingers. I squeezed gently to remind him that I was here.

"Giovanni," his father greeted with a slight nod before turning to me. "Isabella, right?"

I nodded. "*Sí señor*, nice to see you again."

I was lying, but I had to be polite. I had seen Giovanni's father twice and both were interactions I didn't want to remember.

"So, not the pregnant one," he quipped.

"Cecilio!" Marcina exclaimed and looked up at him, a look of horror spread across her face.

I jerked my head back in surprise and turned to Giovanni who was already glaring at his father.

"*¿Que carajo te pasa?*" Giovanni snapped.

I felt as if I had been slapped. Clearly, the animosity between Giovanni and his father had passed the point of no return. I was actually disgusted by his distasteful comment, but I kept my anger to myself for the sake of Giovanni. I didn't need to be reminded of Casey's pregnancy and especially not from his father.

"What?" his father objected. "Is that not public knowledge?"

Giovanni was seething. He didn't take his eyes off his father and I could tell Cecilio was enjoying this. I had never seen two people who were related that acted more like strangers. It was shocking to me. Marcina's face settled on a look of embarrassment over her husband's behaviour.

"And what about you?" Giovanni muttered. "Should we find out how much is public knowledge about your life?"

Before Cecilio could respond, an older couple interrupted to greet him. He switched from hostile father to welcoming host and it was jarring. Both he and Marcina settled into the correct public persona they were supposed to be sharing tonight - the happy couple. Giovanni's hand squeezed mine and I could feel the rage radiating off of him. I pulled him to the bar on the other side of the room away from his parents.

"Giovanni." I turned to him as we reached the bar, his eyes were deadlocked across the room. "Hey." I reached out and cupped his face, turning him to face me. The sadness returned in his eyes but now they were also laced with anger.

"I hate him," he muttered.

I used to think that was an exaggeration, but after witnessing the coldness in their relationship, it wasn't surprising to me.

"He's one to judge, look at the fuck up that is his marriage," Giovanni continued. "But he'll fucking say shit like that. It's ridiculous."

I pushed my own irritation at his father aside. I was here for Giovanni so I was going to be the support he needed.

"I think we could both use a shot," I suggested.

He turned towards the bar and signaled for the bartender. "Two shots of tequila, please."

"Just try to avoid your dad tonight. You know he wants to get under your skin so you need to be the bigger person."

The bartender placed the two shots in front of us and we reached for them, bringing them up to our lips. I tilted my head back as the alcohol burned down my throat. Any nerves I had slowly started to disappear, leaving me with a fake sense of calm.

"Thank you for being here," he murmured.

I reached out and cupped his face, running my nails through his hair. "Of course, I'm happy to be here for you."

"As a friend?" He flicked his eyes to meet mine.

How could I be friends with someone I was completely in love with?

I couldn't believe the clear divide between my head and my heart. My head was constantly warning me not to take this any further. If I did, it would only hurt more if our relationship imploded again. My heart was dying for me to reach out to him. To show him how much I loved him.

And my body was becoming a raging deprived bitch.

I wanted to devour him in any way I could. There was a struggle going on inside of me and the more he looked at me with the intensity that he was, the more my desire was starting to push itself to the front. He slowly started to run his hand up and down my arm, the electricity coursing through my veins.

"As a friend," I repeated, knowing I didn't believe that myself.

He ignored what I said and his eyes wandered down to my lips. "You deserve to be worshipped, Isabella."

My breath caught in my throat.

"And I'll be waiting here until you let me."

I didn't know what to say. I tugged at my lip in an attempt to control my desire from pushing itself through. He was killing me tonight and I didn't know how much longer I was going to be able to keep myself from giving in to my feelings.

***

I was having a great time.

Penelope and I were standing behind Giovanni and Alvaro as they joined a blackjack table. We were cheering them on as the champagne kept flowing. We had worked our way through the program for the evening and now the party really started. Cecilio had given a speech during dinner welcoming everyone and spoke more about the charity that tonight was benefitting. *Beyond Borders* was an organisation that was close to his heart as they helped migrant families who came to Spain with nothing. He shared more about those families and the challenges facing immigrants and it was the first time I noticed a flicker of emotion inside of him. It was surprising considering he didn't have any of that towards his own son.

"Twenty," the card dealer announced to Giovanni.

I shrieked with excitement and slid my hands around his shoulders, leaning my head by his neck. "You're killing it, babe!"

I didn't mean to say it but it came so naturally to me. His eyes lit up at the nickname but he didn't say anything about it.

"Alvaro, come on!" Penelope groaned.

I burst out laughing. Alvaro hadn't won a round yet and Penelope was losing hope in her husband.

"This game is rigged." Alvaro tossed his cards on the table.

"Don't be a sore loser, *hermano*." Giovanni laughed.

"You're stealing my money here."

We all laughed and I was enjoying their company. They arrived shortly after the interaction between Giovanni and Cecilio. Alvaro was helpful in getting Giovanni to calm down. He reminded him that they just had to get through tonight and then they could deal with their family. I downed the rest of my drink and placed it on the empty table behind us. I only had a few drinks, but it was enough for the alcohol to have settled over me. I was feeling really good.

"I need to run to the ladies room quickly," I murmured to Giovanni and reached for my bag.

"Do you want me to walk with you?" he offered.

I shook my head. "I'll only be a couple of minutes."

I reached for my clutch bag on the table and positioned it underneath my arm. I grabbed the bottom of my dress so I didn't walk all over it. I pushed through the crowds of people and made my way to the back where the bathrooms were. The music was no longer blaring in my ears as I strolled up the stairs further away from the party. The building was exquisite. The archaic architecture continued inside with the gothic designs against the wall. Even the staircase was fancy as it spiraled itself to the next floor. Each step was illuminated with light from underneath it and I followed the stairs to the top where the bathrooms were. They were at the end of the hall, but I stopped in my tracks about halfway when I heard my name from behind me.

The déjà vu settled over me as I turned to meet Nate. He stood with his hands in the pockets of his well-fitted navy suit. His hair was perfectly styled in place and I noticed his beard had continued to grow out. He always managed to look so well put together.

"Nate," I breathed.

"I didn't expect to see you here," he said.

I shifted awkwardly. "I'm actually here with someone."

"Giovanni Velázquez?"

I nodded.

"I saw you arrive with him. I didn't know you were seeing him," he commented.

"I'm not. I mean, I was." I sighed and stopped myself from the unnecessary explanations. "It's complicated."

"Well, you look beautiful."

I was surprised by his compliment. He shifted uncomfortably and pulled his hands from his pockets. A couple of women left the lady's room and strolled past us, laughing at something one of them had said.

"Thank you."

We stood in awkward silence and I was dying to get out of this interaction. It was weird to be standing here with him. Someone I had such a long history with and yet, we were complete strangers now. I wasn't sure what to say to him and he clearly felt the same. He ran his fingers over his hair and I noticed his nervous twitch in his hand. He always got like that when he had something to say. I just didn't feel like entertaining this conversation.

"Well, I should go."

I turned towards the direction of the bathroom.

"I'm sorry, Isabella."

I stopped in my tracks. *Why was he apologizing to me?* I took a deep breath in and turned to face him again.

"Why are yo-," I started to say before he stepped closer, interrupting my sentence.

"I never apologised to you for how I left things between us and after I saw you at the airport, I haven't been able to stop thinking about you."

I jerked my head back in surprise. *Where the hell was all this coming from?* His face was riddled with nerves and I had never seen him like this.

"Nate, you don't need to apologize. Everything worked out the way it was meant to."

"Except it didn't," he retorted.

"What are you talking about?"

His eyes were filled with sadness. "I should never have left you that night."

My breath caught in my throat. What was he doing? Why was he doing this now? Now when he had a fiancé and I had moved on with my life?

"Nate, you have a fiancé," I recalled. "You shoul-".

He interrupted me again. "I broke up with Christina."

Now my jaw dropped. They had only been engaged for a couple of months and now here he was standing in front of me telling me that they broke up.

"What happened?"

He lifted his eyes to meet mine. "I saw you again and I realised I made a mistake."

I was shocked. The last thing I expected tonight was for Nate to be saying what he was. *What did he want me to do with that information?* I looked at him and I was reminded of our friendship and the love we once shared, but it was nothing more than a distant memory now. It wasn't something I longed for. Not when I had gotten a taste of what real love was.

"Nate, you didn't want to get married." I was trying to process all the information. "When you broke up with me you said it was because you didn't want to get married, but then you got engaged."

"I know." He let out an exasperated sigh and stepped closer to me again. "I got scared, okay? I got scared of getting married, but then we broke up and when I met Christina I-".

"You obviously loved her enough to propose," I said softly. "And that's gre-".

"I loved you, too." He reached for my hand. "I still love you."

What the hell was he doing?

I didn't want a confession of love from him. I didn't need it. I had moved on with my life and was finally living a life I wanted to live. Granted, I had a lot of my own shit to figure out, but compared to the controlled life I was living back in London, this was so much better. I could never go back to the life I had.

I pulled my hand away. "Nate, I don't know why you're telling me this."

He stepped closer to me again. "I need you to know that I want you back, Isabella. I'm sorry that I left you, I should never have don-".

This time I was the one who interrupted him. "Nate no, you can't be saying this."

"Why not? You need to know how I feel."

I shook my head. "Why are you doing this now? It's been so long since we were together."

"I know and seeing you again just reminded me of how good we were together." He reached for my hand again.

"That's over now," I retorted and pulled away. "That's been over for a long time."

"We can have it again, just think ab-".

I interrupted him. "Nate, I'm sorry but I can't."

"Why not?"

"Because I'm in love with Giovanni."

CHAPTER 44:
Giovanni

Her confession to Nate brought on a sudden wave of happiness. I didn't plan to eavesdrop. I was on my way to find her and as I got to the top of the stairs, I heard their voices. I didn't want to interrupt, but I was also way too nosey to turn away. It wasn't right, but I couldn't help it. It angered me that Nate was so upfront about wanting her back. She clearly said she was here with me, but that didn't matter to him.

"You're in love with him?" I heard Nate mutter.

"Of course I am," she replied. "I've moved on with my life. You broke up with me a long time ago, Nate, and this is probably not what you want to hear, but I'm glad that you did."

"How could you be glad? Did our relationship mean that little to you?" There was a flicker of sadness in his voice.

"No, of course not. I loved you, but I just realized that I wasn't in love with you."

Ouch.

That couldn't have been easy for him to hear. I didn't care about his feelings, but there was no denying that one probably hurt.

"I'm sorry, Nate, but you can't just waltz back into my life and think I'm going to drop everything to be with you. I'm not the same woman you once knew. I've changed and I'm happy that I left London that day."

"I don't understand, Isabella," Nate muttered. "Your mother said that I had a chance of winning you bac-".

"I'm sorry, did you just say my mother?"

I heard the anger in Isabella's voice rise at that new piece of information.

Her mother was a generally disrespectful woman when it came to our relationship, but talking to her ex about trying to win her back was a low blow.

"Yes," he answered sheepishly. "After I saw you, I reached out to her. I needed some advice."

"Here's some advice for you, Nate. Move on with your life."

She was angry now and I couldn't stay in the shadows any longer. I climbed the last few stairs and they came into view. Isabella looked over Nate's shoulder and met my eyes.

"Giovanni," she breathed.

"I came to find you," I explained. "You had been gone for quite a while." I walked over to her and reached for her hand. "Is everything okay here?"

Isabella nodded. "Nate and I were just saying goodbye."

Nate looked defeated. He couldn't hide the very obvious regret in his eyes. He avoided my eyes and didn't even mutter a word to me. Instead, he turned and made his way back downstairs. I watched as he disappeared from view before turning to Isabella.

"What was that about?" I pretended not to know.

She shook her head, trying to get rid of the shocked expression across her face. She strolled over to the small bench against the wall and sat down. I followed her lead and took a seat next to her.

"Just my ex-boyfriend teaming up with my mother to try and win me back," she muttered.

I acted surprised, but I didn't have to pretend when it came to the irritation I felt over that. "Nate wants you back?"

She nodded. "Apparently so."

"And how do you feel about that?"

She clicked her tongue. "I'm more annoyed than anything else. My mother has no boundaries and Nate has no chance. The relationship he and I had is long gone."

She reached out and grabbed my hand. Her simple touch set my body on fire. She had been holding back all night. I could tell she wanted more from me. She wanted me to kiss her but out of respect, I didn't. I wanted her to be sure. If she was sure, she would tell me and I would happily give in to her request.

"Seriously, what the hell is wrong with my mother?" she continued, trying to control her anger. "The last she knew was that you and I were together but she still thought it would be the right thing to help Nate win me back."

She shook her head as I rubbed my thumb over hers, reminding her that I was here for her. She hadn't told her family about us splitting up. That didn't surprise me too much but I was surprised that it didn't come up in conversation with them up until now. Mainly with her father - I figured that she and her mother still weren't on speaking terms.

"What Nate and I had was platonic love. It was never the kind of love that I really wanted." She tucked a strand of hair behind her ear. "That I found with you, Giovanni."

I lifted my eyes to meet hers.

CHAPTER 45:

Isabella

"**I**'ve never loved anyone like I love you," I confessed. "And I know we have so much that we need to talk about and we keep putting off the inevitable, but I don't want to do that right now."

I leaned closer to him, reaching out and resting my hand on his leg. "I don't want to think right now. I just want you, Giovanni."

His hand rested on mine. "You want me?"

I nodded and he pulled into me, his soft lips touching mine. *Finally*, I had been craving this for days. The feeling of what it would be like to kiss him again. I shifted myself closer to him, the desire I had been holding back pushed its way to the surface and there was no going back now. I was giving into what I really wanted and it was enthralling. I didn't want to think. I didn't want to deal with anything. I was so good at running away from my problems, but that was irrelevant right now. I didn't know what tomorrow was going to bring, but I knew I would regret it if I didn't do what I wanted.

And right now, I wanted him.

His hand made its way into my hair and I could feel the intensity of our movements increasing.

I pulled away, trying to catch my breath. "We can't do this here."

We both looked around and a couple of people were walking up and down to the bathroom. I wasn't even embarrassed that they may have seen us making out. I was too high on my desire for him to care.

He stood up and grabbed my hand. "Come with me."

We continued down the hallway, moving further and further away from the party. He stopped at a door and looked around to make sure the coast was clear before pushing it open to reveal an empty office. We stepped inside and he shut it behind me. There was a table in the middle with a couple of files and stationery scattered across it. There was a large leather couch in front of it and big windows against the wall, displaying the nighttime sky. The moonlight peeped between the curtains that remained open and illuminated the room. I turned to face Giovanni who had his head tilted to the side as he eyed my figure. He couldn't hold it back. I could see he wanted me.

I slowly reached behind my neck and started running my fingers down, across my collarbone before continuing over the cleavage my dress had created.

He ran his tongue over his bottom lip. "Isabella."

"Yes, Giovanni?" I flicked my eyes to meet his. "Do you like what you see?"

I had never had the courage to be like this, but with Giovanni it was different. He made me feel desired and that gave me an addictive rush that made me crave more. I wanted to see all the different ways I could get a reaction out of him. I felt comfortable enough with him to explore my own sexual desires.

He took a step closer to me. "I love what I see. You're fucking breathtaking."

This time I took a step closer to him.

"You know someone could walk in at any time?" he murmured seductively.

"I know." I flicked my eyes up to meet his. "And I don't care."

He reached for me and pulled me closer to him, his lips crashing against mine. The previous intensity we had built up had returned and I wanted nothing more than to rip into him. I reached for his jacket and pushed it down his arms, dropping it to the floor. His hand found the back of my neck as he pinned me up against the nearest wall. His lips left mine and started to work its way across my cheekbones and down my neck. Each kiss burned against my skin. Overwhelming desire coursed through me and I couldn't contain the aching pressure building between my legs.

He reached for my dress and started pushing it upwards until he could slip his hand underneath. He grabbed my leg and lifted it as it wrapped around his waist. I threw my head back, soaking in every touch. My hands reached for his shirt and I started to undo the buttons as quickly as I could. I reached the last button and ripped his shirt open, revealing the markings against his body. The moonlight shone through the open curtains, illuminating him enough for me to soak in that body of his. I tugged at my lip, a small groan escaping me.

I reached for his pants. "Giovanni."

He pulled away and reached for the buttons on his pants. I held my dress up to my waist, making sure it wasn't going to be a problem for him. I kept my hand wrapped around the back of his neck, digging my nails into his skin in anticipation. He pulled his pants and underwear down enough to free himself to me.

He was so ready for me.

He lifted my leg up around his waist again and positioned himself in between my legs. He ran his tongue over his bottom lip as he pushed himself inside of me. Both of us let out a small gasp at the feeling of being skin to skin. I tightened around him as his lips returned to mine and we moved, both of us overcome with an animalistic desire. I didn't care where we were. I didn't care that at any moment, someone could walk in here and catch us. It was exhilarating to me. I threw my head back as his hand wrapped gently around the base of my throat. I wanted him to tear me apart. I had handed myself over to my deepest darkest desires and there was no going back.

His strong arms came around me as he lifted me up, my other leg wrapping around his waist as he pushed deeper inside of me. He turned and brought us over to the couch that was directly behind us and he lay me down against it, pushing my dress up to keep from getting in the way. He didn't stop - we couldn't stop. We were consumed by each other. Each thrust deeper inside of me was sending my body further towards the edge.

"Yes, yes," I moaned.

My eyes rolled back, soaking in the feeling of him inside of me. He filled me up and my body started to tighten around him, constantly pushing itself further and further. I opened my eyes and watched as he tilted his own head back, his own pleasure working its way over him. The sight of his clenched jaw and the way he couldn't hold back the small breaths that escaped his lips were sending my body into a frenzy. He reached for my right leg and slowly lifted it up. I didn't know what he was doing, but I followed his lead. He lifted it straight up into the air and started to push it closer to my body, suddenly intensifying the feeling inside of me.

"Oh my God." I threw my head back as he pushed my leg closer to me, testing my flexibility as my knee moved closer to my chin.

The feeling was unreal. He moved his body deeper inside of me and from this angle, he was getting to where he needed to be much easier. Each thrust pushed me further to my climax. I loved every moment of it. I was loving every moment of having him where he belonged.

"I'm close, Giovanni," I murmured as the pressure between my legs escalated.

"Don't hold back, baby."

And I didn't. I allowed my body to be overcome with the delirious pleasure shooting through me. With one hard thrust inside of me, we both came undone. All my senses were heightened now. I could hear the music in the distance but I focused on our heavy breathing. I closed my eyes and took a deep breath in. For a couple of minutes, we didn't move. We soaked in the lingering pleasure and even though that had taken a lot out of me, I was ready for more. I wanted to have as much of him as humanly possible.

"Giovanni?" I murmured.

"Yes, baby?"

"Let's get out of here."

CHAPTER 46:
Giovanni

We somehow managed to make ourselves look decent enough to say goodbye to people as we made our way out of the party. I was more than happy to leave - all I could think about was having Isabella again. I was high on the euphoria I felt whenever I was inside of her. I craved it and I needed her again.

It didn't take long to get back to our rented-out cottage. I unlocked the door and stood back, allowing her to step inside. I followed closely behind her and locked the door behind us. I watched as she leaned down to remove her shoes, suddenly removing the extra inches she had in height. I preferred her this way anyway. She was the perfect height to rest her head against my chest whenever I had her in my arms. I slipped my jacket off and laid it against the couch as we strolled into the small living room. The curtains were drawn closed and there was nothing from the outside world that could disturb us right now.

"Well, that was a fun party," she quipped.

I chuckled and kicked my shoes off. "I guess it wasn't too bad."

It could have been worse, but with Isabella by my side, she was the perfect distraction. I didn't have to focus on the fuck-up that was my parent's relationship and the way they faked their happiness. I didn't focus on the fact I was ready to punch my dad in the face at his mention of Casey being pregnant. His inability to read a situation was beyond me. Or he knew exactly what he was doing and he was trying to get under my skin.

I undid the buttons of my shirt as she turned to face me, lifting her curious hazel eyes to meet mine.

"Do you need something?" I murmured playfully.

A small smile pulled at her lips as she shook her head. "As you were."

I smirked. She was enjoying watching me as I pulled my shirt down my arms and let it fall to the floor. I watched as she took a deep breath in, her eyes never leaving my body. I slowly stepped closer, closing in the proximity between us.

"Do you need help getting out of that dress?" I offered.

I watched as her eyebrow lifted as she nodded. She always got this naughty look on her face whenever she heard something that she liked. She turned to face the opposite direction and pulled her hair forward, revealing the zip on the back of her dress. I reached for it and slowly started to slide it down, careful to make sure my fingertips brushed over her skin. I was ready to have her again. I wanted to worship her body - I wanted to spend time discovering every inch of it in any way I could. I pulled the zip to the bottom and slowly pushed the material of her dress to the side, causing her straps to slide down off her shoulders. I leaned forward and started to kiss the back of her neck. I heard her small breaths as I moved my lips across her skin, sometimes lingering a bit longer as I sucked softly. She was mine and I wanted her to know what I was capable of doing to her body.

I brought my lips up to her ear as I pushed myself up against her. "Do you see what you do to me, Isabella?"

A small groan escaped her lips.

"I think I could do with a shower," I murmured. "What do you think?"

She turned to face me, her eyes burning with desire. "Lead the way."

I strolled into the master bedroom with the en-suite bathroom as she followed closely behind me. I wanted to have her again, but I also wanted to savour every moment I had. I walked over and closed the curtains of the room before turning back to her. She had already escaped into the bathroom and I heard the water turn on. I undid my belt and pulled it off, dropping it onto the floor as my pants followed. I grabbed two towels that were laid out on the chair in the corner before slipping into the bathroom, closing the door behind us. The steam had started to surround the room and I couldn't even make out my reflection in the mirror. Isabella stood just outside the shower and I watched as her hand came around her back, unclasping her bra. She dropped it to the floor and stepped out of her underwear. Just the sight of her naked body was enough to set off my arousal.

I removed my underwear and joined her.

CHAPTER 47:

Isabella

I took a deep breath in as the hot water hit against my skin. I tilted my head back and closed my eyes, soaking in each burning drop against me. I felt his presence behind me. I could feel him anywhere. The constant tension between the two of us was enough to suck the air out of any room. Our bodies called for each other. I felt his hand snake around my waist, pulling me closer to him.

I could feel him hard up against me.

I tugged at my bottom lip and slowly opened my eyes, suddenly overcome with the salacious desire that I experienced at the party. I turned to face him, my eyes landing on his wet body. I watched as the water slid over his chest and down his abs. I allowed my eyes to follow the natural path of the water. My breath caught in my throat at how ready he was for me. Without a second thought, I stood on my tiptoes and reached up for him, my lips crashing against his. He returned the intensity of my kiss and pulled me closer to him, the hot water falling over us. He pinned me up against the wall and I was reminded of the first time with him in Valencia. That was one memory that would be ingrained in my mind for the rest of my life. I was consumed by him. He had always done so well to take care of my body and now I wanted to return the favour. I wanted to see how far I could push him. I pulled away from him and turned so his back was against the wall.

"Isabella, what are yo-," he started to say, but quickly stopped as I bent down, lowering myself to him.

"Joder," he breathed, never taking his eyes off me.

He brought out a side to me that I never knew existed. I wanted to please him. I wanted to show him all the ways I could take care of his body. The water slid down my back as I leaned closer to him, taking him in my hand. I heard a small breath escape from his lips and I started to move. Slowly and careful at first before finding a rhythm that he was enjoying. I watched as he tilted his head back, soaking in what I was doing.

I brought my mouth over him.

"Fuuuuuck," he groaned.

Hearing his own pleasure was increasing the throbbing between my legs. I didn't hold back - I found an intense rhythm that he enjoyed. His hand made its way through my wet hair and he pulled at it. I flicked my eyes up to meet his and they were swimming with desire. Each groan, every hard pull of my hair, every reaction coming from him right now was only making me want to do more. I went faster and deeper, pushing him further and further to his climax.

"I'm close."

I didn't stop. I continued increasing my rhythm as he reached his climax. It was an exhilarating feeling knowing I was the one causing his body to react this way. With one last twirl of my tongue around him, I pulled away and stood up, moving the rest of my body under the hot water again. He stepped forward, the water hitting his head and running through his hair.

He never took his eyes off me. "You are just-".

"Just what?"

"Perfect."

He didn't wait one more second before pulling into me. His tongue flicked over mine and I was engrossed by the heat between us. My body was aching to have him again and the anticipation of what was coming next was edging me further and further. His arms came around me as he turned, pinning me up against the wall again. I gasped at the feeling of the cold wall against me, but also at the way his lips traveled down my neck.

"Giovanni," I moaned his name.

"Yes, baby."

The arousal shot through my veins, begging me to have him take me again. All I wanted was to feel him inside me again. I wanted to be wrapped up in him and focus on nothing, but the way he pushed my body further to its climax. He positioned himself between my legs and with one swift motion, he was buried deep inside of me.

I threw my head back and moaned his name into the night.

CHAPTER 48:

Giovanni

We finally managed to drag ourselves out of the shower, but we didn't stop there. We spent the rest of the night wrapped up in each other's arms, giving in to our burning desires. It must have been the early hours of the morning now and we lay in bed, her head on my chest as I listened to her soft breathing. My body was exhausted. I had devoured her in any way I could get her and the pleasure still lingered.

She turned to face me, her head still on my chest. I glanced down at her and her eyes were swimming with questions.

"What's going on in that beautiful mind of yours?" I murmured.

"Do you even want to be a father?" she asked softly.

I didn't expect her to ask me that. We had both made it clear that we didn't want to deal with any of the outside world right now. We didn't want to think of tomorrow - we just wanted to soak in each other as much as we could. There was a lingering sadness that returned to her eyes and I hated to see it.

"Isabella, we don't have to ta-".

"We do," she interjected. "We can't keep pretending this isn't happening because it is. You're going to be a father and that's a big deal."

I took a deep breath in. I didn't want to have this conversation with her, but she was right. I loved staying in this little bubble with her away from all outside forces, but we were only putting off the inevitable here. She lifted herself from my chest and pulled the sheet over her naked body. She sat upright now facing me while I tried to put together my answer.

"I was pretty sure having kids was never going to be for me. I didn't want them," I explained. "But I can't explain the feeling I got when I saw the scan at the doctor's office."

She remained silent and kept her eyes firmly on her hands in her lap. She had opened up the conversation and I had to be completely honest with her. I wanted her to know everything so we could figure out the next step together. When I was in that doctor's room and I saw the baby for the first time, I was overcome with unexpected emotion. I couldn't explain it.

"It reminded me that this isn't about me anymore and I have a responsibility to that little kidney bean."

"Kidney bean?" She looked up.

"Yeah, the baby is about the size of a kidney bean now," I said sheepishly.

"Oh."

She averted her eyes again and I swallowed, trying to contain the rising guilt inside of me. I shouldn't have said that. It made me feel sick to my stomach. I couldn't help but feel a small attachment to the baby during the scan. I didn't even know for sure if it was mine, but it wouldn't change the fact that in that moment, I felt something.

Tell her about the paternity test.

The voice in my head was screaming at me to do it. Just tell her and maybe things would be different? If I told her, we could figure this out together. I was at war with my head and my heart here. The last thing I wanted to do was hurt her even more and since I didn't know the results, I was going to have to keep my mouth shut. The fear of the unknown kept me from being selfish for the sake of her. I couldn't be selfish with her.

"And have you and Casey spoken about how this is going to work?"

I shook my head. "There is still so much that is up in the air right now."

She lifted her head to the side and stared off into the distance. She was so deep in thought - her eyes had squinted slightly as she clenched her jaw. I didn't want to upset her but I knew I already had.

"Isabella." I reached for her hand.

"I've always wanted kids," she murmured. "I didn't hate the idea of having a family and it may sound so stupid now, but I saw that with you, Giovanni."

"Hey, I sa-".

She stopped me and continued. "I saw it so clearly in my mind. It was something I was convinced we were going to have one day, but I never imagined it would be like this. I know it's not the baby's fault and this probably sounds ridiculously selfish, but I didn't want to have to share you with anyone."

I hung my head in shame. There was nothing I could say to change the facts right now. No matter how much I wanted to.

"What are we supposed to do now, Giovanni?"

I pulled her closer to me. "I don't know, baby, but I don't want to lose you again."

"I don't even like Casey," she added. "I'm constantly reminded of how she told me you guys always find your way back to each other and how do I know that's not true? Look at what's happened."

"I'm sorry, Isabella, I don't know how many times I can apologise for the situation we're in. This was never my intention."

"I know that and I'm not trying to make you feel bad. I just don't know what to do."

"You're the only one who can decide what you want to do now. I will take you any way I can get you - I don't want to have to watch you walk out of my life again, but if that's what you decide, I will let you go this time," I said softly, swallowing to stop the emotion that was building. "If that's really what you want then I'll stay away. I won't keep rocking up unannounced. I won't reach out to you. I'll try my hardest to let you go because your happiness means more to me than anything."

Every fiber of my being was hoping that it wouldn't come to that. I was hoping that she would tell me I was being crazy and that she wanted to be with me, no matter the circumstances. I wanted her to choose me. I wanted us to make this work but it was up to her.

Her eyes met mine and they were overcome with sadness, tears now brimming in them.

"I keep making you cry." I pulled her closer to me. "I don't want you to cry."

"I just know I'm going to have to make a decision and I don't want to," she choked. "I've been putting it off for as long as I could but everyone is right, we can't keep doing this to each other. You already have so much to figure out with the baby, we can't have our relationship so up in the air but I just-"

She stopped, her words getting caught up by her cries. I held onto her and said nothing. I couldn't form the words. Deep down I already knew her answer - she was never going to get past the fact it was Casey having the baby. That was enough for her to walk away every single time she was reminded of it. I wish I had the results of the paternity test already. I could just tell her about it and if all was in my favour, we wouldn't have to keep saying goodbye. I could put all this shit behind me and she and I could build a life together.

Right now, there was nothing I could say to comfort her and that was the worst part.

"I think I need a few days by myself to think about everything," she murmured. "When I'm around you, I can't think straight. You consume me and it's impossible to pull myself away from you. I need some time to really think about what our options are and see what's best for me."

"Okay," I murmured into her hair, leaving a kiss against it.

I had watched her walk away from me a number of times now, but a part of me always believed she would find her way back. I believed we were meant to be together, but with the way she was talking now, I was terrified that this was going to be it for us. If she decided not to be with me, that would be it for real this time and I would have to accept that.

Please God, let those results come back soon.

CHAPTER 49:

Isabella

Why did you do that to yourself, Isabella?

I stood in the elevator of my apartment building being reprimanded by the voice in my head. I had pushed her to the far corners of my mind throughout my weekend with Giovanni, but now she was back in full force. I had convinced myself that it would be no problem to have another weekend rendezvous with him. It wouldn't be an issue at all because I'd be able to handle it.

Turns out I was very wrong about that.

It hurt more than before to pull myself away from him, especially after the weekend we just had. Every moment with him was like a dream, but now that I've woken up, I had to face reality. He was going to give me my space to figure out what I wanted to do next and now that I was away from him, my shattered heart reminded me of why I should never have put us through that in the first place. I was still the same broken woman I was the first time I found out about Casey's pregnancy. I was delusional to think that a weekend away was going to change the facts.

I unlocked my door and pushed it open, surprised to see Lorenzo seated at my kitchen counter.

"Lorenzo?" I gaped.

"Hi, Izzy."

"What are you doing here?" I asked. "How did you even get in here?"

I dropped my bag by the entrance and closed the door behind me. I looked around, but there was no one else in sight.

"Reyna was just here. She told me you'd be back soon so she said I could wait here."

I was completely caught off guard by his unexpected arrival. I didn't expect to see him and if I'm being honest, I didn't want to see him. I didn't want to see anyone. I just needed time to myself. He slipped off the barstool, but remained by the counter, standing awkwardly. I strolled into the kitchen and brought the kettle to boil.

"Coffee?" I offered.

"Yes, please."

I grabbed two cups and placed them on the counter. My mind was swimming with so many thoughts but I couldn't get a handle on any of them. I leaned against the counter and looked over at him.

"Reyna said you went out of town this weekend," he said casually.

I nodded, avoiding his gaze. I know I had no reason to feel bad, but I did. I felt guilty that I just spent the weekend with Giovanni and didn't even give Lorenzo a second thought. The last time I saw him, we didn't really leave things on a good note and he spent the whole weekend trying to get a hold of me. I had screwed up by letting him kiss me. I had probably given him the wrong impression and I didn't want that. I enjoyed Lorenzo's company, but it wasn't going to be the same now.

"I tried to get a hold of you."

"I know, I'm sorry I never returned your calls. There was a lot going on."

He flicked his eyes to meet mine. "Who did you go away with?"

I pulled my gaze away from him again. I didn't want to say it.

Lorenzo scoffed, forcing me to bring my gaze back up to his. My silence gave him the answer he needed.

"Are the two of you back together now?"

I shook my head.

"Then what are you doing, Isabella?" he asked.

A flicker of irritation flared inside of me at his question. It wasn't what he was asking me that annoyed me, it was the fact I didn't have an answer for him. I didn't know what the fuck I was doing. I sighed and reached for the coffee on the counter, attempting to distract myself from having to meet his eyes again.

"What are you doing here, Lorenzo?" I changed the subject.

"I needed to see you. I'm sorry about what happened the other day, I didn't mean to behave that way."

"You don't need to apologize."

"Yes, I do because that's the type of guy I am. I'll apologize when I do something wrong and learn from my mistakes."

Why was he telling me this?

Before I could open my mouth to reply, he continued.

"I'm the type of guy who goes after what he wants and I know you don't want to hear this but if I don't tell you now, I'm going to regret this."

He slipped off his stool and walked over to me, taking the coffee tin from my hands and placing it on the counter. He stepped closer to me, closing the proximity between us. My breath caught in my throat. He was so close to me now that I couldn't help but breathe him in. He was looking at me with an intensity that made me nervous. His light brown eyes were the same kind eyes they had always been, but there was something more to them now. I watched as his eyes traveled down to reach my mouth.

"You deserve so much better, Isabella," he murmured. "You deserve to be with someone who knows what he has when he has you."

"Lorenz-".

"I just need to say this once," he interrupted me politely. "I could make you happy, Isabella. I know I could if you gave me a chance to."

Why was he doing this now? First Nate and now Lorenzo. *What the fuck was going on?* I didn't want to hear any more confessions. I couldn't handle any more complications. I had so much I needed to figure out, I didn't need to add any more information to the mix.

"I haven't stopped thinking about you since the first night we met," he said softly. "And I know I said I wouldn't do this, but I can't keep watching you run back to Giovanni."

"I'm not running back to him."

"You just spent the whole weekend with him."

I swallowed and averted my eyes.

"You need to know that I have feelings for you, Isabella, and it's more than just friendship for me. It always has been and I know I could really fall for you."

The voices in my head were groaning in frustration. I didn't ask anyone for declarations of their feelings and in the last couple of days, three different guys had expressed how they felt.

But my heart belonged to one.

He continued, "And I think you could fall for me too, if you gave yourself the chance."

I had thought about that before. It briefly crossed my mind. I cared about Lorenzo and there was definitely an attraction but I couldn't give anyone else my heart. Not when Giovanni had a firm hold on it. No one would ever make me feel the way he did. He was everything I wanted.

"Lorenzo, I can't do this right now." I pushed past him.

"Why not?" he retorted.

"Because I'm still in love with Giovanni," I admitted and hung my head in defeat. "And I don't know what's going to happen with him and I."

I watched his face fall at my words. I never wanted to hurt him - I never wanted to hurt anyone but I had to be honest. I wanted Lorenzo to be my friend, but I watched as he slowly started to slip away from me.

"You can't tell me you're thinking of getting back together with him," he objected.

"I don't know!" I shouted. "I have no idea what I'm supposed to do right now."

"Isabella, he got someone else pregnant."

I rolled my eyes. "I am well aware."

"Are you really going to be able to be a stepmother?"

"Don't ask me that," I snapped.

"Why not?" he probed. "Are you prepared to stand by and watch while he and Casey raise a baby together? To always be the person on the outside looking in?"

A lump started to form in my throat at his words. This was everything I was afraid of feeling. I was too selfish to be on the sidelines. I was too selfish to come second to Casey and the baby but that's what was going to happen. Of course, Giovanni was going to put his child first. Any good parent would do that and I couldn't expect him not to be that way.

"I don't need this from you right now, Lorenzo." I choked, the emotion catching in my throat.

"I'm not trying to upset you," he softened his tone.

I brought my hands to cover my face as the tears started to spill over. I couldn't hold it back anymore. I was so frustrated with everything.

"Izzy," Lorenzo murmured and walked over to me, pulling me into his arms. "Hey, it's okay."

"No, it's not," I cried. "None of this is okay."

"You don't deserve to be hurt like this." He tightened his arms around me. "I just want you to think about what will make you happy, Izzy. It doesn't feel like it right now, but you can be happy again."

It was impossible to see how that could be true. My heart was shattered and all that was left was an empty hole in my chest. Giovanni walked into my life and everything changed. He was everything I didn't know I needed and I couldn't comprehend how I was supposed to let him go. I pulled myself away from Lorenzo as politely as I could and walked over to the counter. I wiped away the last of my tears and took a deep breath in. I didn't want to keep crying, especially not with an audience.

"Lorenzo, I'm sorry for everything that has happened and for dragging you into my mess."

"Please don't apologize, I'm happy to be here for you."

"But I can't give you what you want right now." I met his gaze. "I don't know what I'm going to do, but I know that I still love Giovanni and it's up to me to decide what I'm going to do about that."

He sighed. "You just deserve better than this."

CHAPTER 50:

Giovanni

"Where are they?" I asked as Alvaro walked through the reception doors.

"The receptionist said they checked out already."

I scoffed. "Seriously? Did you not tell them we wanted to talk to them?"

"I did," he said. "Clearly they didn't think it was that urgent."

I ran my fingers through my hair and leaned my head back, soaking in the cold air around us. The sky was scattered with dark clouds and I was more agitated than usual. Before Alvaro and I could corner our parents for that family intervention we needed, they had already left back to the city. Even after Alvaro told them we needed to talk, they still chose to leave.

Typical Velázquez-family behaviour - always running away from their problems.

"They can't run away from this forever," I muttered. "We need to sort this shit out because I'm sick of having to deal with their marital problems. They need to get a fucking divorce already."

Alvaro crossed his arms. "We're going to have to talk to them on Christmas."

"Do you really think that's a good idea?" I eyed him. "The whole family is going to be there."

"Then after that."

I rolled my eyes. At this point, I was over both of my parents and the shit they were putting each other through. All I wanted was for them to acknowledge what's been done to this family and the fact they shouldn't be together anymore. I couldn't care less about my father - as far as I was concerned, our relationship was past the point of repair but I wanted my mother to be happy.

"Where's Isabella?" Alvaro asked.

"On her way back to the city."

This morning I called a driver to escort Isabella back to Barcelona. She had decided that she needed some time to think about what she was going to do next and I had to respect that. In the past, I was quick to constantly try and see or communicate with her in some way, but I couldn't do that now. She needed to decide what was best for her without me getting in the way. I love her enough to give her that.

"What's going to happen with the two of you?"

I shrugged my shoulders. "It's up to her now. If she wants to leave for real this time then I'm going to have to let her go."

"And what about the paternity test?"

"Well, I can't say anything until I get those results and there's still a chance that the baby is mine."

It had been a couple of weeks now since we did the test and I was itching for the results. I just wanted to know for sure so I could figure out what the next step was. Every part of me was hoping that the results would tell me exactly what I wanted to hear.

"And how do you feel about that?"

"I haven't quite figured that out," I admitted. "I don't want to have to think about any of it until I know for sure."

Penelope pushed through the reception doors with Mateo in her arms. She smiled at us as she strolled over to join the conversation.

"Did you find your parents?"

We both shook our heads.

"They thought it would be fun to play the disappearing act on us," I muttered.

She said nothing more on the topic and instead turned to Alvaro. "They're bringing the car around. We should probably get out of here before the storm hits."

We exchanged goodbyes shortly after that and I walked back to the cottage to clear out the last of my things. I shoved my clothes into my bag as I heard the rain starting to come down hard outside. I needed to head back to the city today as well. There was still so much I had to sort out to get the renovations going for the new *Mala Mía* in Valencia. I was going to throw myself into my work or any other distraction I could get. I didn't want any spare moment to think of her. I couldn't allow myself to do that. It only reminded me of the hollowness that now rested inside of me. I reached for my bag and pulled the strap over my shoulder, turning to do one last scan of the room. The memories of the night before were still fresh. I could still feel her hands on my body and the way it felt having her against me. The way she took control of the situation and made my body bow down to her. I was at her mercy and I would continue to be for the rest of my life.

There was no forgetting her.

Isabella Avery waltzed into my life when I least expected it and became the most important person to me. She lured me in with her innocent charm and beautiful smile, but there was so much more to her than meets the eye. She was compassionate and kind. There was not a selfish bone in her body and I couldn't have fallen harder for her. The dull ache in my chest at her absence was going to have a permanent residence now. As much as I was hoping she would come running back to me, I already knew that she was going to choose differently. I took a deep breath in and pushed that out of my mind. I grabbed my car keys off the counter and locked the door behind me.

After handing the room key back at reception, I made it to my car now soaked from the rain. I shut the door behind me as the intensity of the rain picked up. It was really coming down and the thunder roared through the sky. I pulled my seatbelt across my chest and secured it in place. I wasn't going to be able to drive very fast, not in this weather. I connected my phone and allowed the same *reggaeton* playlist we had listened to on the way here to come through the speakers. There were so many things that reminded me of her and I was going to have to consciously focus on keeping her from entering my mind again.

I turned my car on and I pulled out of the driveway.

CHAPTER 51:
Isabella

"So, my family are arriving tomorrow for Christmas Eve," Reyna explained.

She arrived shortly after Lorenzo left. I told him that I needed time to think about everything - alone. I needed to gather all my thoughts and double down on what I was going to do next. I had to make a decision. Reyna didn't ask me anything about my weekend away which I found unusual. Instead, she came home with a box of some of my favourite pastries and turned on her distraction mode. At first, we ate and drank coffee while she filled me in on what it was like to meet Diego's parents for the first time. Now, we have started a mini spring-cleaning of the apartment. Anything to keep me from having a spare moment to think of anything.

"You know I didn't even realise it was the 23rd," I admitted.

"I'm not surprised. You've had way too much going on in your life over these last few weeks."

I reached for the broom and started to sweep the tiles in the kitchen. "I usually love Christmas but this year it's just not the same."

"Tomorrow you're coming with me so I promise it's going to feel more like Christmas than it does right now."

The Cazarez family had agreed to join Sergio's family for Christmas Eve now that he and Katrina were engaged. They had a large family home about thirty minutes outside of the city and since I was a roommate and newly appointed third daughter of the Cazarez family, I was encouraged to tag along. The last thing I felt like doing was being around crowds of people to celebrate anything but I was not going to spend Christmas alone.

I was not going to be *that* girl.

"What are we in charge of bringing?" I asked as I swept the last of the dust into a corner to throw away.

"Dessert," she announced happily. "Which is great because I technically don't have to make it myself which is why I went out today and stocked up on anything we could need."

She opened the fridge and displayed an array of boxes.

"Holy shit, Reyna, how many people are attending tomorrow?" I gawked.

She chuckled. "Tons. Apparently, Sergio's family is huge and they invited everyone -*los primos, los tíos y las tías, los abuelos* - the whole lot of them are excited to meet Katrina."

The idea of having to socialize with a large group of people was causing a rush of anxiety over me. I was never good at meeting new people. I always found it overwhelming and now it was even worse. I didn't have a handle on my emotions at all, but I was going to have to lock that away in a tight box in my mind tomorrow.

"Katrina must be so excited to meet his family." I bent down and swept up the dust into the dustpan.

"She's pretty nervous actually. This is the first time meeting most of them and now that they're engaged, she's feeling some pressure."

"She'll be fine."

I emptied the dirt into the bin and placed the dustpan and brush in the corner again. I dusted off my hands and turned to lean on the counter. Reyna had hung up the last of the jackets that were lying around and strolled over to sit on the stool across from me. We sat in silence, but I could tell she had something to say. I knew her well enough and she had been quiet about my weekend away for long enough.

Just as I was about to open my mouth, thunder boomed through the sky causing us both to jump.

"*Joder,*" Reyna muttered.

"That's quite the storm outside." I was facing the windows watching as the rain washed over the city.

Reyna turned towards it for a moment before turning back to me with that look on her face again.

I sighed. "Go ahead."

"How did you know I was going to say something?"

I scoffed. "How long have I known you, Reyna? Trust me, I know when you want to say something."

"I just wanted to ask about your weekend away." She eyed me.

I brought a barstool around to where I was standing and pulled myself up onto it. There was a cloth still on the table so I reached out and fiddled with it, avoiding her gaze.

"What about it?"

"You went away with Giovanni for the weekend and you really have nothing to share with me?"

I sighed and met her questioning gaze. I could always count on Reyna to tell me exactly what she thought, but this time I was afraid to know. I hadn't been making the smartest decisions with him but I didn't need a reminder of it.

"He needed a friend."

"Friends don't sleep together."

She wasn't wrong.

"How do you know I slept with him?"

She eyed me. "You don't expect me to believe you went away with him for the whole weekend and nothing happened."

The heat spread across my cheeks confirming that she was right about her suspicions.

"Exactly."

I ignored that and continued. "I need to decide if I want to be with him or not. But for real this time - we can't have this constant back and forth. It's not healthy for either of us."

"You're right about that." She leaned her elbow against the counter and rested her head on her hand. "I told him to leave you alone at *Paradiso,* but then you kissed Lorenzo and that was it for him."

"Lorenzo kissed me," I clarified.

"Either way, that set Giovanni off. I honestly thought he was going to punch him."

"Me too," I admitted. "Instead it was like being stuck in a pissing contest between the two of them."

She laughed and rolled her eyes. "Men."

I laughed and shrugged as I leaned back against the barstool, running my fingers through my hair. My head was pounding and I didn't know if it was from the lack of sleep or from the unnecessary amount of information running around inside of it.

"What are you thinking of doing, Izzy?" she asked softly. "You spent the weekend with your ex-boyfriend. Are you thinking of getting back together with him?"

I lifted my shoulders and dropped them back down. "I don't know what to do. Giovanni has a hold on me in a way no one has ever had before and I can see a future with him."

"And what about Casey and the baby?"

"See, that was never supposed to be part of my future with him," I admitted sadly. "And I don't think anything has changed. I've tried to put off dealing with it because the baby isn't here yet so it doesn't seem real, but I just can't be okay with them having a child together."

A wave of nausea washed over me at the memory of him mentioning the "kidney bean". It just reminded me that they were sharing something special that didn't involve me. The two of them had made a baby together and it made me sick to my stomach.

"Why couldn't he have not slept around?" I said, exasperated. "None of this would have happened if he had just controlled himself."

"That's what Giovanni was like. You are the only person I've ever known him to commit to and I'm sure he never expected that."

"He didn't," I mumbled.

To think our relationship started off as nothing more than a one-night stand was mind-blowing to me. All of this was the ripple effect of that one night - a night I never expected to have. It was the night that changed it all for me.

"Well, you don't need to make any decisions now." She reached out and squeezed my hand. "Give it a couple of days. I'm sure by then you'll have thought about it more and you'll be able to make a more informed decision."

What was she going on about?

I had all the information I needed and deep down I already knew my answer. I would never be able to get past the two of them having a baby and now Giovanni had a responsibility to his child. He was going to have to put that baby first, always.

I wasn't ready to accept the decision I had already made. I needed a couple more days before my life changed for good.

CHAPTER 52:

Giovanni

I had taken the off-ramp leading me down the road back into the city. The rain didn't stop once while on my way back. Instead, the intensity of it continued to pick up. It was a real storm out there and I was trying my hardest to focus on the road in front of me. I couldn't clearly make out the headlights that were in front of me so I kept my distance, careful not to get too close to another car right now.

"Fuck man!" I muttered and opened my eyes as wide as I could, trying to make out the road ahead of me.

This storm was ridiculous. The water wouldn't stop pouring and the thunder roared across the sky, often giving me unexpected jump frights. I slowly approached a red light as my phone started to ring. I reached down for it, glancing at a number I didn't recognise. I answered it over the hands-free kit.

"*Hola?*"

"*Buenos dias*, is this Mr. Giovanni Velázquez?" A polite female voice said on the other end of the line.

"*Si*, that's me."

"*Hola*, Mr. Velázquez. This is Dr. Gonzalez calling, we met a couple of weeks ago."

My stomach dropped. That was Casey's doctor which could only mean one thing - the paternity test results were ready. A rush of nerves came over me at the anticipation of the unknown.

"Mr. Velázquez?" she repeated.

"*Lo siento*, I'm here," I choked, trying to pull myself together. "What can

I do for you, Dr. Gonzalez?"

"We have the results of the paternity test you and Miss Fonseca had done. It's not usually customary to give information like this over the phone, but I decided I needed to call you off the record."

I was surprised by this. I had only met her once, but I was pretty vocal about my reservations about being the father and she clearly picked up on that.

"It's Christmas now and that's a time to be with family so I hardly think it would be appropriate for me to expect you to come and meet me to chat about this," she continued.

"Thank you. I'm dying to know what you have to tell me."

"I tried to get a hold of Miss Fonseca, but she didn't answer so I left her a voicemail to contact me as soon as she can," she explained.

God lady, just get to the point.

"I'm sorry to inform you Mr. Velázquez, but you are not the biological father of Miss Fonseca's baby."

My head jerked as I tried to process what she had just told me. "I'm sorry, Dr. Gonzalez, but did you just say I am *not* the father?"

"Yes sir, the results came back and you are not the baby's biological father."

I had never experienced true joy until that moment. The realization that everything that was wrong with my life could now be rectified. I was overcome with emotion. My first thought was to call Isabella and tell her.

"Mr. Velázquez?" she said again. "I know that this is probably a shock to you."

"This is definitely a shock," I repeated with a huge smile on my face. "You have no idea how this has just changed my life."

"Lo siento, Mr. Velázquez. You should probably speak to Miss Fonseca further about this."

I could hear in her voice that she felt bad for me, but she shouldn't. This was exactly what I needed to hear. She was right about needing to speak to Casey. I wasn't the father which meant that Casey had been lying this entire time. *That bitch.* Did she know that I wasn't the father? Did she do this on purpose? Or was this going to be just as much of a shock to her as it was to me?

"I will. Thank you for the call, doctor."

"You are welcome," she said. *"Feliz Navidad."*

I returned her season's greetings before disconnecting the call. I was so distracted that the car behind me had to hoot to get me to move.

I'm not the father.

Oh my God, I am not the father.

That means everything I just went through with Isabella was for nothing. All the heartbreaks and watching her walk out of my life was for nothing. There was no reason why Isabella and I couldn't be together.

"Joder," I repeated out loud, trying to process the information.

I couldn't focus on anything else but telling Isabella. I needed her to know. I reached for my phone again and dialed her number, this time bringing my phone up to my ear. I indicated to turn down the road and followed the flow of traffic as I tapped my fingers on the steering wheel. We reached another red light.

"Come on, pick up," I muttered, listening to the sound of the ringing on the other end.

The traffic light turned green as I got her voicemail.

Hi, this is Isabella, leave a message.

"Isabella, it's me. I need you to call me back right now." I put my car into first gear and stepped on the gas. "I have to tell you something. Everything is going to be fine with us, but I need you to ca-".

Before I could continue, the sound of shrieking tires caught my attention. I turned towards the sound and watched as a car slid across the road and crashed into me, sending me into darkness.

CHAPTER 53:

Isabella

"Start the popcorn. I'm just getting dressed," I shouted to Reyna from my room.

We had finished off the last of our attempt at a spring-clean and I quickly took a shower before we were going to binge-watch something on Netflix. I was exhausted - mentally and physically so I was looking forward to mindless watching right now. I quickly got changed, ensuring I had multiple layers to keep out the cold lingering breeze that the storm had caused. I heard a phone ringing in the distance. I had put mine on the charger before I stepped into the shower. It had died earlier, but I didn't have the energy to turn it back on. I didn't want to see the messages that I was pretty sure I had received from Lorenzo. I also didn't want to be reminded of the fact that there wouldn't be a message from Giovanni. I couldn't bring myself to change my wallpaper either so I'd have to see his smiling face looking up at me and I just didn't have it in me.

"Isabella!" Reyna shouted from the lounge.

I strolled down the hallway leading into the kitchen as Reyna's worried face came into view.

"What's going on?" I asked, the sudden concern building up inside of me.

She had her phone to her ear, listening intently to the person on the other end. "Okay, let us know which hospital."

Hospital? Now, I was definitely worried.

"Reyna, what's going on?"

"I'll let you know when we get there, Alvaro."

Alvaro? Oh my God. What was going on? What could possibly be the reason for Reyna to be speaking to Giovanni's brother right now?

Oh no.

Giovanni.

A sick feeling entered my stomach and I was consumed by the fear of what could be coming next. Reyna hung up the phone and walked over to me, not being able to contain the fear across her face.

"Izzy, I need you to listen to me carefully okay?" she said gently.

"Reyna, what the hell is going on here?" My voice is shaking now. "You're scaring me."

"Giovanni was in a car accident."

I jerked my head back trying to process what she had just told me.

Giovanni was in an accident?

Oh my God.

My sweet sweet Giovanni. *What was happening?* The sick feeling inside my stomach turned to a deep fear I had never experienced before and I felt my throat tighten. I couldn't pay attention to anything else that she was saying. Her voice became nothing but a distant murmur. I was bombarded with fragmented thoughts about him and the sickening fear of what was going to happen next.

"Izzy? Are you listening to me?" Reyna snapped me out of my trance.

I turned back to her, swallowing as a numb feeling settled over me. "What did you say?"

"I said they're on the way to the hospital with him now. Some drunk driver skipped a red light and hit his side of the car," her voice quaked as she tried to keep it together for my sake. "We need to go meet Alvaro at the hospital."

"Is he okay?" I managed to choke.

Her eyes dropped. "They don't know yet. The paramedics on the scene were helping him, but they don't know yet how bad his injuries are."

A deep pain from within spread throughout my body, suffocating me in its wake. I couldn't comprehend what I was hearing right now. There was no way this could be true. The world wasn't that cruel.

I didn't even realise that the tears were streaming down my face until Reyna pulled me in for a hug and I cried into her shoulder. I was drowning in my own guilt and regret. Here I was trying to figure out if I should be with Giovanni or not and now there was a possibility that it wouldn't be up to me. Everything with Casey and the baby seemed so insignificant now that I was faced with the fear of losing him.

I couldn't lose him.

Reyna let go of me and started grabbing everything we needed. I couldn't move. I stood frozen, trying to process everything. There was no way this was happening. No. I wouldn't accept that. This was all just a big misunderstanding. There was no way Giovanni was in an accident.

No, no, no.

The more I tried to convince myself this wasn't happening, the more the reality of the situation started to settle. My heart shattered into a million pieces. A gut-wrenching pain pulled inside of me and I became short of breath.

There was no way this was happening.

***

By the time we arrived at the hospital, I had gone through the denial stage and went straight to needing answers. I pushed through the doors of the hospital and was welcomed by the all-consuming smell of disinfectant that every hospital had. I made my way to reception with Reyna following closely behind me.

"*Hola,* I'm looking for an emergency patient that was just brought in. His name is Giovanni Velázquez," I didn't even recognize my own voice as I asked the receptionist to point me in the right direction.

She nodded and turned to her computer, but before she could answer, I heard Penelope's voice from behind me.

"Isabella!" she exclaimed.

I turned to meet her worried eyes. She was holding Mateo in her arms and walked over to us, quickly introducing herself to Reyna.

"Penelope, thank goodness." I pulled her in for a quick hug, careful not to disturb a sleeping Mateo. "Where is he?"

"They've just taken him into surgery," I could hear the emotion in her voice. "They were saying something about the blunt trauma and internal bleeding. I'm sorry, it was all so much."

"Where's Alvaro?"

"I'll take you to him."

She led us down the hallway in the direction of the ICU waiting room. Everything was a blur around me under these blinding fluorescent lights. I didn't expect to be back at the hospital so soon and I definitely never thought it would be because of Giovanni. Just the mere thought that he wouldn't make it out of this was sending me off the edge. It was a thought that I couldn't entertain. Not even for a second. I had to hold back the blood-curdling cry that was building up inside of me just at the thought of losing him. We reached the waiting room and Alvaro sat in the corner with his head in his hands.

I walked up to him. "Alvaro?"

He looked up, his dark brown eyes stained with tears. "Isabella."

He stood up and pulled me in for a hug, the emotions suddenly overcoming me.

"What happened?" I managed to get out.

He pulled away and sat back down, leading me to sit down next to him. He wiped his tears and took a deep breath in.

"I got a call from the paramedics on site. They told me a drunk driver ran a red light and the car hit Giovanni's side," his voice cracked. "He was already unconscious when they arrived on the scene."

A huge lump started to form in my throat and I clenched my jaw trying to contain my emotion.

"They said the blunt trauma could be causing internal bleeding. They mentioned something about abdominal swelling and trauma to the spleen. I didn't understand everything they were saying."

I reached out and squeezed his hand. "Is he going to be okay?"

His tear-filled eyes met mine. "They don't know yet, Izzy. They don't know how bad his injuries are."

I swallowed in an attempt to get rid of the pain building up in my throat from holding back my tears. I clenched my jaw and closed my eyes, allowing the pain to consume me. That was all I felt right now. Shooting through my veins was a deep pain I had never experienced before. The hollowness I felt before was nothing compared to the fear of him not making it out of this alive. I couldn't allow myself to think that way. I just couldn't. The air around me became thin and I started to feel dizzy.

"Izzy, hey, look at me," Reyna said, sitting down next to me as she pulled on my hand.

"I can't lose him," I choked, the tears streaming down my face. "This can't be happening."

"Hey, everything is going to be okay." She cupped my face. "The doctors are going to do everything they can."

What if that wasn't enough?

CHAPTER 54:
Isabella

We sat in that waiting room for hours. I was losing track of how long we just sat waiting for answers. Each moment that passed was torture. I was drowning in pain and every time I tried to reach for air, the reality of what was happening kept pulling me further and further from it. I was sick to my stomach with guilt. I felt so guilty that I left Giovanni this morning. I felt guilty that this whole time I was trying to figure out if our relationship was going to last or if I was going to walk away for good. Now, I didn't care about any of that. I didn't care about any of the reasons for us not to be together. I just needed to be with him. I loved him in a way that consumed every part of me. With his witty charm and seductive confidence. The way he would throw his head back in laughter, displaying the deep dimple in his left cheek. His spontaneous and care-free energy that I always found contagious. The way he would pull me into his arms and tell me how much he loved me. He had a raw sex-appeal to him but I had come to fall in love with his heart. The same heart that cared for everyone around him more than himself. He was too good for this world. How could I have ever wanted to give him up?

Now, I would give anything just to have another moment with him.

Giovanni's parents arrived shortly after I did and I couldn't hold my emotions back when I saw Marcina's grief-stricken face. She cried into my shoulder, repeating over and over again how she needed her son to be okay. Cecilio was still in shock but I could see the fear in his eyes. It was the most emotion I had ever seen him show. Sergio and Katrina were the next to arrive after Reyna called them to tell them what had happened. Both of them threw their arms around me when they arrived, trying to console me and repeating that everything would be fine. Each passing moment without a word from the doctors was killing me. I was curled up on the chair in the corner, staring into the distance. I was starting to feel numb again. There was no pain - I couldn't allow there to be. Every time it seeped into my heart, I felt it shatter over and over again. The possibility that the doctor could walk up to us now and tell us that they did everything they could, but they couldn't save him.

That could not happen.

I couldn't lose Giovanni. He was everything to me and I couldn't believe it took me this long to realise that. It took him having to be in an accident for me to get the wake-up call that I needed. I would never be able to live with myself if something happened to him. The regret I was feeling from walking away from him was all-consuming. The guilt of constantly putting him through the back and forth of whether I could accept this new change in his life. All of that was a mere speck in our universe. I needed him more than I had ever needed anyone before.

I couldn't lose him.

"Señor y señora Velázquez?" an older doctor said, bringing me out of my own thoughts.

I jerked my head up as I watched Giovanni's parents stand up and walk over to the doctor standing in dark blue scrubs. He was a much older gentleman with a kind face. He continued to speak to them in Spanish and I looked over to Alvaro for a translation - the anticipation was killing me.

"He says that there was some internal bleeding due to the blunt trauma to his spleen that caused his abdomen to swell."

He listened intently as the doctor continued.

"They managed to remove the spleen and the swelling has been reduced."

"That's a good sign."

I slowly started to breathe a sigh of relief, but still waited in fear over if he was going to be okay or not. That was all I needed to hear. I didn't care about any of the medical lingo. I just needed to know that the love of my life was going to make it out of here alive.

"He's got a broken leg and he is in ICU now, but the doctor thinks the worst is over and he should be fine."

Marcina turned to Cecilio and cried tears of relief into his shoulder. I collapsed back against the chair, bringing my knees to my chest as I allowed my own tears to fall.

Oh my God, thank you.

Reyna's arms came around me, pulling me closer to her as I continued to cry. I was crying out of relief. I was so consumed by the fear that I could have lost him that I didn't even know how to breathe. I had never felt pain like that before and the fact that he was going to be okay was all I needed to hear.

He needed to be okay.

That was all I cared about right now.

"Can we see him?" I asked Alvaro.

Alvaro turned to the doctor and asked my question. The doctor nodded and proceeded to say something further in Spanish. Alvaro thanked him before turning back to me.

"They're moving him into ICU so we should be able to see him before we leave, but they're still waiting for him to wake up."

"That's okay," I answered quickly. "I just need to see him."

I tapped my nails against the armrest of the chair as I waited for them to give us the go-ahead that we could go and see him. I was full of nerves and I just needed to see Giovanni. Just one glance at him and everything would be better now that we knew he would be okay. I wanted to tell him how much I loved him and that I wasn't going anywhere.

Not now. Not ever.

***

After what felt like forever to me, we finally got the go-ahead from the doctor that Giovanni had been successfully moved to ICU and we could go and see him.

"Isabella?" Penelope's voice brought me out of my thoughts and I glanced up at her. "We can go in now."

I turned to Marcina and Cecilio. "You should go in first."

Marcina's eyes were full of tears as she reached out and squeezed my hand before standing up. I was dying to see him, but I had to let his parents go first. I was scared of what I was going to see when I went inside. He was in a car accident and with the injuries they were explaining, he was probably in so much pain. It made my heart ache at the idea of him in pain.

A little while later, Giovanni's parents stepped outside of the ward, Cecilio's arms still around his wife as he consoled her.

"Isabella, you can go in." Alvaro said softly.

I nodded and stood up, taking a deep breath in before taking off down the hall. My heart was beating at an incessant pace as I tried to calm myself down. I pushed myself through the doors and was surrounded by the sound of constant beeping from the machines. There were a couple other patients in the ward, but the nurse pointed me to his bed in the corner. I turned and started to approach his bed, my breath getting caught in my throat as he came into view. He was hooked up to so many machines around him. He had a plastic pipe in his nose and his hand was resting on his stomach, displaying the pipe that the drip was hooked up to. His leg was in a cast and was elevated by the material hanging from the roof. He had marks and dried blood on his face along his cheek and I couldn't hold back my emotion any longer. I allowed the tears to escape from my eyes as I pulled the chair closer to his bed. I was thankful for the small rising and falling of his chest.

He was alive and that was all that mattered to me.

"Giovanni, I don't know if you can hear me," I started, my voice full of emotion. "I can't apologize enough for everything. I am sorry for walking away from you. I am sorry for leaving this morning and for telling you I needed some time. I don't need any time."

The tears were streaming down my face as I gently tightened my grip around his warm hand.

"When Reyna told me you were in an accident," my voice cracked. "I have never felt pain like that before. I just needed you to be okay and now you're going to be and I take it all back. I want to be with you. I have never loved anyone like I have you, Giovanni."

I leaned my forehead against his hand. "I don't care about any of the other shit we have to deal with, I can't imagine living without you."

I didn't know if he could hear what I was saying, but I needed to get it out. I needed to apologize and remind him of how much I loved him. It's crazy how one life changing moment can put everything into perspective. I didn't want to waste another moment being without him.

He is the love of my life.

"So, I'm going to be here when you wake up. I'm going to be here tomorrow and every day after that."

I brought my eyes up to his face. The beautiful face I love so much that was now covered in marks. There was a deep cut under his left eye and I reached out and brushed my fingers over it. The sight of him in pain brought on another wave of emotion. I cupped his face, the feeling of his rough beard brushed up against my hand.

"I love you so much, Giovanni," I murmured. "And I'm never going to leave you again."

CHAPTER 55:
Giovanni

There was nothing but darkness. Complete and utter darkness. I looked around and I couldn't make out anything in the distance. I reached out in front of me and I couldn't see my hands. It didn't matter where I looked, there was no light and I started to feel unsettled.

I didn't know where I was and it terrified me. I felt completely paralysed with no idea how to begin to find my way back. I tried to move but I couldn't - I was riddled with pain across my entire body. I wasn't even able to move and still, my body ached. Every inch of it ached and I couldn't understand where this pain was coming from.

Suddenly, I heard her voice in the distance.

She was close by, but I couldn't figure out where. I looked around again, trying to find her voice, but wherever I looked, there was nothing. Just the constant echo of her voice. I tried to focus on her words. She was speaking to me, but I couldn't piece together exactly what she was saying.

Come on, Giovanni.

The voice in my head was screaming at me to focus. I needed to focus on her voice. I took a deep breath in trying to get a handle on the rising anxiety in my chest.

Focus on Isabella. Focus on her voice.

"...I needed some time. I don't need any time, Giovanni."

What was she talking about?

I could hear she was crying. It pained me to hear the clear sadness in her voice and I tried to call out for her. I repeated her name over and over again trying to tell her that I'm here and I can hear her, but the words never reached my mouth. I couldn't form the words. I couldn't even move.

"When Reyna told me you were in an accident," she continued.

Accident? What was she talking about? When was I in a-

Oh wait.

The memories came flooding back to me. Sitting in the car, driving through the rain as I tried to dial her number and tell her what Dr. Gonzalez told me. I remembered the overwhelming happiness that washed over me as she confirmed I was not the father. I remembered the excitement of wanting to tell Isabella so we could get our lives back on track - together this time. I remember begging her to pick up the phone before I heard the shrieking tires against the road and then there was nothing.

Just darkness consumed me.

The same way it was consuming me now. *Was I dead?* Surely, there was no way that was true? I could hear Isabella's voice which must mean something. I tried to focus on what else I could hear around me. I started to focus on the constant beeping around me before I got distracted by the feeling of her hand in mine. I could feel her. The warmth of her hand spread across mine as she squeezed.

"I'm here, Isabella," I tried to say. "I can hear you and I can feel you."

But nothing came out. No movement. No words left my lips. I was so angry at myself.

Come on, Giovanni - get your shit together!

I repeated that over and over again, but there was nothing. I couldn't move or form the words I needed right now. There was nothing I could do right now to get her attention.

"So, I'm going to be here when you wake up. I'm going to be here tomorrow and every day after that."

I couldn't believe what she was saying. She wanted to be with me again and I couldn't react. I couldn't comfort her. All I wanted to do was tell her how much I loved her and that I just wanted to be with her.

"I love you so much, Giovanni," her sad voice murmured in the distance.

I love you, Isabella. I love you so much.

I kept screaming that, hoping that eventually the words would reach my lips and she would know. I needed her to know how much I loved her and that everything was going to be okay now. We were going to be okay. The more I shouted for her, the further away from me she started to become and then eventually, there was nothing but the darkness again.

CHAPTER 56:
Isabella

Just after three in the morning, I unlocked the door of my apartment and pushed through as Reyna shut it behind us. Now that Giovanni had been moved to a ward, we couldn't stay at the hospital any longer. We had to come back in the morning for visiting hours. Thankfully, that wasn't too far from now since we spent most of the night and the early hours of this morning waiting to hear what happened with the surgery.

"Can I get you something?" Reyna offered. "I can make us something to eat."

I shook my head. "I'm not hungry."

I still had tears in my eyes and the hovering pain from earlier was still present. I was so happy that he was going to be okay, but I just wanted him to wake up. I wanted to hear his voice again and to know that he was fine now. Seeing him hooked up to all the machines and the marks on his face just broke my heart. I hated knowing that he was in pain and there was nothing I could do to take it away.

"I'm going to take a shower." Reyna walked over to me. "I think you should try and get some rest."

"I'll try."

She pulled me in for one last hug before disappearing down the hall. I took a deep breath in and pulled myself up onto the bar stool by the counter. Sudden exhaustion washed over my body and I couldn't hold back a yawn. The emotional rollercoaster I was on tonight had drained me. We had left in such a hurry earlier that I didn't even grab my cellphone. It was still lying on the counter where I left it. I reached for it and disconnected it from the charger.

I turned it on and waited for everything to load. I was tapping my fingers nervously on the counter. I hadn't quite wrapped my head around the events of the evening. I couldn't believe that Giovanni was in an accident and that I had almost lost him. That thought alone brought on a wave of nausea and I couldn't hold back the tears anymore. I allowed them to stream down my face as I glanced down at my phone, my notifications now popping up. I scrolled through them and my heart dropped as I saw Giovanni's name on my screen.

Oh my God, he had left me a voicemail.

My hands were trembling as I reached for my phone and brought it to my ear.

"Isabella, it's me," his voice came through the other side and my tears filled again. "I need you to call me back right now. I have to tell you something - everything is going to be fine with us, but I need you to ca-".

And then suddenly I heard the sound of shrieking tires in the distance before the call disconnected.

The ache in my chest worsened. He was trying to get a hold of me before the car hit him. I couldn't hold myself together any longer. I hung my head in my hands and cried, allowing the pain to consume me. He said he had something to tell me. He tried to phone me earlier and I wasn't there to answer. I just let it go to voicemail and I felt sick to my stomach with guilt. I just needed him to be awake when we went back to the hospital tomorrow.

I needed to apologize to him.

I grabbed my phone again and dragged myself to my room, dropping onto my bed and fell into a deep sleep.

***

When I woke up the next morning, I was convinced that it had all been a horrible nightmare. Until I was reminded of what really happened and I was consumed by the same pain I had felt the day before. Giovanni was in a car accident. He was going to be okay, but they were still waiting for him to wake up. I was sick with anxiety over that. I would only start to feel better once I saw him awake. Then I would know for sure that he was here with me again and he wasn't going anywhere. I was thankful for the few hours of sleep I had managed to get, but I could feel the lingering exhaustion. I was way too eager to get to the hospital so I had already showered and was ready to go.

Reyna strolled into the kitchen, still in her pajamas.

"What are you doing?" she asked. "Are you going to the hospital now?"

I nodded and reached for my handbag that was hanging on our coat rack by the door. "I need to go and see him and visiting hours are soon."

"Visiting hours aren't for another two hours, Izzy," she said softly. "Don't you want to have something to eat first?"

I shook my head and walked back to the counter to grab my phone. "I just need to be at the hospital in case anything happens."

"Nothing is going to happen." She reached for my hand. "Izzy, hey, stop and look at me."

I stopped and looked over at her.

"Giovanni is fine. The doctors said he was going to be just fine."

"But he's not awake yet," I objected.

"He needs his rest. He was in an accident, he's going to need time to recover," she said softly.

She was right. Of course, he was going to need time to rest. I was just far too anxious to see him again. I needed to see him.

"If you give me a bit of time, I can come with you."

"No Rey, your parents are arriving soon," I reminded her. "You have to fetch them from the airport."

"I forgot all about that." She poured hot water into a cup to make herself some coffee. "I can ask Katrina and Sergio to do it."

"You don't have to do that," I objected. "But I don't think I'm going to come through tonight for dinner. I need to stay wi-".

"Hey, Izzy," she stopped me and reached for my hand again. "You don't need to explain. Of course, you should go and be with Giovanni."

I squeezed her hand. "Thank you."

"But I'm not letting you go to the hospital alone so give me 15 minutes tops and I'll be ready to go."

I opened my mouth to object to her offer again, but she ignored me and walked back to her room, cup of coffee in hand. I sighed and leaned against the counter. I was dying to get to the hospital again. I just had to see him. My stomach growled, reminding me of the lack of food in my system so I walked over to the bread bin and grabbed a slice of bread, placing it in the toaster. As I was reaching for a plate from the cupboard, my phone started to ring. I turned back and glanced down seeing my father's name on the screen.

I grabbed it and brought it to my ear. "Hi dad, how a-".

"Hi, Isabella," My mother's voice greeted me on the other end.

I stopped in my tracks. "Mom? Why are you phoning me off dad's phone?"

"Because you wouldn't have answered if I had called off mine."

She wasn't wrong. We had left things on very bad terms when I left London and I had no desire to try and save a relationship that was already so damaged. She had made her feelings very clear and I didn't care for them.

"Why are you phoning me at all?"

"Because I'm your mother, Isabella, and you can't ignore me forever."

I scoffed. "I hardly think you and I have anything to speak about."

"Well, how are you doing?" she asked, not being able to hide how uncomfortable this conversation was making her.

My mother was never one for small talk. She was never one to reach out to find out how people were doing. That would require her to have feelings and she had proven over and over again how incapable she was of that.

"I've been better."

I was not about to get into a conversation about how I was really doing with her. The fact she had called me at all was making me feel incredibly uneasy.

"Are you not coming home for Christmas?" she asked.

"I am home."

I could practically hear her rolling her eyes over the phone. "London is your home."

"Oh God, Mom, not this again," I groaned. "I don't have time to have this argument again with you."

"I'm not trying to argue with you, Isabella," she retorted. "I just wanted to see if you would be joining your family for Christmas. It's Christmas Eve already and you've given no indication that you'd be coming home."

"Because I'm not," I argued. "I already told dad that. I have my own life here and that hasn't changed. Clearly, you haven't changed either it would seem."

"What's that supposed to mean?"

"I mean you seriously called me believing I would be coming home for

Christmas," I argued, "How could you possibly think that would be happening? We haven't spoken in weeks and you've made your feelings about my life perfectly clear."

"I know I was a bit harsh the last time we spoke, but I just thought things would have been different by now."

"You mean you thought your little plan with Nate would have worked and I would have gone back to him and back to the life you tried to force on me?" I snapped.

She was silent for a moment before answering, "You spoke to Nate?"

"Yes, and listened to his attempt to win me back after you advised he would have had a chance." I laughed at that thought. "You really disrespected my relationship with Giovanni by doing that, you do realize that right?"

"You're not still with that club owner are you?" she scoffed.

I didn't have the patience to do this today. I didn't have the patience to deal with this ever again. Time and time again she continued to prove how little she respected me and the choices I made. I spent so much time being sad over our broken relationship, but it's very clear to me now that it was meant to stay broken.

"His name is Giovanni," I clarified. "And that same *club owner* is lying in hospital now after being in a car accident, but you wouldn't know that. You wouldn't know anything about my life because of the choices you have made."

"He was in a car accident?" she repeated, a flicker of emotion in her voice.

"Yes mother, a really bad one," my voice cracked.

"I'm sorry to hear that."

I could hear the emotion in her voice, but I didn't believe her. Even if she was trying to be genuine, I just couldn't accept that because that wasn't who she was. She had no problem disrespecting my relationship with Giovanni so no, I didn't think she actually cared about him.

I ignored her previous statement and continued with my own thoughts. "I just want you to take a moment and think about what you just did. You were the one who called me and for what? So, you could continue to take digs at my life and my choices. It's been weeks since we spoke and you still don't realise why I want nothing to do with you. Just take a look at what you keep doing to me, why can't you just leave me alone?"

"I'm your mother, Isabella," she muttered, a hint of sadness coming through.

"Well, you're not acting like it. You just can't accept the fact that you can't control me anymore."

"I just want my daughter back."

I took a deep breath in before responding. "I am not the Isabella that you once knew and I'm okay with that. I like who I am now and I think you would like me too if you actually gave our relationship a chance. I have made a life for myself here and I am happy with the way I have chosen to live it but until you accept that, you won't be hearing from me again."

She took a moment before responding. "Merry Christmas, Isabella."

And with that, she disconnected the call.

I was shaking with anger and sadness. *What the fuck was the point of all that?* She didn't want to make amends unless it was on her terms. Every interaction with her was making it easier and easier to accept that our relationship had reached a point of no return. I didn't want to have to constantly deal with her general disrespect of my life.

"Seriously?" I groaned, replaying the conversation in my head.

I stopped and took a deep breath in, trying to focus on nothing more than my breathing. *In and out*. I repeated this until I slowly started to feel the anger leave my body with each breath. My toast popped up and I opened my eyes, feeling better acquainted with myself at that moment.

"Okay, I'm ready to go," Reyna announced, walking back into the kitchen.

I reached for my toast and my handbag, placing it over my shoulder. "Let's get going then."

CHAPTER 57:
Giovanni

I opened my eyes and was greeted by the bright fluorescent lights shining down on me. I closed them again before trying to open them slowly, this time prepared for the bright lights. I could hear the constant beeping again and tried to look around to see where it was coming from. I was definitely in a hospital, that much was clear but I couldn't move. There was pain all over my body. I was so disorientated trying to gather my bearings.

"Buenas dias, Señor Velázquez," I heard a voice say and I slowly turned in the direction of it.

A younger-looking nurse walked over to my left side, suddenly coming into my view. She smiled at me sweetly. "How are we feeling this morning?"

"O-okay," I stuttered.

I swallowed, the feeling of my dry mouth urging me to ask for water. I couldn't move so I wouldn't be able to get it myself.

"Water," I managed to get out. "Water, *por favor*?"

"Si, Señor." She turned and reached for a small cup with a straw sticking out. She brought it to my lips and I welcomed it, slowly sucking on it as I felt the water on my tongue. It was like a breath of fresh air after suffocating. I took another sip before she moved it back to the table.

"What happened?" I asked.

"You were in a very bad car accident," she explained. "But the doctor says you're going to be just fine. I'm sure he'll be here soon to explain more."

"Gracias."

She gave me a small nod before she left my side. I was left with nothing but the ceiling for company as I stared up at it trying to rack my brain around what happened. Everything was a blur in my mind. I remembered driving back to the city. I remembered the storm. I remembered Isabella.

Isabella? When was the last time I saw her?

I tried to think back. I remembered her voice and her hand in mine. She was apologising to me. She must have been here because it was after the accident. The memories of the accident came flooding back. The feeling of being thrown into darkness and not being able to move. I remembered the pain which was much worse than what I was experiencing now and I was thankful for that. I remembered trying to call Isabella and tell her about the paternity test.

Oh yes, the paternity test results.

I remembered the fact that I was not the father of Casey's baby and the happiness inside of me returned. I just needed to see Isabella and tell her. I needed to tell her that we were going to be okay. I didn't care about the pain I was in or the fact that I was in an accident at all, I just needed to see her again and tell her.

Between the exhaustion and the pain, my eyes slowly started to close again. I tried to keep them open, hoping that someone would come and see me but I couldn't any longer. I shut my eyes and welcomed the sleep.

***

"Giovanni?" I heard her voice in the distance. "Can you hear me? The nurse said you were awake earlier."

I could hear her voice but I couldn't move again. I was paralysed and the frustration started to build up inside of me.

Come on, Giovanni. Focus on her voice.

"I needed to come and see how you're doing," she murmured.

I focused on nothing but her voice as I took a deep breath in. I needed to see her again and I used all the strength I had inside of me to open my eyes. After a couple more moments of darkness, I was finally greeted by those bright lights again.

"Oh my God!" she exclaimed and her face came into view. "You're awake!"

She had been crying. I could see her eyes were still filled with tears and they were red and puffy. Even with the clear sadness in them, she still looked beautiful. She was a natural beauty - not a drop of makeup was on her face and I had never seen anyone look more perfect.

"Hi baby," I murmured.

"You're awake," she kept repeating as she grabbed my hand and leaned her forehead against it, the tears slowly escaping her eyes. "I can't believe you're awake."

"Hey, don't cry." I slowly lifted my other hand, bringing it over hers.

"I'm so happy that you're okay," she cried. "I was so scared that I was going to lose you. I was here yesterday."

I remembered her words. I remembered her apologising and telling me that she wasn't going anywhere. She didn't know it, but I had heard everything she said.

"I'm so sorry, Giovanni," she murmured. "I am so sorry for everything and for leaving like I did and for saying I ne-".

I stopped her. "Isabella, hey, look at me."

Her hazel eyes met mine.

"You don't have anything to apologize for," I assured her.

"Of course I do." She tightened her grip on my hand. "I left because I needed to think about if I wanted to be with you. How stupid could I be? Of course, I want to be with you. The fact that I almost lost you..."

She stopped her sentence as she was overcome with a new wave of tears. She leaned closer to me, resting her head on my hand again.

"You didn't lose me, baby. You're never going to lose me." I lifted my hand slowly and ran my fingers through her hair as best as I could. "Everything is fine."

"It's not fine," she said. "And I didn't even know you tried to call me till I listened to your voicemail this morning."

Voicemail?

Oh yes - I had called Isabella to tell her about the results when the car hit. That was really bad timing, but I didn't dwell on it for too long. I was far too eager to tell her about the results.

"Isabella," I said softly. "Baby, look at me."

She lifted her gaze to mine again, her eyes swimming with sadness.

"I don't want you to cry anymore. You have nothing to worry about - everything is going to be fine."

She nodded and gave me a small smile. "I was just so scared of losing you. I don't care about Casey and the baby. I want to be with you Giovanni, doesn't matter what it takes."

My heart warmed at her words. She was willing to put herself through that because she loved me enough to be with me.

"You don't have to worry about Casey and the baby," I said.

"Of course, I do," she objected. "And that's fine. I'll be a stepmoth-".

"You're not going to be a stepmother because I'm not going to be a father."

She froze.

CHAPTER 58:
Isabella

"What are you talking about?" I managed to get out after trying to process what he had just said.

"I'm not going to be a father," he repeated. "The baby isn't mine."

My jaw dropped and my hands jerked up to cover my mouth.

Oh my God.

What is going on here? The baby isn't his? My brain was imploding with all the thoughts running around inside of it.

"I don't understand," I said as calmly as I could manage.

I watched as he tried to shift himself higher on the bed. I stood up to try and help, but I wasn't even sure how I could. He managed to move himself to an elevated seated position and I fixed the pillow behind his head to make sure he was more comfortable. I could see the distress on his face just from those small movements.

He reached for my hand and took it in his as he leaned his head to the side to look at me. "A few weeks ago, I did a paternity test to find out if I really was the father of Casey's baby."

"A few weeks ago?" I repeated.

"Yes, it was actually Reyna's idea an-".

"Reyna?" I interrupted. "The two of you knew about this weeks ago and you didn't tell me?"

"Don't be mad," he murmured. "We had a good reason. I didn't want to tell you about it and get your hopes up because there was still a possibility the baby could have been mine."

I wanted to be mad about them not telling me, but I couldn't. I understood why he chose not to tell me. I couldn't imagine the pain if he had gotten my hopes up for the life we wanted for it to be ripped away from me again. My heart wouldn't have been able to take it.

"So, the baby isn't yours?" I asked slowly.

He shook his head.

I couldn't believe it. I leaned back against the chair, staring straight ahead of me as I processed this. All this time lost was for nothing. All the pain and heartbreak was for nothing. All because Casey lied about Giovanni being the father of her baby. Anger deep inside of me started to flicker at the thought of her and her deceit.

"Please say something," he said softly.

"I don't know what to say," I admitted."I think I'm in shock."

He chuckled. "That's understandable."

"Did Casey know this whole time that you weren't the father?"

"I have no idea. I haven't spoken to her. I got the phone call from her doctor and then I tried to call you and then this happened." he gestured to the hospital room. "How long have I been here?"

"Only a day," I said. "The paramedics brought you in yesterday and the doctors took you straight to surgery. It was a long surgery."

"What's the damage?" he asked, attempting to make light of the situation.

"Well, your leg is broken and you have some cuts on your face."

"That's not so bad."

"Oh, and they removed your spleen."

He lifted his eyebrows. "Can you live without a spleen?"

I burst out laughing. "I'm going to say yes since they removed it and you're still here."

He chuckled and leaned his head back against the pillow, closing his eyes.

"I've definitely never spent Christmas Eve in a hospital room," I joked.

He opened his eyes and peeped at me. "Is it really Christmas Eve?"

I nodded. "Our first Christmas together and this is how you choose to spend it."

He laughed at my attempt at a joke and I couldn't help but smile. It was so good to hear him laugh again. It was my favourite sound and I just wanted to keep hearing it. He closed his eyes again and he had a smile on his face that just warmed my heart at the sight of it. I couldn't believe he was here. I couldn't believe that after everything, he and I could be together again. I was so ready to accept anything in his life but knowing now that he wasn't the father of Casey's baby was the news I didn't think I needed to hear today. My heart was bursting with happiness.

I could finally see our future again and this time it was the way I wanted it to be.

***

I had to eventually drag myself away from Giovanni when his parents arrived and wanted to have some time with him during visiting hours. No more than two people were allowed in the ward at a time so I said my goodbyes and stepped outside. I told him I'd be back later because I would. I would be here for every visiting hour because I needed to make sure that he was going to be okay. Seeing him up and speaking again made me so happy. I was so happy that he was alive.

I strolled down the halls of the hospital and into the cafeteria area, spotting Reyna seated in a booth in the corner. She looked up as I started to approach the table.

"And?" She asked, her eyes full of concern. "Is he awake?"

"He's awake," I said and took a seat across from her. "His parents are with him now."

A young waiter walked over to our table and I quickly ordered myself a coffee. I was fighting the mental and physical exhaustion I was feeling.

"You must be so relieved."

"I am," I admitted. "I feel like all the adrenaline has made its way out of my system and it's really hitting me how absolutely terrifying that all was."

Thinking back to how differently this could have gone was shocking to me. I could have easily lost Giovanni yesterday, but thank goodness that was not in the plan for us. We still had so much we had to do together. We still had a whole life ahead of us to live.

And now we didn't have to worry about Casey being a part of it.

I turned to face Reyna. "Giovanni told me he asked Casey for a paternity test."

She couldn't hide the surprise on her face. "Why would he tell you that? I specifically told him not to until he had the results."

"Well, he got the results. He's not the father."

This time her jaw dropped as I watched her process what I had just told her. I hadn't quite wrapped my brain around it myself, but I could feel the happiness inside of me over it.

"He's not?" She finally managed to ask.

I shook my head. "He said the doctor called him yesterday and told him. He was trying to phone me when he got into the accident."

I felt so incredibly guilty over that. He was trying to get a hold of me and I didn't even bother answering his call. What if that was the last I ever heard from him?

Isabella, stop.

The voice in my head was right. I didn't need to think of the *what if's* or the *maybe's*. All I could think about now was that we were given a second chance to be together and we had to take it.

"Oh my fuck!" she exclaimed. "You must be so happy!"

I chuckled. "Of course I am. I can't believe we wasted all this time over something that wasn't true. Why did you tell him to get a paternity test?"

"Well, I was secretly rooting for the two of you," she admitted. "I had never seen the two of you the way you were when you were together. Something just felt off about the timing of the whole thing and I wanted him to make sure before he said anything to you."

"He explained that. Said you guys didn't want to get my hopes up."

She shrugged. "The last thing I would have wanted was for you to get your heart broken all over again."

I reached across the table and squeezed her hand. She had always watched out for my feelings and this situation was no different. She was just being a good friend and I couldn't fault her on that.

"So, does that mean you guys are back together?" she asked.

I couldn't help the smile forming on my lips. "I think I'm just focused on making sure he gets home where he can recover and then we'll talk about all that. After what happened yesterday, I would have been with him no matter what it took. If that meant Casey and a baby then so be it because I've never felt fear like that before."

She squeezed my hand. "That's all in the past now. Giovanni is absolutely fine and the two of you are absolutely fine, too."

The waiter returned with my coffee, placing it down in front of me.

"Gracias."

He smiled before turning, leaving us to continue our conversation. Reyna was telling me all about her parents arriving and how excited they were to meet Sergio's family when a tall, blonde figure caught the corner of my eye. I turned towards the entrance and watched Casey wander into the reception area. I heard Reyna stop mid-sentence as she followed my gaze.

"What the hell is she doing here?" she asked.

Before I could answer, I was making my way in her direction. There was a fair amount of anger I had towards her and she had no right to be here right now. She had already reached the receptionist when I stopped behind her.

"Casey?"

She turned and I could see the surprise in her eyes. "Isabella?"

"What do you think you're doing here?"

"I heard Giovanni was in an accident." She turned to thank the receptionist and stepped away from her. "I needed to come and see him."

The audacity of this woman. After everything she had put Giovanni through, she still believed she had a right to be here right now. I couldn't help but focus on anything but the anger inside of me.

"You have no right to be here."

She crossed her arms. "Now, Isabella, I hardly think your hostility is necessary."

"Oh, please," I scoffed. "I think it's completely necessary. You're the last person Giovanni would want to see right now."

She was glaring at me now. "You don't know what he wants."

"He definitely doesn't want the woman who lied to him about carrying his baby to be here right now."

Her eyes widened and I watched as she clenched her jaw, trying to process what I had said. Now she knew that I knew about the results and there was no going back. It was out in the open and we had to deal with this now.

"I didn't lie to him," she muttered.

"Casey, your doctor told him the results. He knows he is not the baby's father so yeah, I think you did lie."

"No, I didn't!" she snapped. "I knew there was a chance it wasn't his, but I didn't know for sure."

"That's still lying."

I couldn't comprehend the way she truly believed she didn't lie to him. Not telling him the whole truth means she was lying. How difficult was that to understand?

"Do you have any idea what your lies did to our relationship?" I asked. "And the humiliation you put me through finding out in the press! I never thanked you for that."

I was being unnecessarily sarcastic right now, but I couldn't control my tongue when I was angry.

"It's not my fault Giovanni let you find out in the press," she muttered. "I told him before the story broke."

I rolled my eyes. "I'm not going to get into that with you right now because it's completely irrelevant, but you need to leave Casey, you shouldn't be here and you know that."

"I care about him," she objected. "You have no idea what it feels like."

She huffed and walked over to the empty chairs in the reception area. I rolled my eyes and followed her, sitting at the chair across from her.

"What are you talking about?"

"You don't know what it's like to love someone that doesn't love you back." she stared at her hands in her lap.

I took a deep breath in and clenched my jaw, trying my hardest to try and be empathetic to her. She didn't deserve it, but it was the right thing to do. I tried to think of what to say to her, but she continued before I could get a word in.

"I've loved him for years, but he has never looked at me the way he looks at you." I watched her take a deep breath and roll her eyes at her own statement. "I thought we were making good progress before you came along."

I kind of felt bad for her. I remembered seeing her around *Mala Mía* a number of times. I had seen her with Giovanni but he had never reciprocated her very clear interest. He was obviously interested in her at one time and I was pretty sure that sleeping with her wasn't his smartest move. Especially if he knew how she was feeling.

"Look Casey, I'm sorry that he never felt the same about you but how could you lie to him about the baby? It's not right."

"I know that," she groaned. "I'm just so scared to do this alone."

For the first time, I noticed the emotion spreading across her face. She looked terrified and I couldn't help but feel bad at how harsh I was with her initially. She did so many things to fuck up my relationship with Giovanni, but when it came down to it, she was just afraid and I couldn't help but feel a little bad.

"Giovanni isn't your baby daddy, but someone is Casey and I'm sure you know who so you should probably start by telling him."

She looked up at me. "Why are you being so nice to me?"

A smile played on my lips but I held it back. "Because I'm not usually a bitch so I'm not going to start now."

"I'm sure there are some things you'd love to say to me though."

She was right. I'd love to call her a bitch and tell her how wrong it was that she lied. I'd love to tell her that she had no right to sabotage my relationship with Giovanni and that she didn't know the hell she put the two of us through. I'd love to tell her that she caused trust issues I never had before and that I couldn't stop thinking of the two of them together - always replaying in my head how she said they would always find their way back.

But instead, I didn't.

With everything that happened in the last twenty four hours, all I wanted was Giovanni and now I had him. Nothing else mattered to me.

"Giovanni is going to be fine," I changed the subject. "But I don't think he is going to want to see you."

She sighed and stood up, reaching for her handbag. "For what it's worth, I am sorry, Isabella."

I was surprised by her apology. She had never struck me as someone capable of being sorry for the things she had done. She had always been spiteful so this change in behaviour was completely unexpected.

She didn't wait for me to reply before turning on her heels and making her way to the exit. I let out a sigh of relief. Seeing her actually gave me the closure I needed around that entire situation. I made my way back to Reyna who was waiting anxiously at our table.

"So? Did you give her a piece of your mind?"

I chuckled and shook my head. "It really wasn't worth it."

Reyna scoffed. "You're a much better person than I am."

CHAPTER 59:

Giovanni

By the end of the week, I was being wheeled back into my apartment after being discharged. The doctors were happy with the way I was recovering and the only thing I had to deal with now was wearing a cast for the next few months. I ended up spending Christmas in my ward surrounded by Isabella, my parents, Alvaro and Penelope. It was an unusual experience given all the drama that was still going on behind the scenes, but that day, it didn't matter. Even my father was somewhat cordial to me - he even went as far as to say he was glad I wasn't dead which was probably the nicest thing he had ever said to me. My body was still weak and I was pretty sure the painkillers were causing the strange sense of calm I felt over me as I was welcomed back home.

"I'm going to put his medication on the counter," Penelope announced, walking ahead of Alvaro and me.

Alvaro was pushing my wheelchair into the lounge. I insisted on using the crutches, but the two of them were adamant that I didn't need to exert myself. He went over to help Penelope as Isabella wandered in with Mateo in her arms. She was smiling down at him and I could see the intense happiness in her eyes. She walked over to me and took a seat on the couch.

"He has got to be the cutest baby I have ever seen," she gushed.

I chuckled. "Yeah, he's pretty adorable."

He was sleeping so peacefully in her arms. I had gone back and forth about whether I wanted children when I thought Casey was having mine. I was forced to tackle that conversation head-on and I was terrified at just the thought of it. It scared me to think of becoming a father, but now seeing

Isabella with Mateo in her arms, the thought didn't scare me anymore.

With her, I wanted it all.

"Are you going to stay over?" I asked her.

She looked up at me. "Of course. I just have to stop by my place and grab a couple of things. Can I get us something for dinner while I'm out?"

"What do you have in mind?"

"Pizza?"

My stomach roared at the mention of that. The hospital food had been terrible over the last few days. I was never one for hospital food so I was ready to dig into anything I could.

"I'd eat a cardboard box right now if it meant I never had to have that hospital food again."

She threw her head back and laughed. The beautiful care-free Isabella I had come to know and love was back again. There was no pain in her eyes anymore. No sadness. No anger. Everything we had been dealing with over the last few weeks was done now and we could focus on making up for lost time.

"You're not going to have a very eventful New Year's Eve," Alvaro said from the kitchen.

He was right. New Year's Eve was tomorrow and there was no way I was going anywhere. Any other year it would have been disappointing to be stuck at home, but I had Isabella now and I couldn't think of anything better than staying in with her.

"Oh, we have a lot of shows on Netflix to catch up on," Isabella announced. "We had started watching *La Casa de Papel* together a while ago and I've been dying to finish that."

"Whoa guys, please cool it with your rowdy plans," Penelope jokes. "You're making us jealous here."

We all laughed and I couldn't help the smile that was left on my face. It was almost as if everything that happened with Casey was just some bad dream that I had woken up from. Isabella was here and she was talking as if everything was back to normal. Everything was getting back to the way it was and I couldn't have been happier. This was what I had wanted.

Penelope strolled into the lounge. "Okay, we've put all your medicine on the counter there. We need to get going though because this one is fast asleep already which means I need to get him to his bed before I'm up all night with him."

Penelope reached for Mateo and took him in her arms, careful not to wake him. Isabella shifted closer to me and rested her hand on my leg, intertwining her fingers in mine.

"Isabella, can we drop you at your place?" Alvaro offered.

She turned to me. "Are you going to be okay by yourself for a while?"

"Oh, he's not going to be alone," Alvaro announced. "*Mama* is on her way."

"She really doesn't need to come here," I said.

"You know her," Alvaro shrugged. "She's going to want to make sure you're fine which gives Isabella enough time to grab those things from home that she mentioned."

"Good idea," she said, smiling. "I won't be gone too long anyway."

"You better not be," he murmured softly and squeezed my hand. "You're never leaving me again."

She smiled. "Never."

CHAPTER 60:
Isabella

For the first time in weeks, I felt genuinely happy. Giovanni was back home now and all he had to focus on was recovering. We didn't have to deal with any unnecessary drama anymore. There was no more Casey and no more baby. A part of me felt bad for Casey. She was pregnant and scared to do this alone, but another part of me was just relieved that it wasn't my problem to deal with anymore. Everything was back to how it was supposed to be.

Giovanni and I are together again.

I couldn't help the smile on my face as I waved goodbye to Alvaro and Penelope as they dropped me outside my apartment. I needed to pack enough for the next few days. I wasn't going to want to leave his side. The worst was over now, but I just wanted him to recover and all would be well in the world again. Reyna and Katrina had gone away with their parents to celebrate New Years and both significant others had gone with them. They extended the offer for me to join, but I couldn't leave Giovanni so they understood when I politely declined to join. I made it upstairs and pushed through my door as my phone started to buzz in my back pocket. I closed the door behind me and pulled my phone out

Lorenzo.

I sighed. I hadn't returned his calls in days since Giovanni's accident. It wasn't an intentional move on my side, I was just focused on so many other things. I couldn't ignore him forever though so I answered and brought my phone to my ear.

"Lorenzo, hi."

"Hey, Izzy," he said. "It's been a while, how have you been?"

We went through the small talk quite quickly. I was careful not to give too much away since I knew how Lorenzo felt about Giovanni. He was my friend though and I didn't want to be rude.

"Well, I'm glad I finally got a hold of you, I wanted to see if you had any plans tomorrow evening?"

"For New Year's Eve?"

"Yes, there is this great party that they're having close to the beach and I really wanted you to join. It could be really fun."

I couldn't help but feel bad. Even though I knew we were just friends, Lorenzo had made it very clear how he feels about me and I had to be honest with him.

"I actually have plans," I murmured.

"Oh, you do?" He sounded surprised.

"Yes."

The line was silent for a moment.

"With Giovanni?" he finally asked.

"Yes," I replied. "Lorenzo, so much has happened over the last few days. Giovanni was in a car accident and he found out he wasn't the father of Casey's baby and it-".

He interrupted me. "Hold on, did you just say he's not the father?"

"Yes, turns out Casey was lying."

His silence on the other end spoke volumes and I knew that wasn't what he wanted to hear.

"So, are the two of you back together now?"

I didn't want to say it. I felt bad about saying it. I know I didn't owe Lorenzo anything but I couldn't help the compassion I felt towards him. He had been there for me in a time when I really needed someone. He was always willing to help and did his best to keep me distracted from everything going on. Things didn't go the way he was clearly hoping it would have, but I couldn't reciprocate his feelings. Not when Giovanni had my heart.

"I'm sorry, Lorenzo."

"You don't have to apologize, Isabella," There was a new distance in his voice now. "Seems like everything really worked out for the two of you."

"You know I care about you," I murmured.

"Yeah, but not in the way I care about you."

I sighed and hung my head in my hands. "I'm sorry."

"I just want you to be happy," he said softly.

"Thank you. You know I want the same for you and I hope that we can still be fr-".

"Please don't say friends," he murmured. "I think it's probably best if I take a step back now."

"You don't have to do that."

"I do. I want you to be happy, but I can't watch you be with him. Not when I have feelings for you."

It saddened me to know that this was probably the last time I was going to hear from him. I had grown so fond of him and even though I couldn't reciprocate his feelings, I knew someone out there would and he deserved that.

"I understand."

"Giovanni is a lucky man," he said. "You better remind him of that."

"Thank you, Lorenzo."

"Take care of yourself."

And with our last goodbyes, we disconnected the call.

***

"Honey, I'm home," I said playfully as I strolled back into his apartment, bag and pizza in hand.

He was seated on the couch and he peeped his head up to meet my gaze as I came around the corner. I looked around and found he was alone.

"Where's your mom?"

"You just missed her," he said. "She says hi though."

I walked over to the counter and placed the pizza box on top of it as I dropped my bag to the floor. I pushed the whole Lorenzo interaction out of my mind. It didn't matter what had happened, I knew I would have always chosen Giovanni anyway and there was nothing I could do about that. He had a hold over my heart and soul and I was just happy to be here with him again.

"Are you hungry?" I asked, leaning over the couch.

He looked up at me. "Starving."

I smiled and was about to make my way back to the kitchen when he reached out and grabbed my arm, pulling me closer.

"You do realize that we technically have no reason not to be together now right?"

A smile played on my lips. "Is that so? Seems so unlike us."

He chuckled. "I'm serious, Isabella. The last few weeks without you were fucking torture and I never want to feel that again."

"Trust me, neither do I."

He pulled me closer and my lips reached his. I sunk into the kiss, feeling all the fear and pain that previously lived in my body, slip away. There was just him and I now. I felt him smile beneath my lips and that warmed my heart. It was bursting with a happiness I never thought I would feel again.

He pulled away. "Now, I can start calling you my girlfriend again."

It was like hearing it for the first time. The same goofy smile spread across my face and I couldn't help but tug at my lip, trying to contain my happiness.

"Well, your girlfriend is going to get the pizza and plates."

He chuckled. "Don't worry about plates. We can eat out of the box."

I walked back to the counter and reached for the pizza box. I placed it down on the small coffee table in front of the couch. I pulled my phone out and noticed it had died.

"Let me just grab my charger."

I opened the zip of my bag, looking through it to find my charger. There were so many things in the bag that I had to start emptying some clothes to find it.

"Are you managing?"

"Yeah," I said as I pulled it out. "There is just so much shit in this bag. I didn't know how long I would be here for but I'm pretty sure I overpacked."

"You know you wouldn't have to keep packing bags if you just lived here."

I froze and slowly stood up, turning towards him."What did you just say?"

He was reaching for a slice of pizza as he casually turned to me. "I said you wouldn't have to keep packing bags if you just lived here."

I heard exactly what he had said the first time but I needed to hear it again. Did he just ask me to live with him? Did he seriously ask me that? *Oh my God,* my heart was bursting.

I stepped closer to the couch. "You want me to live here?"

He took a bite of his pizza. "Of course I do."

"Like to move in here?" I repeated the phrase differently, trying to wrap my head around it. "To live with you? Like this would be my apartment, too?"

He burst out laughing. "How many other ways are you going to ask me the same thing? Yes, *mi hermosa,* I want you to live here with me in this apartment."

My hands went to cover my mouth.

"Isabella, if I could move right now I would come to you but I'm in a bit of a situation so if you could bring yourself over here, that would be great."

I couldn't help but laugh as I went over to the couch again. He dusted off his hands as he finished the last of his pizza slice and pulled me closer to him.

"Don't you think we're moving too fast here?" I asked.

He shook his head. "I know what I want. Being without you is something I never want to experience again. I want a life with you and that starts with living together so I'm ready if you are."

I didn't know what to say. I was too overcome with happiness to say anything. I just sat in his arms with a huge smile spread across my face.

"If this is too much for you then I understand and we can wa-".

I interrupted him. "I want to do it."

"You do?" His eyes lit up.

Happy tears had started to form in my eyes. "Of course."

CHAPTER 61:

Isabella

8 MONTHS LATER

"That was a really sweet speech you gave," I said as Giovanni pulled me into his arms on the dance floor.

His arm came around my waist and rested on my lower back, sending electricity through my veins at the mere touch of his skin against mine. The dress Katrina had chosen for her bridesmaids was open back which meant Giovanni took full advantage of that by brushing his fingertips against my skin. His other hand was in mine and he pulled me closer to him so we were inches from each other.

"Well, Sergio has always been like a brother to me," he explained. "The least I could do was remind him of that."

I smiled and rested my head against his chest. Katrina and Sergio's wedding was absolutely stunning. Katrina had always wanted to get married at this beautiful vineyard just outside of Madrid and I understood why. The venue was like something out of a fairytale. Beautiful chandeliers hung throughout the room and the wedding planner had done a great job of bringing Katrina's timeless vision to life. From the dance floor, you could see the doors were opened completely and guests were scattered throughout the room and the patio outside overlooking the rest of the property. There was a maze in the distance and with the full moon shining down on it, it truly felt like something out of a movie. I couldn't help but cry during the ceremony - it was beautiful to see the love those two shared. We had started to approach the late evening and the party was just getting started. The DJ was easing everyone in after the first dance and I was happy to have this moment with Giovanni. He looked so sexy in his tight-fitted navy suit and it was taking all my self-control to not have my way with him already.

I didn't realise I was gawking at him until he looked down at me and lifted an eyebrow. "What are you looking at?"

I blushed. "You. You look really handsome tonight."

He had neatened his beard for the occasion and his hair was styled in place. He still had a faint scar under his eye from the night of his car accident. I often found myself running my fingers gently over it, reminding me of that night and what it felt like to nearly lose him. It wasn't a thought I wanted to entertain but it reminded me to never take our time for granted. His leg took a few months to heal and only recently did he get his cast off. After being stuck on crutches for months, he was ready to take every opportunity he could to be on his feet.

"Thank you, baby." He moved closer to me and brushed his fingers over my skin again. "You already know how I feel about this dress."

A mischievous grin played at his lips and I knew exactly where his mind was headed. It took us a while to leave our hotel room today after he saw my dress for the first time. It was a long, deep maroon dress with a slit up my left leg. Between my bareback and leg on display, he was having a hard time keeping it together and I loved it. Even after all this time, I still managed to get this reaction out of him.

"You really didn't want to leave the room today," I giggled.

"Nope. I was ready to take you right then and there," he said in a hushed voice. "But we couldn't be late to the wedding. Not like we were at that other dinner of theirs."

I couldn't help the heat that spread across my cheeks. A couple of weeks before the wedding, Katrina and Sergio had set up a dinner for the friends and family that weren't able to travel to Madrid for the wedding. Giovanni and I didn't even make it past our bedroom door before devouring each other which caused us to be late for the dinner. We didn't plan it. We just couldn't get enough of each other. It didn't matter that we had been living together, the heat between us was only intensified by that. There was no blowing out this flame anytime soon.

"That was so bad," I chuckled.

"Luckily we were on time today and look how nicely everything turned out."

"It was a beautiful wedding."

The song finished and moved onto something more upbeat. We made our way back to our table and sat down next to each other. Giovanni shifted his chair closer to me so he could rest his hand on my thigh. As we continued our conversation, the emcee for the evening interrupted us.

"Can we get all the single ladies on the floor now? We'd like to do the throwing of the bouquet."

"That's me," I announced, standing up.

He grabbed my hand and pulled me closer to him. "Where do you think you're going?"

"They're calling all the single ladies."

"And that's not you," he murmured. "You're mine, or do I have to remind you?"

A smile played on my lips. "I think you should remind me."

He lifted an eyebrow and smirked.

"But they are, technically, calling all unmarried women and I don't see a ring on my finger so..."

He chuckled. "Are you hinting at something, Isabella?"

I shook my head and smiled innocently before making my way to the dance floor. We gathered together as Katrina stood on a chair that was brought onto the dance floor for her. Giovanni was watching me from the table, the desire still burning in his eyes. I loved it when he called me his and I loved all the ways he showed me. He dominated my body and it bowed down to him. He knew all the ways to push it to the edge.

"One, two..." Katrina's voice brought me back to reality. "Three!"

She turned around and tossed the bouquet into the crowd causing all the women to push forward. The bouquet landed right in Reyna's hands and a chorus of cheers filled the room. I looked over at Giovanni who had his arms up as if to say. "Why didn't you catch it?"

I shrugged my shoulders and laughed. That was never my intention - it was just fun to be involved. I walked back to the table, his eyes were on me the entire time.

"Now about that reminder," I murmured closer to him.

He tugged at his lips before smiling. "Come with me."

He grabbed my hand and stood up. I couldn't help but smile as he led me out of the reception hall. The DJ continued the music and everyone was making their way back onto the dance floor. We made our way outside as he led me down the stairs. The fresh nighttime air surrounded us and I took a deep breath in.

"Where are we going?" I asked.

"I think that place over there should be far enough."

He pointed to the small barn-like structure that stood across the lawn just in front of the maze feature they had on the property.

"Far enough from what?"

"Far enough that no one will be able to hear us."

The pressure between my legs came alive and I couldn't help but tug at my bottom lip. Desire rippled through me and I was intrigued.

He stopped and turned to me. "You want me to remind you that you're mine, don't you?"

He was so close to me now that I could feel his breath on me, sending shivers up and down my body. I could feel the pressure building inside and I was dying to have him. He leaned down, his lips touching mine. He was soft and careful with his kiss before pulling away to continue to lead me towards the building. I looked around but there was no one in sight. It was exhilarating - this kind of spontaneity was what I loved about him. We reached the wooden door and he pushed it open.

"Hello?" he shouted.

There was no answer. It was a lot bigger than I realised and had long tables scattered across the hall that they would usually use for wine tasting. There was a small staircase to our left leading up to a second floor.

"Follow me," he said and led me towards the stairs.

I climbed the stairs first as he followed closely behind me. The anticipation was killing me. We reached the top and it revealed a small office. There was an old oak table by the wall and in front of it was a leather couch. There was a window behind the table revealing the night sky to us. I felt his breath on my neck as he stepped towards me. His fingertips ran along my bare back and my breath caught in my throat.

He moved some of my hair to fall over my chest, revealing the back of my neck to him. I held my breath as he brought his lips down to my neck. The heat spread throughout my body sending sensations over every part of me.

"Giovanni," I breathed.

"Yes, baby?" he murmured in between his kisses. "Do you like this?"

"M-hmm."

"I already knew that," he whispered seductively in my ear. "I know what drives your body crazy."

He turned me to face him and his lips found mine with a hungry desire. Our bodies collided as I wrapped my arms around his neck. We stumbled towards the desk as his hand found its way into my hair. We stopped at the desk and he lifted me up on it, opening my legs with enough space to stand in between. I reached for his jacket and pushed it down his arms as my lips found his again. His hand ran up my arm to reach the back of my neck, wrapping around it gently. He pulled the clip holding my hair in place out and the rest of it cascaded down my back. It was already such a mess anyway.

He broke the kiss and placed his hands on my thighs. "Can you follow instructions?"

I nodded.

"Good girl."

He pulled the single chair that was standing behind the desk forward and he took a seat, bringing him eye level with my knees. My breathing picked up and I tugged at my lip again. I was so ready for him. I could already feel my body was awake with desire. He slowly moved the material of my dress over my other leg, leaving both my legs now exposed. I shifted as he lifted my dress, making sure it was out of the way. I knew what he was planning on doing and it killed me. I loved the sight of him between my legs and the way he enjoyed me. My body craved his greedy tongue. He flicked his eyes to me before spreading my legs and reaching for my underwear. I lifted my body and allowed him to pull it down my legs, dropping it to the floor.

He leaned closer to me. "Keep your hands against the table."

I leaned my arms back and tilted my head, watching as he brought my legs up, my heels resting on the table.

"Fuck, these are sexy," he said, referring to my shoes.

He ran his hands up and down my legs. He loved to take his time. He loved to make me wait in anticipation until I was begging him to take me.

"Giovanni," I pleaded.

"You need to learn to be patient, Isabella."

Before I could respond, he brought his head forward and locked his arms around my thighs. With one last naughty smirk, he flicked his eyes to mine as he brought his tongue over me.

I threw my head back. Just the feeling of his tongue against me and the way he explored me was electrifying. I loved it. He was slow at first - flicking and moving at a rhythm that made me arch my hips towards him.

"Giovanni," I breathed.

Hearing his name caused him to increase the urgency. His beard scratched against me but I didn't care. I was too high on the pleasure to care. I rocked my hips against him and my hand found its way to his hair, gripping as he continued.

He pulled away and his eyes reached mine. "I thought I told you to keep your hands on the table."

I lifted an eyebrow at him and brought my hands back against the table, loving every moment of the way he took control. The pressure inside of me was escalating at a fast pace.

He brought his tongue back down against me. I tugged at my lower lip trying to contain the pressure building up inside of me. Suddenly, he slipped a finger inside of me, accompanying his tongue flicking over me.

"Oh myyyy," I purred.

Another finger slipped inside, reaching exactly where I needed him to. I couldn't control the moans escaping my lips. This was driving my body fucking insane. He knew how to perfectly combine both as he pushed me closer to my climax. It was building and building and as he removed his fingers and replaced it with his tongue, my body came undone. I couldn't help but grip his hair as I threw my head back, moaning his name into the night.

He removed his head from between my legs. "I'm not done with you just yet."

My legs were shaking but that didn't stop him. He undid the buttons of his shirt and pulled it open, revealing those sexy markings I'd never get enough of.

"Fuck," I gaped.

"Stand," he instructed.

I dropped my legs to the floor, careful to lean against the table.

He stood closer to me. "Turn around."

My eyes widened. "What?"

"I want you to turn around and bend over."

My eyes rolled back just at the thought of what he was asking. I could feel my body screaming with desire as I turned around. He lifted my dress up and slowly bent me over the table, the cold wood against me. I was so overcome with delirious pleasure that I could have just exploded. I heard him undo his belt and rip open the condom packet. My breathing picked up and my toes curled, dying to have him already. His arms came around the side of my body and I felt him brush up against me. I couldn't hold back my gasp but that was nothing compared to what came when he finally entered me.

"Oh my God!" My eyes rolled back in pleasure as he filled me up.

He started to move his body and he was not gentle about it either. He gripped my hips and pulled me against him, our bodies colliding. The sound of mine hitting his was enthralling. I was already so high on pleasure that I couldn't believe my body had anything left to feel but I was wrong. The pleasure shot through me with each thrust inside of me. I tightened around him as his hand gripped my hair, pulling my head back.

"Don't stop, Giovanni," I moaned.

I could hear the small gasps escape his lips. He pulled me closer to him and his lips found my ear.

"Mine, Isabella." he claimed me. "You're all mine."

"I'm yours." I was absolutely his. There was no doubt about it. Body, soul and heart belonged to him and that was never going to change. Each thrust deeper inside of me pushed me towards my climax again. I tightened around him, the throbbing between my legs increasing.

"Yes, yes, yes," I repeated.

He continued until we both found our climax. I couldn't hold back the moans that escaped my lips. I lay against the table trying to catch my breath as the overwhelming pleasure settled over me. I couldn't move. He pulled out of me with one last small gasp. I slowly brought myself up and turned to face him. He looked up at me, a grin on his face as he tried to catch his breath.

"We are doing that again," I said.

He chuckled. "Whatever you want, baby."

***

After finally making ourselves presentable enough, we made our way back to the party. We rejoined the dance floor and he pulled me closer to him, our bodies moving together. We stopped by the car before coming back to the hall so he could spray some of his cologne on him again. He didn't go lightly with it. I breathed it in as we moved - it was intoxicating. He was intoxicating and he always would be.

"You know, I can see this being us one day," he murmured softly.

I glanced up at him. "What do you mean?"

"The whole getting married. The idea doesn't scare me anymore."

Giovanni Velázquez had come a long way from being that typical bad-boy with commitment issues that everyone warned me to stay away from. Our relationship had become something so sacred and every part of my being knew we were meant to be together. We were meant to meet each other that night at *Mala Mía* - even if I didn't realise it at the time, he was the one for me.

"And I know that most marriages end in divorces," he continued. "Just look at my parents."

It didn't take long after Giovanni's accident for him and Alvaro to finally sit down with them and play open cards. It took Cecilio by surprise to learn that his wife had been unfaithful to him but he had no leg to stand on when he was doing exactly the same. Their family meeting imploded and it took a couple of days for his parents to come to terms with the fact that their relationship was broken beyond repair. A few months later they filed for divorce and now they both lived separate lives with their new partners. Their family was surprisingly better off because of it.

"But I know that's not going to happen with us because there is no one else for me but you, *mi hermosa*."

I couldn't help but smile. My heart was so full and it was all because of him. We had a love that I never believed I would ever be able to have and I often found myself wondering how I got so lucky. I leaned up to him and my lips reached his. My arms wrapped around his neck as we deepened the kiss. I had to remind myself that we were on a dance floor full of people and I slowly pulled away. He was smiling down at me - those deep brown eyes of his filled with a happiness that mirrored my own.

"There you two are!" Reyna exclaimed and turned to Diego on the other side of the dance floor. "Bring the shots here."

"Oh God, Reyna, not shots," I groaned.

She rolled her eyes at me. "Don't be a bore. This is a celebration and you bet your ass we are going to celebrate."

Shortly after I moved in with Giovanni, Reyna and Diego took their relationship to the next level. He moved into the apartment and a few months later, they were engaged. I owed Reyna everything. She took me in with open arms that one day and never looked back. She never asked for anything in return and I was allowed to become the woman I was today because of her. I couldn't be happier that she had found Diego. He treated her right and was completely smitten with her - what more would I want for my best friend?

"If you think this is a party, wait till our wedding," Diego said as he joined our group, handing each of us a shot.

"I'm actually afraid of what that's going to be like," Giovanni jokes. "I don't think my liver is going to be able to handle that."

"Boooooo!" Reyna shouted playfully. "You're such an old man now."

I couldn't help but laugh as we all brought our shot glasses together. I brought it to my lips and tilted my head back, the alcohol making its way down my throat. It was strong but I was just thankful it wasn't tequila. The dance floor filled with more people as the DJ changed the music up, bringing on the real party music now. Katrina and Sergio joined our group and we all moved our bodies to the music. Looking around at all of the people I loved, I couldn't help but feel at ease with life.

I was happy.

CHAPTER 62:

Giovanni

"Okay, come on baby, we're here now," I said to Isabella as she leaned against me, using me for support.

Reyna kept the shots coming and she and Isabella didn't stop. Between all the dancing and laughing, they were downing the shots and I knew it was time to go when Isabella looked up at me with those doe eyes of hers and that goofy smile she always got when she had too much to drink. I opened up the door to our hotel room and we stepped inside. Isabella let go of me and strolled into the room. I closed the door behind me and watched as she stumbled her way to the couch. She was definitely intoxicated but she had a good time and that was all that mattered.

I walked over to the fridge and pulled out a bottle of water, handing it over to her. She kicked off her shoes and took the bottle from me.

"You need to drink all of that," I instructed.

"And what if I don't?" she mumbled, a small smile playing on her lips. "Are you going to make me?"

I smirked. "You're a big girl, you can handle yourself."

"I am a big girl," she announced. "That is quite correct young sir."

She opened the bottle and brought it to her lips. She downed about half of it before placing it on the coffee table in front of her. She leaned back against the couch and looked over at me, a naughty look spread across her face.

"What are you thinking about?" I said as I removed my suit jacket and placed it on the chair in the corner.

"You look fucking sexy right now."

I couldn't help but smile. Whenever she was drunk, she got wildly turned on and her mouth ran away with her. It was like a switch went off in the back of her mind and she couldn't hold back her true desires.

I sat down next to her. "Is that so?"

She tugged at her lip and nodded. She left her hair loose for the rest of the evening since I undid it earlier and now a couple of strands were hanging in front of her face. I reached out and slowly placed it behind her ear. I watched her watch me as I did that and noticed the change in her breathing. Her eyebrow lifted next the way it always did when she saw something she liked. She flicked her eyes to meet mine before they wandered down to my lips. I could feel the heat inside of me start to spread at the sight of her. She looked fucking hot right now and I was dying to have her again.

"Tell me what's on your mind, Isabella."

She shifted closer to me, the material of her dress moving to expose her leg through the slit. I reached out and placed my hand on her knee. She glanced down at my hand before her eyes met mine again with a hungry desire that mirrored my own.

"I'm thinking that we're alone in a hotel room."

"We are."

"And I could think of a few things we could do to entertain ourselves," she murmured.

"Oh?" I lifted my eyebrow. "Do tell."

She couldn't hold back the smile that played on her lips. The happiness radiated off of her and I had never seen her look more beautiful.

"I'm surprised you have any more energy left after earlier," I commented.

"I can't believe we had sex in a barn." Her hands covered her mouth as she giggled.

"Technically, it was in someone's office," I corrected playfully.

"We seem to have a thing for offices."

I giggled, thinking back to the time we had sex in someone's office at the Christmas party. When I wanted her, I had to have her and I didn't care where we were. Thankfully, she was crazy enough to go along with my spontaneity. I knew she loved it as much as I did.

"As much as I'd love to take you right now, I actually think we should order you some food."

Her eyes widened. "Yes! Food - I could so eat right now."

I chuckled and reached for the phone that was placed on the table next to the couch and lifted the menu next to it.

"Pizza or a burger?"

"I could eat both right now," she admitted.

I laughed and dialed reception. "*Hola* - could I please get one small margarita pizza and one of your burger combos with chips sent up to room 205."

She was nodding her head and smiling at my mention of chips. Drunk Isabella could eat her way through a buffet and I thoroughly enjoyed watching her enjoy some good food. Whenever she was enjoying what she was eating, she would do this little dance as she chewed and it always made me smile. Simple things made her happy and I was happy to be one of those. I thanked the lady on the other line and disconnected the call. Isabella shifted closer to me and rested her head on my chest. I wrapped my arm around her and pulled her closer to me.

"You said you wanted to marry me tonight," she mumbled playfully.

"Did I?" I joked. "I think you're making that up."

"I'm - I am n-not," she slurred and looked up at me. "You, technically, said it. I heard you."

I leaned down to kiss her forehead. "Maybe I did."

"You did," she repeated and smiled. "Do you remember when we first met?"

"How could I forget?"

I was supposed to be working that evening. We had hired new bouncers and a new bartender on a trial-period basis as per Alvaro's suggestion. Penelope was already pregnant at the time and running *Mala Mía* had become my main responsibility. Sergio invited me to join their table that evening and so after putting our manager at the time in charge, I was technically off-duty. I'd never forget when I first saw her. She was a new face to me and I was immediately intrigued. She was the kind of woman that wouldn't expect to get noticed in a crowd but I did. I noticed her with her youthful innocence and contagious smile. She had a more reserved demeanour to her in comparison to someone like Reyna but that's what drew me in. Who was this beautiful stranger that stumbled into my club?

"Reyna dared me to have a one-night stand with you," she said.

"She did?"

"Well, technically she dared me to have a one-night stand with anyone," she explained. "But that wasn't why I did it."

"So, why did you do it?"

"Because no one has ever made my body feel the way you did. You had such an effect on me from the first moment we met." She flicked her eyes to meet mine. "I remember thinking how fucking hot you were."

I chuckled.

"And I even went as far as thinking about what it would be like to Netflix and chill with you."

This made me laugh again. "Well, you and I do plenty of that now."

She smiled with a happiness that reached her eyes.

"I hate to have to be the one to tell you but you failed at having a one-night stand," I said.

"Can you blame me?" She lifted an eyebrow playfully. "You just knew what to do to my body."

I leaned closer to her neck and rested my lips against it. "And I still know."

"I tried to fool myself into thinking it could be something casual," she explained. "But I quickly learned that I had to have more."

"And you have it, *mi hermosa*. You have me and you have my heart and that's never going to change."

She reached up and brought her lips down to mine, smiling against them. I wrapped my arms around her and wondered how I ever got so lucky.

Isabella Avery - the only woman who ever made me want more and I wanted it all with her.

CHAPTER 63:

Isabella

"**D**o you really have to go to Valencia today?" I asked and wrapped my arms around his neck.

We had just arrived back from Madrid. Katrina and Sergio's wedding was something out of a fairytale and the two of them were headed on their honeymoon. Sergio had planned it all and it was a surprise so none of us knew where they were going. Giovanni and I stood in our kitchen, my back against the counter.

"Yes, I have to go and meet the new manager and I've got a whole lot of other boring stuff that I have to do there," he explained. "But it's just for the day. I'll be back for dinner."

The *Mala Mía* in Valencia had its grand opening a couple of weeks ago. They had done a great job of getting it ready and I was happy to have tagged along with Giovanni. Despite what happened the last time I was in Valencia, that place held a special place in my heart. His business partner, Pedro, had been running things that side since he lived there and they had recently hired a permanent manager for the place so he needed to head down there to meet them.

"I should probably make us something tonight," I suggested. "How do you feel about seafood? I can get some stuff on my way home."

"You know I love seafood," he said and leaned down to kiss me. "What time is Reyna fetching you?"

I glanced up at the clock against the wall. "She's only coming around lunchtime. Diego had to finish something off for work this morning and then he's going to come help us set up the sign."

After months of hard work, Reyna and I had finally managed to finish off our coffee shop. We eventually bounced names back and forth and decided that *Aroma* was the best one. We were planning to open in two weeks' time and now it was time to finish off the smaller tasks that needed to be done. We had already started interviewing a couple of baristas and after the rest of our stock gets delivered next week, we would be all set to open for the public. A lot had changed over the last few months but it really felt like everything in my life had come together the way it was supposed to. I was no longer that lost woman I was when I first landed in Barcelona. The same woman who had no idea what her life was meant to be like. The same woman who believed she had no purpose. Once I had accepted that my life wasn't going to be what my mother laid out for me, I started to allow myself to really discover who I was and what I wanted. Fast forward to the present and I was a small business owner living with the love of my life. I didn't need more than that.

"I'm so proud of you." he smiled down at me. "You guys have really worked hard to get that place looking good."

I couldn't hold back my own smile. "I actually can't wait for it to be open, but I'm super nervous to see if people are going to like it."

"They're going to love it."

He leaned down and his lips met mine again. I melted against them and tightened my arms around his neck. It didn't matter how long we had been together, he still managed to give me butterflies.

I pulled away but kept my arms around him. "You need to head to the airport so I should probably let you get ready."

He gave me one last kiss before disappearing upstairs.

CHAPTER 64:

Giovanni

I lied to her.

I wasn't headed to Valencia but instead, I was going to London. The day I realized I was in love with Isabella was the day I knew I was going to marry her. A few weeks after she moved in, I bought a ring and I kept it hidden, waiting for the right moment to propose to her. For months she spoke about how it saddened her that her relationship with her family was the way it was and I knew what I had to try and do. I couldn't propose to her without at least letting her family know my intentions. I was a traditional man when it came to stuff like that. I wasn't going to ask for their blessing because I didn't need it. I just needed them to know I was going to take care of their daughter for the rest of my life.

I landed in London and I was full of nerves. Her mother wasn't my favourite person but I was adamant to keep my cool and respectfully let her know that I was going to ask for her daughter's hand in marriage. I hailed a taxi and slipped inside as a light drizzle started to come down.

"The London Herald offices, please," I asked the cab driver and he took off down the street.

I left Isabella a message telling her that I had landed safely. I didn't want to tell her that I was here. She had kept in touch with her dad as frequently as she could and Camila had recently started to make an effort. Her mother was truly a lost cause and although she said she didn't care, I knew that deep down she wishes things could be different. I was prepared for whatever insults Gloria Avery was going to throw my way. None of that mattered to me except doing the respectable thing for the sake of Isabella.

The taxi stopped outside a tall building and I quickly paid him for the ride. I took a deep breath in and stepped outside, trying to gather my composure. My palms were sweaty and I wiped them off against my jeans. I had underestimated how nervous I was. I pushed through the doors and was welcomed by the receptionist sitting behind the desk. A huge sign was against the wall behind her that very proudly announced *The London Herald*.

She smiled and politely greeted me with her thick British accent, "Good morning, sir. How can I help you today?"

"Hi, I'm here to see Oscar Avery," I explained. "I should have an appointment scheduled for one o'clock."

I wasn't sure how busy her parents were so I made sure to make an appointment. I lied and said I was interested in learning more about the ad space in their digital editions. I didn't know shit about that, but it was good enough to get an appointment with her father.

"Yes sir, you can head up to the second floor," she said. "He should be expecting you."

I said my thank you's and turned towards the elevator. The doors opened and I stepped inside. I didn't think I had ever been more nervous about anything in my life and I had to remind myself to keep my shit together. I was here to speak about their daughter and that should be easy enough since I was completely in love with her.

The elevator doors opened and I was surprised to see Camila waiting on the other side. She couldn't hide the surprise on her face as we made eye contact.

"Giovanni?" she asked, surprised. "What in the world are you doing here?"

"Hi, Camila," I said and stepped out of the elevator. "I'm actually here to see your parents. Well, your father mainly."

"He didn't tell me you were coming."

I had spoken to Oscar Avery a couple of times on the phone and via FaceTime. Isabella's relationship with her father was important to her and I made an effort to get to know him as best as I could over the phone. We had never met in person but he definitely knew who I was.

"He actually doesn't know it's me," I said sheepishly. "I made an appointment. I have something important to speak to him about."

Oscar Avery walked down the hall with a file in his hand. He looked much older in person. The grey in his hair had spread to most of his head. The wrinkles around his eye gave away his age but he had a softer look to him than his wife. You knew right off the bat what to expect from Gloria but Oscar's demeanour was much kinder. He was muttering something to a younger man walking with him but stopped in his tracks when he noticed me.

"Giovanni?" He was just as surprised as Camila was by my presence.

"Hi, Mr. Avery," I said politely and stepped forward, extending my hand to him. "It's nice to finally meet you in person."

"It's nice to meet you too." He shook my hand but the shock on his face remained. "Forgive me, but I am quite surprised to see you here. I have an appointment now."

"Yes you do," I said. "With me."

"With you?"

I nodded. "Yes sir. I really need to speak to you and your wife so I made an appointment to do so."

He looked over to Camila who shrugged her shoulders. "I didn't know he was coming."

"Well, I suppose we should move this to the conference room," he suggested. "Camila, don't you want to go and get your mother please."

She nodded and stepped into the elevator. Oscar turned back down the hall and gestured for me to follow him. We stopped at a closed wooden door and he pushed it open, revealing an empty conference room. There was a large table in the middle and chairs scattered all around it.

"I must say I am really surprised to see you here, Giovanni," he said and took a seat at the head of the table.

I followed his lead and took a seat down next to him. "I know and I'm sorry if it's not a welcomed surprise, but I had something important I needed to talk to you about and it felt wrong to do it over the phone."

I rubbed my hands against my jeans again, attempting to get a handle on my nerves. He was not an intimidating man in any way but the entire situation made me nervous. It's not every day you tell your girlfriend's family that you want to propose to her.

"It is very nice to finally meet you in person," he said and before I could reply, Gloria Avery stepped into the room.

It had been a while since I had seen her and she had aged since then. She still walked with the same demanding energy. Her age now sat in the wrinkles on her face and there was a lingering sadness in her eyes that she didn't have before and it surprised me to see.

"Giovanni," she said and walked over to us with Camila following closely behind her. "I never expected to see you here."

That was the general response amongst the three of them and I understood why. I had given them no indication that it would be me they were meeting but I didn't want to give them a chance to decline my meeting proposal.

I stood up respectfully. "Hi Mrs. Avery."

She didn't crack a smile and instead, sat down across from me, crossing her arms as she faced me. Camila sat down next to her and now that I had all three of them in the room, it was time to let the cat out of the bag.

"I know that you're all surprised to see me but I have something very important to discuss with you," I explained.

They were all peering at me, waiting for me to continue so I took a deep breath in before continuing.

"I need to start off by saying that I love your daughter and I've watched what it's been like for her to have the relationships she has with you guys." I looked over at Gloria. "I know that she wishes things could be different with you but I didn't come here to discuss Isabella's relationship with you."

"Then why are you here?" Gloria asked.

"I'm here to tell you that I'm going to propose to Isabella."

I watched as they all reacted differently to my news. Oscar's eyes widened but I noticed the happiness in them. He and Isabella had the closest relationship and he had been able to see firsthand how happy she's been over the last few months. Camila's jaw dropped and her hands flew up to cover her mouth while Gloria's face fell as she processed the information.

"And, respectfully, I'm not here to ask for your blessing but rather to state my intentions. I have never loved anyone like I love Isabella and she and I know we are meant to be together. The only thing I have ever wanted to do was make her happy and I am ready to take the next step with her."

"Does Isabella have any idea?" Camila asked.

I shook my head. "I don't think so. We have spoken about marriage before so that's not new but I don't think she thinks I would do it anytime soon."

All three of them remained silent as I watched them process this new information. It made me sick to my stomach with nerves but I made sure to continue to remain confident on the outside.

"I want you to know that I'm going to take care of Isabella and for the rest of my life, I just want to make her happy. It's what she deserves."

Oscar agreed. "That's all I've ever wanted for her."

I turned back to Gloria. "I know you don't like me and you don't think I'm good for your daughter but I want you to know that you're wrong."

She lifted an eyebrow and shifted uncomfortably in her chair.

"Your daughter is the love of my life, Gloria," I said. "And you never even gave me a chance."

She opened her mouth but I lifted my hand to cut her off as respectfully as I could manage. "I'm sorry, I would just like to finish. You never gave me a chance and I understand that you had expected other things from Isabella but you need to know that your daughter is the strongest, smartest, kindest woman I have ever known and I really think you would be proud of who she is today."

I watched as she took a deep breath in. She tried to hide it but I noticed the small tears filling her eyes. It was the first time I had ever noticed her ability to share emotion.

"I am going to marry her and I am always going to put her needs above my own. All I ask is that you guys respect her choice to be happy and I hope that by the time we do get married, that you will be in attendance because I know that deep down, Isabella would want you to be there."

Camila smiled at me from across the table and I saw the approval in her eyes. Oscar looked over at his wife and reached out to grab her hand before turning back to me.

"We want Isabella to be happy and that's all that matters," he said.

Gloria nodded. "I know I am a difficult woman, Giovanni, and I have made plenty of mistakes with my daughter but I love her."

"You should tell her that," I suggested.

"I must commend you," she said. "You came here knowing very well that I wasn't a fan of you."

"Yes, but I've never given you a reason for that," I retorted. "And I wanted to remind you and make it very clear that my number one priority here is Isabella so however you decide to react, that isn't going to change my intention to propose to her."

A small smile played at her lips before she stopped herself. I was winning her over. I could see it in her eyes. As much as it made me nervous to call her out, I had to. I've never given her a reason not to like me. She just couldn't accept the fact that her daughter wasn't with the man she had chosen for her.

"Well, I think congratulations are in order," Oscar announced and stood up, extending his hand to me. "And even though you didn't ask for it, I want you to know that you have my blessing because I've never seen my daughter happier."

I smiled and shook his hand. "Thank you, sir."

Camila came around the table and pulled me in for a quick hug. "As long as you take care of her, I'll be happy."

"I promise you she's in safe hands with me."

"And I'm sorry for how I have treated you in the past," she said. "You must love my sister very much if you came all the way here just for this."

"It was the right thing to do."

Gloria stood up and came around the table. "I have many faults, Giovanni but I respect you coming here and speaking to us."

That was as good as getting a stamp of approval from her. I didn't know what I expected from this meeting, but it had gone better than I ever thought it would have. I half expected Gloria to throw me out but she and I both knew I had never done anything to her in the first place. She had no reason not to give me a chance and all she needed was to be called out about it.

"Well, can we see the ring?" Camila asked excitedly.

CHAPTER 65:
Isabella

"Can you lift it a little higher on the left?" Reyna asked.

We stood outside the entrance to our shop while Diego balanced on the ladder. We had a sign created with the name *Aroma* on it and Diego was helping us put it up above the big window that peered into the shop. The name was written in beautiful cursive against the background that was the same baby blue we had used inside to paint the walls. It was a delicate but welcoming-looking sign and that was what I wanted. I wanted it to welcome people into our place of tranquility.

Diego lifted it higher and Reyna exclaimed. "Yes! That's perfect."

He leaned back a little to take a look at it while we did the same, admiring it from the bottom.

"I think that looks great," I said.

Reyna turned to me with a huge smile on her face. "It does, right? I am so happy with it."

I took a couple steps back to get a better look at the entirety of the entrance. I couldn't believe that after all this time, we were finally at this point. I felt a sense of accomplishment looking at *Aroma*. I could consider myself a business owner now and I was so excited at the prospect of what was coming next for it. I took a moment to soak in the heat from the sun that was shining down on us.

I turned to face the ocean in the distance and I couldn't help but smile. There was so much I had to be happy about. I finally had my business opening up, I was living with the man of my dreams and we were the happiest we had ever been. Sometimes I wondered if my life was too good to be true but it had taken a lot to get to this point and a lot of sacrifices were made.

"Let's bring in the last of the boxes from the car," Reyna suggested. "We can start organizing that."

I nodded and followed her to the car that was parked on the street just outside our shop. Diego climbed down off the ladder and started to move it back inside. She unlocked the car and opened the boot, revealing the last two boxes we had. We had ordered our personalised mugs to suit the colour scheme of our shop and they had arrived recently. We had tons of stock inside already to unpack and next week the first of the books were arriving to be packed out onto the shelves.

"Can you believe we made it to this point?" Reyna asked excitedly. "For a while, I honestly believed this place was a lost cause and we had wasted our money."

I chucked. "Oh my goodness, me too! When we couldn't sort that leak out, I had accepted that this wasn't going to work."

"We should probably stop being such pessimists," she joked.

We each grabbed a box and made our way back to the shop. I pushed through the door and Reyna followed closely behind me.

"Babe, please can you grab the small box that's on the back seat? I forgot about it."

"Yes, of course," Diego said and disappeared outside.

I placed the box down on the counter and slipped underneath it by the staff entrance. I popped up and picked it up again, bringing it to the counter across from it where the coffee equipment was placed. I opened the empty cupboards above that to start placing the mugs in there. Reyna followed my lead but kept her box on the opposite counter as she had all the to-go cups in hers. I ripped the box open and started to carefully unpack each individual mug that was wrapped in newspaper for safekeeping.

"How long is Giovanni staying in Valencia for?" she asked.

"Oh, just for the day," I replied. "He should actually be heading to the airport soon."

Before she could reply my phone started to ring and I pulled it out of my back pocket to see Giovanni's name flashing across it.

"Speak of the devil," I joked and answered, bringing the phone to my ear.

"I was just talking about you," I said.

"You were?" he asked. "All good things I hope."

"Not really. I'm struggling to find something good to say about you lately," I said playfully as he laughed on the other end of the line.

"I'm on my way to the airport," he said.

"Great! How did your meeting go?"

"It was surprisingly successful. I think we're all on the same page now and things are going to be much better."

"I'm glad to hear that," I smiled. "We finally got the sign up."

"I can't wait to see how it looks."

"I'm excited for you to see it, too. We're packing out some of the cups and stuff but I'll meet you at home."

Even though it had been months of us living together, I still got the same rush of happiness whenever I mentioned *our* home.

"Sounds good baby. I'll let you know when I board."

"Perfect. I love you."

"I love you more, *mi hermosa*."

We said our last goodbyes and I ended the call, placing my phone back in my pocket. I couldn't help the huge smile on my face. *How did I get so lucky?*

"I think we should have dinner this weekend," Reyna announced. "You guys should come over and I'll cook us something."

"That's a great idea," I said. "But can we do it Sunday? Giovanni is taking me somewhere on Saturday."

When we were in Madrid, he mentioned that he made plans for us this Saturday. He said it was a surprise so I had no idea what he had planned. He was usually all spontaneous when it came to our plans, but he had asked me to book Saturday out and he had piqued my curiosity. I tried to rack my brain to what he could have planned, but I genuinely had no idea. I wasn't a big fan of surprises, but I was a big fan of Giovanni so I'd let this one slide.

"Where is he taking you?" Reyna asked.

I shrugged my shoulders and placed a mug in the cupboard. "I have no idea. He said it's a surprise."

"Okay well, let's do Sunday then."

I was curious as to why she brushed past the surprise part so casually.

Reyna was usually nosy as hell, but she didn't even hesitate as she continued about us making plans. I wondered if she knew what Giovanni was up to? She and Giovanni had built up quite a good friendship so it wouldn't surprise me if she knew something, but I let it go.

I would just have to be patient.

CHAPTER 66:

Isabella

"So, you're really not going to tell me at all where we're going?" I asked.

"That would ruin the surprise."

I rolled my eyes and zipped up the zip on my boots before standing up, ready to go. Autumn was rolling around again and there was a cold breeze in the air this afternoon. I had no idea where we were going or what we were doing, but Giovanni assured me that the way I was dressed was perfectly fine. I had decided on a pair of black pants and a tight long sleeve sheer bodysuit that I had gotten a couple months back. Since moving out of Reyna's apartment, I wasn't able to borrow her clothes as frequently as I used to so I had started to fill my own closet up with some pieces similar to what I used to use of hers. He handed me my black jacket as he came to stand by me at the bottom of the stairs.

I placed it over my arm. "You know I hate surprises."

"Can you just trust me?" He laughed and grabbed my hand. "Your boyfriend just wants to take you out."

"My boyfriend has given me no indication of where we're going."

"Because your boyfriend knows it would ruin the surprise."

He pulled me closer to him and leaned down, his lips touching mine. I sunk into the kiss and wrapped my arms around his neck. He had just sprayed some of that cologne I loved. I would agree to anything he asked whenever he had that on - it was hypnotising.

I pulled away from him. "Well, I must say that you look really good today."

He playfully pulled away and spun around, displaying his entire outfit. I threw my head back and laughed at his dramatic theatrics. He was wearing a pair of black jeans that cuffed around his ankles and paired them with a pair of his dark brown boots. He had recently gotten a sexy new leather jacket that I had come to love and he paired that with a white shirt underneath. Our aesthetics were matching and I smiled - what a couple thing to do.

"Shall we?" he asked.

***

He turned into an open parking spot along the street and I suddenly recognized the area. "Wait a minute. Isn't this where the *Magic Fountain of Montjuïc* is?"

He turned the engine off. "I was so close to surprising you, but you just had to go and guess it correctly."

I chuckled. 'Why didn't you just tell me?"

"I was attempting romance here, Isabella," he said playfully. "But the cat's out of the bag now."

"I'm sorry I ruined your surprise but surely you knew that I would have recognized this place when we arrived?"

There was no way I would have ever forgotten coming here with Giovanni. That day with him at the fountain was one of my favourite memories with him and it will be ingrained in my mind for the rest of my life. I was already in love with him that day. I was pretty sure I had been in love with him long before that, I just didn't want to admit it to myself. It felt like a lifetime ago.

He stepped outside and I followed his lead. I shut my door and went around to his side as he locked the car.

"I just wanted to recreate our date," he admitted sheepishly.

A huge smile spread across my face as I looked up at him, his deep brown eyes full of love. Still to this day, he made me nervous when he looked at me. The butterflies were something I still experienced around him and how could I not? Especially when he was going out of his way to do romantic things like this.

"It was one of my favourite dates," I said.

"Mine too." he reached for my hand and led me down the same road. "You didn't know this at the time though, but I was already in love with you then."

I couldn't help the heat that spread across my cheeks and the warmth that appeared inside my heart at his words. I squeezed his hand and smiled. There were no words to describe the way he made me feel. All I could settle on was how much I loved him. We turned the corner as the fountain came into view. The sun was already setting behind it and it was a sight to behold. I remembered walking up here with him, so happy that I was getting to spend the day with him.

"I didn't know that, but I was in love with you too," I admitted. "I tried to deny it though because I was just too scared to tell you."

"Why were you scared?"

"What if you didn't love me back? I couldn't have handled that kind of rejection."

He chuckled. "Did you really think I didn't love you?"

I shrugged my shoulders. "I didn't want to read too much into anything. You were the guy with commitment issues that everyone told me to stay away from remember? How could I have believed you would have loved me?"

"I think the question is how could I have not loved you?" He brought my hand up to his lips. "You are the only person I have ever wanted more with and I think it's safe to say that I am well over those commitment issues."

"Yeah, I'd say the whole living together thing really got rid of those."

We walked hand-in-hand up to the same spot we sat at before with the perfect view of the fountains. When he brought me here that day, I remembered thinking how romantic he actually was. It was difficult to believe that he was the same bad-boy everyone warned me against. Everything he did was just proving that we both cared for each other. We had come a long way since then and I had never been happier. We stopped at the spot and I brought myself up onto the wall, allowing my legs to hang over either side. I noticed that there were a couple of other people scattered around us in the distance.

I turned back to him as he had his hands in his pockets and shifted nervously in front of me. "What are you doing?"

"Huh? What?" he asked.

I had clearly interrupted a deep thought.

He looked so nervous. I had never seen him like this and it was confusing me. We were just casually going to sit here and watch the fountain. Why was he acting so weird?

"I asked what you're doing?" I repeated.

He shook his head and stepped closer, positioning himself between my legs. "Sorry. Nothing, just daydreaming."

I wasn't convinced by his answer, but I let it go. I turned to face the fountains as we watched the sun continue to disappear behind *The Palau Nacional*. The show was only starting at night as they loved to take advantage of the lights they used with the fountain. I watched as groups of people started to form on the stairs in front of the fountain, all of them probably here just for the show.

I looked back at Giovanni who was already looking at me. "What?"

"I'm just looking at you."

I couldn't help the blush that started to spread across my cheeks. "You make me nervous when you do that."

I shied away from him and glanced down at my hands. His hand came up to cup my cheek and lifted so that I could meet his eyes. "Don't look away, Isabella. You're so beautiful."

"Gio-".

He continued. "I'm serious. There are so many things that make you the most beautiful person I've ever met. It's not just the fact that you are ridiculously beautiful on the outside, but I've never met anyone with a more beautiful heart."

His compliments were so unexpected and my heart was bursting with emotion. He was looking at me with so much love that it made my stomach flip. I couldn't believe that this was my life. I couldn't believe he was all mine.

"I never believed I would find anyone," he murmured. "There were so many reasons for me to avoid relationships. It just wasn't worth it for me, but when you came into my life I couldn't believe how everything changed. For the first time ever, I wanted more."

He reached down and grabbed my hands. "And every day I wake up next to you, I want more. I want more of you, I want more of our life together. I want to give you more. I want to take care of you and make sure that you are happy because that's what matters to me."

Tears started to pool in my eyes. I couldn't control it. I didn't know why he was saying all of this but I was experiencing a happiness that was way beyond anything I had come to know. I always believed I was the happiest I could be but then Giovanni came along every day and showed me a new reason to be happy.

"Your happiness is all that matters to me," I said softly.

He leaned his forehead against mine. "You're all I need to be happy, *mi hermosa*. I will always owe Reyna for bringing you to *Mala Mía* that night. I didn't know it at the time but that was the night I met my future wife."

Before I could react to his words, he pulled away from me and took a step back as he got onto one knee.

Oh my God.

He reached for his jacket pocket and pulled out a small black box.

He was proposing to me.

He popped open the box and revealed a diamond ring staring back at me. My jaw dropped and the tears escaped my eyes. My hand went over my mouth as I stared down at the beautiful man I loved so much on one knee.

"I have never loved anyone the way I've loved you and I know I'm never going to," he said. "You are everything to me and I promise to spend the rest of my life making you happy. No matter what life throws our way, you are the only one I want by my side through it all."

I was shaking at this point as I looked into his deep brown eyes that were filled with love and emotion. The image of him in front of me on one knee will be one that I will keep with me until my last breath.

"Isabella Avery. Will you marry me?"

I let out a little cry and pushed myself off the ledge, throwing my arms around him. He stood up and picked me up, my legs wrapping around his waist.

He pulled away to face me. "Is that a yes?"

"Of course!" I cried. "Of course, I'll marry you, Giovanni."

He pulled me closer to him again and I buried my head in his shoulder, the tears of happiness streaming down my face. I couldn't believe it. I couldn't believe the amount of happiness I was feeling inside right now. He slowly put me down on the ledge again and brought his lips to mine as he cupped my face in his hands. My heart was bursting and I didn't know how to handle all this emotion at once.

He pulled away from me, but still kept his hands against my cheeks. "I love you so much."

"I love you, Giovanni."

He kissed me one last time before he brought his hands back down and reached for the ring out of the box. He closed the box and placed it next to me as he reached for my left hand. I was still shaking as he held my left finger, sliding the ring into its new permanent residence. I stared down at the large princess cut diamond around a single thin silver band staring back at me. He had done a great job of picking out an engagement ring. Hell, I would have worn a plastic ring if that was all he was able to give me. I would marry Giovanni in a heartbeat. I reached for him and pulled him back to meet my lips. We were consumed by our emotions and I let it all in. My love for him grew exponentially in that moment and I never wanted it to end.

"You've made me the happiest man in the world," he said between his kisses.

I couldn't help but giggle as I wiped my eyes. I was so overcome with emotion. I wanted to cry my eyes out from the happiness I was feeling. I couldn't believe that he had chosen me. I was his and he was mine. After all the shit we had gone through, we had finally made it to this point. We were together and there was nothing that was going to get in the way of that. I had never been a girl that believed in happy endings but with Giovanni, he made me feel like I was living a fairytale.

He pulled himself up onto the ledge and positioned himself behind me with his legs on either side of mine. He pulled me closer to him and wrapped his arms around mine, reaching for my hand and lifting it to admire his work.

"Do you like it?" he asked.

"Oh my God, Giovanni, I love it," I gaped. "It's so beautiful."

He leaned closer and kissed my cheek as he pulled me towards him. "I'm so glad."

As the last of the sun disappeared, the sky was consumed by darkness. It may have seemed scary to watch the light disappear, but there was something beautiful about it. Even through all the darkness, there was always light. The one cannot exist without the other. For the longest time, I believed I was living in darkness. There was no end in sight to it until Giovanni came into my life and lit up my world in a way I had never experienced before. He made everything brighter and brought out the best in me. He always pushed me to be the best version of myself and allowed me to live unapologetically.

"I hope you're ready for our life together, *mi hermosa,*" he whispered and left a kiss against my hair.

"It's all I've ever wanted."

And for the first time in my life, I was content and I didn't need more than this.

THE END

Printed in Great Britain
by Amazon